And Heavenly Things

And Heavenly Things

Book 2 of the
Clashing Kingdoms Series

Kim Cousins

RESOURCE *Publications* · Eugene, Oregon

AND HEAVENLY THINGS

Resource Publications
An Imprint of Wipf and Stock Publishers
199 W. 8th Ave., Suite 3
Eugene, OR 97401

www.wipfandstock.com

PAPERBACK ISBN: 978-1-6667-4268-8
HARDCOVER ISBN: 978-1-6667-4269-5
EBOOK ISBN: 978-1-6667-4270-1

08/01/22

For Jessie and Jerry, Matt and Heather, Sam, and Cindy:
the Lord make his face shine on you and be gracious to you.

Preface

I DERIVED SOME OF the descriptions of heaven and hell from three books, and personal testimonies of people I hold in high regard. The three books include: *Heaven Is for Real*, by Todd Burpo; *23 Minutes in Hell*, by Bill Wiese; and *Heaven: An Unexpected Journey*, by Jim Woodford. I won't mention the names of individuals who related their stories of hell but I attest to getting more white hair listening to them.

Once again, I cited scripture in my story. Although I used Zondervan's New International Version (NIV) Study Bible, I paraphrased some passages to provide a smoother flow in the narrative. Most of the time, I didn't touch the words in direct quotes because the Bible's poetry is perfect as written.

Acknowledgments

So many people deserve recognition for their help with this book. Those who consistently prayed for the project: Woodie, Sam, Deb and Reece Matoy, Dave and Sharon Conover, and John and Patty Southwick, I thank you wholeheartedly. To the outstanding professionals of Resource Publications: Matt Wimer, Emily Callihan, and George Callihan, thank you for your prompt attention, professional advice, and supportive guidance. You set the standard of publishing excellence which others in your organization exemplify with quality typesetting, editing, and marketing.

And my five greatest assets—a royal flush—are my esteemed editors: Woodie and Sam Cousins, Matt Higgins, John Southwick, and Verla Lockard. Your contributions improved this story immensely and I appreciate your time and expertise. To everyone who helped with this project, I thank you so much!

List of Characters

1. Caleb, Army Intelligence
2. Gabriel, Army Intelligence
3. Jeremiah "Miah," seventeen-year-old teenager
   a. Bill, dad
   b. Nora, sister
   c. Papaw, grandfather
   d. Shadow, Border Collie puppy
4. Jim and Sara Wilkins
   a. Mattie, Australian Shepherd
5. Juan and Rosa Peña
   a. Sydney, Border Collie puppy
6. Valley residents
   a. Alicia, Army veteran
   b. Brant and Toynell Matthews
   c. Homesteaders
      i. Bert
      ii. Gaya
      iii. Kali
   d. Marcus Washington's family
      i. TJ, sixteen-year-old son
      ii. Talia, thirteen-year-old daughter

c. Monica, Army veteran
d. Nellie Markwell
e. Ryan McGuire's family

   i. Jason, fifteen-year-old son

b. Pastor Greg

Week 1

1

"Yee-ouch!" yelped Beth.

Moments earlier, she stared carefree at the crystalline sky—a perfect spring day to walk in the mountains—daydreaming about her future. Disregarding her steps, she accidently stepped on something slippery, causing her to fall down. As she leaned on her elbow to rise, she felt a sharp stab on her ankle. Looking at her feet, she saw an angry rattlesnake uncoiling itself beneath her foot. Horrified, Beth realized that she stepped directly onto the snake as it lay camouflaged in the leaves.

Frozen with panic, Beth simply looked at the snake with thoughts tumbling through her mind. Before she could pull her pistol from its holster, the creature quickly slipped into a moss-covered rock wall, disappearing without a trace. Sitting up to examine her ankle, she saw the snake's calling card: two bloody fang marks.

What have I done? Sara will kill me for not wearing hiking boots. Immediately, she realized, *The snake will kill me for not wearing hiking boots!* Beth turned her head left, then right, looking for her Australian Shepherd, Mattie.

Alone, Beth started screaming as loudly as she could, "Mattie! Mattie, where are you?!"

Exploring the forest, Mattie returned to Beth within minutes of hearing her friend's voice. But instead of seeing her lively, sixteen-year-old mistress, Mattie saw Beth's beleaguered face and heard her labored breathing. Beth's hair already stuck to beads of sweat on her forehead, her eyes wide with fear.

Beth grabbed a broken branch lying on the ground. She stabbed the branch into soft, leafy soil, and hoisted herself up. Inhaling deeply, Beth started to hobble down the mountain using the gnarled branch as a crutch.

Despite her dizziness, Beth stumbled along the path. Mattie stayed close to Beth, watching anxiously. Confused, the young dog whimpered with concern, unsure of what to do. A natural herder, Mattie ran ahead of Beth then sprinted back to the disoriented teen, trying to encourage her mistress to follow. Mattie ran back and forth, finding the easiest path to walk, steering Beth down the mountain, carefully avoiding jagged boulders and fallen trees.

As Beth's pace slowed, Mattie continued to prod the teen. She pushed Beth with her nose, "*Come on; keep moving! Don't stop!*"

But Beth's steps became more sluggish, clumsier. Gasping for breath, her vision blurring, Beth stopped. Clutching the branch tightly—as if her very life depended on the strength of her fingers—Beth struggled to remain upright. She stood shaking, unable to take another step; until at last, she slumped over the branch and fell to the ground like a limp ragdoll.

As Beth lay on the ground, Mattie nudged her friend. The dog licked Beth's face, but when the teen's eyes fluttered then closed, Mattie started to bark repeatedly. Not knowing what else to do, the Aussie ran around the young woman several times, whining, scratching Beth's hand with her paw. Instinctively, Mattie wanted to defend Beth from some unknown enemy but there was no one to growl at—no one to bite.

Mattie stopped. After she looked at Beth, she sniffed the air for danger. The dog didn't smell any intruders but she did smell death. Mattie softly kissed Beth's face, whimpering with fear. Beth was dying. Uncertain about leaving, Mattie crept next to Beth, lying nervously beside her, occasionally licking the teenager's hand.

When she couldn't rouse Beth, Mattie decided to run home. She turned away from Beth and sprinted. Flying over rocks, splashing through creek beds, and snagging her fur on thorny bushes, the shepherd ran with all her might. Nothing slowed her down.

As she approached their home, Mattie yipped sharply, "*Help! Help!*"

She kept barking as she jumped up and down, scratching the front door of a luxurious log cabin in the Appalachian Mountains—the home Beth shared with Jim, Sara, and Rosa. At the insistence of Mattie's barking, Jim ran out of the garage, followed by several neighbors. Sara came out of the house, wiping her flour-covered hands on a towel, looking around fearfully, "Beth! Where's Beth?"

Jim called to Sara, "What's going on?"

Alarmed, Sara cried, "I don't know but something's wrong! Look at Mattie's fur, she's torn up from running . . . and Beth isn't with her!"

"Where was Beth going?" shouted Jim—now focused, in charge, all soldier.

"She went to the south side of Comstock Mountain to pick blueberries," Sara said, her voice shaking.

"When did she leave?"

"Um," Sara hesitated, trying to remember, "about three hours ago."

Jim and two visiting neighbors quickly saddled and bridled their horses. They rode up a path they suspected Beth followed to find blueberries. Jim pushed his horse to step quickly but the steep incline inhibited a rapid pace. Carefully stepping over or around sharp rocks and deep ravines, the trail traversed several mountains to finally converge with a fairly level path along the ridgeline.

Mattie maintained the lead. Undeterred by fatigue or bleeding paws, she guided Jim and his friends to Beth. When Mattie found Beth, she ran up to the teen's prone body, and sat down—panting, licking her dry, thirsty mouth, watching with worry.

The men swiftly slid off their horses. Jim dropped to his knees beside Beth; he gently lifted her head and shoulders into his arms. He touched his cheek to her cold forehead. He felt her pulse. Nothing. Jim (a battle-tested Army medic) wrapped his arms tightly around Beth, bent his face into her golden hair and wept bitterly.

⁀⊙⊙∿

In a world far from Jim, TJ opened his eyes and instantly felt sheer terror, an indescribable sense of dread. He remembered grabbing Carly Parsons's wrist when he tried to kidnap her, but Carly stood her ground. *What happened next? Oh yeah, she poked a stick into my eye!* He paused to remember those last few moments, *She . . . killed . . . me. Wait a minute—where am I?*

"Where indeed?" croaked a wicked voice.

TJ turned around frantically trying to identify the source of this ghastly sound. Although he saw nothing, he struggled to inhale, suffocated by panic. Absolute darkness. Steaming heat. Putrid smells. Screeching, wailing, tortured souls pleading for mercy.

Collapsing with fright, TJ curled into a ball, unable to control his trembling. He felt completely exhausted: too wobbly to stand, too weak to move. Bony, sticky fingers—possibly tentacles—grabbed his arms, lifting him into an upright position. Unable to breathe the oppressive, sulfuric fumes, the teen's legs crumpled beneath him again. This time he didn't fall to the ground because two stinking creatures on either side of him jerked him up by his elbows. Their violent action wrenched both arms out of their sockets. As they dragged him through an uneven, rocky corridor, TJ's head hung limply to his chest. He moaned pathetically—suffering agonizing pain.

TJ choked, "At least, give me new clothes." Mortified, he explained, "I . . . I messed myself." His oppressors exploded in mirthless laughter—a choking, howling racket.

As they pulled TJ through oily puddles and over sharp protrusions, the creatures spoke some freakish language. Splintering sounds that hurt TJ's teeth: nails-on-a-chalkboard or stepping-on-a-cat's-tail type of sounds, but TJ actually understood the meaning of the words. *How can this be? What's happening to me?!*

One of his tormenters shrieked to his partners, "Clothes?! This worm thinks he'll wear clothes." Still unable to see his persecutors, TJ felt the creature's nauseating spittle strike his face as it spoke.

Another monster gloated, slapping the teenager on the back of his head, "He'll never feel clean again; a filthy body and clothes are the least of his worries."

Laughing malevolently, a third demon corroborated, "He doesn't understand, the worthless slug." With his yellow, slanted eyes staring into TJ's face, he snarled, "We delight in humiliating humans; your horror is our honor."

"Your anguish, our accolade," croaked his accomplice.

Licking his parched lips, TJ asked with a trembling voice, "Where am I?" Hideous laughter filled the corridor.

TJ tried to suck in air but his lungs burned whenever he inhaled the scorching vapors. Dangling helplessly between his captors, TJ looked into three sets of glowing, evil eyes. Without waiting to hear their answer, TJ suddenly grasped, *I'm in hell! There really is a hell!*

Instantly, TJ realized he would never receive relief from this excruciating pain because *he would never die again.* This was the end of the road, the result of his choices!

Suddenly the three loathsome beings clawed his skin fiercely, cackling maniacally, slashing great gouges in his skin. Smelling vile odors of decay and being ripped apart by demons he couldn't see terrorized TJ! Horrified, the teen screamed at the top of his lungs.

Yet his screams brought no relief. Little did TJ know at the time, but he would scream in pain and anguish every few seconds, for eternity; because in hell, torment and abuse never ends. Forever means for . . . ever.

⸎◉⸎

Beth felt a strange lifting of her spirit. As she gazed down at her lifeless body, she watched Mattie courageously trying to protect her. She saw leaves blowing and smelled the fresh mountain air. As she floated upward, she realized that clean air continued to fill her lungs. In addition to the rich, earthly fragrance of leaves and soil, her nose picked up a distinct, wispy aroma of incense. *I know these scents*, she reflected distractedly, *gum resin, frankincense. Sara had these items in her apothecary.*

A beam of light appeared. She turned in the direction of the light. Smiling expectantly, she ran into the light. Beth saw a lone, dark figure standing in the distance. Without any doubt, she knew who was waiting for her.

Crying tears of joy, Beth approached the figure waiting for her and she fell into Jesus's arms. He held her tightly, stroking her golden hair. When Jesus loosened his embrace, Beth dropped to the ground, kissing his feet, wrapping her arms around his legs, thanking him profusely. Laughing, crying, praising God, she couldn't contain the elation bubbling inside her.

The Lord's eyes sparkled, "Welcome to my kingdom, dear child." His gentle grace made Beth's heart swell with joy. "Here you will lack nothing. You will never suffer, nor face hardships again. You have eternity to explore the love and goodness of my Father and his never-ending blessings."

Jesus reached down to hold both of Beth's hands in his hands. Smiling, he said, "Stand, for others also want to greet you." Even as she stood, Beth kept her eyes on Jesus's face; she never looked away from him.

Jesus put his right hand tenderly on her chin to turn her face toward a gathering of souls. Beth saw the shining faces of her parents, her grandparents, and her brothers. Everyone she lost on earth now stood eagerly waiting to meet her in heaven.

Beth looked back at Jesus. Jesus nudged her, "Go, my daughter, your family awaits you."

Beth ran into the arms of her loved ones. In the midst of the crowd, Beth felt hugs, kisses, and pats on the back. She heard the group cheering, laughing, and talking enthusiastically—all at once.

In the excitement, she also saw a bear standing off to one side of the crowd. Overwhelmed by this heavenly welcome, Beth quickly discounted her vision as an overactive imagination; but when she hugged her small grandmother, Beth looked over Nana's shoulders to see the black bear again. *Wait a minute—that's not a bear.* Narrowing her eyes then opening them wide with surprise, Beth whispered with incredulity, "Happy? Is that you?"

⁂

Within the depths of hell sat an ugly, wretched being. Hideous, frightening, contorted. A beautiful angel at one time, now a deplorable beast with greenish, leathery, blistering skin, gnarled hands and feet at the ends of skeletal arms and legs—an abomination of his once proud, handsome physique. Satan. The fallen angel Lucifer. The manifestation within the Antichrist. The enemy of mankind, a deceiver with exceptional shrewdness.

Although Satan spent much of his time lately within the Antichrist's body, when that measly puppet slept, Satan returned to hell to oversee his dominion. As Satan considered humans, he scoffed, "Morons! As long as these mindless humans don't think I exist—or that I'm a ridiculous Halloween character—I can continue to deceive them, capture them, *enslave* them." A smile, of sorts, spread across his pitted, pustule face.

Disrupting Satan's reflections, one of his lieutenants entered the moldering office in abject submission. Crawling on his deformed hands and knees—refusing to look into Satan's countenance—the demon stretched flat on the stone floor before his master's throne. With his eyes closed and his hands placed on the floor in front of him, the demon said loudly, "Hail, Satan, king of the underworld. I have come at your request."

Satan cast a malicious glare at his subordinate. "What have you to report?"

"Much success, your majesty! Every day more of these senseless humans relinquish ownership of their souls as they receive your mark. They do it without thinking! They would rather receive your mark to buy groceries than stand in allegiance to that crucified martyr."

Mustering his courage, the demon stood in front of Satan's stone throne, his knees trembling. With his face cast downward, the lieutenant pulled an itemized list from his pocket, and continued to speak, "Our numbers grow exponentially. Teenagers and young adults are hell's fastest growing populations."

Leaning back on his stone throne, "Go on," snarled the beast.

"Wizardry books, pornographic videos, sadistic music, gory movies—all the corruptible areas of adolescence that parents ignore—feed our coffers with blood. Do you know what we hear parents saying? 'Well, I'm glad Suzy's finally reading books!' or 'I don't care what the rating is for that movie or video game, I just want my kids outta my hair for a few hours.'"

Satan rocked with laughter. "And how do you use those few hours?"

Smirking, the demon responded, "We fill young people with fear, desensitize them to violence, teach them vulgar language, instill distrust for God, bolster their vanity."

"Splendid!" Satan remarked, unsurprised by human ignorance and pleased with parental indifference.

The lieutenant lifted his head slightly to look at Satan's knees. "We have more young people filled with lust, anger, depression, and sorrow than we ever dreamed possible!"

"Well done! What else have you to report?"

Drawing a breath to steel his nerves, "We're still having trouble breaking into some of those Christian enclaves."

Despite his greenish tint, Satan's face darkened to near black, "Do not say that cursed name in my presence!"

Cowed, the demon cringed as he imagined the penalty he'd receive for speaking Christ's name. With his eyes closed—awaiting his punishment—the only thing the demon heard was Satan's labored breathing and the incessant screams of prisoners outside the office walls.

Heaving a sigh, resigned to work with imbeciles, Satan growled with measured control, "And how will you deal with these . . . *enclaves*?"

Exhaling deeply for being spared a beating, his lieutenant added quickly, "We're working with people within their ranks to cause disruption, cast doubts about their faith. Destroy community cohesiveness."

Standing abruptly, towering over his minion, Satan screamed, "Then do it! Do it now before I hang you over the flaming pit to blister your miserable hide!"

Shaking violently with fear, the demon stood and slammed his fist once across his chest: a salute of respect. "As you wish, master." Relieved to be out of the office, the lieutenant straightened to his full twelve-foot height in the corridor.

Clenching his clawed fists, he spotted a lowly jailer. The jailer walked down the corridor, looking at his feet as he hauled a pail of something vile and smoldering. The lieutenant hit the demon across the face for no other reason than to bolster his own ego. This sudden action caused sizzling waste to fall onto the lieutenant's lopsided, furry feet, singeing the hair and scorching his skin. Hollering with pain, the officer beat the jailer with his fists, until the lowly creature could no longer stand.

"Let that be a lesson to you, maggot!" the lieutenant shouted. "Even when you don't see me, you should *sense* my presence. Fall on your knees, put your head on the ground, and *do not* look at me." Lowering his face to growl into the underling's ear, "You are nothing more than navel lint!"

He kicked the jailer in the ribs and stormed out of the cavern to carry out his majesty's orders. He would destroy every Christian compound that he and his followers found. Without being told, he knew Satan's time on earth would soon end. Consequently, he relentlessly searched everywhere for more souls to join him forever in hell. He sneered when he thought of humans, *They deserve life in hell, punishment for turning their backs on God*; afterward he moaned, remembering his own pride and foolishness, *Just like I did so long ago.*

Week 2

2

ONE OF THE COMPOUNDS could be found in a semi-isolated valley in the southwest corner of Virginia, just a few miles away from Tennessee. Surrounded on all sides by the Appalachian Mountains, the quiet glen provided sanctuary and sustenance for the few remaining residents living there. Despite hordes of homeless people wandering the former eastern United States, this valley remained fairly obscure to travelers because of its mountainous obstacles.

Even a year and a half after the United States collapsed, valley residents still felt protected. Most of the families lived within a community surrounded by an earthquake fault and a fence. The fault line and fence discouraged outlaws from stealing their food, but these barriers didn't completely discourage renegades from trying to breach their protected perimeter.

It didn't matter. Compound residents were now seasoned fighters. They fought against human invaders wishing to steal their livestock, insect and plant pests that attacked their crops, and outside governmental decrees that threatened their existence.

They only refrained from fighting each other. A family of different races, genders, ages, and cultures, they seemed unbreakable but nothing is perfect. Even in a close community dedicated to serving one another with mercy and grace, dissension sometimes occurred.

Although the compound included several large farms managed by individual landowners, residents considered Marcus Washington their general leader. Standing over six feet tall with skin as black as coal, the muscular and easygoing, middle-aged man was a natural leader. Marcus worked as hard as anyone but always found time to listen to the concerns of his neighbors. His patience and fair-mindedness endeared him to everyone within the compound.

Although no one referred to the old calendar anymore, Marcus looked up at the sky one summer day, felt a slight breeze in his hair, and said quietly, "Thank you, God, for this beautiful, June afternoon." Taking off his leather work gloves, he wiped his feet on the welcome mat and entered his house to get something to drink.

Because of his open-door policy, Marcus wasn't surprised to see Alicia standing inside his kitchen, gazing out a kitchen window. "Hey, Allie, how're you doing?" He removed his baseball cap, slapping it against his jeans, filling the air with dust from his pants and cap.

Alicia turned around to face Marcus. A handsome young woman, thirty-five years old with long, brownish-blonde hair pulled into a ponytail, Alicia was the epitome of a soldier. As an Army veteran, she always studied her surroundings, understood battle tactics, and executed orders with efficiency. She was not a person to provoke; thus, most people—especially the compound's women—gave her a wide berth when she entered a room.

In contrast, Marcus felt completely relaxed with Alicia's company. She was someone he could count on; in fact, he was the only one who called her "Allie." The other person close to Alicia was her friend, Monica, another Army veteran, which meant that Alicia could count all her good friends on one hand.

Alicia smiled at Marcus, "Hey, buddy."

Marcus reached into his cupboard to find a drink. Moving a few bottles around, he found what he was looking for, a sealed quart bottle of apple cider. "Want somethin' to drink?" He held up the bottle as he shook the cider.

"As tempting as that looks, I think I'll pass today."

"Arright," he feigned disappointment, "it's your loss." He poured himself at tall glass of cider and sat at the kitchen table. Leaning back in his chair and stretching his legs in front of him, he asked, "Is there somethin' I can do for you?"

For the first time since Marcus knew her, Alicia acted uncomfortable talking with him. Rather than initiating small talk, Marcus just smiled, took a long pull of his drink, and waited for her to speak.

"I don't know quite how to say this, Marcus." She chewed on her bottom lip. She looked in the air—as if words would mysteriously appear on the ceiling—but she remained speechless. Smiling, Marcus continued to watch her but said nothing to ease her discomfort.

Finally she blurted out, "Marcus, I think you're really attractive." She blushed, "There I said it. Now I feel stupid."

"Was that so hard to say?" his eyes flashed lightheartedly.

Alicia started laughing, "Honestly? Yes. That was very hard!"

"Well, let me make this a little easier for you," offered Marcus. He reached for an oak chair next to him and pulled it out from the table, "Sit down and relax. Let's talk awhile."

Alicia sat on the edge of the chair, her feet planted firmly on the ground. She looked as if she might jump up and run out of the room unexpectedly. She stared at Marcus sideways, "You're not going to give me any breaks, are you?"

"Naw, this is really fun!" He enjoyed teasing this serious woman.

"Humph!" She closed her eyes but kept speaking, "Every man I ever dated treated me like I was a competitor. Rather than accepting me the way I am, they wanted me to be different. One guy stopped dating me because I scored better than him on the rifle range. Another guy told me that I needed to be 'softer.' My last boyfriend left me because he said that I could probably beat him arm wrestling!"

Marcus chuckled, "Arm wrestling? Are you kidding?" As he thought of that ridiculous excuse, he added, "I can honestly say I never wanted to arm wrestle a woman."

"Well, laugh all you want, big fella, but that's the truth!"

He raised his arms in mock surrender, "I believe you; no one makes up stuff like that." He leaned back in his chair, crossing his arms, "Listen, why don't we just take it easy? I've only been a widower a little while. I could use some time to figure out why a beautiful woman like you could see anything in a relic like me."

"I think you're wonderful! In fact if you want, I could make dinner for you and your daughter tonight." Although Alicia acted innocent, Marcus suspected she already planned a meal before she walked into his house.

"Dinner, huh? This was my night to fix supper." He stalled, shrugging his shoulders indifferently, "But I'm completely out of ideas."

Her eyes brightened, "Would you like me to give you a few pointers in the kitchen?"

"Yeah, but I don't have anything to pay you for your instruction." Looking at her mischievously, "Hey, I got an idea, let's arm wrestle! If I win, you can make us supper!"

Alicia's jaw dropped open. She picked up a wooden spoon from the counter and flung it at Marcus. "You're a jerk," she said with good humor.

Marcus dodged the spoon, letting it clatter on the floor. "You'll get no argument from me!" he confessed. Marcus got up, walked over to a wooden crib next to a closet and opened the lid. He rifled through the vegetable bin, pulling out a few potatoes, "Whatta ya say? I'll peel some potatoes as an apology."

"Deal!" she said agreeably.

For the next half hour, the pair stood at the kitchen counter, chatting easily, chopping vegetables. Alicia talked about subjects that interested her: repairing firearms, brewing beer, and shoeing horses, while Marcus listened, amused by her stories. Just two friends enjoying a conversation while sharing a single glass of apple cider.

3

BETH ADAPTED QUICKLY TO her new world in heaven. Everything was so lovely! She saw unimaginable colors everywhere, heard music and laughter floating through the trees, and smelled pleasing aromas that teased her nose when she walked. Or flew, no less!

As she strolled through a meadow filled with waist-high grasses and wildflowers, she hummed to herself. When she brushed flower petals gently with her hands, the flowers released a dewy, fresh fragrance. Inhaling deeply, Beth closed her eyes, grinning contentedly.

In her reverie, she didn't notice a companion quietly following her. She opened her eyes suddenly when she heard a deep voice rumble, "Beth, I am so glad to see you again."

Beth turned around to behold the heavenly Happy. Although impressive as an earthly dog, the Newfoundland now took Beth's breath away. Taller, more muscular—with a luxurious coat of black, silky fur— Happy gave Beth her best smile.

"Happy, you look beautiful!"

The dog grumbled amiably.

"I really didn't expect to see animals in heaven," Beth admitted.

"I will not surprise Juan." Hap wagged her tail, "Juan is very smart."

Beaming, Beth agreed, "Yes, he is."

Still standing, Happy scratched one of her ears with her back foot. Happy reminded Beth of a bashful man trying to talk with a woman, tripping over his words, fumbling with a hat in his hands. Unaccustomed to speaking out loud, Happy blurted, "In the truck. You talked with Miah."

To help the big dog, Beth prompted, "Yes, Miah and I talked about a lot of things."

Happy nodded her head, "Come. I want you to meet Miguel. You can ride on my back. You will not hurt me."

Beth hugged Happy's neck, burying her face in the dog's fragrant fur. "I'd love to go with you, Happy." Beth slipped onto her back, wrapping her arms around Hap's neck. She held on tightly as Happy ran across the meadow. Beth laughed with delight. *Who would ever dream that such a clumsy-looking dog could be so graceful?* The wind blew Happy's soft fur across Beth's face, tickling her nose, making her sneeze and giggle at the same time.

Exhilarated, Beth wished she could ride on Happy's back all day; but within minutes, they approached a young man staring into a violet, translucent pond. Happy slowed her pace and padded up to the pensive young man, clearing her throat to announce their presence.

Recognizing Hap's voice, Miguel turned around with a ready smile. His eyes widened as he looked at Beth. Words failed him. Riding on the back of his gigantic friend, was a vision! A young woman with long blonde hair, cobalt blue eyes, and porcelain skin gazed at him, smiling warmly.

"Hi," she said shyly, "my name's Elizabeth." Self-conscious, she quickly stammered, "But you can call me Beth, that's what Happy calls me."

Miguel stood up. He held her left hand to support her as she slid off Happy's back, "It's a pleasure to meet you, Beth." He motioned to the mossy rock he was sitting on, "Would you like to sit by the pond with me? The moss is surprisingly soft." Before they sat, he guessed, "Are you new here?"

When Beth nodded, yes, Miguel asked excitedly, "Have you seen a pond dance yet?" Reacting to Beth's bewildered look, Miguel added excitedly, "You gotta see this." He pointed to the small lake, "If you watch the water, you'll notice the ripples on the surface spurt and spin with the music in the air."

Beth tiptoed carefully to the pool. Not wanting to disrupt this otherworldly dance, she watched the water expectantly. She listened to the soft music blowing through the air and saw the synchronicity between the music and eddies in the water.

"Unbelievable," she said breathlessly.

The two young people sat beside the pond, quietly—unwilling to disrupt the water's movements. Beth held her breath, mesmerized by the whirlpools moving with the music. Shaking her head in wonderment, "I can't believe how beautiful everything is in heaven."

"I only know heaven," Miguel said matter-of-factly, captivated by the lovely person sitting next to him.

Startled by this news, Beth looked more closely at Miguel. *What an interesting face*, she noticed for the first time. *His skin looks like coffee with cream. Mocha colored.* The breeze ruffled his black dreadlocks. Miguel grinned at Beth, his emerald green eyes sparkled with good humor.

"Pardon me for staring but . . . you're beautiful," she said boldly.

"Thank you," he said, "but everyone in heaven is beautiful."

"Yeess," she said slowly, as if she'd missed this obvious detail—which of course, she had. "If you don't mind me asking, why do you only know heaven?"

"I was never born," he answered simply. "My mother aborted me."

Beth held her hands to her mouth, embarrassed by her question, "Oh, I'm so sorry. I didn't mean to pry."

"It's okay," Miguel said, as he tossed a stone into a placid part of the pool. "Jesus loves me. So does my Father and the Holy Spirit. I'm fine."

Beth shifted slightly, brushed a flower petal off her dress. She wanted to ask another question but she didn't know how to say the words without sounding insensitive. Ultimately, she cleared her throat but said nothing.

Miguel smiled at her discomfort. "You're probably wondering why I'm a young man and not a baby."

"Yes," she answered timidly.

"I lived in heaven's nursery. It's a wonderful place. Kind people sang to me, fed me, rocked me, loved me. I never felt rejection or fear as I aged, only love."

"But you aged," Beth added, a bit confused, "I guess I don't understand age in heaven."

Miguel thought a moment then asked, "What did you see when you met your family in heaven?"

Beth looked up, remembering all the joyful faces, "My mom and dad." She paused, "Come to think of it, they looked young."

"What about your grandparents?"

Following his logic, Beth spoke excitedly, "Now that you mention it, Nana had brown hair and . . . no wrinkles. No glasses either!"

"Exactly," Miguel said.

"But honestly," Beth recalled, "I was so curious about the bear watching us that I forgot about Nana's face."

"Bear? What bear?"

Happy barked loudly, her tail wagging. "Me." She made a throaty sound, a dog laugh.

Miguel chuckled, his face beaming. "Happy the bear. I like that!"

"So old people look younger in heaven and babies grow older, is that it?"

"Almost. If you study the faces in heaven, you'll notice that most people are in their thirties. Same age as Jesus when he returned to heaven. This is the age where we can do the work our Father designed for us to do. So babies grow older in heaven and old people get younger."

"We have jobs?" Beth asked. "What's your job?"

"Occasionally I greet souls coming into heaven. Some people don't know anyone; so Jesus asks me—and a lotta others—to welcome new-comers into paradise. It's fun!"

"That does sound fun," agreed Beth.

Miguel nodded his head, adding wistfully, "Actually I kinda hope someday I'll meet my parents here. I dream that Jesus will introduce us; then we'll have eternity to spend together." He added softly, "That's my prayer, to meet my parents in heaven."

Beth reached over to hold Miguel's hand. "That will be my prayer too, Miguel."

Flashing her dog smile—squinty eyes and rounded cheeks—Happy sat next to Miguel. "When I see Juan again, I will kiss him and kiss him," she stated confidently. Her wagging tail swept dust into the air, "He likes my kisses."

Miguel put his arm around Happy's shoulders, "Who wouldn't?"

Happy gave him a kiss on the cheek. Raised by a good man, Happy learned that all compliments deserve a show of thanks: a tail wag, a paw shake, or a soft kiss. Juan would still be proud of her.

On a nearby hilltop, Jesus watched Beth and Miguel holding hands, captivated by the swirling pool. As the two young people talked, Jesus smiled and gently whispered, "Father, you are so good, so kind, so faithful to a thousand generations! Thank you for bringing these tender lambs into my fold."

Responding again to Miguel's request, Jesus said, "Dear Spirit, penetrate the hearts of Miguel's parents; saturate their minds with my love and forgiveness. Pursue them. Sing to them as they dream, pique their curiosity as they read. Stir in them a desire to seek my salvation while they still have time to find me."

⁓◌◌⁓

Mountain people who knew Beth mourned the young woman's death, but no one grieved more than Jim. Despite his rugged exterior, Doc Wilkins, Jim to his friends, felt as if something died inside him—something that he may never again revive. Jim continued to practice medicine, chop firewood, or hunt game, but he felt like a phantom. His feet moved, his brain worked, but his chest felt hollow—empty.

His wife, Sara, also mourned Beth's passing but she endured. She trusted that she would see Beth again in heaven. This knowledge gave her the willingness to push forward, to carry on despite the heaviness in her heart.

Sara watched Jim carefully. Without acknowledging Jesus as Lord and Savior, Jim didn't understand her hope in eternity. He was a lost soul that cared for his ailing patients but grieved for his adopted daughter and longed for his absent friend, Miah. Jim was almost robotic, he functioned well enough to accomplish tasks, but he sorely lacked emotion or ambition.

One night after dinner, Sara addressed her concerns. "Jim, you need to talk with me about your feelings. Please tell me what you're thinking."

Pursing his lips, "That's just it, Sara. I don't have any feelings at all. I'm completely numb inside." He sighed, "I loved Beth so much," he paused, "it felt like my heart was torn out of my chest the day she died." Fumbling for an analogy, "It's like a bomb exploded inside of me and blew my heart into a thousand little pieces." He bit his upper lip, thinking aloud, "I don't know if I'll ever put it back together again."

Sara touched his hand, her brow creased with worry. "Do you still love me?" she asked bravely.

He looked at her face, "Yeah, I do. You're the only person that keeps me together. Without you, there's no point in fighting day in and day out."

"You don't have to fight any of your battles alone." Sara placed her hand on Jim's arm and sang a peaceful melody. When she finished singing, she pressed her cheek to Jim's cheek and prayed. As she prayed, Jim closed his eyes, relaxed, and allowed Sara's gentle spirit to minister to his wounded heart.

After the prayer ended, Sara promised him, "I will never give up on you. I love you."

Unseen by Sara, tears welled in Jim's eyes. Maybe somewhere deep within his soul, he would love another person unconditionally, but for now, he would guard his heart from loving anyone new. It would take someone very special to break his defenses.

The Holy Spirit watched while Sara prayed for her husband. Although Jim had not accepted Jesus as savior, Sara was saved. As she prayed for serenity to fall upon Jim, the peace of the Lord mysteriously filled both Sara and Jim. Comfort filled their minds and bodies. The anxiety that haunted their thoughts during the day and caused sleeplessness throughout the night slipped away. Mercifully, tonight they would sleep soundly, and for a while, forget the pain of Beth's untimely death.

ಞೋఴ

In the dark recesses of hell, Satan screamed, "Whatta you mean you can't get close to that backwoods pill pusher! We almost had him in our midst!" Spittle drooling from his mouth, Satan growled threateningly, "You said he held a pistol under his chin last week. He almost forfeited his soul to me!"

Satan's underling, Depression, a contemptuous, slouching figure, covered his scaly face with disjointed fingers to prevent blows to his head. "Sire, I whispered into his ears night and day, 'You are unworthy of love,' 'There is no life after death,' 'You will never see Beth again.'"

"So why didn't he kill himself?!" raged the beast.

"His wife," whined the twisted creature. "Just as he tightened his pull on the trigger, she called his name." Watching Satan's black eyes, he explained rapidly, "He was in the barn, ready to kill himself, when she said it was dinnertime." The demon swallowed, pursing his lips, "He stopped! He looked at the weapon, his hands were shaking, and then he threw his pistol across the barn."

"Go on . . . ," threatened Satan.

"When he walked into the kitchen, she looked at his face, and knew something was wrong. Ever since that evening, she's been relentless! She prays for him throughout the day or whenever she wakes up at night. Her constant prayers brought in a small army of angels that continually guard him against us. A circle of fire surrounds him. We can't even get close to his dreams anymore!"

Satan screamed furious invectives at Depression. When he regained his composure, the devil stepped inches from Depression's face and hooked a clawed nail into the demon's nose. With supernatural strength, Satan dragged the stinking demon across jagged rocks on the floor of his throne room. At the entrance, Satan stopped, picked up the massive gargoyle and heaved him over the heads of thousands of tormented souls in hell.

Depression landed on top of a group of lost souls and demons lining the great hall that encircled a massive, blazing pit of fire. Seething with hatred, Depression crawled across the hall to find a hiding place. Determined to make amends to Satan, Depression schemed: *I won't let my failure with Jim Wilkins discourage me. I'll find another unsuspecting soul to deliver to my master.*

Unable to think clearly amid deafening screams, the hateful spirit left the hall. As he stomped down a sweltering passageway, he planned his journey back to the earth's surface in search of another fragile person to destroy. Smiling contemptuously, running his tongue over razor-sharp fangs, Depression plotted, *This time I'll invite Suicide to join me. Together, we'll destroy as many of those detestable humans as we can before our work on earth ends!*

His eyes narrowed. His face cracked hideously. He could almost taste the blood of humans on his lips.

Week 3

– Day 1 –

4

Traveling in the Tennessee Smoky Mountains, a strapping seventeen-year-old named Jeremiah continued to plan his future with Beth. Unaware of her passing two weeks earlier; Miah wanted to marry Beth as soon as possible. As an outsider, Miah—and others like him—no longer used electronic communication that government agencies can easily monitor. So in Miah's mind, Beth was still very much alive and he wanted to hurry home to see her again.

"Hey, amigo," his traveling companion Juan Peña said, "are you ready to leave your granddad's place?"

"I am. It looks like we'll take Nora, Dad, and those two new guys we met."

"What about the Border Collie pups? Should we take 'em?"

Miah scratched his head, "Ya know when Happy was alive, we didn't have any choice but to take 'em; she wouldn't leave those puppies for anything. But now that Hap's gone, I'm not sure that's the best idea. They might slow us down."

Juan smiled, "Lemme see if I got this right: we're carrying a wiggly three-year-old on our backs and expecting your dad to keep up with us. But you're worried about puppies slowing us down?"

"We still have to cross the Tennessee River—"

"Yeah, I haven't forgotten the river," the Latino sighed. "I'm just afraid someone will mistreat these pups if we leave 'em here. I don't know if you've noticed, but there aren't many animals left anymore."

Miah rubbed the back of his neck, "It's your call. I'm the one bringing my baby sister and dad."

"Okay, since it's up to me, we'll take the puppies. I love dogs. Even with their short, little legs, they can't be any slower than Hap was on the trail."

"Done deal!" said Miah. "I'll tell everyone to get ready tonight. We'll leave first thing in the mornin.'"

⸛᯽⸛

Despite Miah's insistence that everyone be ready to leave at daybreak, Miah's dad, Bill, was foggy headed and insolent in the morning. "What does it matter if we leave now or at noon?" his dad said heatedly. "Do we hafta catch a train?"

As Miah stuffed Nora's chubby arms into a sweater, he spoke pointedly, "No, but we have a long way to go and the sooner we get started, the better." After Miah laced his sister's shoes, he set her on her feet, and turned her around to make sure she wore enough clothes to keep her warm on the journey. "If you get too hot today, baby girl, we'll start peeling some of these duds off ya."

Nora hugged her big brother's neck and gave him a messy toddler, grape-jelly kiss.

Miah threw Nora's small knapsack over his left shoulder and lifted her up in his right arm. "C'mon, Dad, we're leavin.' If you wanna stay here, you're welcome to go back to bed, but I'm takin' Nora with me."

Surprised by his son's independence, Bill quickly slipped on his jeans and grabbed his boots. Sitting on a cot, pulling on his boots, Bill responded, "Hey, wait for me. I just need to pack a few things for the trip!"

Without turning around to look at his dad, Miah answered, "We're takin' the main road up to the river. Catch up with us when you get yourself together."

When Miah left his dad's cabin, he looked into the faces of three hardened soldiers. Intelligent men averse to accommodating the whims of self-centered people like his dad. Miah apologized, "I'm sorry for the delay. Nora and I are ready to go."

The three men, Juan and their two new traveling companions, cast sideways glances toward Bill's cabin then looked knowingly at each other. No one said a word. To break the silence, Juan said good-naturedly, "Lemme take Nora."

Juan put his arms into a makeshift child carrier Miah made for his sister. Miah carefully maneuvered her little body into the backpack as Juan rolled his shoulders. "I think I got the best job today, fellas, she's as light as a feather."

The two other men smiled at the toddler. They hoisted their fifty-pound rucksacks onto their backs and started to walk down the road, followed by two rambunctious Border Collies.

Juan glanced at Miah, "Cheer up, compadre. Your dad will either man up or he won't. In either case, we'll all take care of Nora."

With that promise, Juan marched up the road toward their destination, a beautiful log mansion that he and his wife, Rosa, shared with Miah, Jim, Sara, and Beth. Juan dreamed of the cabin nestled deep within the Tennessee Mountains, a retreat that offered plenty of opportunities for growth and safety.

As he walked, Juan decided to get more familiar with their newest traveling companions. "All I know about you guys is that you're Jewish and you did something with Army intelligence. I don't even know your names."

The biggest man—bearded and roughly two hundred pounds of hardened muscle—looked at Juan, "My name's Gabriel. Gabe." Indicating his friend, a shorter, bearded man with a swimmer's physique, Gabe added, "And this is Caleb." Caleb nodded to Juan and Miah.

"You already know Miah and me," Juan said, "and the bundle on my back is Nora. You guys are pretty tight-lipped so why don't you tell us a little about yourselves?"

"Hmm, tight-lipped, that's a pretty accurate description," said Caleb.

Looking at Caleb, Gabe answered, "Yeah, I like it." The group marched up the road in silence.

Juan looked at the two soldiers, shrugging his shoulders, "It's cool. You don't have to say anything." With a roguish glint in his eyes, "But my guess is, you're gonna ask Miah all kinds of questions before we get home."

As they marched, Gabe and Caleb looked at each other with puzzled expressions. *What's he talking about?* Juan chuckled to himself and Miah stared at the ground without saying a word.

As they approached the Tennessee River, Juan's party stopped to strategize their next move. Standing on high ground on one side of the main road, they watched hundreds of people milling around a heavily guarded ferry station. PeaceKeepers studied everyone's traveling papers and checked each person's mark of fidelity.

Miah spoke first, "I've been wondering about the best way to cross this river. I think we need to build a raft downstream," pointing to their left, "and float across the river at night."

Gabe, Caleb, and Juan watched the troops without speaking. Although they stood near the barricade, they remained hidden behind trees.

"Let's move across this mountain ridge, staying in the forest. I don't want anyone taking an interest in us," said Gabe.

Heading downstream, the four men walked silently through the forest. They stepped cautiously, using hand signals when necessary. After they moved a klick along the ridge, they stopped to reassess the situation.[1]

Caleb removed a pair of binoculars from his rucksack to study the troops below. "It looks like they're closing the gate for the evening. I see people building campfires along the shore; they're probably gonna spend the night on the beach and try to cross the river tomorrow."

"Let's find a secure place to set up our camp," suggested Juan. "Before we build a raft, I'd like to explore the abandoned homes around here. We might find a rowboat or an inner tube we could use."

"Great idea, Juan," said Miah. "I really don't want to build a raft if we don't have to."

---

1. A klick is one kilometer or about 3/5 of a mile.

Week 3

– Day 2 –

5

THE ONLY REMAINING FARM in the valley outside of Marcus's compound belonged to Nellie, Brant, and Toynell. Although the three homesteaders didn't have the safety of a fault-and-fence boundary, they maintained constant vigilance against intruders. Nestled close to mountains and forests, they found places to hide, especially a large cave hidden within a rocky crag near their farmhouse.

Whenever they saw strangers, Toynell and Brant immediately moved large livestock into the obscure cavern. As a precaution, they already kept chickens, turkeys, and geese in the cave but the big animals needed to graze outside in grassy meadows. Today was no exception. Nellie sounded their alarm, two blasts from a whistle, and the young couple swiftly herded cows, horses, and goats into their hiding place.

Unfortunately, Nellie didn't have time to join them. She spotted a team of PeaceKeepers just as they walked up her driveway. The unit moved with stealth and silence, catching Nellie completely off guard.

Rather than looking guilty, Nellie put on her work gloves, swept her bangs over her eyebrows, and started to sweep the porch nonchalantly. "Mornin' fellas. What can I do ya for?"

Tipping his hat slightly, a sergeant leading the troop said with an easy inflection, "We need to fill our canteens, ma'am."

Nellie smiled openly, "A Southern boy! Land sakes, I haven't heard that drawl in a pig's age, darlin'."

The sergeant walked up the porch steps, extending his right hand. Nellie reached her right arm out to shake his hand. When she did, the sergeant grasped her wrist and twisted her arm behind her back.

Pulling the old woman in front of him tightly, the sergeant growled in her ear, "How long did you think you could evade us?"

Mimicking surprise, Nellie said, "Whatta ya want with an ole' gal like me?"

Turning her around to face him, the sergeant pulled off her work gloves and noticed her unmarked hands. He swept the hair off her forehead to verify her unlined—and unmarked—brow. Speaking now in his native New England accent, "Oh, I think I'll take this 'old gal' and arrest her for sedition."

Nellie sighed, looking down at her feet. As they began to bind her wrists with zip cuffs, she sniffed, "May I wipe my nose first?"

Scoffing, the sergeant nodded his approval. Nellie pulled a red handkerchief from her apron pocket, wiped her nose, and held the handkerchief as they roughly secured her wrists behind her back. As they dragged her off the porch, Nellie indiscreetly dropped her hanky on the ground. The troops pushed her forward roughly—trying to make her stumble—but Nellie braced her steps and walked down the driveway without faltering.

When they reached her gate, Nellie saw a van parked discreetly in a grove of bushes. She mocked the men with an exaggerated twang, "Why I declare, sergeant, you musta thought I was some big criminal with all this fuss."

Recognizing her thinly veiled sarcasm, the sergeant struck her in the stomach with the butt of his rifle. Nellie doubled over and this time, fell to the ground writhing in pain.

The sergeant looked at the old woman disgustedly. "Stop staring at the old bag, private! Pick her up and chain her in the van with the rest of our prisoners then let's get outta here. We have more hillbillies to arrest before we reach Marshall City."

Toynell and Brant witnessed Nellie's arrest from a thicket of trees. Without adequate ammunition, the pair knew they were no match to attack PeaceKeepers. With one hand over her mouth, the young woman mouthed a silent prayer, never taking her eyes off Nellie. As the van drove past them, Brant already devised a plan.

"Toy, we need to move our livestock to Marcus's compound." He held her hand, "I want you to stay in the cave tonight with the animals. We'll make a small living area for you so you can eat and sleep without being bothered by cows. I'll talk with Marcus about getting you and our animals to safety. Afterward we'll find a way to rescue Nellie."

Toynell agreed; she understood his reasoning. She surprised her husband by adding, "You know the cows don't bother me. They're big, simple animals, but after milking them for months now, I know all their personalities. They're sweet girls."

Surprised, Brant stepped back, "My girl! The woman who could out shop anyone on Chicago's Miracle Mile has a herd of sweet milk cows."

She jabbed him with her elbow. "Every one of our animals—the cows, horses, goats," she gestured, "all of them—are sweeter than most people." She looked into his eyes, "I'll take care of everything while you're gone."

Brant and Toynell stood up, facing each other. He placed his hands on her shoulders, awed by her steely determination. "You're the best *woman* in the world," he said affectionately.

She smiled humbly, "Help me take care of the animals first then we'll set up my sleeping area. Noah spent over a year with a boatload of animals; I think I can manage a few days with our animals in a cave."

∽◌◯◌∾

After dinner, Marcus sat down at his kitchen table, spreading several pairs of work gloves across the tabletop. Leaning into the pale glow of an olive oil lamp, he studied each battered glove. His gloves needed mending. Since he didn't have anything else to do, he threaded an embroidery needle and started to stitch up torn seams.

He was still mending his first glove, when Ryan McGuire's fifteen-year-old son, Jason, knocked frantically at the front door. Marcus's daughter, Talia—two years younger than Jason—bounced out of her chair in the living room to open the door.

"Hiya, Jay!" she said gaily.

"Hey, Talia, is your dad home?"

Hearing the anxiety in Jason's voice, Marcus got up to meet the teen. "C'mon inside, Jason," invited Marcus. Jason removed his hat and walked into the warm cabin. Talia shut the door slowly, alarmed by Jason's nervousness.

"What's wrong?" asked Marcus.

Breathlessly, Jason responded, "Brant sent us a long Morse code message. It's Nellie; she was arrested by PeaceKeepers today." Talia gasped. Jason paused, "He wants to come over to our place tonight to talk. He has Toynell tucked away in a cave with their animals but they need to move everything across the fault." Dry mouthed from running, Jason cleared his throat, "He also wants to know if we can help rescue Nellie."

Marcus sat in his chair again, absorbing this news. He placed his elbows on the table, folded his hands, and rested his chin on his thumbs. Thinking. He lifted his eyes from the table to stare at the fire as he spoke, "Send a message back to Brant. Tell him to get here as soon as he can. He needs to stay off the roads and watch for PeaceKeepers. Tell him that our guards will keep an eye out for him." Marcus stood up to look at both teenagers, "When he arrives, he can spend the night here at our house."

When Jason turned to leave, Marcus added, "Tell your dad and Pastor Greg to come here as soon as they finish dinner. We'll talk about our options so I can update Brant when he arrives. Who's on guard duty tonight?"

"Alicia and I," answered Jason.

"Good," Marcus looked toward the ceiling, nodding his approval.

As he considered the situation, Marcus felt his daughter's presence behind him. She put her hand on his arm, "Dad, is there anything I can do?"

Marcus put his hand over hers and said thoughtfully, "Pray, Talia . . . pray."

⁂

While Marcus stared at his fireplace thinking, Miah and his group sat in front of their small fire cooking dinner. "I snared two rabbits so we won't go hungry this evening," smiled Miah as he held his quarry in the air.

"Alright, Miah," congratulated Juan, "I'm hungry."

The two puppies fell over themselves in their excitement to eat. The men grinned as they watched the rambunctious pups wrestle with each other and Nora. Eventually, Caleb picked up one of the wiggly puppies and the dog licked his face repeatedly, growling playfully as she tried to chew his gloves.

"Man, puppies are the best contraband we ever smuggled, Gabe," said Caleb.

Gabe's eyes shined, "I don't know who I want to hold first, that fat baby girl or a fuzzy puppy."

Already liking his new traveling companions, Juan said, "We should name these pups."

Pointing to the bigger collie, "Did you watch this guy today?" asked Caleb. "He never left Miah's heels. If Miah stopped, he stopped; if Miah sat down, the puppy sat down. It was like Miah had a living shadow following him."

"Hey, that's a great name," declared Juan, picking up the stout, male puppy, "we'll name this tough guy Shadow." Juan held the puppy in front of his face, "How does Shadow sound to you, Miah?" The puppy wagged his tail furiously, yipping brightly.

Miah said, "I like it!" Miah never had a dog of his own before and he liked this puppy. All day Shadow stayed near his heels—always watching, learning Miah's movements, never making a sound.

"Alright, that's one puppy." Juan put the male pup down and picked up his smaller sister. "Now what should we call you?" She wagged her tail, panting happily.

Gabe piped up this time, "She reminds me of a private I once knew. A little woman that did everything the men did without complaining." Looking skyward as he reminisced, he said, "She trained twice as hard as the others so she could keep up with the unit, but she also made sure that we all stayed on task. Our mission was everything to her."

Gabe leaned back against a rock, his fingers laced behind his head. He motioned his head at the puppy watching him, "This little pup never wandered off the trail or caused problems today. As small as she is, she matched us step-for-step without whimpering. She reminded me of Pvt. Markham." Gabe turned to his friend, "Do you remember her, Caleb?"

"Yeah, I do," laughed Caleb. "Markham even had a streak of white hair that ran right through the middle of her black hair. Kinda like a Border Collie."

"Or a skunk," joked Gabe.

"When I asked her about it, she said everyone in her family had white hair before they were forty."

Picturing this young woman, Miah asked, "What was the private's first name?"

"Sydney."

"Sydney . . . I like it. Let's call her Sydney, Syd for short," said Juan.

After they finished naming the puppies, the men returned their attention to Nora. As soon as Juan took her out of her backpack, she ran around the campsite: picking up sticks, throwing pebbles, and playing in the spongy, forest soil. Now Nora's face and hands were crusted with mud.

Miah picked up his sister and tossed her chubby body in the air. Nora squealed with delight. After he caught her, Miah told the others, "I'm going to take this messy kid down to the river to wash some of dirt off of her."

"Good idea," said Gabe. "Make sure there's no one around when you get to the river. We're just starting to like you two."

Caleb joined in, "Yeah, it'd be a shame to leave 'em."

Miah smiled at the men, picked up his babbling sister, and walked down to the river's edge, staying beneath the dense growth of a willow tree. When Miah was out of earshot, Caleb said softly, "I saw Miah's dad, Bill, milling around a few fire pits this evening. I think he was looking for Nora and Miah."

Gabe snarled, "Well, we half expected to see him again."

"That's not what concerns me," stressed Caleb. "I'll see if I can find Bill with my binoculars tomorrow. But tonight, it sure looked like he had a brand-new tattoo on his forehead."

❧☙

While Miah bathed his sister, Brant began his journey to the valley compound. He didn't take any chances. He carried his rifle and enough food and water to sustain him for days if he had to hide from government troops, but his primary goal was to reach Marcus's farm in three or four hours. The heavy cloud cover obscured his trail but he walked in ditches near the road so he wouldn't get lost.

Brant preferred to think that PeaceKeepers monitored valley roads continually, even at night. With this mindset, he stayed alert, hiding behind bushes or crouching down in ditches because he knew Peace-Keepers routinely wore night optical devices (NODs) to find insurgents. Although he couldn't see anyone, that didn't mean his enemies couldn't see him. *Better safe than sorry.*

When he finally arrived at the fault bridge, Brant ran briskly across the sturdy structure. Once he crossed over the crevasse, he jumped back into a ditch next to the road. As he lay flat on the ground, he listened for any troop movement.

All he heard was the rapid beating of his own heart. *I'm okay. I only have a few more miles to go. Once inside Marcus's fort, I'll send a quick message to Toy; then I'll talk with Marcus and Ryan.*

Brant stayed in the ditch, walking in a crouched position. Suddenly he heard large, military vehicles rumbling through the valley. *Probably filled with PeaceKeepers,* he thought grimly. Brant stretched out flat on his back with his face sticking out of the ditch's muddy water. Remaining motionless, he watched three trucks roll by him on the road leading to the enclosed compound.

The trucks stopped about two miles away from the compound's gate. A commander stepped out of the lead truck to talk with his subordinates in other vehicles. After a few minutes of discussion, the truck drivers quietly moved their vehicles into a dense forest for cover. Masked by darkness, troops slipped out of the trucks armed with M4s and NODs, moving quickly through the forest toward the sleeping compound.

Brant knew tonight's compound guards would be searching for him but he hoped they wouldn't mistake a PeaceKeeper for him. Brant whispered, "God, help the sentries distinguish between me and the PeaceKeepers." Unfortunately, the invading soldiers remained so well hidden that Jason and Alicia didn't see the enemy pressing closer to the compound gate.

Brant couldn't play it safe any longer. Knowing that troops would focus on the fenced compound in front of them, he slipped out of the ditch behind the PeaceKeepers. Ignoring the chill from his drenched clothes, he ran swiftly down the road. He found a grassy ridge behind the troops to set up a defensible position. Lying on his stomach with his elbows resting on the ground, he braced his rifle against his right shoulder. Brant whispered, "Lord, make my aim true." He found his first target, exhaled slowly, and pulled the trigger.

Once Brant's shot fired, everything in the valley erupted. Brant's target fell to the ground. Dead. The shot stunned PeaceKeepers who—at that moment—stood in an unprotected field near the gate. The vulnerable troops began to shoot in Brant's direction and toward the compound guard towers.

Alicia and Jason quickly returned fire from their fortified positions above the advancing army. Within minutes, half-dressed men and women in nightgowns ran to the walls carrying weapons to shoot from fire ports cut into the fence's metal wall. Children stood behind their parents, loading weapons or bringing ammunition.

Everyone now functioned on high alert. Awakened without warning, residents heard weapons firing, people shouting, and bullets ricocheting off the corrugated metal fence but they didn't panic. Hours of weekly training overcame the initial response to flee during an attack. Each person understood their role and position in battle. Everyone fought fearlessly because if captured, they would most likely face execution.

Because of Brant's warning shot and their fortifications, compound residents repelled the PeaceKeepers' attack. Realizing their folly, surviving PeaceKeepers retreated to the closest truck hidden in the woods. Grinding through gears, throwing gravel into the air, and fishtailing up a mountain road toward Kentucky, government soldiers narrowly escaped the valley with their lives.

Disappointed, the leading NCO thought, *I'll report this area but our detachment is spread so thin, we might not ever send more troops back here.*

Ryan carefully aimed his 50 BMG at the fleeing truck. He wanted to shoot the vehicle's engine, but the light was so faint—and the angle so poor—he decided not to waste a bullet. He took his finger off the trigger and rested his cheek on the scope. Narrowing his eyes, he continued to watch the truck until its taillights disappeared over the crest of a hill. When he sensed someone standing next to him, Ryan turned around.

Ryan simply nodded at Marcus. Marcus laid a hand on his friend's shoulder. "Well done, Ryan," Marcus said gravely. "We need to look at our wounded; then see if there are any injured troops outside the fence."

"Whatta you want us to do if we find wounded PeaceKeepers?"

Marcus knew the New World Order ordered the annihilation of all unmarked citizens: in other words, everyone within their community. Marcus replied, "We'll take them prisoner. Maybe they have information that'll help us."

"And if the prisoners won't cooperate?"

Marcus asserted, "They'll stand trial."

Ryan arched an eyebrow. *Stand trial? This is something new.*

Before Ryan questioned him, Marcus continued, "See if you can find Brant out there. Once we remove PeaceKeepers from the field, gather their tactical weapons and body armor, we'll need them. We'll also requisition any vehicles left in the forest." Speaking almost inaudibly, "They'll be back, with reinforcements." As Marcus looked around the compound to assess the damage, Ryan and several other men walked toward the gate to clean the battleground and gather weapons.

Week 3

– Day 2 –

6

ON THE SAME NIGHT Toynell slept in a cave and Brant fought PeaceKeepers, Nellie endured the indignities of captivity. Her trip began in an innocuous, white van that rumbled inconspicuously through the countryside. The van looked more like a mail truck than a prisoner transport, exactly the misperception PeaceKeepers wished to send.

Accustomed to having snipers fire upon their vehicles, Nellie's abductors kept a low profile to reduce surprise attacks. Even though insurgents didn't like government agencies, no one wasted precious bullets on mail trucks. So the truck meandered through the valley—appearing harmless—carrying private citizens to reeducation centers. Although detainees would eventually face a tribunal, they were quietly arrested without any disturbance from the local population. Very few onlookers knew the mail truck contained their shackled friends and family instead of packages and letters.

The van contained seven people: four PeaceKeepers and three prisoners. While one guard drove, his commander issued orders from the front passenger seat. The remaining people assembled behind them. In the back of the mail truck were two metal benches welded on both walls, with a small window on one of the back doors. Two guards sat next to each other on one bench: an older, grizzled man and a nervous teenager. Across from the guards sat three prisoners, chained together: Nellie, a slight ten-year-old girl, and a despondent old man. The seating arrangement was snug but not unbearable.

As they drove toward Marshall City, they passed a farmer trying to break ground with a pick. The farmer looked up at the mail truck, waving enthusiastically.

The driver spoke to his commander, "Is he one of ours?"

The commander flipped through a few pages on his clipboard, "Yeah, a recent convert."

The young guard in the back scoffed at the farmer, "Hah! Toothless moron! He's got no idea this van is filled with his neighbors."

The older guard sitting next to the teen said, "These 'toothless morons' are the ones reporting their friends and families to us. There's big money in being a snitch."

Nellie gasped as she quickly looked out the small window in the back door. Horrified, she thought, *Bobby Joe! We went to school together.*

Watching Nellie's face, the older guard said, "You knew him, didn't you?" Nellie shifted her eyes but remained speechless.

Smiling at Nellie, the commander glanced over his shoulder, "That's how we knew where to find you. People are creatures of habit." Looking at some documents, he explained, "Our problem was trying to locate you. Whenever our troops got within a mile of your house, you disappeared. But your neighbor . . ." looking at his list again, "a Robert Joseph Miller, reported that you and your friends stayed close to the house every morning. That's why we arrived early today."

Nellie sighed.

"Whether you know it or not, you also revealed how we can catch the others that disappeared into the woods." Nellie looked at the commander with a doubtful expression. "Two blasts from a whistle, isn't it?" he ventured smugly.

Inscrutable, Nellie continued to look into the commander's eyes without flinching.

"You don't need to say anything." Reaching into his shirt pocket, he pulled out Nellie's red bandana, "I'm just curious . . . what does a handkerchief on the ground mean?"

Nellie thought, *It meant danger. It meant I've been caught.* Without missing a beat, she answered curtly, "It meant that I needed to wipe my nose but your thugs made me drop it."

"Yeah, whatever," sneered the teenager.

Nellie raised her chin to look at the insolent young man sitting across from her. Pimple faced and snaggletoothed, the teen didn't look much older than fifteen.

"What will you do when you reach Marshall City?" Nellie asked the pompous teen.

The young guard glared at Nellie. *How dare she address this unit's newest PeaceKeepers recruit!* "Be quiet, you old bat, or I'll blast you in the belly again!"

The trembling girl sitting next to Nellie cringed. She'd been beaten so many times by this sadistic guard that she feared for her life. The girl whispered faintly, "Shhh. He's insane."

Nellie licked her split lip and stared at the teenaged guard defiantly. *Take it easy,* Nellie told herself; *maybe you can reason with this kid. He doesn't seem very bright. None of the men respect him so I might be able to talk with him.*

Nellie changed her demeanor, softening her tone. Looking at her feet in a defeated posture, she asked the teen, "Where'd ya grow up?"

"What's it matter to you?" he asked sarcastically, sneering hatefully.

"Just passing the time with conversation," Nellie responded evenly.

"No place in particular. Everywhere I guess."

Feigning interest, she asked, "Whatta you mean?"

"My old man left Ma when I was a kid; I don't even remember 'im. Ma got busted for selling dope so I been in foster care mosta my life. What a waste a time! A bunch a do-gooders, like you, tryin' to help me 'become a respectable man.' I hated 'em all."

He glared at Nellie, hoping to get a rise out of her. Nellie met his gaze, but said nothing.

The teen leaned over closer to Nellie, "I hate all of you, Bible readin' hypocrites! You say one thing but do somethin' else. There ain't a one of you who iddn't twofaced."

"You're right," she said. "Not one of us is perfect. No one can stand before God alone."

"Humph, God! I ain't got time for God. He never done nothing to help me."

"Maybe you never asked."

Infuriated, the teen sat up, began to swing his rifle butt at Nellie's face when the older guard jammed his forearm into the teen's throat. The seasoned guard snarled quietly into the teen's ear, "You hit this lady again and *I'll* kill you."

Chastised, Pimple Face slouched back against the wall of the mail truck, sulking. The two men in the front seats gazed at each other, rolling their eyes.

Looking at Nellie with a deadpan expression, the old guard warned, "Don't try to make friends with us. Our job is to get you to headquarters alive. Nothin' more. You don't mean anything to me, but I do get paid to deliver live bodies. People spend lots of money to buy tickets to watch unmarked insurgents lose their heads."

∽❧∾

While Nellie endured the hardships of imprisonment, Juan's group spent a peaceful evening around a small campfire. In addition to roasting rabbits, Miah made a salad of water cress, purslane, and dandelion leaves. As the other men picked at the salad, Miah added, "These greens taste better with vinegar but you get used to 'em dry too."

Chewing on the greens unenthusiastically, Gabe grumbled, "They're probably good for us, right?"

"Yep," replied Miah.

"I'm done," said Juan. "Once you guys finish dinner, I'll wash our plates and forks in the river." Nodding, Gabe stuffed the remaining salad into his cheek and passed his utensils to Juan. Miah and Caleb followed suit.

Noting Miah's practiced dinner preparation, Caleb noted, "I'm surprised you didn't save the rabbit pelts, Miah."

As he stirred the fire, Miah answered, "If we were at home, I would've. I can't think of softer fur to make a blanket for Nora."

Gabe chuckled, "Someday, you're gonna make a great wife."

Miah blushed but said matter-of-factly, "When we killed a pig, Nellie used to say, 'Use everything but the oink.' I guess her advice really stuck in my head."

"I'm glad it did, buddy," Juan said as he stood up with the dishes, "because without your training, we'd probably go hungry tonight." Despite the tasteless salad, the others grudgingly agreed.

Even after traveling one day together, the group began to coalesce. Although they shared similar talents, each man brought his own specialties to the team. A warrior and tactician, Gabe was their leader. Caleb, an expert marksman with a strong medical background, became the party's doctor. A generalist, Miah liked to solve mechanical problems. And Juan, a brave soldier and hard worker, offered the group his natural finesse to tell stories.

Tonight was no exception. As the men settled around a dying fire, Juan gazed at Nora curled between two exhausted puppies—three sleeping babies. He stared at the fire then looked into the eyes of his companions.

"These coals remind me of a time when our unit was stranded at night, on a hill just above Jalalabad. We didn't see anything, but we knew we weren't alone." The others shifted forward—gazed at the glowing embers—and imagined city lights halfway around the world. With crickets chirping in the background and stars flickering overhead, the men sat quietly and listened intently as Juan spun another one of his colorful, spellbinding tales.

✐

Nellie sat on the cement floor of a dismal jail cell. The frightened girl from the white van sat beside her, still trembling. Nellie wrapped her arm tightly around the girl's fragile shoulders and hummed a melody. Eventually, the girl's head rested on Nellie's soft shoulder and she fell asleep. Too cold and restless to sleep, Nellie continued to hum quietly.

Nellie watched the other women in her cell. Most of the captives were Christian, but some were Jewish or people simply too independent to receive the beast's identification mark. Whatever their reasoning, they were all sentenced to face a tribunal judge in the days ahead, one last opportunity to renounce Jesus Christ and receive the mark, or face execution.

What will I say? Nellie wondered.

As she listened dully to rats scampering among prisoners, Nellie noticed a young woman across the cell watching her closely. Nellie smiled weakly. Emboldened, the young woman slid over to the old woman.

As she touched Nellie's hand, the woman whispered, "Why aren't you afraid?"

"Oh, darlin', I *am* afraid."

"Do you know what you're going to say when you face the judge?"

Nellie sighed, "Not yet; but I prayed that the Lord will give me his words when the time comes." Nellie studied the young woman's dirty, terrified face. She smoothed the woman's dark, oily hair, gently touching her face.

Emboldened, the young woman proceeded, "I'm not a Christian; I'm an Orthodox Jew. We're not supposed to get tattoos but I'm tempted to put my faith behind me to avoid the guillotine."

"What's your name, sugar?"

"Rachel."

"Rachel, we live in a strange world. Stars fallin' from the sky. Seas and rivers turnin' to blood. Starvation, wars, diseases . . . how long do you think any of us will live—marked or unmarked?"

"I don't know," Rachel moaned, "but I'm so scared!"

"So am I. But I keep my eyes on heaven and Jesus's promise of salvation."

"How do you know you'll be saved?"

"Because I believe what Paul wrote: If you declare with your mouth, Jesus is Lord, and believe in your heart that God raised him from the dead, you'll be saved."[1]

Somewhat hopeful, Rachel asked, "What's Jesus like?"

"He is so kind, so wonderful."

A raspy, smoker's voice cackled from another corner, "How could a kind, wonderful savior subject you to this?" A middle-aged woman spread her arms wide, indicating the deplorable cell where they sat. "What sorta 'God' is that?"

"A perfect, righteous God."

"Humph! I'll take my chances with our Sovereign Leader," the belligerent woman declared. She ran gnarled fingers through her thinning, shoulder-length hair.

"That's your decision," Nellie answered. "But as for me and my house, we will serve the Lord."[2]

"You're an idiot!" In a huff, the woman gathered her coat around her chest, pulling the collar up to cover her ears. "Keep your humming and praying to yourself. I wanna sleep!"

"You will never rest peacefully, not now, and certainly not in hell," warned Nellie. "If you want to talk about Jesus, you know where to find me."

"Yeah, yeah, yeah. Here's my last question to you: how will you be able to talk without a head?" snarled the woman contemptuously.

Demons slithering through the prison cells, attached their tentacles to some of the quivering girls and women. The unclean spirits whispered lies into prisoners' ears. "You will never find redemption in this world." "Your only hope of survival is to renounce Jesus Christ." "There is no life after death, there is only death; and death will be a welcome relief to this painful existence."

1. Rom. 10:9.
2. Josh 24:15.

Yet within the same, wretched cells were glowing angels: tall warriors wearing brilliant, white tunics, standing beside stalwart Christians, their swords drawn, ready to attack. As Christians softly sang praises to God, the Holy Spirit flowed through the women, encouraging them, strengthening their bodies and souls, and giving them life-affirming words to share with fellow captives. Christians spoke boldly to their cellmates, "Believe me, sister, there is life after death." "Jesus is our hope and salvation. I will see him face-to-face when I reach heaven." "No matter what you've done—if you receive Jesus as your Lord and savior—your sins will be forgiven."

Colliding within the jail cells were conflicting viewpoints with two very different results: forgiveness or condemnation, humility or pride, hope or despair, life or death. In other words, the basic issues that all rational people consider sometime in their lives. *This is the battle.*

Week 3

– Day 3 –

7

As TIME PASSED, JIM became stronger. Although he still mourned Beth's death, he no longer contemplated suicide because too many families depended on him. He continued to minister to sick people and animals using medical skills he learned in the Army. When he wasn't caring for patients, he helped Sara settle into their new home.

A millionaire's dream lodge. The abandoned log house sat in a lush, green cove between two imposing mountain ridges. Once they moved their meager belongings into the house, they repaired fences and barns for their growing herds of livestock. After settling their animals securely, they concentrated on making the house a home—dusting furniture, rearranging wall coverings, and organizing the kitchen. Delightful tasks for people accustomed to living with practically nothing.

But the Wilkins were not alone. Rosa Peña, Juan's wife, lived in the same house. With eight bedrooms, several sitting rooms, a large, open living room, and an amply supplied kitchen, many families could live comfortably in the mansion. Realizing the value of living with others, Sara and Rosa cleaned the entire house to make room for newcomers that might join them later.

Rosa adapted quickly to her new surroundings; she loved the Wilkins, the house, and her new life. Having lived on a farm, Rosa understood animal husbandry so she helped Jim with his veterinary practice. Furthermore, she knew homesteading practices so she helped Sara with gardening and food preservation. Pregnant with her first child, Rosa took precautions with some of her activities, but she always worked without complaining of muscle aches or her ever-increasing baby bulge. Rosa looked down the driveway daily hoping to see Juan's swarthy face, but she knew he would return to her as soon as he could.

She smiled, *Juan is a good man.*

"Ahh, there's nothing like coffee brewed in an old sock first thing in the mornin," joked Juan to his buddies.

"Yeah, I thought you'd like it," said Miah. "When I found a can fulla coffee in that old shack, I did a double take to make sure I wasn't dreaming it."

"It was a good find, guy. Maybe tomorrow morning, you won't add as much coffee to the sock. This batch could take paint off a barn."

Gabe and Caleb cautiously took sips from their tin cups then looked at Juan, nodding in agreement. Caleb added optimistically, "It'll open your eyes; that's for sure. We'll have lots of energy when we search empty houses."

Still on the opposite side of the Tennessee River from the log mansion, the men hiked downriver in search for some kind of watercraft. While they hadn't found a boat, raft, or even an inner tube, they found other sundries in empty houses. Whenever they uncovered anything valuable, they stuffed the item into their backpacks. So far they requisitioned extra cans of food, matches, and batteries. Although the explorations slowed their progress to cross the river, everyone enjoyed foraging for supplies.

Despite the men's amazing discoveries, the puppies brought home the weirdest acquisitions. After the first day of travel, the puppies learned to hunt. At first the pups just gulped down mice they caught in fields but soon they worked together to catch rabbits. When Sydney brought a rabbit to Gabe, he made such a fuss over her that both puppies sought bigger game to please the men.

Three days after leaving Papaw's farm, the group settled down near their evening campfire. Suddenly they heard the trampling of many feet. Grabbing their weapons, the men braced for an attack. Seconds later, Gabe burst out laughing when he saw Shadow and Sydney deftly herding three goats into their campsite.

"What are we supposed to do with goats?" chuckled Gabe. Looking at Miah, "How does roasted goat taste?"

Before anyone made another comment, Miah said hurriedly, "Wait a minute, don't do anything!" He pointed to a specific goat, "That poor doe needs to be milked. She's so engorged she probably *followed* the dogs into our camp."

Juan's eyes sparkled; he read Miah's mind. "I'll bet there's a dark-haired girl who would love a cup of goat's milk."

"My thinking exactly!" exclaimed Miah. Nora walked over to the tame goats and started petting them. "I hope the puppies didn't take the goats from a farm."

"I don't think so," noted Caleb, petting the head of a nanny goat. "When they came into camp, they looked lost and afraid. Now they actually seem *relaxed*."

Gabe offered a cracker to one of the goats and the small herd gathered around him, begging for more food. Gabe petted the animals hesitantly, a bit unsure about how to treat these friendly, horned creatures. "They smell kinda . . . musky," Gabe said.

"Yeah, kinda like us," added Juan.

By this time, Miah tied the engorged doe to a tree. As she nibbled on a bush, Miah sat on a stump and started to milk her. Raised in cities, both Caleb and Gabe watched Miah with fascination.

What else does this kid know? thought Gabe. He looked at Caleb and noticed his friend watched Miah with curiosity. Gabe asked his friend, "Do you know how to milk a goat, Caleb?" Caleb simply shook his head, no. "Me neither. The kid stays."

Playing along with their ribbing, Miah looked up at the new guys, "What about Nora?"

Juan piped up, "Oh, bringing Nora was never in doubt. That's the cutest, little girl I ever saw! Hey, I have an idea for dinner . . . I saw a patch of wild asparagus not too far from here. How does cream of asparagus soup sound?"

"Made with goat's milk?" asked Caleb. Juan nodded his head. "Sounds fantastic!"

"Alright, I'll go cut the asparagus," responded Juan. Gazing at the three goats and two growing puppies, Juan smiled, "Looks like we're gonna need a bigger boat."

෴

Although Miah's dad, Bill, hesitated about walking to Miah's new home, he finally relented. When Miah left with Nora, Bill realized that no one would pamper his selfish whims anymore. Without his dutiful wife, his industrious son, his precocious daughter, or his forgiving father, Bill really didn't have much in his life.

Oh, he did have his special interests, his own hobbies. He'd never give up those pleasures but it didn't look right to desert your children. He could say his entire family died in one of the countless disasters plaguing the world but he didn't feel like using that excuse yet. Miah was too important—probably his most valuable asset—and Bill didn't want to burn any bridges.

The kid could do practically anything but he never expected payment in return. To Bill, Miah was the goose that laid golden eggs. Bill always brokered deals with anyone willing to pay for Miah's labor, with some of those people paying handsomely. Miah always brought home his earnings to put food on their table but Bill managed to siphon off enough money for liquor, drugs, and gambling.

Actually, Bill was partially responsible for Miah's separation from their family. After he came home from work one day, Miah grabbed his rifle to begin hunting game for dinner. When Miah waited by the front door for his dad to accompany him, his mother said, unconvincingly, that his father felt "under the weather." Miah bit his tongue. He knew his dad was just recuperating from another bender but his mom didn't want to belittle her husband—especially in front of the children.

While Miah hunted, Bill continued to sleep, unconcerned about his family's welfare. Unfortunately after Miah left, others watched their house with interest. Completely oblivious to danger, Bill woke up when his wife shook him frantically, whispering, "Bill, someone's trying to break into our house!"

Bill pulled off his blanket, stumbled out of bed, and tried to adjust his bleary eyes. His wife seized him abruptly, pulling him and Nora into a small, hidden storage area under the staircase. Just as she closed the recessed door, the family heard vandals break into their house.

"Hellooo! Anyone home?" snickered a young man.

"Pizza delivery!" shouted an arrogant male voice. He rang out in a singsong manner, "Come out, come out, wherever you are."

A desperate female voice uttered, "If they wanna hide, let 'em hide. Let's get some food and get outta here!"

Mr. Arrogant replied, "You're such a spoilsport. Go check out the kitchen, Miss Goodie Two-Shoes. Junior, see if you can find anything valuable that we can use for tradin'."

"What are you gonna do?" complained Junior.

Twirling a baseball bat in circles, Arrogant said, "I'm gonna play ball." With that announcement, he gritted his teeth with a menacing snarl and started to swing the bat. He charged through every room, smashing lamps, wooden tables, windows—anything breakable. Whenever he made a spectacular noise, he'd say, "Strike one!" or "Woops, foul ball!"

When he heard a grandfather clock chime six times in a back room, the vandal ran down a hallway, located the clock, and proceeded to pulverize it with his bat. "Strike one," he hit the pendulum; "Strike two," he broke the clock face; "Ball one," he splintered the wooden cabinet; and finally, "Home run!" he pushed the clock over kicking it and tearing it apart with his bare hands.

Miah's mother heard light steps run down the hall. "What's the matter with you?" screamed the girl. "Are you nuts? We just need food!"

"I need to rip somethin' apart!" Using his bat to crush the glass on the clock, "I love bustin' stuff, especially glass!" He cackled ecstatically.

"Let's get outta here!" screeched Junior. Miah's parents heard two sets of feet run from the house. The final intruder—the bat swinger—broke a few more items on his way out, stomped down the porch steps, leaving a deadly silence in his wake.

Within the dark, cramped storage room, Miah's family listened intently. They heard nothing. Nora's mother continued to hold her daughter tightly to her chest, keeping the child quiet. Nauseated by the smell of moth balls and Nora's dirty diaper, Bill almost got sick but he controlled his churning stomach—at least for the time being.

Eventually, Bill opened the storage room door to catch a breath of fresh air. Sensing stillness in the house, Bill tumbled out of their snug quarters, gasping for breath, holding his stomach. Miah's mom crept out of their hiding place with more caution, still holding Nora close. "I think they're gone," she said hesitantly.

"Ya think?" snarled Bill contemptuously. "We need to get outta here as fast as we can."

Stunned, his wife objected, "What about Jeremiah? We can't leave without him . . . maybe we could write him a note, something." Her eyes swept the room frantically searching for a pencil and paper. Despite his wife's pleas, Bill yanked his coat off a chair and declared that *he* was going to his father's farm in Tennessee.

"At least in Tennessee, we'll be safer," he stated, his head still pounding from his blinding hangover. "If you want to stay here with Nora to take your chances that Miah may—or may not—return, be my guest. I'm leaving!"

Miah's mother looked at her baby girl then looked weakly at her husband. Without writing a note, she started packing. She opened dresser drawers, clutched some clothes, frantically stuffed everything into a backpack kept under their bed, and reluctantly followed Bill out of the house.

When Miah returned home several hours later carrying two doves for dinner, he found his family gone and the house torn apart. The young man thoroughly searched each room before he accepted the fact that they left without him. Remembering to go to his granddad's farm if they ever got separated; Miah hastily planned a trip from his West Virginia home to the Tennessee Mountains.

It's possible that I may catch up with them before they get too far, he told himself. As the doves roasted over a small fire, Miah gathered supplies for his trip. A few crushed packages of potato chips, several pairs of jeans, tee shirts, water, and his rifle—the bare necessities for survival. After eating a small portion of roasted meat, he stowed the remaining food in his backpack because he assumed he'd find his family soon. As Miah walked out the front door, he turned to look at his home one last time. Exhaling, Miah walked away silently. He didn't bother to lock the door; he just slipped into the obscure blackness of night, hoping to find his family by morning.

✑⊙⊙✑

Now (almost two years later) Bill walked idly toward the Tennessee River in search of his son and daughter. Bill didn't understand the hardships Miah endured during their separation. Moreover, he didn't realize the changes Miah experienced, physically and spiritually. At first his son's growth didn't matter, but then Bill reconsidered his opinions. *I can charge more money for his strong back*, Bill thought greedily, *but I hate his conversion to Christianity*.

Vaguely aware of Miah's influence on his spiritual deliverance, Bill discarded the importance of discipleship. *I don't need God, I need liquor!* Bill chuckled dismissively. He was an easygoing guy, paid his bills, kept a roof over his family's heads. He wasn't an alcoholic or a druggie. He was a social drinker and a recreational drug user.

Bill was in control. His life wasn't bad. Granted, life was better before all the craziness started, but he adjusted. He made friends.

"That's right," the demon, Alcohol, hissed into Bill's brain. "You don't need God, you need a stiff drink."

Another voice whispered, "And a cigarette, a cigarette would taste great with a shot of bourbon."

Licking his dry lips, Bill approached the Tennessee River and noticed that PeaceKeepers locked the ferry station for the night. Bill turned around to observe groups of people huddled over fires on the beach, talking casually. Suddenly Bill heard the roar of laughter and cursing from a crowd bent over a blanket, throwing dice.

"A craps game!" the gambling demon exclaimed to Bill's psyche. Bill riveted his attention to the loud, raucous shouting. He sauntered over to the party, trying to look naïve: an easy patsy.

Bill smiled at the revelers and walked over to a man blowing smoke rings. Bill sniffed the air like a bloodhound searching its quarry. "Hey, buddy, do ya have another cigarette?" Bill asked. Now he was the guy's best friend.

"Got anything to trade?" the smoker asked, warily.

"Nope. Maybe a few good stories."

Patting a package of cigarettes in his coat pocket, the man lamented, "I could use a good story." After Bill shared some amusing gossip, the man gave Bill one of his precious cigarettes. Bill lit it and took a long drag. As he blew the smoke out, Bill asked the man, "Know anyone with some liquor?"

The guy looked at him with amazement. He rolled his head to the right, "Yeah, there's a feller over there with a flask but it'll take more than a story to uncork his bottle."

Eyes twinkling, always open to a dare, Bill responded, "I'll make a bet with ya. If you see me talk him outta a swig from his flask, will you gimme another cigarette?"

"You're on! But if you lose, I get that cap you're wearing."

"Deal!"

Bill walked over to an elderly gentleman standing outside the firelight. The smoker watched as Bill started talking with the gentleman, both men laughed together, and within five minutes, the old man offered Bill his flask.

Bill smirked, glanced over at the smoker, smiling radiantly. *I own this place.*

As his minions—Alcoholism and Gambling—screeched with delight, drooling over another reclaimed victim, Addiction murmured into Bill's mind, "Yeah, Bill, you're in complete control."

Week 3

– Day 3 –

8

In the early morning hours after their battle with PeaceKeepers, Marcus, Ryan, and Brant talked about bringing Toynell and their livestock into the compound. They wanted to move quickly and quietly. Despite their concern to clean the battlefield, they felt more compelled to bring Toynell into their secure camp rather than burying dead PeaceKeepers.

Knowing that Ryan's team scoured the battlefield, Marcus inquired, "Any surviving PeaceKeepers?"

Ryan shook his head, "Nope."

Marcus pondered that answer for a moment. He looked into Ryan's steady gaze then proceeded, "Brant and I will ride over to Nellie's farm first thing in the mornin'. Do you need anything before we go?"

Ryan shook his head, "No, I think we've got everything we need."

Marcus resumed, "We'll pack up Brant and Toynell's supplies and bring the herd back by evening." He studied Brant, "We may not get everything you want, but at least you'll have Toynell and your animals inside fenced walls by tomorrow night."

Relieved, Brant said, "I can't thank you enough."

Marcus patted Brant on the shoulder, "You can thank us once we're safely inside these walls again. Until then, let's pack our gear tonight and get a little shut-eye."

A few hours later, Marcus awoke to sounds outside of his bedroom window: horses snorting, men and women talking, and buckboards creaking. Marcus rubbed the top of his head, yawning. He shifted his weight to sit upright on his bed. He felt every new bruise and strained muscle resulting from last night's skirmish. He stood up, threw his shoulders back, let his spine snap into place, and walked stiffly to the window.

He pulled away the drapes, pushed open the old, squeaky pane, and watched his friends. At first they didn't notice Marcus smiling at them, but it doesn't take long for people to feel the eyes of a watching person. Still jumpy from the skirmish, the crowd started to glance around, looking for intruders. Alicia was the first to notice Marcus.

"Hey, sleepyhead, when did you decide to wake up?" she teased.

"Ah, I was just enjoying the view. What's with the big production?"

"It looks like you got a lotta helpers today. What's with the secrecy anyway?" The tall woman walked over to his window, "Didn't you know that we'd all want to help you and Brant?"

Marcus leaned against the window frame, crossing his arms in front of his chest. A grim expression fell over his face, "The last time I asked for volunteers to go to Nellie's house, everything ended badly."

Alicia remembered. The last group that ventured from Nellie's farm became victims of renegades; and many of those innocents died. No one needed to remind community members of the hazards beyond their perimeter. Nevertheless, at least twenty people stood ready to help Brant and Toynell bring their belongings into their commune.

"That's why so many of us wanna go with you," she stated firmly. "This time everyone's gonna come back alive."

Glimpsing over Alicia's shoulder, Marcus spied Brant talking with some ranchmen. Always eager to learn new things, Brant enjoyed listening to his neighbors pass on general knowhow. Brant looked over at Marcus, gave him a broad smile and tipped the brim of his hat.

Marcus looked back at Alicia. "Let me get dressed and grab somethin' to eat."

"There's no hurry," she remarked, "the sun's not even up yet." She turned back to the gathering crowd. When she rejoined the group, she accepted a mug of strong, black coffee from an elderly neighbor pouring drinks for everyone.

The old man squinted at her with watery, gray eyes, his weathered face crinkled as he spoke, "I'm not much help at herding livestock no more, but I can make a mean cuppa Joe."

Alicia took a sip of the thick brew, opening her eyes wide, "Whew, you're not kindin'." Before she left, she added, "I think I'll check out the rest of this outfit but I'll bring your mug back before we leave."

"Sounds good."

Alicia strolled nonchalantly behind Marcus's barn. After greeting a few more ranchers, she tossed the remainder of her coffee on a sickly-looking bush. Glancing over her shoulder then again at the plant, she mumbled, "I don't know if there's much life left in you but this coffee will either kill you or make you bloom!"

Alicia snickered to herself, but turned back to the crowd when she heard a ringing dinner bell. She rounded the barn, grabbed her mount's reins, walked over to the old neighbor and handed him her mug. "Thank you very much," she said politely. "Now I don't think I'll need to sleep for a week."

The man nodded his head graciously, *Always glad to help.*

Marcus stood on his porch greeting his friends. A towering man, he never planned to oversee such a large group of people. It just happened naturally. Marcus assumed primary leadership because he respected everyone and that respect bolstered his authority. Landowners within the fenced community had complete control over their animals and property but they allowed Marcus to serve as the judge if personal conflicts arose.

"It looks like this is gonna be a good day to herd livestock," he opened. The crowd agreed with cheers and applause. He glanced over everyone's heads to watch Ryan join the group. Addressing Ryan, "Are you coming with us?"

"Nope, I just wanted to rally some volunteers to help us finish cleaning the battlefield and rebuild the fence. Who's in?" Several men broke away from their buddies to offer their help.

Marcus appreciated their sacrifice. Nobody likes to clean battlefields or repair fences. Encouraging more people to help Ryan, Marcus suggested, "If we split this group in half, we could get both jobs done by the end of today. Tomorrow, I'll donate one of my steers to roast: we'll celebrate Brant and Toynell's arrival *and* the repair of our wall." The crowd murmured their approval, dividing into two fairly even detachments.

Once everyone reorganized, Marcus announced, "Arright, let's get these groups movin'!" He hoisted himself into the saddle, enjoying that familiar, creaking sound of leather as he adjusted his position. He counted everyone in his party: six people riding in three horse-drawn wagons; three stockmen on cattle ponies accompanied by dogs; and Brant, Alicia and himself following the others. Twelve people now and thirteen when Toynell returned with them. "God be with us," he prayed under his breath.

Ryan and his team waved as Marcus's contingent left the compound. "Flash us a coded message when you leave Nellie's farm so we'll know when to expect ya."

"Will do!" shouted Marcus.

Talia, Marcus's daughter, held her hands high as she jumped and waved. Marcus blew her a kiss. She always hated to see her dad leave but she understood the importance of this endeavor. She chewed her fingernails absentmindedly, watching her father leading a small group of people into no man's land.

Talia whispered worriedly, "Jesus, please bring my dad home again."

꧁꧂

Although no one in the valley mentioned her name that morning, everyone thought about Nellie. Where was she now? What was happening to her? Was she still alive?

꧁꧂

Living is sort of a relative word, thought Nellie as she shifted her position on the cold, stone prison floor. *I'm breathing, eating some kinda gruel, but this is sure a grim place.* Nellie studied her cellmates: diseased, emaciated creatures. Some young, some old, but it was really tough to guess anyone's age because starvation makes even children look ancient and withered. *Lucky for me, I have so much reserved fat to draw upon*, she smiled ruefully.

"Whatta you smiling about?" her nemesis snarled.

Nellie gazed across the cell at the belligerent woman. "Honestly? I was thinking about my chubby arms."

"Well, give yourself a few weeks in this hole; you'll be as skinny as a super model."

Despite the woman's rude intent, Nellie broke out laughing. "Mercy me! No one—absolutely no one—in my life ever compared me to a super model."

A grin twitched at the corners of the grouchy woman's mouth. Nellie's outburst woke several sleeping women. Although drowsy, the women remained quiet because nobody wanted to incur the wrath of the ill-tempered woman speaking with Nellie; they just stared, scratching lice bites.

"You ain't bad lookin', considerin' where we's at," continued the woman.

"Thank you." Nellie felt Rachel rustling next to her. She shifted her gaze away from the harpy across the cell to look at the dark-haired beauty. "Hey there, sweetie pea, how're you doin'?"

Rachel grasped Nellie's hand. As the young woman kissed Nellie's fingers, she started to cry. Nellie wrapped her soft, warm arms around Rachel and rocked her gently. Nellie hummed a calming melody, brushing stray hair away from Rachel's face. Soon Nellie added words to the tune— odd words, foreign words—but words that made Rachel's fear melt away.

A few other women slid beside Nellie to listen to the strange song. The music was comforting, strengthening. Nellie opened her embrace of Rachel to hold the hands of several women snuggling closer to her. Despite the darkness of the cell, Nellie's face glowed.

Surprised by Nellie's radiance, the scornful woman across the cell said, "You ain't so ugly . . . for a fat, old woman."

Nellie threw her head back, laughing at the woman's backhanded compliment, "Thank you again. And you're not so vicious . . . for a broken, scared woman."

⊷◉☙

That same morning, Juan's camp bustled with activity. While Caleb brewed coffee, Miah milked the goat and kept a watchful eye on Nora. Gabe created trail mix from the nuts, cereals, and dried fruits they found in abandoned houses but Gabe stood up quickly when he heard Juan crashing into the camp.

Wanting to maintain a silent presence, Gabe asked sharply, "Juan, what are you doing?"

"It's not me, mijo," Juan explained in a hushed voice, "it's this herd of animals."

As Juan and the puppies walked into camp, they ushered the entrance of a workhorse mare with her foul, two heifers, and a gaggle of geese.

Despite his normally quiet demeanor, Caleb exclaimed, "What's this?!"

Juan answered, "I don't know, man. I heard some noise in the bushes so I grabbed my rifle to check it out. First, this elephant horse crashed through the trees. Then the cows started licking me with their big, slimy tongues." Spreading his arms open, "And all around my feet were these geese." Juan noticed the geese were already trying to snatch seeds from Gabe's hands, honking noisily. "This is the weirdest thing I've ever seen!"

Sydney sat near the campfire, her head tilted slightly to the right. "*What should we do, Shadow?*" she asked her brother.

Shadow sat down, watching the activity. "*I dunno. Leave them, I guess?*"

The mare walked over to Shadow, pushing him with her nose. "*No, don't leave us here. Take us with you. There are bad people everywhere.*"

Sydney stepped cautiously to the mare to touch noses with her. The mare nickered, "*You're a good dog. Take us with you; we'll be safe with your people.*" The two young cows crowded next to the mare, not wanting to be excluded.

"*I don't know,*" said Syd, doubtfully.

Shadow pranced playfully, stepping around the noisy geese, "*What's wrong, sis? They're not gonna hurt anybody.*"

Miah observed the men and animals without saying a word. Finally he said quietly, "I've been around animals all my life but I've never seen anything like this before."

Juan turned to face his young friend, "Whatta ya mean, buddy?"

"I've never seen new livestock act this friendly with complete strangers. It's like they wanna be near us."

"What?" Gabe asked, puzzled.

Miah explained, processing this phenomenon, "These animals walked into our camp like they belong here. I think . . . they were invited."

"Now, *I'm* not following you," added Caleb, frustrated.

"I think God invited them into our camp."

Juan stared at Miah incredulously. "You mean—"

Miah watched the geese walking near the fire, eating food from Gabe's hand, nestling close to the men's feet, talking incessantly among themselves. The young man nodded his head slowly, "It's kinda like Noah's Ark . . . on dry land."

Now it was Gabe's turn to gape at the young man. "Noah's Ark? Are you kiddin' me?" The gruff man heard that fairy tale when he was a kid, but he was a man now: a hardened soldier. This was no time for stories.

Miah held up his hands, bewildered. "I can't explain all these animals coming out of the woods. For the past two years, every animal I've seen has been terrified of people. Humans are their greatest enemy."

The other men studied the livestock: geese, goats, horses, cows— a veritable children's zoo—that wanted attention! None of the soldiers knew enough about animals to pass judgment, but they also hadn't seen livestock out of their pens before. In fact, they hadn't seen many live animals in a very long time.

"Look at 'em," marveled Miah, "they're eatin' out of our hands. They're lying down! It's like they've been around us for years."

Following Miah's rationale, Caleb reasoned, "They should be afraid of us. Afraid that we'll kill them, right?"

"Exactly," responded Gabe, stroking a gander that sat in his lap.

Juan stood transfixed. Perplexed. "So what should we do?"

Unconvinced of Miah's theory, Caleb and Gabe remained undecided about their next move. These strangers were definitely stranger than anyone they knew.

Miah suggested, "I think we should keep doing what we're doing: moving down river, staying away from people, searching for a boat in vacant houses. If the animals leave, they leave; but if they stay with us, we'll take care of 'em."

Caleb stared intently at each man in the group, "We won't be inconspicuous anymore."

Gabe ran a hand through his thick beard, concerned. The gander in his lap started to nuzzle his arm with light pecking—not spiteful goose bites—just friendly nibbling. Idly, Gabe stroked the bird's feathers again. He looked at all the animals, clearing his throat, "I'm okay with Miah's idea. Let's keep looking for some kinda boat to cross this river. Maybe we'll get over to the other side before we collect any more animals."

Juan scratched his chin, thinking, "Hopefully, they'll swim across the river because we're not going to find a boat big enough for horses and cows."

"Alright," agreed Caleb. "Let's break camp and go to that fancy subdivision about two klicks away. We need to cross this river, no matter what." He studied the horse and cows, "If we don't find any boats, we might end up riding these guys to the other side."

Week 3

– Day 4 –

9

Riding on their cattle horses, Marcus and his group quickly passed over the gorge. As they rode south, he noticed a wisp of smoke from a far off fire. Wary, Marcus stopped moving and pointed to the smoke.

Alicia volunteered to check out the fire but Marcus restrained her. "You and I'll go together in a minute." He asked a reliable rancher to lead the others to Nellie's farm without delay. "Get Brant's stuff packed quickly and head back over the bridge as soon as you can. I don't know who—or what—we'll find by the fire but I'd like to see y'all back home where it's safer."

Accepting Marc's decision, the group left without delay. They pushed their wagon teams of oxen and horses a bit faster; moreover, everyone did one last press check on weapons to make sure they were ready to fire. No one bothered to admire the scenery or talk casually; there was work to do and very little time to accomplish it.

Nellie woke up in a knot of sleeping women—heads leaning sideways, hair covering faces, feet touching legs, arms splayed randomly—all breathing deeply, a few even snoring. Sometime in the early morning hours, Nellie stopped singing and peacefully dozed off. Now she needed to stand up and stretch. Stiff from the cold rock floor, she tried to carefully unwind herself from her cellmates without waking anyone. Most of the sleepers continued to doze, but one woman with blazing red hair and striking green eyes, woke up. Nellie put a finger to her lips, indicating silence, and Red helped Nellie to her feet.

"Gracious! That's a miserable bed for old bones," whispered Nellie, rubbing her sore knees and back. "Thank you for helping me stand," she smiled, "I might'a been struggling there for a long time." The red-haired woman nodded kindly. Nellie reached out her hand, "Name's Nellie."

The red-haired lady shook her hand, "Cassie."

"Short for Cassidy?"

"No, short for Cassiopeia."

"Whoa, that's a ten dollar name. So how did ya land in here?"

"Hmm, let's see . . . besides being unmarked, I'm what they call an academic heretic, a menace to society, and now—although it's not a crime—an untenured faculty member. So if you talk with me, you may become wiser, but your wisdom will be considered politically incorrect, possibly even subversive."

"Ahh, an insurrectionist," Nellie grinned.

Cassie's green eyes flashed wickedly, "You have no idea of the depth of my insurrection."

Nellie laughed with this conspirator, "I'll betcha we know some of the same people."

Cassie liked this old gal. *She's smart, kinda sassy.*

The two women sat in a corner and began to talk quietly, comparing notes, exchanging ideas, discussing philosophies. Cassie marveled that despite their dissimilar backgrounds, they actually shared a lot of common beliefs. She couldn't remember the last time she spoke with such candor without suspecting she would be reported to authorities: the department chair, the university president, or the compliance officer.

Inside academe she was considered a pariah, ostracized by peers for her unconventional thinking. Unconventional ideas. Isn't that why higher education was created? Wasn't it intended to be a safe place for unbridled exchanges of divergent ideas? What was higher education now? An expensive channel designed to indoctrinate young, curious minds to become mouthpieces for the elite cabal: undiscerning students trained to speak and act without questioning their instruction. A perversity of learning. The antithesis of enlightenment.

No longer could faculty facilitate scholarly discussions among differing viewpoints. Rather than expanding one's thinking by politely listening to other opinions, students now yelled at dissenting voices, called classmates cruel names, denigrated the values of anyone that thought differently from them. Universities no longer expanded knowledge; it simply redefined knowledge into a single ideology. *A single mindset that students accepted with blind enthusiasm and I fought against vigorously,* Cassie thought with disgust.

As Cassie described her frustrations and challenges, Nellie listened attentively. When Cassie finally finished her tirade, she looked at Nellie. Nellie smoothed her dress, "Sounds like the government could charge you with a laundry list of crimes. What did they arrest your for?"

"Racial discrimination."

As wagons rolled toward Nellie's farm, Marcus and Alicia rode toward the chimney smoke rising from a small farmstead. They stopped their horses on the crest of a hill. Below them—lying in a gulch of deep prairie grass and wildflowers—sat a one-story log barn remodeled into a small house. The riders watched activity around the farm to assess its danger before riding closer.

Their new neighbors seemed harmless. A few chickens wandered around the yard, clucking, eating bugs, rolling in the dust. Two fenced pens held a pair of pigs and three horses, respectively.

They counted four people moving about the property: three women and one man. With blonde, disheveled hair, the man walked with a limp, sometimes leaning on a crutch to stand upright. The three women were far more interesting. One woman sported a short haircut, almost a buzz cut, and covered her hair with a broad, man-sized hat. The other two women looked very similar: each wore a simple, cotton dress, tied her hair in a loose braid, and wore heavy-duty leather gloves. Simple, hard-working farm people.

"I don't think they'll give us any trouble, Marcus," remarked Alicia, already bored.

"Nope. We might as well stop by and say hello before we head over to Nellie's."

Marcus and Alicia rode their horses leisurely down the hill so they wouldn't alarm the newcomers. The woman wearing the broad hat first noticed the pair, stopped her work, and waited. Marcus waved to let her know that they wished her no harm, but the woman continued to watch them closely with a brooding, unwelcome stare.

As they rode into the yard, the woman with the broad hat said distrustfully, "Whatta ya want?"

Marcus leaned forward in his saddle, "Nothin'. We just stopped to say hello. We live on the other side of the fault and we were just passin' through."

By now, the other three homesteaders joined the lady with the hat. Observing their body language, Marcus already guessed that Big Hat was their leader, but he also sensed animosity between the lame man and Big Hat. Marcus introduced himself and Alicia but the four homesteaders just looked at them guardedly, not sharing their names.

Before they left, Marcus tipped his hat to wish them well. As they rode up the hill toward the road, Alicia said, "I kinda feel sorry for them, Marc."

"I don't trust 'em any farther than I could pick 'em up and throw 'em," judged Marcus.

⌒⊙⊙⌒

"Alright!" shouted Miah. After exploring dozens of houses, he found the one item he hoped to find: a Holy Bible. He held the battered, leather book tightly in his fist, smiling broadly.

Juan stuck his head into the room when he heard Miah shout. He thought the teen discovered a cache of gold, weapons, or food. The Latino stopped suddenly when he saw Miah clutching the Bible to his chest.

Juan smiled, shaking his head. He understood his young friend. "I knew you were looking for something special; I just never thought it was a Bible."

"Ever since I lost my Bible in the river, I've been trying to find another. This is so great!"

Gabriel and Caleb stood behind Juan, watching Miah. The two intel guys looked at each other. As he glanced sideways at Miah, Caleb raised his eyebrows to Gabe, *What's going on with the kid?* Gabe just rubbed his chin.

Walking out of the deserted house, Gabe said, "Let's see what we found today."

Caleb threw a blanket from the house on the front lawn. Each man placed his discoveries on the blanket and, as a group, they appraised the value of each item. This became a game to them; at the end of their game, the man with the most points for the day got the first, and biggest, helping of food at dinnertime.

Each man arranged his findings on one corner of the blanket. As the men emptied their packs, a menagerie of farm animals encircled them. The pair of bashful heifers stayed back a couple of steps, but the mare and her foul bent their heads down to look closely at odd things on the blanket. The geese tried to walk onto the blanket, but Sydney briskly chased them off.

"*Behave yourselves*," Sydney growled to the noisy birds. The geese squonked, flapping their wings indignantly as they ran away from the blanket. Once the geese knew the willful dog wouldn't bite them, they stamped back to watch the goings-on.

Caleb thoroughly enjoyed leading this game. Rubbing his palms together, "Okay, whatta we have today? Let's start with Juan."

Juan didn't find too many things, but what his discoveries lacked in value, he made up in showmanship. He held up a can covered with his handkerchief. "I found a can of," whipping off the handkerchief, "lima beans!"

"Ugh!" all the men said in unison. Nora, sitting on Miah's lap, clapped her chubby hands together.

Gabe spoke first, "Juan, you just lost three points!"

"You're going to have to do something really incredible now, buddy, if you wanna redeem yourself," laughed Miah.

Juan proceeded to show off a multimeter, a hammer, and a sharpening stone. Gabe made an exaggerated yawn. "And last, but not least," Juan held his hand behind his back, "I found this." And when he displayed a corked bottle of wine, the men were suitably impressed.

"It's gonna be tough to beat Juan's score, even with that lame can of beans," speculated Caleb.

Caleb went next. As a medic, he continually searched for first aid kits, and today was no exception. He found assorted bundles of bandages, fresh aspirin, and herbal tinctures. He talked about the therapeutic supplies with such fervor that everyone gave him a high score.

Trying to maintain a straight face, Gabe finally took his turn. He brought out some freeze-dried food and a handheld water filtration system. The score was very close, but he wasn't through yet. The big man straightened up and walked over to his gear. Keeping his back to his friends, he wrestled something out of his rucksack. Turning around, Gabe held up a two-person, inflatable, canvas raft!

His onlookers all yelled at the same time, "Oh, man!" "Touchdown!" "Gabe, you did it!" "No one's gonna top that!" Gabe just beamed with pleasure. He didn't say anything; he just held the crinkled boat above his head proudly.

Miah threw all of the tools he found into his pack without showing them to anyone. Gabe looked at the quiet, young man, and said, "We're not done yet, Miah. You need to take your turn."

Miah said simply, "I found a few tools . . . and a Bible."

Gabe walked over to the unassuming teen. "Stand up, Miah." When Miah stood, he balanced his sister on her feet and she stood beside him, wobbling a bit on the lumpy soil. Gabe put his left hand on Miah's shoulder, shaking his right hand. "What can I say? You found a Bible! I know when I've been beaten. You won, Miah. Hands down."

⁓᪥⁓

The games and banter glued these men together; soon they became a team. They understood each other's hand signals, their moods, their temperaments. While Gabe was the leader, Juan assumed Gabe's second-in-command; when trouble arose, Gabe depended on Juan's intellect and resourcefulness to carry out assignments. With Juan assuming the secondary role, Caleb concentrated on collecting therapeutic plants in the forest and stocking prescription drugs from abandoned bathroom cabinets. Miah simply filled in the gaps with his diverse specialties: tool repair, livestock maintenance, and childcare. As a unit, they each took turns hunting, cooking dinner, and guarding the camp.

After spending several days scavenging supplies, they finally found a boat to cross the Tennessee River. That night during dinner, Juan glanced at the river and said, "Well, fellas, how do you wanna do this?"

"I'd like to cross the river at night," said Gabe. "Government troops walk along the river during the day. I wanna avoid them."

"Okay," said Miah, anxious to start moving forward, "let's do it tonight. With such a little boat, we'll need to make several trips to get everyone across."

The men discussed different courses of action. They finally agreed on who would travel first, second, and so forth, until they all landed on the far shore. They walked until they found a place where the river was only a click wide; this would be their launching site.

According to their plan, Gabe, Miah, and Nora would cross first. Miah would row across the river while Gabe held Nora, once Miah and Nora disembarked, Gabe would row back to the other side alone. In the second crossing, Caleb would paddle across the river, this time with Gabe and Sydney on board. After leaving Gabe and Caleb on the far shore with

Nora, Miah would paddle back to get Juan. On the final leg, Juan would paddle while Miah and Shadow rode as passengers.

Miah would paddle the river twice. Each man volunteered to take the double duty; so to end their debate, they drew straws. Miah won; he drew the longest straw. Miah had the strength and stamina to complete the task so everyone accepted God's choice without further comment. Thus the youngest man would paddle the farthest.

The livestock would either stay on the far shore or swim alongside the boat. This was a difficult decision because they enjoyed the animals but they only had room on the boat for the puppies. Furthermore, everyone realized that with each successive passage, their presence would become more conspicuous to PeaceKeepers, so they limited their crossings to three.

When Marcus and Alicia reached Nellie's farm, they saw everyone steadily working. Women packed household items while men cleaned the barns. With only three wagons to haul their worldly goods, Brant and Toynell understood they couldn't take everything. Consequently, Brant chose which implements to stow in wagons and Toy managed the domestic goods.

Carl—Nellie's fat, orange cat—sat on a wagon seat watching the activities. The cat enjoyed sitting by a fire and drinking milk, but no one wanted to build fires or milk cows today. The big tabby stretched his front legs in front of him, arched his back in a long stretch, and sat down again to clean his paws and face. He eyed the busy people with feline nonchalance, closed his eyes, and felt the warm sunshine on his fur.

No use tiring himself now, traveling was tiring in itself. *I might do a little prowling before we leave*, he thought dreamily, *but it looks like I have all day*. Never one to neglect a nap, Carl closed his eyes again, and dozed.

Maybe Carl's dreams drifted into Nellie's mind that day because Nellie told several of her acquaintances about Carl. "I wouldn't actually say that he's my cat; he's sorta his own cat. He does what he wants, when he wants, but when I sit by the fireplace at night, or shell peas on the front porch, that big, old rascal sits on my lap, purring."

Conversations about the simple joys of life always lifted her cell-mates' spirits. When she noticed women becoming listless and quiet, Nellie brightened the atmosphere with stories about the valley. She talked about Carl, Mattie, her friends, even her favorite flowers.

As she reminisced, others added their own stories. Despite the dismal darkness of the cave-like prison, stories lightened their hearts. The women told anecdotes about people no one else knew, but these stories sustained everyone who heard them. They laughed, they cried, they became friends.

One day, a woman asked, "How long do you think they'll keep us here?"

"Who knows?" answered another, "but the longer we're jailed, the closer we get to actually seeing Jesus's return."

"Do you really think Jesus is coming soon?" the first woman wondered.

"Absolutely!" chimed a third voice. "I wouldn't be here if I didn't believe that. He's comin' back for us, ladies, just you wait and see."

Those who doubted the stories about Jesus sat resolute, yet despondent. They thought about their own lives, their decisions, and ultimately, their deaths. They didn't look forward to anything. Life had no value and death just ended life. To them, life was meaningless, a cosmic aberration, an unplanned event.

Conversely, Christians encouraged each other and the disheartened. They endured imprisonment because they felt free, they disregarded the present despair because they believed in eternal hope, and they loved others because they understood love. They were an anomaly, a strange group of people. Their eccentricity did not escape the attention of unbelievers.

One woman turned to her friend, "You know, Sylvia, I can't wait to get away from these Holy Rollers." Her friend giggled. "Every word they say sets my teeth on edge. Listening to them is like hearing fingernails scrape across a blackboard!"

Women old enough to remember that nerve-wracking noise cringed. "Ugh, I hated that sound!" someone declared, grimacing.

"Yeah, well now you know how much I hate these Christians."

Nellie didn't bother to look at the person speaking, she already knew. It was that greasy-haired woman, the expert-on-all-things-spiritual, who loved to chastise her. Normally, Nellie just ignored her comments but sometimes she said something.

Today, Nellie spoke, "Your name is Darla, right?"

"Yeah . . ." Darla answered. "What's it to you?" she challenged.

Nellie looked up at the ceiling thoughtfully, "It's a pretty name, but I think from now on, I'll call ya, Darlin'. It suits ya better." Darla remained speechless; she opened her mouth and stared across the room.

Nellie continued, "Whenever you say anything cruel or nasty to *anyone* in this cell, I'll try to remember all the people I called darlin' in the past. I'll answer you with the same love I had for those dear people. You may not like me—or anyone else for that matter—but whenever you speak, I'm gonna call you darlin', and mean it."

Darla leaned her back against the stone wall. Numb. No one ever treated her with kindness before; at least no one she could remember. Not her mom, not her teachers, no one loved her. She was never anyone's darling, ever. Until today. *Is this some kinda trick?*

Week 3

– Day 4 –

10

MISSING HIS OPPORTUNITY TO travel with Miah, Bill still looked for his son and daughter along the river. Bill tried to forgive Miah for deserting him but he couldn't muster the compassion. "There was no reason for him to leave without me," Bill grumbled, "I just slept in a little."

As he searched for his family, Bill stayed entertained with his new friends. He gambled and drank every night, but he never became so obnoxious that PeaceKeepers arrested him. He also never ran out of money.

This was the beauty of living in a crush of strangers. He moved through crowds inconspicuously, picking pockets, earning a fine income. No one suspected the good-humored man with a charming smile and a self-effacing demeanor of any wrongdoing. He was just an average guy with a quick wit, and even quicker fingers. By the time people realized their money or personal treasures were missing, there was no one around. It was as if the items vanished into thin air.

Bill never tallied stolen items; he just spent them leisurely every night as he gambled. One day, a steely-eyed man, who lost quite a bit of money to Bill several nights in a row, questioned Bill's deep pockets. "How much money do you really have for gambling?"

Bill gave him a startled look, "Who, me?"

"Yeah, you, wise guy. I been watching you real close like and there ain't no way you got all that money in your pockets without stealin' it."

Assuming a cool attitude, Bill dusted off his new jacket (won a few nights ago from another chump), and acted as if the man disputed his expertise at craps. "Well, if you'll pardon me for saying, I know when to walk away from a game before I lose too much money."

"That's just the point," the man said, inching closer to Bill's face, "you don't walk away! You stay until you're pulling lint outta yer pockets.

But lo and behold, the next night, you're in fat city again, playing like there's no tomorrow."

A PeaceKeeper standing nearby suspected a dispute brewing so he moved closer to listen to the quarrelers. Lately, people complained to government troops that they lost their life savings by simply walking through congested campsites. Their commander asked soldiers to apprehend anyone caught stealing, and maybe today, he found one of the culprits.

Still maintaining his innocence, Bill turned his back on the sore loser. He put his hands in his jacket pockets and tried to walk away. But this time his casual behavior didn't work. The PeaceKeeper collared Bill, dragging him away from a growing crowd of gawkers. Doubtful of Bill's virtue, the soldier decided to take Bill to his commander.

The soldier brought Bill into a canvas tent which served as the makeshift headquarters. Behind an olive green, metal desk—a holdout from last century's military décor—sat a weather-beaten, white-haired officer. When Bill stood before the commander, he had very little to say. The commander asked Bill to empty all his pockets. Bill reached into his pockets withdrawing a few silver coins, cigarettes, a girl's locket, candy bars, a man's watch, bullets, and two lighters; he placed the assorted sundry on the officer's desk.

The commander smiled. Although these things looked like ordinary junk, he knew better. These were valuable trading items—small, insignificant pieces easily snatched from unsuspecting marks, but highly negotiable.

The officer picked up the girl's locket. "Tell me about this necklace."

Bill cleared his throat, "That belongs to my little girl."

"Really?" the commander arched his brow. "What's inside the locket?"

Bill cleared his throat, *This isn't so bad.* "Who knows what girls put into lockets?"

The officer opened the locket, "It's empty.'"

Bill exhaled a sigh of relief. He reminded himself to stay cool.

The commander made an abrupt change of tact, "Tell me about your watch; the watch you chose *not* to wear on your wrist."

Cagey now, Bill shrugged his shoulders, "Well, I don't want anyone taking it off my wrist so I carry it close to my heart."

The officer stroked the back of the watch. "It's a fine watch, I wouldn't want to lose it either. By the way, who manufactured your expensive watch?"

Bill removed that watch from a man's wrist minutes before his arrest. He hadn't even inspected it yet. Bill opened his mouth to speak but he couldn't think of a believable explanation. He looked at the commander, shut his eyes, dropped his chin to his chest, but said nothing.

"You know this watch is very interesting: a man just reported losing one exactly like this five or ten minutes ago." The commander's eyes sparkled with malice. He turned to an aide, "Corporal, is that man still around?"

"Yes, sir, he's finishing up the paperwork."

"Good." A smile spread across the officer's face, "Could you please bring him to me?"

The commander sat quietly, staring intently at Bill. When the young soldier returned with a middle-aged man, the commander addressed the victim. "You reported that your watch was stolen. Is that correct?"

"Yes, sir."

"You didn't sell it, misplace it, or let someone borrow it?"

Surprised by this question, the man answered, "No, sir. It's too important to me."

"Can you tell me anything distinctive about your watch?"

"Yes, my wife gave it to me on our anniversary. On the back it says, 'To my beloved husband—'"

"That's exactly what my watch says too!" interrupted Bill.

Smiling, the commander coaxed Bill, "What's your name?"

He responded slowly, "Bill."

The commander leaned back in his chair then he looked at the other man standing in front of him. Now the victim understood the commander's line of questioning, so he repeated the inscription on the back of his watch, "To my beloved husband, Harvey." The man pointed to himself, "That's me!"

The commander placed the watch on the table again; this time with the back of the watch facing up, revealing its inscription. "Well, look at that! I believe we found your watch . . . Harvey." He gave the watch back to the disgruntled man, dismissing him. Afterward, the commander looked at Bill, sneering. He growled, "Arrest him."

The time spent packing and loading Toynell and Brant's belongings into wagons passed quickly. The couple took only bare essentials because they assumed someday they'd return to the farm to set up housekeeping again. The stockmen with their dogs, gathered livestock and prepared to drive the herd back to the enclave.

Although it was late afternoon, Marcus felt confident they would return to their secure area before nightfall. Just before leaving, Marcus sent Ryan a quick Morse code message across the canyon. Jason saw the flashing light, noted the time of their departure, and confirmed to Marcus that he received the message.

The return trip through the valley was uneventful. As former residents of the valley, many of the herdsmen recognized changes: farms destroyed by the earthquake, rows of wheat replaced by fields of wild grasses, and a new, unrelenting pack of wolves stalking their progress from a safe distance away. When some men suggested that they kill the wolves, Marcus refrained. He was more concerned about wandering two-legged scavengers in the area than wild animals.

Wanting to keep his party together, Marcus said, "The pack's keeping an eye on us right now. If they get close enough to threaten us, we'll attack. But watch the livestock, especially the young'uns." Consequently, the stockmen kept the herd in a tight group, pressing them forward, watching the predators.

As they drew close to the canyon bridge, Alicia stopped her horse to look in the direction of the settler's homestead. She saw four heads, bobbing above the deep, prairie grass, watching them. *They're sitting in the grass,* she guessed, *but they're not making any aggressive movements. They're just staring at us. That's creepy.*

Marcus edged his mount next to Alicia. "I've been watching 'em too. How would you like to ride over and talk to them for a while?"

"Anything you want me to say to them?"

"Nope, just make small talk. Keep 'em distracted while we get everything over the bridge."

"Will do, boss," she smiled. Making small talk was not easy for her, but she'd rather be sitting on a horse above these people now, than fighting them on the ground later. Alicia galloped over to the quartet, careful not to increase the strangers' anxiety.

As she got within hearing distance, Alicia waved, hollering, "Hello, again!"

Big hat stood up, dusted off her jeans, and placed her thumbs in the waistband of her pants. She looked like a stone monument against the setting sun. A solid, boxy silhouette, with her feet apart, elbows bent by her sides, and that ridiculous hat sitting lopsided on her head. There was nothing friendly about her manner, but nothing markedly hostile either.

Alicia deliberated, *Watch yourself, Allie, this one acts like a viper.* "Hello again!"

Their leader responded, "Seems like you got yourself a regular wagon train."

"Yeah; but we're only passing through. No big deal."

Remaining seated on the ground, the grouchy male uttered something to a woman beside him. Not bothering to look directly at Alicia, he just ogled her with rude, sidelong glances. Alicia decided to ignore him and continued to address the entire group. She spent over half an hour talking about incidental subjects—the weather, their travels, their hobbies—just to distract them for a while. From her peripheral vision, Alicia watched the wagons and livestock pass over the bridge. When she noted that only Marcus remained on her side of the canyon, she paid her respects to the group, and turned to leave.

"You can come visit us whenever you want," said Big Hat.

"Well, before I come back, I'd like to know your name."

The broad woman nodded toward her friends, "They call me, Bert. Name's really Bertha, but I like Bert."

"Alright, Bert. I'll come by occasionally to check on you. See if you need anything." Alicia flashed them a grin and turned her head toward Marcus, her hair glinting gold in the evening sun. She rode off to join the wagons.

"She seems nice," one woman said.

"Yeah, she's somethin'," answered Bert, never taking her eyes off Alicia.

That night when they steered livestock into the compound gate, everyone breathed a sigh of relief. Talia ran over to her dad, greeting him with a kiss. Several women introduced themselves to Toynell, hugged her warmly, and welcomed her and Brant into the fold.

"We spent the day tidying up a small house not too far from here," bragged one of Talia's friends.

"Yeah, we even wiped out all the cupboards and drawers. All you have to do is put your stuff into 'em," added another teenager. Both girls giggled self-consciously.

"Thank you so much," Toynell said, smiling. "I can't think of a better housewarming gift than clean cupboards!"

Ryan approached the party of movers. "Marcus, we figured you'd all be hungry when you got back so we fixed dinner for everyone."

"You read my mind, buddy! I'm starved."

Without further comment, the assembly wandered over to picnic tables, sat down and ate dinner together. It would be days, possibly weeks, before Toynell and Brant completely settled into their new surroundings, but they would rest peacefully tonight. Their animals ate grain in sheltered pens; their possessions sat neatly stacked in their new house; and they felt safe. Sleep would come easily tonight for the young couple.

⌇⌇⌇

On this same night, none of the men in Juan's group planned to sleep. With just a sliver of light, the moon cast very little illumination on the placid river. Gabe appreciated the darkness. He hoped the dimness would increase their chance to elude PeaceKeepers and decrease Juan's anxiety of passing over deep water for a second time.

If Juan felt any nervousness, he didn't voice his concern. He worked quietly, thoughtfully. He checked his rucksack, packed weapons and ammo in watertight containers, and spent time with the animals.

Just before the first launch, the men gathered to pray. Miah opened and closed the prayer, but each man added his own words. Neither Caleb nor Gabe felt comfortable praying aloud, but nothing in this world felt comfortable anymore, so they adapted. Flexibility is indicative of an intelligent mind and these men were nothing if not intelligent. So if praying produced positive results, Caleb and Gabe would learn to pray.

Long after Nora (wearing a child-sized life vest) fell asleep in Gabe's arms, the men continued to wait. They waited until most campfires upriver died out and they no longer heard voices carried by the wind. Around 2:00 a.m., they slid out of the forest with the inflated raft. Gabe and Miah each wore a backpack on his shoulders. Since they weren't taking any puppies on the first trip, they placed the large rucksack between their feet. The raft was filled to capacity.

Juan and Caleb quietly shoved the raft away from the thick shrub growth which obscured their presence. Once the raft floated away from the shore, the two men slipped under the shrubs again to watch their friends. Miah immediately rowed the raft as quickly as possible.

Conscious to keep the oars from splashing, Miah dipped his paddle into the water carefully but smoothly. He made no mistakes. By the time they traveled halfway across the river, his shoulders burned, his arms ached, yet he pushed forward, unrelenting. Three-quarters of the way across the river, Miah thought he heard voices on the opposite shore but he refused to alter his speed. He refused to look behind him, he pressed on.

When they reached the other side, Miah and Gabe slipped into a shadowy cove, beaching the raft in shallow water. Miah quietly pulled the raft into a tangle of dense forest growth. The young man breathed heavily, exhausted but exhilarated. He reached over to take Nora's limp, sleeping body from Gabe. Gabe kissed the top of Nora's head before he gently laid her in Miah's arms. Gabe swiftly unloaded their gear without Miah's help.

Clapping Miah firmly on the shoulder, Gabe murmured, "Good man, Miah. Find a secure place on the hill, lay Nora down then hide our gear up there and wait for us." Gabe studied the land across the river. He pointed at an outcropping of rocks, "Keep watch for us. We can't see very far upstream because of that bend in the river. But if you see anyone coming toward our boat, warn us with that bird whistle you taught Caleb."

Miah nodded. He knew the bird whistle Gabe referred to: mockingbirds. He could imitate the birds fairly well because mockingbirds played with tunes. During their mating season, these songbirds warbled beautiful night melodies; fortunately, the birds rested quietly this evening. If the boaters heard a mockingbird tonight, it would be Miah. As often as he tried to mimic this delightful bird, Miah prayed that he wouldn't be whistling a message to his friends tonight.

Gabe took one last look at guard fires several miles upriver from their original launching point. *We're still good.* Gabe sat in the boat and adjusted his position; afterward he focused his eyes across the river then signaled to Miah. Still holding Nora in one arm, Miah stepped into the shallow water and shoved the boat into the current.

Gabe applied the same quiet rowing technique Miah used. Wearing his NODs, he could see his landing site, but he still felt incredibly exposed on the wide, flat Tennessee River. He paddled steadily. Although the river pushed the boat south, Gabe continued to compensate for its current. He sat low in the inflatable raft and paddled carefully, never taking his eyes off his mark.

From the opposite shore, Juan and Caleb watched Gabe's progress. Despite the weak light, Gabe still looked like a man paddling a boat across the river. No camouflage could disguise his activity. They impatiently watched the big man glide closer to them.

Fidgeting, Juan whispered, "Paddle faster."

When Gabe noiselessly drifted the boat into some tall bushes by the shore, Juan quickly tied the inflatable to a tree. Gabe held the paddle with both hands in front of him and pulled his elbows down to flex his back then twisted his neck. His muscles hurt but he wasn't going to linger in the bushes.

Using only hand signals, Gabe motioned Caleb into the boat. Caleb stepped in carefully, holding Sydney in his arms. Caleb handed Sydney to Gabe and Gabe gave his paddle to Caleb. The puppy wanted to jump out of the boat but Gabe held her tightly, nodding his head to Juan and Caleb. *I'm ready*, he indicated, *Syd's not going anywhere.* Caleb held the oar on his lap, motioned for Juan to push the boat into the current then proceeded to float across the river.

Even though the men moved without speaking, the livestock were now fully aware of their abandonment. This time as the boat sailed across the river, a gaggle of geese followed. The lead gander flapped his wings alerting his flock to follow him. Without delay, ten geese stepped into the river to follow the boat.

"We shoulda killed those noisy geese and ate 'em when we hadda chance," grumbled Gabe, holding the whimpering, squirmy puppy.

Initially, Caleb tried to paddle in front of the geese but the geese prevented his passage. Within seconds Caleb realized, "This might work to our advantage. Look at them; they're all swimming around our boat." Sure enough, the geese surrounded them, from bow to stern, swimming effortlessly, murmuring softly. Both men instinctively crouched low, trying to blend in with the flock of geese. The geese talked among themselves, maintaining the same speed as Caleb, completely oblivious to the men's subterfuge.

From the opposite shore, Miah watched with amazement. "Are you kidding me?" he said, awestruck. Still entranced by the perfect alignment between the boat and geese, Miah murmured, "God, you are so good! So good!" He chuckled as he watched the geese slide gracefully across the wide river, never revealing the boat hidden within their flock.

When the small boat reached the rushes, Miah stepped into the water to pull it ashore. The geese stepped out of the water, muttering groggily, flapping wings, grooming feathers, and settling into the deep grass along the river.

"I can't believe what I just saw," breathed Miah. "It's like you had an army covering you."

"We couldn't believe it either," said Caleb.

Gabe released Sydney. The puppy anxiously leaped out of the boat and stood in the grass, next to the geese. She wagged her tail, panting heavily, nervous from the voyage. Gabe reached down to pet her, "You did good, Syd. I guess you're not the only trained animal we have." Gabe glanced at the geese, shaking his head in wonder. Turning back to Miah he asked, "Where'd you hide our gear?"

Miah led Gabe and Caleb to a nook in the shrubs. Nestled snuggly in the grass, between two backpacks and a rucksack, lay Nora. Miah bundled her in a blanket and the toddler slept contentedly without waking. Miah patted the ground beside his sister, "Come, Sydney." Sydney rushed over to Miah, lying down beside Nora—her head between her paws—looking up at Miah expectantly. "Stay." The puppy remained still; she understood her job.

"Well, Miah, are you ready?"

"I am."

Caleb and Gabe escorted the young man back to the raft. Caleb sat on the ground to blow more air into the boat. Once the craft was firmly inflated again, Caleb closed the air valve, and looked up at Gabe.

Gabe said encouragingly, "We're almost done. You just need to get Juan and Shadow across the river. When we're all together again, we'll put some distance between us and the government troops before daybreak."

"Sounds like a plan," said Miah. After Miah stepped into the boat, the men pushed him out into the current. They watched Miah glide away from the shoreline. Before Miah began to swiftly row toward Juan, several ganders stepped back into the water to follow the boat.

"What are those crazy geese doing?" wondered Caleb.

"I don't know but they sure protected us on our trip. Maybe they'll give Miah and Juan the same good luck."

Caleb watched Miah leave with his goose escort. "I hope so . . . but something just doesn't feel right." Gabe looked at Caleb then returned his worried gaze toward Miah.

Week 3

– Day 5 –

11

WHILE MIAH ROWED ACROSS the Tennessee River, his dad, Bill, sat moldering dejectedly in an old root cellar converted into a PeaceKeeper jail. Bill hated this situation. Oh, he'd been in jails before but he never adjusted well to the inconveniences of imprisonment.

He was too smart to live like a caged animal! He deserved a better life. Although his wrists were zip cuffed together, Bill could tap his fingers on his chin, thinking. As Bill pondered his options, he realized that he had a bargaining chip. Not just some small token for the commander—he had a major bargaining chip!

Inspired by his idea, Bill made a commotion to get the guard's attention. When a guard finally arrived, Bill said he wanted to talk with the commander as soon as possible.

"Why?" questioned the surly man.

Squaring his shoulders and sticking out his chest, Bill announced, "I have some information about a large group of unmarked people." When the guard's eyes widened, Bill continued, "But I'll only deal with the commander. Not you."

"Well, you'll have to wait until reveille." Turning to leave, "I'll include your claim in my written report."

Bill narrowed his eyes threateningly, "You'll do no such thing. You'll report directly to your commanding officer first thing in the morning. Otherwise, I'll tell the officer that you delayed my message and possibly lost several insurgents while you wrote a report."

The PeaceKeeper scowled at Bill. He disliked people, but he hated to be manipulated even more. He especially hated to be manipulated by a skinny, worthless rat; except this rat might actually have information the commander could use to capture more rebels. *Maybe I'll get a promotion*, he thought selfishly.

"Okay, hot shot, I'll tell the commander when he gets into his office. But if you burn me on this, I'll make your life pure misery."

Bill rubbed his cuffed wrists. "No need to worry," he smiled assuredly, "you'll look like a hero." Bill sat on his cot, leaning his back against the cool, cement wall. *If this plan works out, I'll not only get free, I might leverage a pretty sizeable bounty.* He smiled proudly; *I'm still in control—even in jail.*

⋘∘⊙∘⋙

As Miah paddled toward Juan, he watched the distant shore carefully. He heard voices and sometimes saw flashlights flicker in the darkness. He didn't think they made much noise crossing the river, but someone might've heard the geese muttering. A goose dinner in the midst of starvation would be a cause for great celebration. He glanced at the three ganders swimming beside him, and thought grimly, *I don't know why you're following me, but if you start honking, you're gonna die.*

Juan was also aware of the voices on his side of the river. He stood in the swallow water, holding Shadow in his arms and wearing his backpack. As soon as Miah coasted up to him, Juan planned to leap into the boat, take the paddle, and start across the river. As much as he hated this river, he wasn't going to waste one second standing near the shore.

But Juan and Shadow were not alone. Standing beside Juan was the horse and her foal, two heifers, and three goats—all wide awake and moving around nervously. "God have mercy on us," groaned Juan.

When Miah slid under the shrubs along the river, Juan jumped into the boat. Immediately, he handed Shadow to Miah and started paddling with fury. When the goats saw Miah leave them, they bleated loudly. Tragically, the goats mournful wailing made the geese start to honk. As all three goats flung themselves into the water, frantically trying to keep up with the boat, the geese flapped their wings, practically running on top of the water, squawking and honking. Frightened by men's voices behind her, the mare and her colt jumped into the water and swam toward the boat.

Only the two heifers waited onshore, unsure about what to do. They had little chance to move before a group of three men with rifles and flashlights overtook them. The men screamed at each other as they tried to capture the terrified cows. Scurrying about and waving their arms, the men not only tripped over logs—falling helplessly to the ground—they lost the cows. Skirting past the clumsy brawlers, the heifers ran frantically up a hill, away from the river.

Ignoring the swimming animals, the men pursued the cows. Still shouting to each other, they continued to chase the heifers through a dense copse of trees. Barberry and raspberry shrubs snagged their clothes and ripped their skin, but the starving men persisted. Despite the dim light, they searched for the cattle tirelessly, still yelling at each other, which caused the heifers to run even faster away from them into more thickets.

Juan took advantage of this distraction. He paddled with all the strength in his arms and shoulders. With his muscles burning, he pushed through the pain, refusing to slow his pace. By this time, Juan neither cared about paddling quietly nor crouching down in the boat. Obviously two men were crossing the river in a boat, followed by a host of loud, frightened animals.

Halfway across the river, Juan and Miah noticed two goats struggling to stay afloat. The goats screamed in terror, gulping water, flailing their legs, trying to keep up with the boat. Miah reached over the raft to grab one of the goats. To save the animal, Miah extended his body over the water to hold the goat in one hand while he kept Shadow under his feet in the boat.

The other frantic goat tried to put her legs into the boat, beating the sides of the inflatable watercraft with her sharp hooves, shredding the canvas, destroying the raft. Although Juan knew the boat was quickly taking on water, he continued to paddle, never stopping. Using a stabbing motion, Juan screamed with anger each time he plunged his paddle into the water, "Not again! Not again! Not again!"

Miah yelled, "Juan, grab the big horse's mane! Hold onto her neck, she'll take you to shore!" Juan swung around to see the mare swimming next to the ragged boat. He grasped the mare's mane and held it firmly. He pulled himself out of the boat, using her hair as a lifeline. While the raft withered beneath his feet, he wrapped his arms around the horse's neck. Knotting his hands into her mane, Juan pressed his head against the horse's powerful neck and held onto her with his remaining strength.

The giant mare swam the river, followed by her foal. Instinctively she knew her only chance of survival depended on the men across the river. When her hooves touched the bank on the opposite shore, the horse stopped and turned, restlessly watching, waiting for her foal. After her baby reached shallow waters, she nuzzled the quivering colt and allowed Caleb to wrap a rope around her neck. As Caleb steadied the horse,

Juan stiffly released his death grip on her mane and slid awkwardly off her back. Shaking from fear and rage, Juan patted the horse a few times before he collapsed on the ground, exhausted. Juan sat on the beach with his knees bent, his head between his knees, his wet hair dripping, every muscle trembling.

Caleb touched Juan on the shoulder, "Juan. You okay?" Juan nodded his head, too tired to look up. Caleb took a few steps back to give Juan time to catch his breath and control his racing pulse.

After Juan and the mare broke free of the raft, Miah and the remaining animals swam. Rather than losing Shadow, Miah let go of the goat and rolled over onto his back to float downstream. He paddled with his feet using one arm to steer and his other arm to hold the puppy close to his chest. Once they got near the shore, Miah released Shadow and let the pup dog-paddle the last stretch. It took Miah and Shadow much longer to reach the other side of the river but they crossed the river, and lived.

Not all of the animals landed near Miah. Some floated farther downstream but when Miah looked across the river, he didn't see any animals swimming, or any people pursuing them. Because of the current, he and Shadow were the last to reach the banks—and they missed their landing site by almost a quarter of a mile—but they lived. In the dim starlight, Miah counted five geese (mumbling to each other), the mare and her foal, two goats, two puppies, and all his friends. *Thank God!* He waved to his friends so they knew he reached landfall.

Miah sat on the ground, heaving a sigh of relief. The young man earnestly spent some time in prayer before he stood up and walked the last stretch to rejoin his company. Gabe and Caleb didn't push their friends; they waited until Juan and Miah were ready to move again.

Eventually, Juan walked up the hill where Nora slept. He picked up a backpack, slung it over his shoulders and said to the others, "I'm ready." Gabe nodded, pulled on another backpack and started to lead the group away from the river.

As they walked deeper into the woods, the men noticed the sky brightening on the eastern horizon. The sun would rise soon. They heard birds singing and listened to the wind rustling tree leaves. After hiking awhile, Gabe said, "This looks like a good place to rest. You three sleep. I'll guard the camp and keep an eye on Nora."

Caleb and Juan accepted his offer without argument. Miah sat down on the ground, thankful for the reprieve. As the others removed their packs, Gabe started to set up a campsite; he chatted with Nora and helped her gather sticks for kindling. Considering Gabe's offer to stand watch, Miah relaxed, *Gabe's as tired as any of us but he'll protect us.* Without any worries, Miah leaned back against a tree, closed his eyes, and fell fast asleep, knowing that Gabe would wake them if danger arose.

Week 3

– Day 5 –

12

In Nellie's world, one day bled into the next. Nothing very exciting ever happened. They received a rancid gruel for breakfast and dinner from lascivious guards, but the rest of the day was filled with mindless chatter.

For dull-witted women, the schedule wasn't much of a hardship—but for thinkers or doers—this routine inflicted grinding boredom. Nellie endured imprisonment by recalling scripture verses she memorized, Rachel sometimes sang songs, Darlin' and her friends played games with pebbles, but Cassie seriously thought she'd lose her mind.

One day, Cassie finally broke their mundane pattern. She stood up, ranting, "I've had it! I need to talk with somebody about the charges filed against me." She started banging on the cell door, "I need to talk with someone in authority!"

Always quick with a comeback, Darlin' said, "Who are you to ask for anything?" Her friends tittered. "You're just some highfalutin, know-it-all."

Cassie bent down, looking directly into Darlin's face, "I don't know everything" she snarled, "but I know *trash* when I see it."

Darlin's hair-trigger temper exploded, she pounced on Cassie, and the fight began. Darlin' grabbed Cassie's thick, auburn locks, trying to yank out fistfuls of hair. Cassie hit Darlin' right in the nose; and the sound of bone crunching under the blow made every woman in the cell cringe. The quarreling women rolled on the floor, screaming, biting, and kicking each other. Several people tried to break up the fight, but each mediator received a bloody lip or a bruised eye.

Knowing she needed to get their attention before guards arrived, Nellie rushed to the cell's corner where a rancid, waste bucket sat. She picked up the bucket, and held it over the fighting women. "That's it! You either stop fightin', or I'm gonna empty this bucket on yer heads," Nellie threatened.

Cassie and Darlin' froze. They looked at the bucket, saw Nellie's determined expression, and immediately let go of each other. By now, all the other inmates stood against the prison walls, desperately trying to avoid the contents of the bucket and the three furious women in their cell.

When Darlin' and Cassie stood up, still half ready to fight again, angry guards entered their cell. Armed with clubs and Tasers, the men quickly took action. One of the guards hit Nellie in the stomach with his club. As she doubled over, Nellie dropped the bucket, spilling its contents on the floor, drenching the guards' shoes. Cursing with disgust, another guard stunned Darlin' with his Taser, leaving her writhing on the floor; and the third guard wrapped his arm around Cassie's neck, choking her.

The lead guard with a stranglehold on Cassie yelled to his friends, "Let's get these three outta here!" Aware of the overturned bucket and its disgusting contents, he turned to the women cringing against the walls. He said spitefully, "A jailer will bring you some buckets of water and towels. I want this cell scrubbed clean before I return tonight with your dinner. If it's not clean, you don't eat!"

The three guards forced their captives out of the cell. The guard with the Taser dragged Darlin' out by her hair. Shaking, Nellie tried to stand upright, but the man with the club pushed her in the back, making her stagger headfirst out the door. Following his subordinates, the lead guard loosened his grip on Cassie's neck, causing her to retch and gag. He forced Cassie out of the cell, locking the jail door behind them.

"Take these smelly vermin to solitary," ordered the leader.

They pushed the stumbling women down several corridors until they reached an empty cell. They threw Darlin', Cassie, and Nellie into the dungeon, together. The three fell on top of each other onto the hard, stone floor. Without a barred window or illumination from the corridor, the women felt buried alive surrounded by suffused light, stifling heat, suffocating air. The door slammed shut on the battered, rejected women, the last nail in an institutional coffin for society's outcasts.

"What if they start fightin' again?" asked one of the guards.

"Let 'em," said his partner, "three less mouths we have to feed." The guards chuckled sarcastically, leaving Nellie, Cassie, and Darlin' alone in the cell. With even less to do with their time than before, the women now suffered tedium in the dark.

◡◉◉◡

Demons indwelling Bill drooled with anticipation for the upcoming meeting with the PeaceKeepers commander. Although demons argued with each another, they retain a hierarchy in leadership. Bill invited a host of minor demons to enter him: Larceny, Alcoholism, and Gambling; but these troublesome fiends were no match against the heavy hitters of Addiction and Pride.

For Bill, Pride was the ace of spades; the demon that trumped everyone else, the leader of the pack. Bill felt that no one was smarter, more cunning, or deserved greater honor than he. So as guards escorted Bill to their commanding officer, he walked with purpose and determination. *The sooner this commander recognizes what I have to offer, the better off we'll both be.* Bill entered the commander's tent with his chin in the air, ready to negotiate.

Sitting behind his desk, the same commander that arrested Bill a day earlier looked at the brazen criminal with disbelief. "Why are you here?" he asked, annoyed by the interruption.

Bill straightened his jacket. He spoke to the commander as a peer, not a prisoner. "I want to negotiate with you."

The commander threaded his fingers behind his head, leaned back in his seat, smiling at the man's audacity. Curious, he asked, "What do you have to bargain with? Another stolen watch?"

"No," Bill answered, unruffled. "I know where your troops can find fifty or sixty unmarked people."

Now this was good news! The commander sat up in his chair, interested. "Go on."

"But before I tell you anything, I need some guarantees from you first."

The commander slanted his eyes, distrustfully, "Uh-huh, what kinda guarantees?"

"Well, first of all, I want my freedom."

The commander opened a folder on his desk and started reading the first page, completely disinterested in Bill. Without looking at Bill, he stated, "You better keep talking, because so far, I don't hear anything worth my time."

Bill shook loose of the guard's hold to approach the commander's desk. "If I reveal the whereabouts of this large group of people, I want your promise that I'll be given my freedom, a sizable bounty for the captives, and access to government officials."

Revealing surprise by this final request, he asked, "Why do you need access to government officials?"

"That's my business, not yours," Bill stated firmly.

The commander bristled. Bill's lack of respect enraged him. He glared at Bill, "Maybe I'll just throw you back in jail."

Bill turned aside, calling the officer's bluff, "Okay, but you might lose your one chance to make a major impression on the territorial proconsul."

The officer scratched his cheek, thinking. He spoke slowly, trying to uncover Bill's angle, "If you can hand over this group of people, I'll give you your freedom and any bounty that's due to you."

"Not good enough," Bill responded stubbornly.

"Okay." The commander considered his options then added, "I'll give you credit for the find and introduce you to the proconsul. Any further conversation between you and the proconsul depends on the proconsul, not me."

Just get your foot in the door, Bill, his brain interceded. "It's a deal!" agreed Bill. "When I get your pledge in writing and signed by you, I'll lead your troops to a farm that's brimming with unmarked souls."

The two men shook hands; neither one trusting the other. When their eyes met, they each recognized the other man's pride. *That's good,* Bill thought, *at least we speak the same language.*

The commander tightened his grip on Bill's hand. "You best keep your word because I refuse to face reprisal because of you." This was not a man to be trifled with; in fact, the commander's self-importance and ambition actually exceeded Bill's exaggerated vanity and lofty aspirations. They understood each other completely.

⎰⎱⎰⎱

After their strenuous river crossing the night before, Juan, Miah and Caleb awoke refreshed before noon. As the men roused, they smelled a pot of coffee percolating and fish roasting on sticks over a campfire. Juan stretched his arms over his head, Caleb started to fold his poncho liner, and Miah sat up, pushing a lock of his sandy, blonde hair out of his face.

Nora ran to her brother's blanket. She loved seeing Miah sitting on the ground, eye level with her. She placed her grubby hands on his cheeks, stared into his eyes, and kissed him on the lips.

"Mornin', baby girl," laughed Miah. Glancing at Gabe, "Has that big, old gorilla been keepin' you busy?"

Excited to talk with Miah, she babbled, "I take Snidley and Shallow for walk. We find prebby rocks." She held up a couple of quartz pebbles for Miah to inspect. Whispering to Miah, "Me play game."

Miah nodded his head, smiling at his little sister. No matter what any of the men found today, he already knew that Nora would win their game tonight. "This is a real treasure, peanut. I'll keep your secret."

As Juan strolled around the campsite, he noticed a few new animals. "Hey, Gabe, did you herd some more livestock while we slept?"

Gabe shook his head, bewildered by the odd behavior of farm animals. "I left the dogs with you while Nora and I went fishing. When we got back, we found these sheep standing around with the goats. Either the dogs brought them over or they wandered in by themselves."

Juan chuckled, shaking his head, "Let's see now, we have horses, goats, sheep, and geese. I don't know . . . what're we missing, Miah? Some pigs? Maybe a few chickens?"

"I'd kinda like to see an otter," mentioned Caleb. All three of his friends swiveled their heads to look at Caleb. Astonished. They roared with laughter. Otters?!

Shaking his head in amazement, Juan said, "This trip is so weird, we'll probably find a unicorn tomorrow."

"Or Big Foot," Miah added quickly, stifling a laugh.

Listening to friendly jokes in the background, Gabe finished making lunch. He knelt down to check on the fish. Pulling a chunk of meat off the stick, he tasted it, and announced, "Dinner's ready." He gave each man a stick with a fish on it. He handed the largest fish to Miah because he knew the young man would share his meal with Nora. "After we break camp, I'd like to head over to a rock ledge I saw with my binoculars. It's gonna be a hike over a couple of mountains but it looks like a good place to spend the night."

"Sounds like a plan to me," said Juan, his mouth watering from the smell of charred fish.

After Miah said a brief prayer, the team sat down on logs or rocks to eat breakfast. Blowing on the hot fish, they used their fingers and knives to pull tender meat off the bones. Famished, they ate the fish quickly then scrounged through their packs, looking for more food to eat. They found stale crackers, a box of granola, and a package of crumbled chocolate chip cookies—not the most nutritious meal—but one that filled their empty stomachs and the puppies' round tummies.

Licking grease off his fingers, Juan praised Gabe's grilling skills. Gabe smiled humbly. He accepted the compliment because he had to admit, the fish tasted great. He usually ate MREs (meals ready to eat) when he traveled with Caleb but Gabe really enjoyed cooking over a campfire. Having lived most of his life in a city, Gabe now discovered the pleasures of living off the land. This was a lifestyle that really suited him.

"Huh?" Gabe responded when he heard his name.

"You were kinda daydreaming, dude," said Juan. "I asked if you'd like to take a nap before we hike over the mountains."

Rubbing his weary eyes, the big man said, "Nah, let's keep moving. We should get up to those rocks this afternoon, so I'll have plenty of time to sleep later."

Before they left, Miah made a few adjustments to the loads each man carried. He fastened a couple of rucksacks together to form a simple pack to throw over the mare's back. Afterward, he made a halter using rope he found on a farm. Calmly, Miah walked over to the mare, stroked her coat, and talked mildly to her as he slipped the halter around her face. Accustomed to people, the docile creature waited patiently as Miah adjusted the packs on her back, tying them securely to her belly.

Miah stepped back to inspect his work. Nodding his head, he looked at the men in his party, "There. That should make our walk a little easier." Miah slipped Nora into her pack and Juan lifted the toddler onto her brother's shoulders. Miah adjusted his shoulders, "Okay, I'm ready."

The others finished packing their supplies. They stuffed a few more things into the rucksacks before closing them. The horse carried most of their gear now which allowed the men to hunt when opportunities arose.

Since the group preferred to stay off roadways, they planned to take a more indirect route back to the mansion: or the lodge as the men now called it. Fortunately, Juan had a compass which he checked throughout the day. He wanted to get back to Rosa as soon as possible; he knew the exact degree heading. If all went well, he would hold his beautiful wife again in a few weeks.

As the party set off, they walked through the dense forest single file. Gabe led the group, followed by Miah and Nora. Behind Miah was Juan who led the mare, with her foal trudging closely at her heels. Caleb assumed the tail end. Caleb liked staying at the back of the lineup because he collected herbs throughout the day. After Caleb cut and stashed the plants in his pockets, he always caught up with his friends without disrupting their pace.

But behind Caleb was a wondrous sight: a long line of animals which, by all accounts, was growing daily. They followed the men without coaxing or prodding, intimidation or temptation. They moved liked a trained army, quietly and in formation.

Nothing seemed to deter the animals' progress. When the men stopped to rest, the animals grazed. When the men climbed rocks, the goats and sheep bounced sure-footed over boulders. Admittedly, the geese honked and flapped their wings in frustration as they maneuvered their flat, webbed feet through rocky areas, but eventually they rejoined the cavalcade.

Although still young, the puppies adapted to their role as livestock overseers. Sydney and Shadow ran continuously in wide circles, constantly observing the landscape, protecting their perimeter, tireless in their efforts. They learned quickly and began to mature into thoughtful, working shepherds.

As Border Collies, the pups inherently knew how to herd animals. When they ran around their charges, Sydney and Shadow barked directions to each other, keeping their stock moving together in the same direction. It was a beautiful configuration: men leading a group of animals to a safer location and their dogs protecting those animals from getting lost or hurt.

As Jesus studied the proceeding party from his lofty throne, he smiled and said softly, "Well done, my good and faithful servants."

Week 4

13

WITHIN A WEEK, TOYNELL and Brant felt comfortable in their new surroundings. They set up housekeeping in a small, rundown cabin on the outskirts of the community. With help from her neighbors, Toynell made new curtains, stocked a root cellar, and started a vegetable garden. Brant repaired the cabin's roof, split firewood, and built a pen for his ducks and chickens.

Fortunately, all the large livestock in the compound grazed together in a vast, open field between the houses and the crevice, so Brant didn't need to worry about fencing his dairy herd. He used Ryan's barn to milk his cows in the mornings and afternoons, but afterward, the cattle returned to the field. The young couple's life was simple inside the boundaries of the compound; consequently, they accepted their home with grace and thanksgiving.

One morning while Toynell swept the front porch, she spied Alicia and her friend, Monica, riding up the road to her cabin. Toynell waved a greeting and both women waved back. Once the riders reached a hitching post near the porch, they dismounted, tied their horses to the rail, and walked casually toward Toynell.

"Hi, sweetie!" called Monica. The lovely Asian American woman grinned at Toynell. She swept her jet-black hair into an elaborate knot on the side of her head which highlighted her already-stunning face. "Allie and I are going to visit the settlers on the other side of the fault. Do you wanna go with us?" Monica asked.

Happy to join her new friends, Toynell jumped at the invitation, "Wait a minute. I'll see if Brant needs my help with anything today. If he doesn't, I'd love to join you!" Without wasting a moment, Toynell ran off the porch to talk with her husband.

While they waited, Alicia sat on the front porch, admiring the scenery. She extended her legs in front of her, crossed her boots at the ankles, and closed her eyes, basking in the morning sun. She suddenly snapped her eyes open when she felt something brush against her legs.

She laughed heartily. On the step beside her legs sat the chubbiest cat she ever saw! She reached over to stroke his orange fur, "What's your name, Bruiser?"

Carl stood up again and started to rub his head against her legs. He leapt into her lap so she wouldn't need to reach far to stroke him. Alicia continued to smile as she petted him with both hands. "You're a monster! What does Toynell feed you? Sides of beef?"

"He's about the size of a bobcat," commented Monica.

Alicia picked Carl up under his front legs and held him so she could look into his brown eyes. "Bob? Is that your name?" she giggled.

When Toynell came back around the corner of her cabin, she saw the women sitting on her steps, talking with her cat. Toynell walked over to the porch, stopping in front of them to watch, but said nothing.

Alicia looked up, "Hey, Toy. Are you gonna come with us?"

"Yeah, Brant said he can take care of everything today." She watched Monica and Alicia, adding, "I see you've met Carl."

"Carl? That's about the last name I'd give this hooligan," remarked Alicia, patting the tabby. Carl jumped off her lap, landing gracefully on the ground. He strutted past the women, swishing his tail in the air, a prince among cats and nobody's fool.

"Funny cat," Monica said. She turned to Toynell, "Do you have a horse to ride?"

"Brant's saddling her up right now. He'll bring her around when he's done." While they waited for Brant, the women talked about insignificant things: the weather, the latest news, just idly passing the time.

When Brant joined them, he stayed to talk for a few minutes. Afterward, he helped his wife onto her horse and gave her little pointers on riding this particular mare. Once confident that Toynell would be fine, he left the trio to return to his chores.

The three women rode through the community, waving at everybody and shouting a few insults at some men fixing a barn roof. The men laughed. They waved their hats at the women, and shouted their own playful banter before resuming their work.

Although Toynell was excited to take a short trip with Monica and Alicia, she felt a peculiar sense of foreboding. *What's the matter with me?*

she wondered. The day couldn't be prettier: a clear, blue sky, the smell of rich soil, a gentle breeze blowing through trees, birds filling the air with music. *Why do I feel . . . so weird?*

She tried to rationalize her discomfort by assuming that she didn't want to leave the safety of her home. But even that excuse didn't pacify her spirit, she liked adventures! Toynell was always the first in line to try something new; but rather than say anything to Monica or Alicia, she decided to remain quiet. She listened to her friends talking, straining her ears for any odd noises.

Monica noticed Toynell's unusual behavior, her quiet intensity. After watching Toynell out of the corner of her eye, Monica finally asked, "Hey, are you okay?"

"Yeah," Toynell said, her voice quavering. She sighed. She could remain silent or she could say something to these very capable soldiers. Toynell straightened her back, admitting, "I have a really bad feeling about something, but I don't know what it is."

Concerned, Alicia stopped her horse to look directly at Toynell. She never discounted intuition; she saw too many bizarre things happen after somebody felt uncomfortable. An enemy waiting in a bombed-out building, snipers hiding in obscure, high positions, children wearing explosive vests, the world was crazy—and unpredictable. "Do you wanna turn back, Toy?" Alicia asked. "This visit isn't important. We're just getting to know some newcomers in the valley."

"No," Toynell responded uneasily, "I'm okay." She smiled apologetically. "I guess I just haven't been away from Brant in a while."

The three sat still on their horses in the middle of the road. Neither Monica nor Alicia believed Toynell's lame excuse; something was really bothering her. They listened carefully to sounds around them as they scanned the horizon: lovely weather, nothing threatening. Monica glanced over to Alicia, raised an eyebrow, and tilted her head toward the compound. "Do you wanna go back?"

"Nah," Alicia said, "let's move on. We'll check on those settlers, give 'em a few groceries and head back home." Alicia clicked her tongue and gently prodded her horse to walk again; except this time, they traveled at a faster pace. Toynell and Monica followed Alicia; they remained quiet, staying acutely aware of their surroundings.

After crossing the fault bridge, the women rode to the top of a ridge overlooking the settler's cabin. They stopped their horses to look down at the farmstead below. Monica and Alicia watched four people moving about the yard doing everyday jobs: weeding vegetables, feeding chickens, hanging laundry, and carrying firewood. Nothing unusual or frightening.

Toynell gasped. As she looked at the farm, her pulse raced, her muscles clenched in alarm. *This . . . is . . . a dangerous place.* When demons surrounding the cabin sensed Toynell's presence, they instinctively slipped into dark nooks and crannies; they had no intention of being discovered by anyone, but especially not by a young woman with very little understanding of spiritual warfare.

ᴄᴖᴖᴄᴜ

Conversely, demons in the PeaceKeepers camp walked around taunting each other with very little concern of Christian or angelic interference. This was their master's domain, Satan's playground. Insurgents were processed for imprisonment, larcenists beaten for their petty crimes, and victims blatantly ignored by government officials. A little bit of hell on earth.

Bill felt completely at home with PeaceKeepers. Without shackles, Bill walked around the area as if the commander promoted him, rather than pardoned him. After making his deal, Bill bathed, got a haircut, and received a fresh set of clothes. Knowing he possessed important, inside information, he even made a few snide remarks to privates. He held the upper hand. Smiling smugly, *I like it here. My life's finally turnin' around.*

Bill entered the commander's tent at the appointed time. The commander sat behind his desk with other soldiers—officers and enlisted men—also in attendance. These men intended to carry out their commander's orders to arrest a large group of unmarked people living somewhere in the mountains. Bill beamed. This was his hour to shine.

The commander gave Bill a flinty stare, "Are you ready to guide my troops to the rebel camp you described to me?"

Bill stepped forward. All eyes watching him, "That's my plan," he said smugly.

"You realize that if you mislead my troops or set them up for an ambush, I'll have you shot?"

Bill swallowed, "Yes."

The commander looked at an officer next to his desk, "Captain, gather your unit. I want your men to depart this evening. Be in position at 0000 hours to keep watch of the insurgent's camp. Encircle the camp and attack the compound at 0200 hours. I want to see all the prisoners lined up in front of this tent first thing in the morning. Is that clear?"

"Yes, sir."

The commander nodded to a grizzled sergeant standing near his desk. The sergeant moved next to Bill. He stood so close that Bill smelled tobacco on the man's breath. The commander resumed his icy glare at Bill, "After you lead my men to the rebels' camp, Sgt. Stafford will escort you back to my office. I don't want to lose you in the shuffle."

Bill looked up at the imposing figure beside him. Stafford—a callous soldier with a long scar running across his cheek—turned his head toward Bill. The sergeant hated snitches, but this snitch was the worst of his kind. He betrayed family and friends. *Yeah*, Stafford grinned at Bill, *try to make a run for it. I'd love to kill you.* His black eyes drilled into Bill.

Bill recognized that look; unconsciously, he stepped away from the threatening man. Stafford took a step closer to Bill and bent his head down to mumble into Bill's ear. As the man spoke, Bill's eyes widened, his face became ashen, his mouth dropped open.

As the commander watched the exchange, a smile flickered slightly on the corner of his mouth. He didn't care what Stafford said to that weasel, he chose the right man to guard his informant. He would see this necklace-stealing thief again or the thief would die: he didn't care. It was a win-win for him. He would present a group of unmarked insurgents to the proconsul or he'd have one less criminal in the camp. Either way, he approved the outcome.

Clearing his throat, the commander ordered his men to prepare for the night's raid. Prepped for battle, his officers and NCOs (noncommissioned officers) already knew their roles, but the commander sometimes spoke to hear the sound of his gravelly voice. He liked control. He liked to give orders.

Life for Nellie, Cassie, and Darlin' moved at a glacial rate. Seconds dripped into minutes, minutes seeped into hours, and hours ground into days; time pulverized any stony resistance the women possessed before their isolation. The threesome felt entombed inside this dark, cold chamber where time virtually stood still.

With only each other for solace, they grew close. They could either depend on each other or go mad; they chose to fight as a team, not as adversaries. Nellie encouraged Cassie and Darlin' with her testimony and she used scripture to support her beliefs. Ultimately, all three women—confined to this filthy, dank cell—devoted their lives to Christ.

This final outcome did not escape the notice of demonic spirits controlling the prison. Something must be done to correct this problem before a higher demonic authority discovered their lapse of attention. The demons initially thought the women would kill each other; but now they realized the group must be separated permanently.

A demon manipulating the women's jailer, whined, "What should we do to correct this situation?"

His supervisor, a menacing fiend who influenced the prison warden, hit the sniveling demon in the face. "Fool! Why didn't you inform me of this problem earlier?"

Looking downcast, the demon started listing excuses, "I had more pressing issues: starving prisoners by neglect, spreading cholera through their water, breaking the ventilation system."

"Liar!" roared the warden's demon. "You were busy tormenting female inmates, leveraging favors from your subordinates, and neglecting your responsibilities."

The jailer's demon trembled, rationalizing his actions, "Prisoners usually go crazy in that dark cell. I didn't think—"

"That's the first smart thing you've said to me. You didn't think. You stupid, pathetic parasite!" Desiring to squeeze the neck of this senseless creature, the stronger demon clenched his fists in fury but refrained from touching him.

Hating the weaker demon, he turned his head to ponder their dilemma. Not a brilliant fiend, the warden's demon relied on tried-and-true remedies to overcome the unity of adversaries. He would divide and conquer. This scheme usually caused enough chaos to throw humans into confused panic. It worked to overthrow world governments, split churches, even destroy families.

Warden Thompson looked directly into the eyes of the jailer. "Listen to me carefully. Separate the women today into three, individual cells with cots. Give them food, drinks, and clean water for bathing. Tomorrow I'll interview each woman alone." Glaring at the sniveling man in front of him, the warden barked, "Can you do that without screwing up?"

"Yes, sir!" the jailer responded quickly.

The warden dropped his chin, massaging his aching temples, *I work with imbeciles.* He glanced up, peering at the jailer's eager, dim-witted face, "Then do it! And get out of my office!"

Turning abruptly, the jailer practically ran out of the warden's office, his keys jangling loudly. He bumped into a chair, almost knocking it over, but he grabbed the chair before it clattered to the floor. Once he exited the warden's office, the jailer slowed his pace because he didn't want to reveal his chastisement to anyone walking the corridor.

As he walked hurriedly down the hall, he wondered, *How could I know those women would become Christian?* He stopped for a moment to regain his composure then kicked the wall angrily; *Christians are so stupid!*

The jailer heaved a sigh, trying to make sense of those wretched, pathetic martyrs. He asked himself questions his warped mind could not fathom: *Why couldn't those women just renounce their faith in Jesus? Where's the glory in facing a guillotine?* He shook his head, *Why wouldn't they submit to the Supreme Leader and spare themselves all this trouble?*

14

"REDEMPTION? WHO NEEDS REDEMPTION? What this world needs are people taking care of each other," stated Bert. She tossed her big hat onto a table in her cabin, continuing a conversation started a few minutes earlier in the front yard.

The conversation began when Bert first saw Toynell approach the barnyard, she recognized the Holy Spirit within the quiet woman. Rather than ignoring Toynell's unassuming manner, Bert accosted her. Grabbing the reins of Toynell's horse, Bert looked up at the astonished rider and said, "Who're you?"

Surprised, Toynell introduced herself. Afterward, she sputtered a few words about being neighborly, welcoming them into the valley, offering awkward pleasantries. Alicia furrowed her brow as she watched the interchange. Addressing Bert's animosity, Alicia raised her hand in the air, as if stopping traffic, "Hold on, Bert, we came to bring you guys some food. Nobody's trying to upset you."

Backing off, Bert resumed her role as the group's spokesperson. "Oh, sorry." She pursed her lips, "I don't have very good people skills."

Monica studied the brash woman, but decided to let bygones be bygones. She turned to her saddlebags and began to pull out assorted items: fresh biscuits, canned jams, and rock candy. Embarrassed by the unwanted attention, Toynell slipped off her mount. She also turned to her saddlebags; her fingers fumbled with the buckles as tears seeped out of her eyes.

Alicia continued to talk, removing food from her saddlebags. As Alicia, Monica, and Toynell walked toward the settlers' cabin carrying food, the dialog made another abrupt turn. Bert began peppering them with questions about their political leanings, social status, and religious beliefs.

"Wow, Bert, you really don't know how to talk to people, do you?" chastised Alicia, already getting tired of this abrasive woman.

"Is it wrong to know which side of the line your neighbors are on?" Bert asked.

"I guess not," Alicia responded guardedly. By now they stood on the front porch.

Bert opened the cabin door, "It's nothing, really, but sometimes I wonder about life. I mean what's the point?" She stared intently at Toynell, "Are you perfect? Is that why you brought food for us?"

Reflexively, Toynell answered, "Oh, no, none of us are perfect! We're redeemed by the blood of the Lamb."

And that's when Bert threw her hat into the cabin. She caught her little mouse in the trap. *Yeah, let's talk about redemption.*

Up until this instant, Bert wasn't sure if Monica or Alicia were even Christians so she wanted to test the waters. Now her suspicions were answered. Bert could tell that Toynell was young in her faith—a mere baby, in fact—and her friends were sitting on the fence, uncommitted to anything. Oh this meeting was going to be delicious!

Over the next hour, the settlers—led by Bert—hammered the trio with perplexing questions and misquoted Bible verses. Before long, Toynell, Alicia, and Monica couldn't answer the settlers' questions or offer any justification for their beliefs. The settlers' theories seemed off kilter but without a strong Christian foundation, the threesome sank deeper and deeper into befuddlement.

Finally, Toynell stood up, "I need to go home. It's getting late and my head hurts." As she turned toward the front door, one of the pale women moved smoothly over to Toynell and offered her some herbs to overcome her headache. Toynell shook her head, "No, thank you. I just need some fresh air. I'll be fine." The woman pressed a small envelope of herbs into Toynell's hand, but Toynell gave her back the package. Smiling weakly, she repeated, "Honestly, I'll be fine."

Monica and Alicia followed Toynell outside. None of the women spoke to each other. Bert, followed by the rest of the settlers, escorted the women to their waiting horses.

Before they left, Bert invited the women back to their house. "Hey, why don't we meet, say once a week just to talk? Let's get to know each other better, maybe swap ideas, and philosophize a bit."

"Yeah," added the snarly-haired man. "Next time, we'll bake something sweet to eat and you won't have to bring anything."

"I'll chill some wine," added one of the pale women, "so we'll have food and drinks for everyone."

Alicia studied Monica and Toynell. Toynell refused to acknowledge the invitation, but Monica said, "Sure, why not? When do you want us to stop by?"

Bert smiled broadly, "Same time next week?"

"It's a date," confirmed Alicia "we'll come back next week."

The settlers waved goodbye to their new acquaintances. The three riders began their trip back home, each woman immersed in her own reflections. With the sun sitting low on the horizon, the women wanted to return home safely and ease their puzzled minds.

As the settlers watched the backs of the three women leaving their farm, one of the pale women asked Bert, "What did you think of today's conversation?"

Bert smirked, licking her dry lips. "I think we fed them just enough misinformation to stimulate their thinking but not enough to alarm them. I can't wait for next week."

✎⊚⊚⊘

Gabe escorted his ever-growing entourage over several mountains. Although bone tired, the big man didn't want to stop for the night until they reached a ledge of rocks he spied earlier. He simply put one foot in front of the other, pushing through his fatigue, nearing their destination.

When they sighted the cave, the horse snorted with fear, stopping stiff legged in her tracks. The mare threw her head back, widened her eyes, and started to lash her head back and forth. Holding her rope, Miah stopped to brace himself and Juan swiftly pulled Nora out of Miah's backpack in one graceful, fluid movement.

Miah tightened his hold on the horse's halter, refusing to release her. Despite Miah's strength, the horse fought violently against his grip. She danced around him in circles, unable to escape his grasp but too spooked to stay in one place. Miah stood his ground, holding her rope, praying aloud in the Spirit. He spoke his commands boldly, unafraid of the horse's actions.

The others stood back. They honestly didn't know what to do, everything happened so fast. They watched the mare roll her eyes, lashing her front legs, whinnying in fright. Even Nora, normally very boisterous, clung to Juan's neck in silence, staring at her brother, horrified by the horse's distress.

When the mare realized she couldn't escape Miah, she began to relent, but only slightly. She pranced constantly, snorting nervously. Miah kept praying out loud. He was not going to release the horse; something shocked her but before they could uncover what that "something" was, he needed to bring her under control, for everyone's safety.

Miah and the mare continued this shuffle for several minutes. At last, the horse stood in one place: lifting her feet, but not stomping; dancing, but not fighting; panting, but not screaming. Miah spoke softly, stroking her neck, trying to calm her, looking around for danger. Once he regained control, Miah guided the horse to a stout tree and tied her securely to its trunk. He spent a few more minutes running his hands over her body, murmuring to her, helping her to relax. Afterward, Miah took a few steps back to watch her closely. When he turned around, Miah saw four human and dozens of animal faces staring at him in wide-eyed wonder.

"What was that all about?" asked Caleb.

Miah shook his head doubtfully, "I don't know but horses have very keen senses. Somethin' really startled her, maybe a rattlesnake." Instantly, the men looked around their feet, listening carefully, their pistols drawn.

Gabe wrinkled his nose as he pushed leaves and sticks around, "What is that smell?" He glanced at Shadow who sat by his feet. When Gabe ruffled the hair on Shadow's head, he noticed the fur on Shadow's neck was matted with something dark and sticky. *Something gooey.* He sniffed his fingers, "Oh man, Shad, what did you get into?"

"Something dead," Juan responded knowingly. "I don't know why dogs do it, but they love to roll in dead stuff."

"That might be what's bothering our mare," said Miah. They started to follow their noses now, searching for a dead body. It didn't take them long to find the offending corpse: a decomposing bear, not too far from the cave entrance.

With his hand over his nose, Juan turned to Miah, "Do you think that's what scared the horse?"

Miah studied the dead animal, "It's possible," he said uneasily. "Horses don't like bears," he scratched his head. "Maybe she didn't like his smell—even though he isn't dangerous anymore."

Then they heard a soft squall on the other side of the bear. Gabe stepped cautiously toward the sound; he stopped, a smile quivered on his lips. The big man bent down and picked up a small, baby bear. The little cub hung limply in his hands, weak from starvation. The others gathered around to look at the cub.

"Let's try to get some milk into this little guy," Miah said urgently.

Almost as frightened as the horse, the female goat trembled; but she was more concerned about being milked on time rather than standing too close to a live cub. The men set up a hasty milking station. Juan tied the nanny goat to a tree away from the bears; Caleb carried a log over for Miah to sit on; and Gabe retrieved the milking bucket. With everything in place, Miah began to milk the goat.

It was a team effort because no one wanted to see the cub die. Once Miah had a few ounces of milk in the bucket, he poured the creamy liquid into a glove Caleb gave him. While Caleb poked a tiny hole into one finger of the glove, Gabe cradled the cub in his arms. Caleb dribbled a few drops of milk into the cub's dry mouth and massaged its throat to help him swallow.

The cub's eyes fluttered then his mouth started to move, instinctively trying to suckle the glove's finger. The milk flowed from the small hole. The cub's front paws moved slightly toward the glove's finger, sucking. As the cub sucked harder, the milk flowed faster.

Gabe sat down on a rock, embracing the cub in one arm, and holding the bulging glove with his other hand. Excited by the prospect of food, the cub started to chew on the glove ravenously, trying to get all the milk into his stomach—now! Gabe pulled the glove out of the cub's reach for a moment to let him catch his breath. Once the cub discovered he couldn't eat the glove, he suckled slower, never taking his gaze off Gabe. When the cub swallowed all the milk in the glove, Gabe passed the glove to Caleb who added more milk.

"Let's start him out slow," cautioned Caleb, "he doesn't need to eat everything at once."

Nora stared at all the proceedings with awe. She watched Miah milking her goat, Caleb filling the glove, and Gabe feeding a baby bear. She listened to the cub greedily sucking on the glove, making satisfied growling noises, wiggling his feet. She toddled next to Gabe, placing her hand gently on the big man's hairy arm. She looked at Gabe's weatherbeaten face.

When Gabe glanced at Nora, his expression softened. She regarded him with kindness but said knowingly, "Baby bears no eat milk. Bears eat purr-age."

~∘⊙∘~

"This is such a pain," Bill moaned inwardly. He led a group of soldiers out of the PeaceKeepers outpost toward his father's farm. The night was dark; a heavy cloud cover obscured light from the moon and stars which provided perfect conditions for an assault. A captain flanked Bill on one side and Sgt. Stafford flanked his other side, one skinny man sandwiched between two seasoned fighters.

"Did you say somethin', weasel?" taunted Sgt. Stafford, itching for a fight.

Pulling his head deeper into his collar, Bill mumbled, "Yeah, I said you gotta lot to gain."

The sergeant cast a wizened glare at Bill, he hated the rat. "I have nothin' to gain; I'm just doin' my job. You, on the other hand, will live like a prince if we catch a group of rebels."

Bill smiled knowingly. *If I become a prince, you'll be the first person I destroy.* Suppressing his hatred, Bill replied sarcastically, "It's kinda hard to think of that group of misfits and old men as rebels. Your troops probably won't fire a single bullet when you overtake 'em."

"Well, just for your information, I have a bullet in the chamber just in case you decide to do somethin'," pausing for effect, "contrary."

Bill shuffled his feet, stirring up dust as he walked. He moped because he wasn't getting the recognition he deserved, but things would be different tomorrow. Tomorrow, he'd be a new person. He'd wash his hands of that self-righteous old man that fathered him, and he'd put Sgt. Stafford in his place. Because, tomorrow, he'd be redeemed by his good works.

~∘⊙∘~

Juan volunteered to take the first watch that night. He got enough sleep in the morning to hold him for a while. Besides, he was too agitated to sleep but he was okay. In fact, he was more than okay. He chuckled as he looked at all the animals and people sleeping in their camp.

"Jesus, this is the craziest mix of oddballs I ever saw," he spoke softly. "But that's alright." He studied the cub snoring loudly by the fire, his little, round stomach moving up and down as he breathed. "I like it. It's cool."

Juan wasn't alone in his contentment. Gabe and Caleb—two technically sophisticated soldiers—blended perfectly with this strange group of travelers. Moreover, Miah and his little sister adjusted quickly to the rigors of living outdoors. But it wasn't just that they lived outdoors and moved with stealth, they did so with an ever-growing host of animals.

"Jesus, I don't know what your plans are but I'm counting on you to get us through each day," Juan sighed. He leaned back against a tree, listening. He knew the noises well enough to distinguish between danger and safety, chaos and peace. Juan relaxed his muscles, tonight was going to be an uneventful, soothing break.

For the next three hours, the night did pass restfully. Just before waking his relief, Juan threw a few more logs on the fire and started to circle the camp's perimeter one last time. That's when he heard the sounds of struggling by the campfire, someone winded, out of breath. Juan ran back into the camp. The dogs were awake. They sat up with bright eyes and uplifted ears; they too knew something was wrong.

But the struggle was not caused by an outside source, it was Miah! The young man thrashed about, yelling in his sleep. *A nightmare*, thought Juan. Juan was tempted to poke Miah with a long stick to avoid being shot, but he decided to stand on one side of Miah to shake him and call his name. Miah's screaming woke up everyone.

Miah opened his eyes with a start, sweating and breathing heavily. He grabbed his rifle unconsciously, standing up quickly. With hair hanging in his face, he looked sharply at his surroundings, alert, braced for action. At the same time, Caleb and Gabe scanned the forest beyond the campfire; each man armed and ready to fight.

"What's happenin', Miah?" whispered Caleb, still watching the woods.

Pale and trembling violently, Miah stared at his companions, speechless. He closed his eyes, and did something none of his friends expected, he began to cry. Miah remained in place, almost paralyzed. He hung his head low and prayed softly through his tears. Juan, Gabe, and Caleb gawked at the young man, perplexed.

For a few moments, no one moved a muscle. They knew exactly how to strategize a battle, how to set a broken leg, or how to hold a woman, but none of these men knew what to do about a crying friend. *Look at the ground? Ignore his tears? How could they help a buddy without embarrassing him?* Before they made a decision, Miah exhaled heavily.

Nora crept over to Juan, reaching her arms up to him. Juan bent down to pick up the child. With her arms wrapped around Juan's neck, Nora looked at her brother and said, "Mea, fine?"

Miah looked at her face, smiling weakly, "Yeah, baby girl, I'm fine." He brushed his blonde hair out of his eyes, wiped away his tears. "Something really bad happened tonight . . ."

"What?" asked Juan.

Miah looked at everyone, his expression filled with sorrow. "It's Papaw," the young man answered, "PeaceKeepers raided his farm tonight."

"Are you sure?" Gabe asked. "Maybe you just had a really bad nightmare."

"No," Miah shook his head, "it wasn't a nightmare. This was different." Miah stared at the ground, his face worried.

He continued slowly, "I was standing on a hill above Papaw's farm. There was someone else next to me. I didn't look closely at the presence beside me, but out of the corner of my eye, he seemed incredibly tall, like thirteen or fourteen feet tall." Miah swallowed with difficulty, he still felt like a statue, his feet frozen to the ground. "The tall man pointed his sword straight in front of us. When I looked down at the farm, I saw people getting tossed out of their beds, children running around crying, blood running down Papaw's face." Miah's chin quivered, tears welling in his eyes again. "I believe I saw a vision."

Gabe met Caleb's eyes, they both doubted paranormal experiences. *Visions, a tall presence with a sword . . . is he kidding?*

Juan, on the other hand, knew his young friend. He expected nothing less than the supernatural when Miah reacted strangely. "What do you want us to do?"

Miah smiled ruefully, "We need to move quickly. The same people that captured Papaw's group will come after us now."

Recognizing certainty in Miah's manner, Gabe asked, with slightly less doubt, "How can you be so sure?"

Miah looked directly into Gabe's questioning face, his blue eyes flashing. "Because I saw the man guiding the PeaceKeepers," his face reflected a mix of rage and sorrow, "it was my dad."

15

NELLIE COULDN'T BELIEVE THE absolute joy of feeling human again. In the morning, a guard brought her a warm breakfast of scrambled eggs, fried potatoes, flaky biscuits, and spiced applesauce. He also brought her a carafe of hot coffee, real coffee, not some watered-down version of boiled roots. Initially, she pounced on her meal like a famished beast; but after gulping down her first mouthful, she slowed down to savor every bite. She shut her eyes to relish the tastes, the smells, the textures of food. It was glorious!

After she finished eating, another guard brought in a large galvanized tub filled with hot, steaming bathwater. The guard's assistant set a fresh towel, an unwrapped bar of soap, and a new set of orange prison clothes on her cot. Both men asked her if she needed anything else!

Nellie gasped. *Needed anything else?* "I can't think of anything," she said, "but if this is a dream, please don't wake me."

For a brief moment, the guard gave her a quick smile, "No dream, but no cake walk either. You'll talk with the warden sometime today. That's not a pleasant experience for anybody," he shot a glance at his partner, "guards included." His buddy nodded his head, a clear look of dread on his face.

Nellie cleared her throat, "Well, I'll pray before I visit the warden." She touched the new set of clothes on her bed, thinking about her upcoming appointment, "God will give me words to say."

As he gathered Nellie's breakfast dishes, the assistant replied meekly, "I sure hope so. I get so scared around the warden that I can hardly breathe—let alone talk."

Nellie simply looked at the pitiful, skittish man. His forehead displayed the mark of the beast, his twisted, bent body bore signs of repeated beatings, and his conduct revealed a man without hope. Nellie's heart broke.

"May I do anything for you?" she asked gently.

He pointed to the tattoo on his forehead, "No thanks, I already signed my death warrant." His partner observed him silently. "Like you," he pointed his chin toward Nellie, "I'm a dead person walking." He crept out the door without uttering another word. The lead guard followed him.

Nellie heard the lock click on her cell door. She whispered, "I may die soon but I'll live again." As tears rolled down her cheeks, she said softly, "Jesus, have mercy on us all."

༄༅

The dreaded warden sat on his swivel chair behind an ornate, walnut desk. Neither his desk nor his office displayed pictures of family or friends. On his beige office walls hung prestigious awards given to him during his professional career: university diplomas, letters of commendation, and certificates of service. The absence of mementos practically screamed that others gave him professional accolades but no one wanted to personally associate with him.

Strangely, when he admired his office walls, he never noticed the lack of pictures, but he had memorized all the words written about him. As he glanced at his advanced degrees, he shut his eyes, muttering, "Through the authority vested by the Board of Higher Education . . ." then he repeated the words on each of his diplomas, smiling smugly. He tilted back in the chair with his hands behind his head, confident that he asserted great power within his circle of influence. After reflecting upon his successes, the warden reopened his eyes to view three folders on his desk. He sighed.

Despite his many attempts to rise above this pedantic position, his superiors still kept him in this wretched prison. They said he was a rare man with specific skills to oversee a penitentiary with complete efficiency. The warden accepted their compliments—after all his superiors were correct—but he continued to search for a more fulfilling career; something that emphasized his talents.

He could never imagine the contempt his superiors really felt about him: his ego prohibited such foolishness. He believed someday, someone would give him the recognition he so justly deserved. He merely needed more exposure.

He looked down at the folders again. Maybe this last woman would give him information he so desperately desired. Nellie Markwell. *Ah well,*

I hope she'll be more helpful than the other prisoners, he thought dismally, *I almost ended my career with that last one.*

The first prisoner he interrogated? Darla Something or other: a real loser. Even after a bath and a new set of clothes, she looked like a cracker. Oh, her eyes were bright enough and she seemed somewhat intelligent, but she couldn't give him one name of another insurgent. She said she became a Christian *after* being incarcerated, not before! Who would consider becoming an enemy of the state, in a state-operated prison that executes Christians? It's ludicrous! The woman was mad!

Furious with her uselessness, the warden screamed insults at her. Rather than melting with fear, she stood defiantly in front of him, sneering. Her lack of intimidation increased his rage. The warden grabbed her by the hair, dragged her out of his office, and ordered a guard to immediately remove her from his presence before he killed her.

Rather than ask any questions, the guard quickly hustled Darla back to a cell she once occupied with a group of women. He tossed Darla into the cell without speaking to her. She crumpled onto the floor, breathing heavily. Rachel ran forward, rolled Darla over, and gently placed Darla's head in her lap.

"Darling," Rachel whispered, "can you hear me?"

"Yeah," croaked Darla.

"Would you like some water?"

Darla licked her swollen, bruised lips, "Maybe just a taste."

Rachel lifted her head upright while another prisoner dripped some rusted, foul water into Darla's mouth.

Darla put her hand up, "That's enough."

"It's been ages since we saw you last. Where are Nellie and Cassie?"

Darla looked at Rachel with a pained expression, "I don't know. I honestly don't know."

eᴔᎉᎅᴠ

The warden looked at the second folder; someone wrote *Dr. Cassandra O'Leary* in bold handwriting. The warden shifted uncomfortably in his seat, adjusting his arm, as he read her name. His interrogation of Dr. O'Leary was another failure. When the beautiful woman walked into his office, she cast a level gaze at him, carelessly brushing aside her long, thick, auburn hair. For a moment, the warden said nothing. He looked deeply into her green eyes, transfixed by her pale, luminous skin, her red lips. She stood confidently in front of him but remained silent.

Wanting to impress this enchanting woman, the warden stood up, clasped his hands behind his back and started to pace in front of his wall of diplomas. *She might as well know that she's speaking with an academic peer, another scholar*, he conceded. Turning his head to give her the full benefit of his chiseled features, he breathed deeply giving himself time to think of the best opening line.

"Ahem, Dr. O'Leary, I have a proposition for you."

Cassie studied him coldly, inwardly seething with hate. She remained unwavering, rigid. She took note of his "Bragging Wall," the heavy bookends on a bookshelf, the wilted plants on a window sill, empty energy drink cans in the trash, the letter opener sitting on his desk. Nothing escaped her quick inspection.

"As you may know, I am a very busy man with many responsibilities." He walked closer to her, so near he could smell her clean hair, hear her breathing heavily. *She's interested in me*, he thought conceitedly, *why else would there be perspiration on her lip?*

He reached up to brush aside a stray wisp of hair on her forehead. Cassie clenched her teeth, narrowing her eyes. He turned abruptly, walking over to his desk to retrieve her folder. "In your arrest report, it says that you were charged with racial discrimination and disturbing the peace. Is that true?"

"Why do you care?" she said boldly.

He turned to look at her, his eyebrows arched. He rarely tolerated back talk. He straightened his stance to exaggerate his six-foot frame, "Well, I considered having you work for me as my assistant, but I need to verify your qualifications."

He stopped hastily. Although he said nothing, they both understood his sustained pause. He also needed to consider her personal liabilities, her possible treachery.

Once he made his point, he ventured on, "You could do inquiries for me, help me write papers," waving his hand flippantly, "um, do whatever needs to be done around the office." With this last suggestion, he gave her a leering smile which made her skin crawl.

Cassie inhaled to control her temper; she might as well clear the air, or at least appear willing to appease this shrewd man. "I did some postdoc research with a brilliant professor of psychology. After working together for several years, we had a falling out." She was not going to bare her soul to this malignant toad. She refused to say, *I made the mistake of falling in love with him, a married man. And I made an even bigger mistake getting pregnant.*

"What kind of falling out?"

She clenched her teeth, now she wanted to fight. "He stole my data and plagiarized my writing. I brought my complaint to the research committee, but they sided with him." Remembering the meeting still made Cassie furious.

The warden reread an insert in her folder again, *Ah, I see that now. The university wanted to keep their "star performer" so they removed a dissenting voice.* He closed the folder but held it to his chest. He remained undecided. Although she was gorgeous, he didn't know if he could trust her with inmate files.

Cassie recognized his doubt but she also wanted to prolong this conversation a few more minutes. She opened her hands as if pleading for her life, reaching closer to his desk. "Rather than admit that he stole my research, my mentor—a renowned, African American doctor of psychology—claimed I was trying to ruin his reputation with slanderous, racial accusations. The university not only removed me from my position, they filed charges against me."

He reopened the folder to check dates in her file, "They didn't arrest you immediately?"

For the first time in their discussion, she turned her face away, *No, I had time to get an abortion, pack my bags, and say goodbye to friends.* When she felt his gaze drilling into her, Cassie turned back to him slowly, and said menacingly, "No, I was arrested a couple weeks later and charged with discrimination."

"What about disturbing the peace?" he taunted her.

"I don't like to be pushed around." With those words, she lunged for the letter opener. Scooping the slim knife off his desk, she plunged it deeply into his cheek, missing her intended target, one of his eyes.

Surprised by the attack, the warden screamed with pain and humiliation. He hit Cassie in the face, knocking her to the floor. She dragged herself to the bookshelf and grabbed one of the heavy bookends. As he bent down to grasp a fistful of her hair, Cassie swung the metal weight upward with all her strength. Crunch. She broke his arm.

He screamed again, this time with murderous fury. When she tried to stand up, the warden kicked her in the face with his steel toed boot, knocking her back to the floor. A guard promptly ran into the office. The guard looked at the enraged warden, clutching his useless arm, cursing the woman; and there on the floor laid a woman, her red hair tangled in a pool of blood, motionless. Instinctively, the guard knelt beside the woman to take her pulse. Nothing.

"Remove this vile woman from my office!" screamed the warden. "And send for my personal physician, now!"

The guard used his shoulder radio to call for help. Before his backup arrived, the guard called the warden's physician on speed dial. In the meantime, the warden stomped behind his wooden desk, slouched in his swivel chair, and gritted his teeth in anger, glaring at the bloody woman on his rug.

In addition to his broken arm, he only had one more chance, from this sorry group of females, to extract information about other insurgents. He was going to conduct this last interview differently. He would not be kind. If she wouldn't produce the results he demanded, he would make an example of her in front of the other criminals.

⌘

Cassie felt her spirit flowing upward, toward heaven. She looked down and saw the guard kneeling beside her broken body, searching for a pulse. Cassie heard the warden screaming his interminable demands, but as she floated above the turmoil, his voice was nothing more than a clanging gong, a senseless noise.

She became aware of two divine beings escorting her into the heavens. Two imposing angels wearing bright, linen tunics. Each angel held one of her elbows; their mighty wings carrying her swiftly to another place, a warm place, a place with soothing music, a place of rest.

When they reached their final destination, her feet touched a soft, spongy surface, and the angels released her arms. As she walked between the angels, Cassie asked her escorts countless questions. Overwhelmed by her surroundings, she chattered excitedly about everything.

The smaller angel studied her compassionately, "Daughter of Man, soon all of your questions shall be answered. But before we speak of higher things, let us first introduce you to someone you have not yet met."

Cassie closed her mouth, waiting, twisting her hands nervously together. Walking from behind the taller angel, a young man stood in front of her. A handsome young man, skin the color of café au lait, shoulder length, black dreadlocks, and sparkling green eyes. Her eyes.

The taller angel spoke, "Cassiopeia, may I introduce you to your son, Miguel. Miguel, this is your mother." Cassie's knees buckled beneath her. Before she fell to the ground, the young man sprang to his mother, and caught her. Protectively embracing his mother, Miguel lifted Cassie back onto her feet.

Pressed against his chest, Cassie wept with all that was in her, "I'm sorry. I am so sorry. Oh Miguel, please forgive me!"

Miguel stroked her hair, whispering gently into her ears, "Mother, there are no tears of sadness in heaven—only tears of joy." She looked up to see tears running down her son's smiling face. He added, "I'm so happy you're here with me; you're an answer to my prayers. Now we have an eternity to get to know each other."

Cassie started laughing, and crying, but this time, she cried tears of elation. A son! She had a son; a magnificent son, a son who loved her and forgave her. *Is there no end to this amazing joy?*

"No, my child, there is not."

Cassie pulled away from Miguel for a moment to look at the newcomer. No introductions were needed for this speaker. "Jesus!" she cried. This time Miguel let her fall to her knees. She crawled on the ground to grasp the Lord's ankles. She kissed his feet repeatedly, weeping and drying his feet with her long hair.[1]

Jesus reached down to touch her flaming red curls. "My dear lamb, your faith has set you free. Now come, tarry with me, there is so much for you to see." Jesus held her hands as she stood up again. He looked tenderly into her eyes, "I have waited a long time to explain the universe to you. Would you like to study the constellations?" Cassie looked at Jesus expectantly, "Let us begin with Cassiopeia."

1. Luke 7:37–38.

16

FOUR MEN SAT AT the rough, oaken table in Marcus's kitchen. On the table sat a pitcher of water, four empty glasses, some apples, and a hunk of cheese. None of the men felt like eating or drinking.

Marcus began, "Okay, there seems to be some kinda grumbling goin' on in the camp. What's happenin'?"

Brant exhaled, he looked at the ceiling. "Ever since Toy came back from the settler's place, she's been moody. At first, I just blew it off, but she isn't gettin' any better; in fact, I think she's gettin' worse."

Ryan leaned forward, addressing Brant, "Have you tried talking to her?"

"Yeah, all the time, but she's not saying anything."

The men overheard offhand remarks and exchanged personal observations, but no one knew how to help Toynell. Pastor Greg listened intently but remained still. When the conversation lagged, the pastor said, "Someone needs to talk with Toynell, Alicia, and Monica. Something might've happened that day but none of them are talking."

"That sounds like a real good job for a pastor," Ryan added.

Greg nodded his head; he agreed. He rested his left arm on top of his head, "I actually asked Monica about their visit right after they got back. She said they had a lively discussion about scripture but she didn't hear anything offensive. Monica did say that Toynell wasn't herself that day." The pastor rubbed his chin absentmindedly with his right hand, thinking.

"I've got an idea," mentioned Brant, "Greg, why don't you come over to our house tonight for dinner? Maybe you can talk with Toy. See if there's anything to worry about."

"Toynell won't be upset when I pop in at the last minute?"

"Yeah, she might," Brant admitted, "but she likes you a lot. She'll warm up to the idea if you look really pathetic."

All the men laughed together. Marcus clapped the young pastor on the back, "There ya go, Greg, just be yourself."

Pastor Greg rolled his eyes. "What do you want me to do? Come up to your door, limping with a rock in my boot?"

"No, no, no," interrupted Ryan, "carry a bouquet of flowers and comb your hair!" Now the men had fun. They started shouting in unison, firing off ideas; each suggestion became more ridiculous than the last.

Finally, Marcus cleared his throat, wiping tears from his eyes. To sum up their teasing, he said, "Greg, hobble up Toynell's porch, knock on her door, hand her some flowers . . ."

"But be clean, comb your hair . . . ," repeated Ryan.

"Yeah, yeah, yeah, clean clothes, hair combed," Marcus said, "hand her a dead chicken and say, 'Toynell, I don't know how to cook a chicken. Could you help me?'"

The men threw their heads back, laughing and pounding on the table. The mental picture of this shy pastor presenting Toynell with a dead chicken—a delicate woman in her own right—was beyond comprehension, it was ludicrous. This wouldn't even happen in another dimension.

When the chuckling died down, Brant scratched his head, "Pastor Greg, don't do anything outrageous. I'll tell Toy that I'd like you to join us for dinner and she'll fix something special."

The pastor looked at Brant, relieved.

Still smiling broadly, Marcus said to his pal, Ryan, "Looks like the young guys got it all under control, buddy."

"Yeah," agreed Ryan, reaching for an apple, "I guess we didn't need to worry about anything. By the way, Greg, what're you gonna wear?"

"I don't know yet," admitted the pastor, "but I guess I need to comb my hair."

☙◎◎❧

That evening, Pastor Greg walked from his small shack on the compound to Brant and Toynell's cabin. He prayed quietly as he walked; he hoped to receive divine guidance to say the right words to this couple. Newly ordained before the United States fell, he lacked practice counseling people, until now. Now people came to his house almost daily for encouragement or prayer, insight or forgiveness. He wondered what would occur tonight.

He didn't need to wait long for the answer. While they ate a pleasant meal of fresh vegetables and biscuits, they chatted about the daily news in their community. After the men took their dishes to the kitchen, Toynell returned to the table with a teapot of steaming spearmint tea.

She set the teapot on the table beside three chipped coffee mugs. As she sat down, she said tactfully, "Pastor Greg, I always enjoy talking with you, but I have the strangest feeling you were sent here on a mission." She glanced at her husband, who suddenly looked away, "What would you like to talk about?"

Greg poured tea into everyone's mug then leaned back in his seat. "Toynell, there are a lot of people worried about you." Her lips started to quiver. She placed her hand over her mouth and looked at the tablecloth. "I just want to know if you'd like to talk about . . . whatever's bothering you."

Toynell looked at Brant accusingly then back to the pastor. "What have you heard?"

"Somethin' has you pretty shook up. And we, Brant, me . . . well, really all your friends, wanna help you. That is, if you'll let us."

That's when she burst out crying. Not little sniffles or perturbed whimpers, she cried those big, "I-gotta-lot-on-my-mind" tears. Brant wrapped his arms around her and simply let her cry.

She didn't cry long but when she attempted to speak, she swallowed a large breath of air; so instead of weeping, she started to hiccup. Sheepishly, she smiled about her hiccups but she couldn't stop the infernal spasms. Wiping her eyes, embarrassed, she said between the hiccups, "I". . . hiccup . . ."can't seem to". . . hiccup . . ."stop this." Brant and Greg watched her—they wanted to do something, but honestly, they tried even harder not to laugh.

Toynell put both hands on her mouth. Now rather than a hiccup, she made kind of a "Blurp!" sound every few seconds. She blurped and tried to talk, but neither man could understand her. Toynell looked at the men in frustration.

"Hey, I've got an idea," said Pastor Greg. "How about if I ask you some questions and you can kind of answer me with signals?" Toynell gave him two thumbs up.

"Did something happen to you when you went to the settlers' cabin?"

Two thumbs up.

"Did someone say something unkind to you?"

She shook her head, no. She coughed then blurped again.

"Did someone say something unkind about someone you love?"

She nodded her head vehemently, yes.

"Brant?"

She shook her head. No.

"Alicia?" "Monica?" "Marcus?"

No. No. No. Toynell pantomimed the word "write."

Brant found a piece of paper and a pencil; he brought the items back to his gulping, hiccupping wife.

She wrote, "Jesus," then patted the Lord's name for emphasis. Toynell sat back in her chair and crossed her arms, satisfied that the men understood her. When the hiccups started to slow down, she caught her breath and cleared her throat.

Both Pastor Greg and Brant looked blankly at her writing. "Jesus? They talked badly about Jesus?"

Relief washed over her face, "Yes," she answered plainly. As suddenly as the hiccups appeared, they now disappeared. Toynell wiped tears from her face as she described the sensations she felt as they rode to the settlers' homestead: dread, danger. Death.

Death? Pastor Greg sat up straighter, listening intently to Toynell's observations and opinions of the farmyard.

The settlers' homestead had all the typical sights and sounds of a farm. Chickens clucking and scratching the dirt, sheep grazing in a nearby field, firewood chopped next to the house, even hay stacked near the barn. At first glance, everything seemed normal, but it wasn't.

Something was very wrong with the place. The animals were edgy, listless; the cabin seemed like a stage prop. And the people? Well, the people looked and acted like caricatures, not like real human beings. Toynell quivered unintentionally as she recalled the settlers' mannerisms.

"The whole area was weird, but the people," she stopping, trying to find the best words to express herself, "the people were . . . like ghosts." She looked down at her hands, afraid that she'd see doubt in Brant and Greg's faces.

"Otherworldly," Pastor Greg stated mindfully.

"You mean like aliens?" Brant asked.

Toynell looked bravely into her husband's eyes, "No, like demons." There she finally said it. Demons. She said the word that plagued her dreams, worried her mind, and stole her happiness. She said the word that drove her to read the Bible night and day in search of insight.

She said the word out loud for everyone to finally hear. Toynell turned to look at her pastor. "I'm not crazy, Pastor Greg. I know what

I felt. I know what I saw." She inhaled before concluding, "The settlers' place is dangerous."

Pastor Greg reached over and clasped Toynell's hands. "I don't think you're crazy." She smiled slightly. "Toynell, what do you know about spiritual warfare?"

"Nothing."

"The Bible tells us that we don't struggle against flesh and blood, but against the rulers, against the authorities, against the powers of this dark world and against the spiritual forces of evil in the heavenly realms."[1] Greg encouraged her, "How did you know that you might be dealing with demons?"

She licked her lips. "You're probably not going to believe this . . . but as we rode close to the settlers' place, I heard the word 'demons' in my head."

"Did you hear a voice?"

"No, not really," she confessed, "it was more like a very forceful idea."

Greg pondered her explanation. Still holding her hands, he repeated, "Toynell, I don't think you're crazy, but you may have the gift of discernment."

"What's that?" asked Brant, worried about the direction of this conversation.

"Discernment is a gift of the Holy Spirit."

Brant responded, "Pastor, you gotta understand, Toynell and I are brand-new Christians. We don't know anything about the Holy Spirit, or his gifts for that matter."

"You don't need to apologize for being new Christians—you're saved, you're free. We'll discuss the Holy Spirit some other time, but for now, just know that the Holy Spirit gives special gifts to followers of Christ."

"And discernment is one of those gifts?" ventured Toynell.

"Yeah. Christians with the gift of discernment can plainly distinguish the power of God, Satan, the flesh, and the world." He looked at Toynell, "Just remember your earlier comment." She looked at him, mystified. "A person with discernment can advise others of dangerous situations, or they can warn us of false teachings."

Toynell leaned back against her chair, reiterating, "You don't believe I'm crazy."

Pastor Greg shook his head, no.

"You think I may have the gift of discernment."

1. Eph 6:12.

He nodded his head, yes.

She took a deep breath, "Okay. Now I guess I have another confession to make . . ."

Brant grasped the seat of his chair, *What else was going to happen tonight?*

"Go ahead," urged the pastor.

Toynell sighed, shaking her head, "Against my warnings, Monica and Alicia have been going to the settlers' homestead every day for weeks now trying to learn more about finding their inner goddesses."

৩৩৩৩

"*What's that?*" Sydney yipped sharply to Shadow, her wits cloudy from sleep.

Shadow growled menacingly, "*Nothing yet,*" his eyes focused on the forest. He stood up, walked over to the edge of their camp. The hair on his shoulders bristled and his muscles tensed, ready to attack. As he stared into the trees, he snarled, showing his teeth, growling louder.

By this time, Caleb—the man on guard duty—stood next to Shadow, holding his rifle. Caleb also heard the snapping of underbrush, the rustling of leaves. Wearing NODs, he looked in the direction of the noise. He rattled the bushes making the intruders flee.

Caleb reached down, patting Shadow on the head. "You're a good dog, Shad. The raccoons are gone."

Shadow glanced up to admire the man. He appreciated Caleb's gentle hands and quiet spirit. No one, other than the animals, woke up from the disturbance. Shadow lay down again, relaxing a bit, but not ready to sleep.

Sydney walked over to her brother, snuggling beside him. She was not alone. Whenever Shadow settled for the night, all the geese gathered around him to sleep. The chatty birds ruffled feathers and fussed with their beds, but they all insisted on sleeping near Shadow. He was their protector. As Shadow placed his nose on his paws, his eyes shifted around the campsite, observing everything. Smells, sounds, sights: he didn't miss anything.

Neither did the man on guard. Once satisfied that the danger passed, Caleb stirred the small campfire. He removed a coffee pot nestled in the coals with a long stick. After he filled his mug, he sat on a rock, placed his rifle on his knees, and continued his duty as he sipped coffee.

The gigantic mare, standing in the shadows of the fire, nickered softly. As her foal nursed, the mare also listened for trespassers. She twitched her ears, listening keenly. The nanny goat walked over to the mare to nudge her nose—the two had become good friends.

"*Is everything okay?*" asked the goat, uneasily.

The mare looked at her friend, "*Yes, I don't hear anything.*" She whipped her tail to chase away a bothersome fly.

Curious with their newest arrival, the nanny goat ventured toward the cub. She stepped cautiously, sniffing the air around the baby bear. Naturally intelligent, the goat couldn't help herself; she wanted to meet this strange, smelly fellow. She pushed him with her head, not a forceful butt, but a shove to wake him.

"*Umph . . . Mama?*" the cub opened his sleepy eyes.

The goat smiled, "*No, dear, but I suppose you'll be drinking my milk. I just wanted to meet you.*"

"*I hungry.*"

"*Of course you are,*" the goat replied. The goat strolled over to Miah. She grabbed the corner of Miah's blanket and walked away, dragging the blanket with her.

After a few minutes, Miah twitched. He shivered, blindly reaching around for his blanket, still half asleep. Snorting, he curled into a ball to stay warm. He breathed heavily, still snoring intermittently.

The goat, chewing on Miah's blanket, stood by the mare. The two mothers watched the sleeping man, sniggering. The cub wandered over to the nanny goat—after all, she was his only friend. Now three animals stood together, staring at Miah, waiting.

"*Do you want me to say something?*" offered the mare, twitching her withers.

"*Oh no, this is too funny. Let's just watch,*" answered the goat.

Chilled again, Miah started feeling the ground for his blanket, his eyes shut. Exasperated, Miah finally sat up and looked around. "Where'd it go?" he asked himself, confused.

Caleb broke the silence with laughter. "Man, I watched these animals play with you for five minutes!" Trying to suppress his voice to let the others sleep, Caleb said, "I think the horse and goat woke you up because the cub is hungry."

Now everyone started rousing. They all looked at Miah, who was still trying to figure out what happened to his blanket then they looked at Caleb. The nanny goat stood off to one side of the campsite, watching the people, munching on Miah's blanket, enjoying the show: live dinner theater . . . for animals.

Miah stood up, rubbing the sleep from his eyes. He flashed a lop-sided smile as he looked over at the chewing goat, the mare and her foal, and a bawling bear cub. While he dusted off his pants, he grinned at his friends, shaking his head at the absurdity of life.

Miah summed up what happened, "Let's see if I got this right . . . we're being chased over mountains by PeaceKeepers. But I can't sleep since a goat is eating my blanket because *Gabe's bear* is hungry." Everyone laughed at Miah's expense.

While Juan poked Miah in the ribs, Gabe asked everyone excitedly, his eyes sparkling, "Is he really my bear?"

17

AFTER NELLIE WAITED AN interminable time in a foreboding hallway, a sergeant finally escorted her into the warden's office. She stood in front of his large desk, her hands clasped in front of her. She smiled, patiently waiting for him to speak.

Hunched over folders, his reading glasses perched on the end of his nose, the warden suspiciously gazed over his glasses to look at her. He didn't raise his chin; he just stared at her with a brooding expression. He shifted his arm, wincing when a sharp pain ran up his broken arm inside the new cast.

The warden growled, "State your name, prisoner!"

"Eleanor Markwell, but everyone calls me Nellie."

Although she tried to lighten his mood, the warden's face darkened further. "I don't care if you're the Queen of England. Unless you can give me some credible, pertinent information, you might as well be called mud." He pushed a folder aside.

Nellie's smile faded. She clenched her hands tighter but refused to let this petulant man intimidate her. She looked openly at him, "What do you want to know?"

"I want to know how you lived so long without getting the mark of our valiant leader." Scowling, he openly ogled her broad figure, "How did you eat?" Narrowing his eyes, "Where are your friends?"

"I'm the last of a dying breed," Nellie replied matter-of-factly.

"Humph!" he snorted. "I don't believe you. You're a liar just like your friends."

Nellie pursed her lips, standing steadfast, neither quavering nor crying. Usually, browbeaten women started to tremble and blubber at this point of the interview. Intrigued, the warden leaned back in his chair, assessing this woman's unusually calm demeanor.

"The last of a dying breed," repeated the warden slowly. "You realize that if you don't give me any information—you will die." He waited for his words to penetrate the room and settle heavily on Nellie's shoulders. "If you cooperate, I'll grant you some special privileges," he waved his good hand nonchalantly, "extra rations, maybe clean water, but you must tell me the whereabouts of others like you." He crossed his good arm over his broken arm, "Otherwise, you're useless to me."

Nellie revealed nothing. She didn't flinch or speak. She just watched him, contemplating his next move.

The warden smiled, *She wants to play hardball, huh? I think I'll enjoy this.* He loved to play games, particularly games of strategy, like chess. He liked to lead prisoners into compromising positions and then take advantage of their weaknesses to score victories.

This pathetic woman was no exception. She was not without her frailties. She was old, feeble, helpless. Pitiful. As he considered her circumstances, his smile dissolved into a sneer. *She's powerless*, he told himself as he envisioned a chess board, *and I'm about to capture her king.*

But little did he know that Nellie understood his tactics. She played chess too so she knew his thoughts. She already identified her liabilities: *He reduced my defenses, limited my movements, and anticipated my actions.* Assuming she was as good as dead anyway, Nellie decided not to play safe anymore.

"I have nothing to tell you about anyone else," she said, "but I do have a message to give you." The warden sat up, his eyes widened: she had his undivided attention. "Your days are numbered, and one day, you will face judgment from a holy, righteous God."

This was not the response he expected to hear. He hated her! The warden bellowed to his sergeant, "Get this repulsive woman out of my office!" He pointed to the door, "Take her to the proconsul, now! Fill out the paperwork to release her from this prison; she's an insurgent, a traitor!"

Red faced and furious, the warden stood up abruptly, knocking his chair over. Suddenly he looked panic stricken. His face contorted in pain, he grabbed his heart, and instantly fell lifeless to the ground—dead from a massive heart attack.

Two guards ran into the warden's office. They stopped momentarily to scan the scene then rushed to assist the sergeant. While the sergeant checked the warden's vital signs, a guard called for immediate backup. The second guard yanked Nellie by the arm, almost dislocating her shoulder.

The guard dragged Nellie out of the warden's office, pulling her down an empty hallway. He was taking her to the proconsul, just one step closer to the guillotine. Clearly recognizing the futility of her situation, Nellie acknowledged grimly to herself, *Checkmate.*

ↄⓄⓄↄ

On the same afternoon Nellie mentioned God's name to the warden, Alicia and Monica participated in yet another workshop on discovering their inner goddesses. The four settlers believed that every woman has an inner goddess but many women don't know how to develop this special, natural radiance. The inner and outer glow of beauty and happiness derived from discovering one's own divinity.

Monica and Alicia accidentally fell into a conversation about inner goddesses when they visited the settlers a week after their initial visit. The pair brought some extra bread and canned vegetables as a neighborly gesture of good will, but they didn't expect anything in return. When Alicia knocked on the cabin door, Bert answered and ushered them into the main room.

Seated on the floor were the two women that said very little during their first meeting. Instead of long, peasant dresses, both women wore comfortable, stretchy clothing. One woman had her ankle behind her head and the other woman stood on her head, legs erect, toes pointed.

For a moment, neither Alicia nor Monica said anything. The sight of these women moving languidly on the floor with absolute muscle control captivated them. Their flexibility was astounding!

Bert broke the silence, "You probably didn't expect to see yoga when you came here today, did you?"

Without removing her eyes from the exercising women, Monica shook her head. Her long, bluish-black hair flowed elegantly back and forth. Regaining her composer, she said to the pair on the floor, "I never saw anyone bend and twist the way you do."

"Me neither," agreed Alicia, spellbound.

Both of the lithe settlers smiled calmly. As they completed their routine, they chanted a mantra together, gradually withdrawing from their trancelike meditation. Still seated on the floor, a plain-faced woman, her mousey brown hair tied in a loose bun, finally introduced herself, "My name is Gaya. My friend's name is Kali." Kali nodded politely, but said nothing.

"Ahem, pleased to meet you," said Alicia. Fidgeting with the groceries, she looked around the room; finally, she set the bags on a table. Never one to mince words, Alicia pressed, "Can you teach me how to do that?"

"Do what?" Kali asked temptingly.

"Well, to move like that. It looks like great physical training."

Kali closed her eyes, smiling peacefully. "It is great training, but this is much more than just exercise." She looked at Gaya, "We sing. We dance. We look inside ourselves."

"We become aware of the divinity within us," added Gaya.

"Would you like us to help you find your inner goddess?" invited Kali.

Mesmerized by the women, Monica and Alicia answered in unison, "Yes!"

"Then come again tomorrow. We'll start to teach you how to look into yourself, to find balance in your life—" encouraged Gaya.

"To be happy," interrupted Kali.

Gaya smiled gently at her friend, "Yes, to find happiness."

Alicia and Monica beamed. After years of fighting battles, they both sought peace, enlightenment. They both wanted balance and happiness. They longed for the contentment that emanated from Gaya and Kali. They wanted to discover their personal divinity, and these strange, new neighbors offered an opportunity to fulfill this innermost desire. Without further debate, both Alicia and Monica knew that even wild horses couldn't drag them away from this compelling compound!

❦

Although Bill reveled in his elevated power in the PeaceKeepers camp, he wanted more recognition, more authority. After revealing the location of Papaw and his community of devoted believers, Bill received a reward for every insurgent arrested but he didn't get the respect he desired. He knew what soldiers called him: a snitch, a rat; but he preferred to think of himself as a good citizen of the New World Order.

The only way he could increase his importance—or notoriety, to his jealous colleagues—was to continue to locate other loathsome Christians. Now that his father was safely in custody, never again to be a pain in his neck, he needed to find more rebels. Sometimes he told himself that not all unmarked people were insurgents; maybe they were just misled, or misunderstood the Supreme Leader's divine plan, like his son, Miah.

What was it that Miah said about his mental breakdown after his wife died? Demon possession? Unclean spirits? Nonsense! There's no such thing as demons. Aliens? Yeah, well maybe, but every rational person knows that demons don't exist.

You see, that's the problem he needed to overcome with his son: Miah was simply brainwashed. If Bill found Miah, he could send his son to a psychologist who would straighten him out. But if Miah doesn't come around to Bill's way of thinking, the government would know how to care for his son. There must be some kind of home for mentally unstable people who pray to unseen gods, talk of demons, or hope for eternal life.

Eternal life, Bill snorted, *what a ridiculous idea!*

As Bill thought about Miah, he became increasingly convinced that it was his responsibility—no, his duty—to find his delusional son. Bill needed to bring Miah back to his senses and he needed to rescue his baby girl from his lunatic son. Bill could raise Nora in a normal household where she wasn't surrounded by a bunch of wackos. Well, Bill wouldn't exactly raise Nora, but he'd hire a government-approved nanny that would take care of everything.

Bill realized his folly. "I've been so busy hunting for rebels for our Sovereign Leader that I forgot my place as a father!" he exclaimed, hitting his forehead with his palm.

Bill began pacing around his apartment, muttering to himself, adjusting furniture absentmindedly. Without thinking, he lined up his desk blotter perfectly: an inch from the desk's bottom and exactly twelve inches from either side of the desk's edge. After he oriented his stapler in its proper place, he sharpened all his pencils to the same length, making sure that the pencil tips were ground identically. He required sharp tips on all his pencils to write properly.

As he talked out loud, he went into the bathroom to look at his reflection in the mirror. Disgruntled by a lock of stray hair on his forehead, he looked inside his bathroom cabinet for a comb. He pulled apart the plastic package surrounding a brand-new comb, ran the comb through his hair carefully, patted his hair down, and tossed the comb into a trash can.

As he continued moving about his apartment, his behavior became even more feverish. He picked up bits of fuzz on the floor, confirmed that all his kitchen spices were shelved in alphabetical order, washed his hands with a fresh bar of soap then threw away the used bar of soap. He moved about feverishly, uttering his plans, arranging and rearranging his household.

This was how his brain worked. This was how he developed new ideas. Thinking, talking, organizing. Sometimes Bill marveled at the complexities of his brain, the sheer enormity of his intellect was amazing.

"Yeah, Bill, you're the man," Pride whispered into Bill's mind.

"Take another look in your refrigerator, Bill, there might be something outdated in there," coaxed Compulsion. The other demons within Bill cackled. Bill furrowed his brow as he walked toward the kitchen. Did he remember to check the stamped date on his milk carton?

Obsession nudged Compulsion, "I'm sure glad we joined this horde, this guy is so easy to manipulate."

Compulsion added, "Isn't he? And it sounds like this party's gonna keep growing. I just heard that Larceny invited Murder to join us."

18

ANXIOUS TO RETURN HOME, Juan was always the first to rise. He preferred to take the last watch of the night because he automatically woke up around 0300 in the morning anyway. In those hushed hours when he perceived no danger, Juan read Miah's Bible and prayed.

Strangely, he quickly grasped everything he read now. Whenever he opened the Bible, he prayed for wisdom and the Lord honored his prayer. He remembered trying to read the Bible when he was overseas but the words made absolutely no sense. Juan couldn't logically explain this change in his understanding.

Now as he read the Bible, God came alive. Juan was excited to read the Word, but more importantly, he realized the words transformed him. The scriptures seeped into the very marrow of his bones giving him strength and encouragement. Before long, Juan realized he could live several days without food but when he didn't read the Bible daily, he became distracted, less effective. He craved God's word; it was his food now, his manna.

"I don't know what's happenin' to me, Lord," Juan whispered, "but if you have a job for me to do, just let me know. I'm your man."

Lying on his side, Miah lifted himself up slightly, leaning on his elbow. He heard Juan's mumbled prayer. He also knew Juan wanted to learn more about Jesus, so he asked, "Do you want to receive the gift of the Holy Spirit?"

"You mean the guy who orders wolves to run away or casts out demons?"

Miah grinned, "Yeah, that guy."

"I've been waitin' for weeks to ask you about that. What do I have to do?"

"You have to confess your sins and earnestly seek the Lord's gifts."

"I've already done that," replied Juan.

"Let me lay my hands on you to pray." Miah stood up, brushing pine needles and dust off his clothes. "When you feel words forming on your tongue, just talk. It's alright if you don't know what you're saying, just let the words out. You're speakin' somebody's language." Miah smiled, "The gift of tongues is an outward sign of the baptism of the Holy Spirit. We'll look at the gifts of the Spirit again, but for now, let's just take one step at a time."

"I'm ready," Juan responded bravely.

Miah walked over to the log where Juan sat. Placing both hands on Juan's shoulders, Miah closed his eyes and began to pray. Within a few minutes, Juan spoke a few words haltingly. Soon both men prayed together; Juan speaking cautiously, Miah speaking confidently. In the stillness of morning, their prayers streamed back and forth as the Spirit issued prayers to their Father in heaven and their heavenly Father showered blessings upon them.

As the minutes passed, Juan bathed in the empowerment of the Holy Spirit. He felt stronger, more attuned to his surroundings, closer to God. He inhaled deeply, trying to fathom what was happening to him.

Suddenly, a thought slammed into his head. He snapped his eyes open, automatically looking up. Juan rushed over to the fire to throw a bucket of water over the glowing embers. Miah tensed, freezing in place; he too gazed upward then he glanced back at Juan.

Juan pressed his index finger to his lips and mouthed wordlessly, "Drone."

Both men rushed to wake Caleb and Gabe with nudges, pointing skyward. The intel men understood the danger immediately without hearing a word. They grabbed their weapons and slipped under a rock shelf near their bedrolls.

Miah swiftly scooped Nora into his arms as he ran toward the rocks. The four men squeezed under the rock ledge. Although their legs and feet tangled together when they sat down, there was enough head room to allow them to sit upright.

As they listened, they shifted into more comfortable positions. They heard the low, whirring sound of a drone flying directly over their position. Although the team always chose campsites in densely forested areas, the drone still hovered over their site, its pilot trying to decipher the images relayed back to him.

By this time, the animals started to rustle. The puppies stood up, wagged their tails, curious about the men's unusual behavior. Before Shadow even moved toward him, Miah softly commanded his dog to stay. Shadow and Sydney sat, but looked at the men with their heads cocked sideways. The mare snorted, pawing the ground. The geese talked among themselves, a sleepy, low muffling; their bills still tucked beneath thickly feathered wings. The goats also muttered, standing up unsteadily. The cub snored loudly, a lump of black fur stretched out on the ground, oblivious to the goings-on.

As the animals shuffled around the area, the drone's pilot discounted his first impression. *Not a fire, just dust from a bunch of animals.*

Looking over the pilot's shoulder, Bill asked, "What're you looking at?"

"It looks like a herd of farm animals," said the pilot.

"Farm animals? In the middle of nowhere?"

The pilot pursed his lips, *Man I hate this guy.* "Yeah, farm animals. You know, horses, sheep, dogs, a partridge in a pear tree," he replied sarcastically.

"What are farm animals doing in a forest?" Bill said again, more to himself than to the pilot.

"How should I know?" the pilot snapped irritably. "Maybe this is a really smart group of animals that learned how to avoid being the main course for dinner."

The pilot would much rather be in bed with his wife than scouring the mountains looking for a small group of insurgents. Because of one lousy infraction, he had to spend his nights flying a drone around hundreds, maybe thousands, of acres of forest looking for this jerk's phantom rebels. *Oh, well, I only have a couple more weeks pulling this duty then I'll go back to my regular day job.*

"Fly over the area again," ordered Bill.

Heaving a sigh, the pilot maneuvered the drone over the campsite. They studied the animals *again.* Dogs sitting in a clearing, watching a couple of horses, and what's that? Goats, not sheep, geese, and maybe a dead dog on the ground.

"Are you satisfied?" the pilot countered peevishly.

Bill stepped back, rubbing his chin thoughtfully. "Honestly? No."

Despite Bill's curiosity, the pilot manipulated his drone over the mountain, into another ravine. The four overlooked men and a wide-eyed, little girl sat under the rocks waiting silently. Once they no longer heard the drone's hum, they began to whisper.

"Someone's still interested in us," sighed Juan.

Miah said doubtfully, "I don't think it'd be my dad; he has no access to technology."

"Well, whoever it is," growled Gabe, "they got too close to us this morning." Studying Juan and Miah, "What's the quickest way back to your home?"

Juan answered, "The mountain road." Gabe frowned. "If you want, we can walk in the woods, parallel to the road for a while. Eventually, we'll turn into a narrow trail that will take us up to the lodge."

Miah suggested, "I have an idea, but you might not like it."

"Go on," said Gabe.

"I could move ahead of you to stake out a trail. If PeaceKeepers get too close to you, I can lead them off in another direction."

Juan sniffed, "That sounds great, buddy, but you're Nora's brother and the only guy who can milk that stupid goat."

"I've heard all kinds of special duty assignments," chuckled Caleb, "but never goat milking."

By this time, Gabe's cub woke up, snuffled the ground for food, and rambled over to his big, hairy nursemaid. Gabe stroked the cub's fur, considering their options. "Any one of us could move ahead of the group—"

"I'll do it," volunteered Juan. "I wanna get home as soon as we can. I'll get my gear together and leave in a few minutes." Rummaging in his backpack, he pulled out a large ball of twine, "I'll mark the trail with some string. Once you settle in for the night, I'll come back and have dinner with you."

Everyone agreed to Juan's plan. The two weakest members of the party, Nora and the cub, needed Miah and Gabe. A novice herbalist, Caleb preferred to take the rear position to gather plants; consequently, assigning Juan as their scout made the most sense.

Juan rubbed the fat cub's saggy coat, "Hey, before I go, I think you should name this guy."

"His name's Griz," answered Gabe.

"Griz!" retorted Juan. "He's a black bear, not a grizzly."

"Yeah, I know but I don't like the names Blackie or Brownie."

Caleb nodded, "Griz sounds tougher."

"Yeah," Gabe smiled, "that's what I thought." He pulled a stale cookie out of his coat pocket, unwrapped the package, and placed the cookie in his palm. He offered the treat to Griz and the cub licked the cookie off Gabe's hand, swallowing it whole. The bear started snuffling Gabe's other pockets for more food to eat.

Juan crawled out from under the rocks. He smiled as he watched the massive, bearded soldier play with the mischievous cub. Looking over his shoulder, Juan said, "Miah, you better start milking that goat. I might come back some night and find all of Gabe's clothes chewed up by a hungry bear lookin' for cookies."

19

THE DREADED MOMENT FOR Nellie finally arrived: her arraignment with the proconsul. With her wrists and ankles shackled, Nellie shuffled down a highly polished marble floor to the expansive courtroom. One guard led the entourage, while another held her elbow, and two guards followed. All Nellie's guards carried loaded pistols in their holsters. An old woman in restraints, she was such a flight risk.

Passing through the double doors of the ornate room, Nellie glanced around at the packed seating; it was a full house. The guards led her to a designated area and motioned for her to sit. She sat on a hard, wooden bench between two beefy guards to watch the proceedings from the front row. Nellie wasn't the only defendant on trial. She was just one of many insurgents scheduled to face His Honor today; but trials created major excitement in Marshall City for anyone, and everyone, who could snag a ticket.

Little did Nellie know that in the far corner of the balcony sat a tall black man and a fair-skinned Irishman. Both men wore their hats and gloves inside the courtroom, but people ignored their crude manners— no one expected much from country folks. Besides, a couple of hillbillies didn't merit the crowd's attention; they wanted to watch the live court proceedings.

Those that didn't get a seat in the courtroom filled the outside courtyard. In the middle of the courtyard sat the Supreme Leader's crowning edifice of punishment: the guillotine. Brant and Toynell stood among this crowd of rowdy onlookers. The couple wore long cloaks and gloves which covered their faces and hands, but just as in the courtroom, no one paid much attention to spectators. Everyone came to watch rebels receive the penalty they so justly deserved, death by beheading.

As part of his royal fanfare, the proconsul demanded that trumpeters announce his entry. Ten men wearing colorful, medieval costumes with tights and waist-length capes walked down the center aisle. Once trumpeters reached the front of the courtroom, they separated into two, separate straight lines, five men in each line. In unison, the musicians raised three-foot-long brass trumpets to their lips and blew a triumphant blast to herald the proconsul's arrival.

In front of the courtroom, bailiffs grabbed the gleaming doorknobs on a pair of enormous mahogany doors. They slowly opened the doors because they adhered to their number-one priority: pageantry. The audience grew quiet. No one stirred. Then standing in the doorway, his silhouette accentuated by a light shining behind him, stood the proconsul.

The proconsul took one step forward then stopped. Jutting his chin in the air, he scanned everyone watching him. The audience inhaled a collective breath of awe. He was beautiful! He wore a distinguished black robe with purple velvet striping on its long elegant sleeves; when he walked, his regalia flowed so elegantly around his body that it looked as if he floated into the room. On his head, he wore a purple velvet tam that set off his glossy, white hair and highlighted his violet eyes.

He walked next to his judgment seat and lifted both hands in the air. In his loud, professionally-trained voice, he said, "May all glory and honor be given to our Sovereign Leader."

The audience responded robotically, "May we be found worthy to serve his every need."

When the proconsul lowered his arms, the musicians lowered their trumpets, holding the instruments perpendicular to the floor, in front of their bodies. The proconsul sat in his chair, behind the imposing bench. He dismissed the trumpeters who formed a single line and marched down the center aisle, exiting the courtroom. A bailiff in the back of the courtroom closed the doors, which signaled the start of official business.

The magistrate reached into his vest pocket to retrieve a pair of reading glasses. He perched the glasses on the end of his nose. As he studied the proceedings from his vaulted position, he looked very intelligent, very professorial. He shuffled some papers on his desk, clearing his throat.

"Before I begin listening to defendant testimonies, I must ask: are there any defendants who want to renounce their insurrection and receive the mark of loyalty to our Supreme Leader?"

At first, no one moved or spoke then several defendants raised their hands. Timidly, several more raised their hands. They didn't expect to be *killed* for their insolence, they just didn't want a tattoo. Expecting this reaction, the proconsul—or "His Honor," as he preferred to be called—motioned for the repentant malcontents to come forward.

Shuffling to the judge's stand, still shackled at the ankles and wrists, three men and four women approached His Honor. They stood before the proconsul, their heads bent in shame as people in the audience threw trash at them, calling them derogatory names. The proconsul let the prisoners stand for a few minutes in front of the raucous crowd; he liked to watch people squirm.

Once he tired of the spectacle, His Honor asked the remaining defendants, "Anyone else?" No one raised a hand or stepped forward. He slammed his gravel on the desk, "Then let the court records show that the remaining defendants received the opportunity to pledge their allegiance to our Sovereign Leader, but decided to abstain."

"Kill the traitors!" a red-faced man screamed.

"Off with their heads!" screeched a woman, waving her clenched fist in the air.

Provoked by hecklers, the crowd roared with anger. They threw rotted vegetables, rocks, and lit matches at the defendants seated on the front row. As Nellie and her cohorts tried to dodge the flying debris, the indignant proconsul quickly crushed the riot.

"Silence!" His Honor thundered. "I will not tolerate this behavior in my courtroom." Glaring at the crowd, "Bailiff, remove everyone in the courtroom that threw garbage or shouted obscenities."

Having noted the belligerent participants, the bailiff and his team began singling out offenders. Initially, they touched a troublemaker's arm and motioned for the person to stand. Most stood obediently and filed out of the courtroom without further complications. Conversely, stubborn agitators received swift blows to their heads and rough handling by court officers before they left the assembly.

Watching the procession leave his courtroom, His Honor sighed wearily, *They'll no doubt join others in the courtyard to watch the executions.*

Putting aside his dreary musings, he organized the order of the defendant list. He preferred to question men first, leaving the women until the end of the proceedings. Very often, after hearing his judgments and listening to the courtyard guillotine swiftly carry out his penalties, women reneged on their original pleas and asked for clemency. This was

His Honor's preference; even with his corrupted heart, he hated to sentence a woman to death.

Clearing his throat, the proconsul announced, "I have decided on the order of the defendant list. We will have a fifteen minute recess so court officials can organize the prisoners and prepare their defenses." The proconsul gave his list to the bailiff. He slammed his gravel on the judgment stand, stood up, and exited the courtroom without fanfare.

Nellie asked the guard next to her, "Could you see where I am on the list?" The man nodded slightly. He, and several other guards, conferred with the bailiff. When he returned to his seat, Nellie asked, "Well?"

"You're the very last person."

In the balcony above Nellie, Ryan leaned over to Marcus, whispering, "Whadda ya think?"

Marcus exhaled, "I'm prayin' for a miracle. We can't get close to Nellie so there's not gonna be a Hollywood-style rescue. I'm just hoping the judge will find some obscure law to grant her a reprieve. I heard he sometimes gives life sentences to women, especially older women."

"If that happens, we might be able to help her escape later."

Hopeful, Marcus admitted, "That's my plan."

Constantly listening for any drones hovering in their vicinity, Juan set out to plot a trail ahead of the others. Already the group's pathfinder, Juan added the dimension of security to his responsibilities. He wanted to stay at least one click or more ahead of his friends so if he noticed danger, he could change his course of action.

When he saw a river in a mountain ravine, Juan found the narrowest place to cross. None of the mountain streams compared with the Tennessee River in size; nevertheless, he always paid attention to the difficulty in crossing bodies of water. As he walked, Juan marked the trail with pieces of twine attached to tree limbs. He tried to keep the markers obscure to PeaceKeepers but noticeable for his team—especially since he also dropped cookie crumbs on the ground for the puppies, or Griz, to find.

Whenever he reached the crest of a mountain, he took a compass reading, looked over the landscape, and charted the swiftest course to their final destination, the lodge. Besides taking map readings, Juan studied the panorama with his binoculars. He first made sure that Gabe's team found his trail. When he reassured himself that they read his markers accurately, he looked for enemy troops. So far they escaped detection.

He couldn't understand why anyone would want to look for them, they hadn't caused any trouble, but Miah's dad, Bill, was a crank. Maybe Bill figured out a way to solicit the help of PeaceKeepers. *Stranger things have happened*, the Latino thought dismissively as he continued walking, constantly studying his surroundings, trying to find the fastest way home.

⸎⊙⊙⸎

Bill examined a topographical map of the Smoky Mountains posted outside a clerk's tent. Despite the pilot's conclusion that the cluster of animals was just an anomaly, Bill felt differently. Generally, farm animals don't wander through dense forests—too many predators live in the woods.

This just doesn't feel right, Bill reasoned, pacing around the drab, hot tent.

Finally acting on his suspicion, Bill went to the camp commander to address his concern. After a lengthy discussion about assigning troops for an incursion without substantial intelligence, Bill convinced the commander to give him a small contingent of PeaceKeepers for one week. One week would be enough time to either find Miah or concede that he lost his son and daughter somewhere in the wilderness.

The commander enjoyed toying with Bill about troop availability, so he acted as if Bill's request was unreasonable. Eventually the commander grudgingly relented, but it was all a show. Honestly? The commander wanted the whining guy out of his hair for a while. Maybe if he was lucky, Bill would shoot himself in the foot or fall off a cliff. *Ahh! What a pleasant daydream.*

The commander sighed. "I'll dispatch a squad with my second lieutenant, a corporal, and three privates to search for this supposed band of rebels." Glancing up at a young officer standing in his headquarters, he ordered, "Lieutenant Anderson will command the troops; any civilians attached to this unit," he eyed Bill contemptuously, "will only serve as advisors." Hiding his grin when he noticed Bill's disappointment, the commander continued, "Report back to post in seven days, with or without prisoners. That is all."

The lieutenant saluted his commander, turned, and brushed past Bill. Bill stood in the tent, astounded, not sure what to do next. "You're dismissed!" growled the commander.

Bill swiveled around, exiting the tent as quickly as possible. He wasn't exactly sure about the details of this search but at least he could spend a few more days looking for his children on the government's dime. He might even earn another reward for helping to capture more renegades: groups that may—or may not—include Miah. He really didn't care anymore.

20

WITH THE ONSET OF summer, Jim, Sara, and Rosa began to worry about Miah and Juan. They knew that neither man planned to take a leisurely trip: Juan hated to leave his pregnant wife, Rosa; and Miah longed to spend time with Beth. Although Miah wouldn't learn of Beth's passing until he returned home, Jim knew Miah would search relentlessly for his family and then promptly return home.

After they left, Jim announced to Sara and Rosa that he planned to follow Juan and Miah's route through the Smokies to find them. Both women agreed wholeheartedly. Both Rosa and Sara nursed the same lingering doubts as Jim and they welcomed his proposal.

Sara asked, "When are you going to leave, sweetheart?"

"Tomorrow morning," he answered. "I keep thinking I'll travel a few miles down the road and find them walking slowly home; Happy prancing ahead of them." Rosa smiled and walked into the kitchen.

Jim touched Sara's elbow to lead her further away from the young Latina. "Help me pack for a long trip," he said in a low voice. "I want plenty of ammo and food, just to be on the safe side."

Sara bit her bottom lip, nodding her head. Jim still mourned over Beth's death and she hated the thought of Jim's reaction to also losing Miah. Never one to mince words, Sara spoke the unspeakable, "Jim, will you be alright if you can't find Miah or Juan?"

Jim looked directly into her eyes, knowing her thoughts, "You mean if I learn that one or both of them is dead?"

"Yes."

Jim held both her hands between his hands, "I'll do what needs to be done. I need to find them, Sara, dead or alive. It's important."

Having returned to the room unnoticed, Rosa interrupted, "Juan and Miah are still alive. I know it. Don't tell me how I know it, but it's true."

Jim and Sara watched the young woman approach them. "I'll replenish your doctor bag because, for some reason, I know that's important too."

Jim wrapped one arm around Sara and his other arm around Rosa. "I'm so lucky to have both of you in my life."

Rosa added tersely, "Jim, I know you're not a believer, but I pray for your salvation every day. Right now, I'm going to pray for you to find my husband and Miah. Whatever happens, know this . . . Sara and I will be on our knees every day praying for your safety, and the safety of Juan and Miah."

Jim smiled at the beautiful woman, her eyes blazing with determination. "I'd like your prayers now, before I leave." Rosa and Sara wrapped their arms around Jim and blessed him with a prayer of strength, guidance, and wisdom. Afterward, with his head still bowed and his eyes closed, Jim humbly thanked them.

With the help of Sara and Rosa, Jim packed his bags quickly. He set out a few sets of clothes to wear, but the women gathered most of the extraneous items: remedy supplies, simple tools, dried food, and water bottles. Once they assembled everything in one place, Jim inspected his supplies. He made a few adjustments in his medical bag and added another rifle and ammunition, but overall, he was satisfied with his gear.

"I have more stuff now than when I first came into the valley," Jim noted. He glanced over at Mattie, now a mature, intelligent companion. "Should I take Mattie with me?" Mattie sat up, her bright eyes watching him hopefully.

"I think that's a great idea," said Sara. "We already have lots of animals here to protect us. I'd feel better knowing that Mattie was with you. Besides, she'd enjoy exploring new places."

"Alright," Jim said. He scratched Mattie behind her ears, "Tomorrow, little lady, we're gonna take a trip in the mountains." Her stumpy tail wiggled furiously. Remembering her friend, Carl, Jim continued, "Maybe we'll find another tabby to bring home with us." He added wistfully, "I wonder whatever happened to Carl?"

At that very moment, Carl twitched his ears. He lounged on Toynell's porch with his eyes closed, purring to himself, sunbathing. Every afternoon, Carl wandered over to Ryan's dairy barn for a saucer of thick, frothy cream. When Carl found Jason milking the cattle, he rubbed against Jason's legs. Jason always picked up the fat cat, stroked his fur, and talked to him.

Granted, Jason's attention wasn't as pleasant as sitting on Nellie's soft lap, but Carl was flexible; he could adjust to changing environments as easily as landing on his feet from a fall. Despite his adaptability, Carl missed Nellie. As he thought about Nellie's gentle voice, Carl purred louder. "*Yep, I'm gonna sit on her lap again and listen to her talk to me while I act like I'm sleeping.*" As he dreamed of sitting in front of a fire with Nellie, Carl twitched his whiskers, smiling contentedly.

❧❦☙

As the crowd returned to the courtroom, Marcus and Ryan shifted slightly in their chairs. They didn't leave for fear they'd lose their seats, but sitting on a folding chair offered no comfort in the cramped balcony. They could still see Nellie from their vantage point so they endured the stiffness in their legs and backs by stretching occasionally to loosen their tense muscles.

As they sat, they studied the audience: roughnecks, rednecks, lawyers, doctors; the washed and the unwashed; the educated and the ignorant. Representatives from almost every walk of life. Some women held dainty handkerchiefs over their noses to protect their fragile sensitivities from being overwhelmed by the smell of others sitting nearby.

One unshaven man nudged his friend to look at a debutante feigning disgust by their mere presence. She placed a handkerchief delicately over her mouth in case she gagged. His buddy smiled and spit some tobacco into a pop can he held in his hand. The lady practically fainted. The lady's escort gave the men a snarling look but said nothing.

The escort looked at his shiny, black shoes, *What's happening to our world? Look at me, a Captain of Industry mingling with the masses. This is a complete travesty, a mockery of decency! I should demand that these men be removed immediately.*

The guy holding the pop can, thought, *I outta step on that fussy punk's shoes and wipe my lips on her hankie the next time I spit.* He grinned when he imagined their reactions, but decided against doing anything. *Nah, they'd just have me arrested for being offensive. Geez, whatta stupid world!*

Before either man reacted to his contemplations, their minds refocused to the front of the courtroom. His Honor returned. This time the proconsul arrived without trumpets, but with the same "hear ye, hear ye," attention devices used to rivet everyone's attention back to the trials and away from their petty rivalries.

This was a terrifying moment for Nellie. Whenever frightened or worried, Nellie always held her husband's hand but her hands remained in restraints on her lap. As she stared at the proconsul, Nellie unconsciously reached over to grab a guard's hand. Rather than pull away from her, the guard held her hand firmly, affirming his presence beside her. She stayed locked in that position, clutching the hand of the man next to her but watching the man in front of her. Nellie never removed her eyes from His Honor. Today, he would decide whether she lived or died.

So began the bizarre circus, the trials of five men and two women, facing charges of insurgency against the Supreme Leader. As planned, the guards ushered each man to the front of the magistrate's podium to state his defense. Unfortunately, without the beast's mark on their hands or foreheads, the men really didn't have any defense; they were automatically guilty of not following the Antichrist's decree.

His Honor issued the death sentence to the first man. With his wrists and ankles shackled, the man hung his head resignedly and shuffled out of the courtroom. As guards escorted him into the courtyard, the crowd outdoors screamed with anticipation of the day's first beheading.

Those in the courtroom remained frozen in their chairs, listening to the commotion outside. No one inside uttered a word. Nellie heard an official in the courtyard mumble something amid the catcalls and jeers from a disorderly, belligerent crowd. A few more minutes passed, the listeners in the courtroom sat in excruciating silence.

Before long, Nellie heard the shriek of a heavy metal blade sliding down its smooth, metal track—screeeeech—until the blade stopped moving. Thunk. The crowd erupted: screams of terror, shouts of delight. Applause, laughter, wailing.

Nellie fainted.

The afternoon hours passed as slowly as mud draining through cheesecloth. His Honor would not proceed with the next defendant's case until each remaining prisoner listened to the guillotine complete its grisly task. After executing all the men, only two women remained: a slight, middle-aged woman and Nellie. This was the hour most hated by the proconsul but most loved by the crowds.

When summoned to approach His Honor's stand, the first woman couldn't even walk. She was so frightened that guards dragged her forward by her shoulders, supporting her on either side. She looked like a discarded rag doll: bedraggled clothes, black eyes, unkempt hair.

Noticing she was unable to speak, His Honor asked mildly, "Do you wish to renounce your sedition against our Supreme Leader?" The woman nodded her head in accord, completely defeated. "Will you receive his mark of allegiance?" Again, she nodded her head. Yes.

"Very well." He signed a document and handed the piece of paper to a court clerk. "You shall receive the mark of loyalty this very hour. As punishment for your crime of treason, you will serve the rest of life in prison, with no chance of parole." He slammed his gravel on the desk, accentuating his final decree.

The guards dragged the woman out, crying uncontrollably. No one could tell if she cried tears of euphoric relief or utter despair. But no one cared. She didn't matter. None of these traitors mattered to the audience. All that mattered was the drama of life and death, or more accurately, the gruesome entertainment of life and death to fill their insignificant lives.

His Honor looked at the last name on his list, "Eleanor Markwell, please come forward."

Nellie rose. She tried to walk steadily toward the proconsul's imposing bench but her knees shook, her pace faltered. The guard beside her supported her back with his left arm and led her forward by holding her elbow with his right hand. She quietly thanked the guard, who nodded his head, almost imperceptibly.

His Honor studied the poor woman. He noticed a slight hitch in her movement. *She probably has arthritis,* he guessed, *like my mom.* Although he made rulings on hundreds of people facing charges of sedition, he still struggled with sentencing older women. He loved too many older women: his mother, his aunts, his sisters.

He swallowed with difficulty. *I hope this woman gives me a chance to reduce her sentence.* He exhaled, "Mrs. Markwell, how do you plead?"

Nellie looked up at the magistrate; her gentle gaze pierced his heart. She spoke simply, without apology, "I'm a Christian, your honor."

He sighed. "Does this mean that you will not renounce your loyalty to this false religion?"

"Christianity is not a religion."

Caught off guard, His Honor straightened his shoulders. He had never heard this answer before. "What do you mean Christianity isn't a religion?"

"It's a personal relationship. A pure religion is one that cares for orphans and widows in their distress, and keeps a person from being polluted by the world."[1]

"Does Christianity care for orphans and widows?" he asked, slightly amused.

"Yes, but it's much more than that," Nellie answered.

The proconsul snorted disdainfully. "We're not going to have a theological debate, Mrs. Markwell. I am here to ascertain your fidelity to our Supreme Leader." Talking in a slow, controlled voice, he repeated his primary question with more emphasis, "Will you renounce Christianity and receive the mark of allegiance to our Sovereign Leader?"

Nellie breathed deeply before answering, "No." The guard clutching her elbow, squeezed tightly, trying to send Nellie a nonverbal cue to modify her answer.

Giving the obstinate woman one more opportunity to change her mind, His Honor asked a final question, "Do you realize that I have the authority to grant you a life in prison?"

Nellie nodded knowingly, "You'd have no power over me if God didn't give it to you."[2]

"It was given to me from above; our Supreme Leader granted it to me!" He wanted to stress his point, "You don't have to die today."

"We all die someday, your honor. I cannot deny my God or his son, Jesus."

Shaking his head with dismay, "So be it." He signed the same document he signed for the five men who stood before him earlier. "Bailiff, you may escort Mrs. Markwell outside to face her sentence."

As the bailiff grabbed Nellie's arm, His Honor asked Nellie, "Do you have any last words you'd like to say to the court?"

Nellie turned around to face the crowd. A frightening sea of faces glared at her with hate. As her eyes wandered around the assembly, she looked up at the balcony to see Marcus and Ryan watching her. Unwilling to betray their presence, Nellie quickly shifted her gaze back to the main courtroom.

1. James 1:27.
2. John 19:10–11.

She smiled wistfully, "Yes, if I may, your Honor. I have only one more thing to say."

The proconsul waved his hand dismissively.

Nellie placed her bound hands on her heart and proclaimed in a loud voice, "The Lord is my God, my Peace, and my Righteousness. The Lord is my Salvation and my Strong Tower. Praise be to the Lord my God!"

The crowd broke into a violent uproar, their fury unleashed. Men and women, the elite and the downtrodden, the refined and the slovenly, all spoke in a single, unified voice, "Kill her! Kill her!" Weary of the battle, the proconsul slouched back in his chair without issuing his usual warnings of courtroom behavior.

The bailiff rushed forward. He hurled Nellie in front of him, causing her to trip over her restrained ankles. As Nellie fell to the floor, the crowd cheered and shouted curses at her. Before Nellie could stand, the bailiff grasped the bindings on her wrists, and dragged her out of the courtroom, tearing the sleeve of her prison garb.

As His Honor made some final pronouncements in the noisy courtroom, Marcus and Ryan stared in disbelief. Ultimately the two men slipped through a swamp of people pushing to go outside to watch the last execution. Keeping their heads lowered and their hands covered, they squeezed out the courthouse without detection by the violent mob.

Marcus whispered, "We need to find Brant and Toynell."

Ryan pointed his chin to a deserted back alley, "Let's go to our meeting spot now. If we're lucky, they'll already be waiting for us." Moving in the opposite direction of the crowd, the two pushed through boisterous revelers gathering outside the courthouse; unruly people drinking, fighting, swearing, and laughing.

Although tall and strongly built, Marcus pressed through the surging masses without creating much attention. Draped in a pathetic, handmade poncho, he looked more like a vagabond than a warrior, a person of no consequence. His precautions were almost unnecessary because the crowd desired to watch a beheading, nothing else mattered to them.

Nothing else mattered to Marcus and Ryan either; both men seethed with rage at their helplessness. Although they tried to develop a rescue plan, there was nothing, absolutely nothing they could do to free Nellie! Oh, they could disable a few guards but they couldn't save Nellie, not with the barrage of people that surrounded her. While Marcus and Ryan walked briskly onward, they quietly debated desperate schemes to save Nellie's life, but each idea evaporated in the scorching heat of the crowd's wrath.

During a lull in their conversation, they realized they already reached the outskirts of town. The mobs thinned. Occasionally, people brushed against them, but the rabble presented less resistance to their movement; so the pair pressed forward at a faster pace, keeping their heads low, their manners subdued. Rather than concentrating on Nellie, both men now resolved to get Toynell as far away from this madness as possible.

Looking down the road, they recognized two indistinct figures, probably Toynell and Brant, waiting for them at their designated meeting place. The men continued their steady pace without uttering another word. As they drew closer, they saw their friends.

Marcus lifted his right arm in the air briefly to signal their approach. When the foursome reconnected, Marcus and Ryan mumbled a few words to the pair. Toynell's eyes filled with tears but she placed her hands over her mouth to stifle any sound that would create attention. Brant wrapped his arm around Toynell and started to lead the group home; Ryan and Marcus followed the pair. They started to walk the long way home from Marshall City to their protected valley enclave, as four, inconspicuous travelers with nothing of value to steal, discouraged by life's inequities.

At the same time Marcus and Ryan tramped the city streets, Nellie made her final ascent up a metal staircase to a solid concrete platform. She no longer saw bustling masses, heard loud insults, or felt trash pelting her. She was completely at peace.

Amazing! Nellie mused.

The executioner stared at the female prisoner's face. When she smiled, her face glowed. She looked radiant! *This is extraordinary!* the executioner thought. He shook his head, bewildered, then asked the beautiful woman, "What's your name?"

She turned to him, "Nellie Markwell."

"Why're you smiling?"

She looked toward heaven, "I can see the Son of Man standing at the right hand of God."[3]

Immediately, the man felt a dreadful heaviness fall upon him. Despite his grave misgivings, he completed all his duties that day as the High Executioner, even fulfilling Nellie's sentence. At the end of the day, the

---

3. Acts 7:55–56.

executioner left his post, never to return, but never to repent. No one ever saw him again; yet in his fruitless wanderings, the executioner never forgot that woman's face: the angel's face that tormented him every day, and every night, for the rest of his meaningless life.

⁓∾ᎯᎯᕲ∾

Despite the crowd's mocking criticism of Christians, the Lord heard every prayer of his obedient children. Always. Although he knew the fate that awaited Christians held in prisons, Jesus made no attempt to rescue anyone today. He knew some unbelieving onlookers would repent after witnessing the deaths of his courageous children but this knowledge did little to pacify his grieving heart.

He walked the corridors within his Father's house. As he entered a hallowed room, he saw under the altar, souls who had been slain because of the word of God and the testimony they maintained. "How long, Sovereign Lord, holy and true, until you judge the earth's inhabitants and avenge our blood?" they cried. Before Jesus answered, each person received a white robe from attending angels.

"Wait a little longer;" promised the Lord, "until the full number of your fellow servants, your brothers and sisters, will be killed just as you have been."[4]

---

4. Rev 6:10–11.

Week 5

21

As he walked up a mountainous gravel road toward the Tennessee River, Jim enjoyed the peace of nature. He listened to songbirds trilling, frogs croaking, and leaves rustling. The hardwood forest exploded with vibrant colors and textures of summer: leaves of varying shades of green, barks of rough browns or smooth grays, the yellows and whites of black-eyed Susans and Queen Anne's lace bobbing their flowery heads above a sea of waving grass. Even the earth smelled alive, exuding the sweet, tantalizing—almost edible—aromas of leaves and flowers.

Smiling, Jim realized that he and Mattie already spent over nine months in this very special place. Although he currently lived in the mountains, he began his life in the valley. Now all his wanderings, all his concerted efforts, centered on his love and concern for those he only recently met.

He watched Mattie scampering ahead of him; she ran straight up a mountain and then straight down the same mountain without missing a step. She flushed birds from the dense forest undergrowth and chased squirrels up trees. Every few minutes, Mattie returned to check on Jim before she ran down the road again, exploring this new, unfamiliar wonderland.

Accustomed to walking miles to provide care for his neighbors, Jim hiked easily up the road's slope. A strikingly handsome man—tall, with black, curly hair—Jim still moved with the agility of an athlete but the wariness of a soldier. Habits he developed early in life and still used every day.

After walking a few hours, Jim sat down to rest under a tree. When Mattie didn't hear his footsteps crunching on gravel, she ran back to find him. Jim greeted his friend with the same gentleness he showed her on the first day they met.

"Whatta ya say, Mad dog, would you like a treat?"

Mattie sat down, her stubby tail twitching furiously. Jim rustled through his pack to find some dog biscuits Sara baked the night before they left. When he pulled out a biscuit, Jim commanded, "Stay." Mattie watched the biscuit with complete focus, remaining perfectly still, maintaining her manners.

"Good girl." He offered her the biscuit and Mattie politely took it from his hand.

As Jim petted Mattie, she stopped chewing and looked abruptly over her shoulder. She listened intently, standing stock still, ears upright, eyes studying the forest. Jim quickly grabbed his rifle, listening to the forest, expecting to hear twigs snap or leaves crunch. Nothing.

For a few more seconds, neither Jim nor Mattie moved; afterward, she ran over to the side of the road, staring down the mountain. Suddenly she burst down the incline, a flash of color disappearing into the thickets. Jim ran over to the place where she ran but saw nothing. He heard her yipping excitedly as she bounded through the forest, her voice growing fainter as she ran farther away from him.

Jim called for her. He fired his pistol in the air hoping to catch her attention; then he heard a terrible squall from Mattie. The sound was somewhere at the bottom of a mountain where a small creek meandered through the forest. He frantically called her name, stepping swiftly over rocks and fallen logs.

When Jim reached the bottom of the ravine, he finally saw her limping back to him; her head hung low, deeply ashamed. As he ran up to her, Jim realized her predicament. A porcupine pelted Mattie with its quills; lodged deeply, the quills covered her muzzle, chest, and two front legs. Jim looked up in the trees to find the porcupine, but he didn't see anything. When he noticed a burrow under several large boulders, he assumed that's where the porcupine found safety.

He turned back to his dog, "Oh, man, Mattie, this is gonna take a while." He picked her up as carefully as possible to carry her back to the road. She winced whenever he made a misstep, but she didn't whine. Instinctively, she assumed full responsibility for her pain, payment for ignoring Jim's call.

Once he set up an impromptu nursing station—a blanket spread on the ground with his doctor kit beside him—Jim began the laborious process of removing porcupine quills. Designed like arrowheads, quill tips enter skin easily but detaching buried quills is painful business. Each quill takes its pound of flesh; a porcupine's retribution for messing around with him. Quills can become infected if overlooked, so Jim methodically re-moved each quill, one-by-one, tearing skin each time he pulled out a barb.

He spent the rest of the afternoon plucking quills out of Mattie's tender nose, chest, and legs. Fortunately, Jim gave her a mild sedative to relieve some of the discomfort; nevertheless, she cried every time he pulled a quill out. After Jim removed five or six quills, they both rested a few minutes then he'd resume the task. Jim talked quietly to her as she suffered through the extractions, but finally by dusk, he felt confident that he removed all the quills. He carefully stroked her hair—watching to see if she flinched when he touched a hidden barb lodged in her skin—but she remained still.

"Well, little lady, I think all the quills are gone, but just to be on the safe side, I'm giving you an antibiotic too." Numb from an afternoon of painful tugging and tearing, Mattie apathetically accepted the shot with a low moan.

Jim made a modest camp in a snug, wooded recess, away from the road. Mattie lay down near the fire in a bed Jim made for her from a horse blanket. Although stiff from the stinging wounds all over her chest and legs, her nose caused her the greatest pain. Overall, she felt exhausted and sick.

While he gathered firewood, Jim watched her carefully. He fried some bacon over the fire, normally a thrilling event for Mattie, but today it hardly triggered any interest at all. He put some cooled bacon in a small roll and offered it to her. Mattie ate it feebly then rested her head on her sore front legs.

"We'll take it easy tomorrow," Jim assured her. He petted her back easily and rested his hand on her neck. "You're a good dog, Mattie." Knowing her keen curiosity, but her even greater intelligence, Jim added, "I'll bet you'll never bother another porcupine again."

Just hearing Jim's calming voice prompted Mattie to wag her tail. Weary from the day, she shifted uneasily in her bed and closed her eyes. Jim gave her enough painkillers to allow a good night's sleep without too much discomfort.

Jim spread his bedroll beside the tired dog, placing his hand protec-tively upon her back. Mattie sighed when she felt his touch. As he listened to her steady breathing, Jim reminisced about some of the wounded sol-diers he guarded in the battlefield.

I hope all those patients lived, he thought, *I only patched 'em up long enough to hold 'em until the choppers came.* Unfortunately, his wartime memories only prolonged his sleeplessness. To halt his worries, he examined the night sky, listened to croaking frogs, and muttered, "I wonder what we're gonna find tomorrow?"

⋞◎◎⋟

At daybreak, Bill, Lieutenant Anderson, Corporal Stevens and three privates gathered in the orderly tent to prepare for their search of a small band of renegades. Considering all the variables, the lieutenant seriously doubted they'd find anyone important. First of all, the commander only had hearsay about the enemy's position; secondly, the supposed "renegade sighting" was somewhere in the mountains; and thirdly, his troops were raw recruits. He regarded this outing more as unofficial field training, rather than an actual manhunt, but he kept his opinions to himself.

Having just graduated from college, the lieutenant wasn't any more prepared for this mission than the three privates. Sure, he had ROTC training but that hardly made him a competent tracker or fighter. Yet instead of becoming discouraged, Lieutenant Anderson presumed the commander gave him this special assignment to develop his leadership skills; consequently, he tackled this task with the same enthusiasm he used during college finals week. *This is just another exam I'll ace*, he believed conceitedly.

Lt. Anderson noticed Bill and the privates watching him so he outlined his objectives for the mission. They would carry enough logistics to sustain them for a week. While they hunted for this small band of outlaws, the lieutenant wanted to develop each man's wilderness survival skills, sharpen shooting aptitudes, practice map reading, and reinforce unit cohesiveness.

He smiled at his resourcefulness, *A practical textbook project. When the commander reviews my unit next week, with or without enemy insurgents, I'll look like a hero!*

After Anderson's briefing, the three privates looked at each other, slightly bemused. Out of the lieutenant's earshot, one soldier commented to his buddies, "It feels like we're traveling with a boy scout."

"Yeah," acknowledged his buddy, "but at least Corporal Stevens will keep us alive."

As they hoisted rucksacks over their shoulders, another private added, "Enjoy yourself. We're going on a camping trip; it sure beats pulling duty this week." His friends agreed.

Bill assessed the five young PeaceKeepers with disdain. As he listened to the privates' banter, Bill realized that no one believed that they would find Miah and his cohorts. Contrary to his initial excitement, Bill now carried a deep-seated resentment for these troops; they questioned his information, doubted his reliability.

If they found anyone this week, Bill presumed he would be the man to get the job done. "It isn't like I'm not already doing enough; now I have to babysit four junior explorers!" he mumbled.

"Did you say something, Bill?" Anderson asked.

"Naw," Bill scowled, "let's just get on the road to find the rebels." He stomped out of the tent with his usual, temperamental attitude. The privates looked at each other, rolled their eyes, and followed the others outside.

❧◎◎☙

At the same time, Bill's group started their excursion into the mountains, Miah spent the early morning hours guarding the camp and brushing the big mare. Although he didn't have a proper brush, he used fresh pinecones—ones with stiff, hard surfaces—to comb her coat. Because of the various things stuck in the mare's hair, Miah needed to replace the pinecones often—they simply fell apart after he brushed her for a few minutes. All the while, Miah talked to her, working out stickers and cockleburs, enjoying their quiet time together.

When Juan woke up, he watched his young friend for a while, appreciating Miah's attentiveness to animals. Finally, he spoke up, "Did you sleep well last night?"

"I did."

Juan stood, casually extended his arms over his head then walked over to Miah. He didn't want to wake anyone up too early but he liked talking with Miah. Juan began stroking the mare's neck. "This is a massive horse! What kind is she?"

Miah shook his head, "I don't know for sure, some kinda draft horse. She's probably not a purebred Shire or Percheron, but she's huge." Miah ran his hand down the horse's neck, "Somebody used her as a work horse, but they weren't very kind to her." He pointed to scars on her chest and nose, "See these marks? Healed wounds from a harness." Miah scowled; he didn't say what he was thinking.

Juan stood in front of the mare, petting her muzzle. "How tall is she?"

"Oh, I'd guess about fifteen hands high, that's about five feet to her shoulders."

"Man, I'm five nine and she towers over me."

Miah smiled, "Yeah, she's a beaut." After he tossed a flattened pinecone on the ground, he picked up another fresh one to continue brushing her.

Juan took a step back to watch. "Have you named her yet?"

"Yep," Miah answered. He glanced sideways at Juan, saying nothing.

Juan opened his hands, as if to say, *Yeah, and her name is . . .*

"Well, I kept telling everybody, 'Let me take the mare here or let me take the mare there.' Even when I talked to her, I'd say, 'Let me help you, mare.' And the name just kinda stuck."

"So you named her Mare?" Juan guessed.

"No, I named her Mary."

"Okay," Juan nodded, "that makes sense. So did you name her colt?"

Miah rubbed his neck, a little embarrassed. "Well, I don't know how big he's gonna get, but I'm guessing he'll be gigantic too. Most people give male draft horses short names: like Ben, Clyde, or Max."

"Uh-huh."

Miah went on, "So I thought, 'What name goes with Mary?'"

"Joseph?"

"Yeah. So I named him Joe."

Juan chuckled, "Mary and Joe. Miah, I swear if I live to be a hundred, I'll never be able to second-guess you."

With sunrise still a few hours away, the friends talked about whatever came to mind. They both longed to see home again—the sooner, the better—and they felt good about the progress their company made in the last few days. In those relaxed, lingering hours of night, they reminisced about their original trip to Papaw's farm.

Juan said, "You know, it's kinda funny but we saw all kinds of miracles on our first trip, but I haven't seen too many strange things on our trip back."

Miah grinned. "Are you serious? We're livin' in a supernatural bubble."

Juan furrowed his brow, looking confused.

Miah lifted his arms, "Just look at our campsite. Every day, more animals join our zoo. Besides Mary and Joe, we have ducks, geese, chickens, goats, a burro, a bear, a woodchuck, *and* a raccoon."

He pointed to the two hardened soldiers with them, "Griz cuddles so close to Gabe that it's hard to tell where the man starts and the bear ends. And look at Caleb; that raccoon curls up right next to him like a cat. Bears and raccoons sometimes *eat* chickens and geese, but not here, our bear and raccoon eat grubs, berries, and crackers!"

By now, Juan cleared his throat several times trying to stifle his laughter. He understood Miah's reflections: their world was crazy, upside down. Despite the bewildering contradictions, living with a herd of animals was funny . . . and refreshing.

Miah added, "I wouldn't be surprised if you came back from scouting someday to find a mountain lion staying with us, eatin' *grass*! Not eating us—or the animals tagging along with us—but munchin' on grass next to Mary, neither one bothered by the other."

"And wagging his tail to keep flies away," grinned Juan.

"Yeah!" Miah shook his head with disbelief, "Honestly, Juan, every single day, I'm in awe of the miracles happening around us."

Suddenly their reverie was shattered when Mary flared her nostrils, snorting. She quickly stormed over to the fire, reared up on her hind legs, screaming the cry of a war horse. Her front feet landed so forcefully on the ground that the coffeepot hanging over the fire fell into the coals. She pawed the soil viciously a few times then stepped back to inspect the ground.

By this time, everyone in the camp was awake. Caleb and Gabe stood up, their weapons in hand. As the smaller animals cowered on the ground, afraid to move, the puppies sat at attention, willing to help.

"What's going on?" shouted Gabe, anger masking his surprise.

Juan and Miah ran over to Mary to see what agitated her so much. There on the ground lay a mangled, flattened, and very dead rattlesnake. Apparently, the fire's warmth enticed the snake out of hiding. Sometimes horses shy away from snakes, but not Mary, and not today.

Mary stomped her feet a couple more times, huffing, and shaking her head. Miah slipped a rope gently around her neck, whispering to her. As Miah stroked her neck and praised her, he discovered she wasn't the least bit afraid. She was mad.

Juan said, "Well, I guess not every animal is welcome to this party, after all."

"It looks that way," agreed Miah, "but I don't think she broke our miracle bubble." Miah studied the snake, "She just reminded us to be careful of snakes."

Juan scratched his chin, "You know what, Miah? Maybe some of these animals aren't following us for *their* protection; they're following God's orders to protect *us*."

22

WHEN MARCUS AND RYAN met Toynell and Brant, neither couple spoke; but the older men studied Toynell carefully. They knew how much Toynell loved Nellie and they wanted to make sure she was ready for a three-day hike back home. She gave them each a straightforward gaze, which said, *I'm okay, let's go.* The foursome left Marshall City together: Brant and Toynell in the front, Ryan and Marcus in the rear, walking in the opposite direction of the crowd.

Few people wandered away from the city, especially on such a beautiful, summer afternoon. The road they followed was crammed with people pushing into the city. Visitors wanted to view the courtyard's carnage, shop in open street markets, and celebrate the advent of summer solstice.

Barricades blocked downtown streets for the celebrations. In the late afternoon, families gathered in parks and thoroughfares to enjoy the citywide entertainment. They laughed at clowns juggling bowling pins, and stared, mesmerized, as actors dueled with swords. Children begged parents for ice cream and parents begged children to cease screaming. The pandemonium was pervasive!

Amid the chaos, music floated into every nook and cranny. On one street, drummers beat sticks rhythmically on trash cans; on another street, musicians played sweet melodies on flutes. Percussion and woodwind, madness and reverie, folly and sanity, all these contrasting elements mixed into a city pulsing with energy. No wonder people for miles around Marshall City gathered for the summer festival. This was a time to break loose, to be free, to do whatever they wanted!

When twilight arrived, wise parents took their children home. Despite the drudgery of dealing with children stuffed with sugar, parents recognized the greater dangers lurking on city streets after dark. Parents said, tongue in cheek, "This is when the demons come out!" Yet without even knowing it—no truer words were spoken.

The summer festival in Marshall City was Satan's playground. Unbridled anarchy. Drunken revelry. Salacious desires dripped from demonic fangs and fingertips, saturating the minds of those victims who carried unclean spirits within their bodies. Unaware of these dark manipulators, partygoers reeled with excitement and abused their bodies, hardening their hearts against anything holy or righteous. Besides, no one said the words "holy" or "righteous" anymore. These were antiquated words, inflammatory words, bigoted words.

Their Sovereign Leader was the one to worship; he was the one who endorsed uninhibited freedom. He was the one who defined sexuality, placated murderers, and condoned liars. No wonder the masses loved him: he didn't hamper them with worn-out sayings about loving God or loving one's neighbor.

He told them that each person would know what was right. Everyone had an internal compass that would guide them to make correct decisions specifically designed *for them*. They didn't need an invisible God to place a yoke around their necks, directing their every move. They were free to be the men and women they wanted to be!

Or were they free? Where was their freedom when they woke up the following morning in a strange house with a bottle of pills next to the bed? Where was their freedom when they returned home with pounding headaches, reeking of alcohol, and looking into the sorrowful eyes of children tired of this behavior? Where was their freedom when they remembered cruel things they said to friends?

There was no freedom; that was the great deception. When they remembered their detestable words, Sarcasm clamped an invisible, metal collar tightly around their throats, strangling them. When they overindulged in drinking, Alcohol snapped shackles on their ankles, causing them to stumble. And when they woke up in strange houses, Lust bound their wrists with restraints, prohibiting them from covering their faces. Granted guilt, pain, shame, and suffering abounded but there was no freedom. There was only abject slavery; the slavery of heavy constraints, connected to chains controlled by demons.

The Supreme Leader packaged slavery in a gorgeous box with shiny paper and a big, red bow; but after unwrapping the package, his slaves discovered his actual motivation, his true, dreadful nature. He doesn't want subjects that serve him, he enslaves them. He doesn't want subjects that love him, he hates them. He hates people with every fiber of his being because his greatest enemy, God Almighty, loves them!

Make no mistake; Satan reveled in this festival. Let disorder, carousing, and desire abound! Let no one speak of righteousness or holiness; words of paltry significance in today's vocabulary. More importantly, let no one say society's most contemptuous word in front of lawyers, educators, or counselors. A word labeled as prejudicial, sexist, offensive, and demeaning. A word that describes man's true character, highlighting his most pronounced inclination. What word causes such controversy, such animosity among its detractors?

Sin.

❧

Leaving in the afternoon, Marcus, Ryan, Brant, and Toynell escaped Marshall City's carnal festivities. They walked briskly for several miles before talking. To everyone's surprise, Toynell spoke first.

"Marcus, Ryan, thank you for bringing Brant and I with you. I know it wasn't easy."

As they walked, Ryan looked down at the young woman, who continued to look straight ahead, never taking her eyes off the road. "How are you doin', Toy?"

She licked her lips, "My heart is . . . broken." She took a deep breath, choking back her tears, "I loved Nellie so much." The men walked silently; knowing she wanted to say more. She said, almost in a whisper to herself, "Nellie never hurt anyone," then big, burning tears filled her eyes.

Brant wrapped both his arms around his wife. Marcus and Ryan closed in to cover the pair with their strong arms, making a tight huddle of three strapping men and one slight woman. The older men prayed for Brant and Toynell bathing them in warmth and protection. Within this circle of love, all four people wept for Nellie, prayed for each other, and allowed the Holy Spirit to blanket them with comfort.

At last they stepped back, still holding hands. They looked into each other's faces. Toynell smiled weakly, nodding her head. She was going to be alright; she just needed to mourn.

As they began to walk again, Brant said, "You know, this is really weird. We've been keeping a low profile all day, not wantin' anybody to notice us. Then without thinkin', we stop in the middle of a road to cry and pray—in front of the whole world!" He held out his arms, spinning on his heels, "But look . . . there isn't a single person around to see us, or report us. Not. One. Person. It's like we're invisible."

"Praise God," breathed Ryan with relief.

಼ು⊙ಱ

Even though they missed their primary leaders, the valley community within the compound thrived. They maintained their routines of livestock management, fence repair, food preservation, clothes washing, and childcare. This certainly didn't include all their daily concerns but these undertakings topped their lists.

In the afternoon, residents usually took a break to relax and visit with each other. Whenever someone mentioned their monotonous lives, another person reminded them to look through the fence portals to see desperate homeless wanderers shuffling down the road, kicking up dust. The sallow cheeks of starving, distressed people immediately altered any misgivings about subsistence living.

They were blessed. They were safe from intruders. They ate two meals a day, worked hard, played regularly, and slept well. They had nothing to complain about.

Then one day, without warning, it felt like the circus came to town! A wagon carrying bright, multicolored merchandise rolled down the road, slowing down in front of the compound's gate. A figure wearing a big hat, stopped the team of horses, locked the wagon's brakes, and started giving orders to three other people in the wagon.

Everyone in the compound ran to watch the excitement through slots in the fence's metal wall. The four new people hung ropes between trees to display glorious, tie-dyed dresses, banners with hand-painted designs, and glimmering streamers made to frighten birds from crops.

A man, with wild, spiky hair, set up a mini-blacksmith's station. After he arranged his tools around a fire, he heated metal and started banging it into interesting sculptures. He forged pinwheels, strange topiary frames, and beautiful trellises.

Awed residents stared at the proceedings with their mouths open, their hearts beating rapidly. Children begged their parents to let them go outside the fence to look closer at the sights. Parents held their children back until one slender woman outside the fence began to pop corn over an open fire; this temptation became too great for anyone to resist.

The floodgates opened. Residents rushed outside their sanctuary to touch silky fabrics, smell tantalizing foods, and hear enchanting music. Even grizzled, old farmers stared at the goings-on as if they'd never seen such unique gifts, such exquisite artistry. Maybe in their secluded lives they hadn't, but today offered these backwater farmers a taste of the wonderful, a kaleidoscope of colors, a breath of savory scents, a change from the ordinary.

But stacked inside the wagon laid the most wonderful vision of all: books, books, everywhere books! The driver displayed books about magical charms, vampire romances, dungeons with dragons, astrology, numerology, decoding mysteries, a vast array of reading material beckoning the compound's starved readers.

Since very few people carried books in their bug out bags, reading new titles or flipping through pages of best sellers enticed the community. But the driver with the big hat gave residents even more incentive to read. She gave away most of the books! She said she couldn't stand to think of parents and children not having books to read so she passed out books like candy. Anyone could have a book!

Even without the giveaways, no one wanted to be excluded from the festivities. Only two guards manning the security towers remained inside the compound. Fortunately on this day—or perhaps *because* on this day—Monica and Alicia sat in the guard towers, without complaint, remaining steadfast in their security positions.

The sentries understood everyone's fascination with the four strangers, the settlers from the other side of the valley. Earlier in the week, Monica and Alicia helped the women dye dresses and paint banners. From their high positions, they watched the surly man forge metal creations, and smiled as Bert managed all the operations. Both women knew the community would welcome this diversion. The settlers brought vivid sights, sweet tastes, and joyful sounds into the lives of those used to hard work, muddy hues, and rugged living conditions.

What harm could come from this meeting? Although they considered this question, Alicia and Monica couldn't think of one problem. Their community would become more rounded, more sophisticated by interacting with worldly, talented individuals. That's why they invited the settlers to meet their friends!

Watching everything from their posts, Monica called Alicia on her walkie-talkie, "Won't Toynell be surprised when she sees our old friends mingling with our new friends?" Alicia smiled, nodding her head.

As shadows started to stretch across the valley, the foursome re-loaded their wagon for their trip home. They excused themselves from dinner invitations because they wanted to return home to check on their animals. Sad to see these newcomers leave, children chased the wagon, cheering the names of their newfound neighbors.

After visiting a sick congregant in the western mountains, Pastor Greg watched everyone wave farewell to a departing wagon. As he crested the last hill, he thought, *Hmm, that's interesting. I wonder who those people are.*

⸺∘⊙∘⸺

At the same time the pastor spotted the wagon, four separate groups of travelers (Jim, Marcus, Juan, and Bill's groups) prepared their evening meals. Jim caught several fish in a mountain stream and shared them with Mattie. Although Jim still felt uneasy about the trip, he enjoyed this quiet time with his lively, inquisitive dog. Marcus's team ventured off the main road to locate a secluded place to set up camp. After crossing several creeks and scaling a steep incline, they safely hid in a rocky crag near the top of a mountain to eat their cold dinner. Juan returned from scouting to find Gabe frying goose eggs over a fire, Nora watching her brother milk the goat, and Caleb teaching his raccoon a new trick; no one seemed too concerned about drones tonight.

Yeah, Juan predicted, *this is gonna be another uneventful evening.*

Interestingly, the PeaceKeepers—those with the least amount of worries—seemed the most dissatisfied. They weren't concerned about being attacked, but they were unhappy with their provisions. They pulled MREs out of their backpacks and opened the shelf-stable foods apathetically.

"Man, what I wouldn't give for a hamburger right now," moaned a private.

The corporal shook his head, disgusted with the young man's grumbling. "Get used to it, guy, you're a soldier now." The corporal sat on a log near the fire and started opening packages in his MRE kit. As he ate, he sniffed forest scents and watched the darkness swallow shadows.

Another private reached into his pack to retrieve a liquor flask. He nudged his buddy, encouraging him to take a drink. His friend, the hamburger guy, unscrewed the lid and took a deep swallow. It tasted like peppermint—peppermint with a bite.

"Ahh," the young imbiber replied. "A couple more gulps of that and I could eat anything." The friends chuckled.

"Listen," the flask owner said, "keep an eye on your food around that other private."

"The skinny one?"

"Yeah, the skinny one," smiled his friend. "That guy can eat more food than ten men!"

"Are you kidding?" his friend asked, taking another gulp before handing the flask back.

Watching the skinny kid walk over to them, the flask guy added with a grin, "Let me put it this way . . . I wouldn't walk in front of him if he had a knife and fork in his hands. I'd be afraid he'd eat me!" His listener gawked at the skinny private, not knowing what to believe.

The skinny private sidled next to the private holding the flask, "Can I have some of that?"

"Sure," the first private answered, handing him the slim, metal flask.

The skinny guy asked nervously, "Aren't you afraid you'll get busted for drinking on duty?"

"Naw," the first guy replied. "What are they gonna bust me for? Having minty, fresh breath?" The three privates laughed. While they talked, they found a cluster of boulders overlooking a river. Sitting on the rocks, slightly out of earshot from the three older men, the privates ate their dinners, joking, and talking.

Actually, the only "older man" in the group was Bill. The privates were all eighteen years old, the corporal twenty-three, and the lieutenant twenty-two. The fact that the commander sent a bunch of kids with him, really irritated Bill. Although Bill didn't like most of the older sergeants and lieutenants, he believed the commander doubted the truth of his claims. Rather than equipping Bill with battle-hardened soldiers prepared to overtake a group of insurgents, the commander sent him on a snipe hunt with children. Revolting!

Bill muttered to himself throughout dinner. He finally moved to a place in the trees far from the corporal and lieutenant. Despite his anti-social behavior, Bill started mumbling, "Chill out. These guys won't get in your way when you find Miah. If you're lucky, Miah and Nora will be with those three Army guys. You'll look like a champion when you bring them all in, single-handedly."

Bill smiled at this mental picture. He'd parade back to post, holding Nora in his arms. Behind him would be Miah and his three Army chums, hands bound. Miah's head would be cast down with shame, but those three other grunts would look at Bill hatefully—powerless to do anything.

Bill sniggered. He licked his lips, relishing the dream. At the same time, Pride licked his lips, relishing the demise: puppet and puppeteer, slave and master, both visualizing the firstfruits of their labor.

23

Despite Satan's plans to overtake Miah's contingent of men and animals, God had other plans. Jesus sent Miah a dream to warn him of their pursuers. When Miah woke up, he immediately told Gabe—the guard on duty—about his dream. Their conversation woke up Caleb and Juan, but Nora remained fast asleep in that deep, unconscious, never-never land of children. No one bothered to wake her.

Juan looked at Miah, "What do you wanna do?"

"I want to see Dad's camp for myself."

Gabe glared ominously at Miah, doubting the sincerity of Miah's vision, "Do you think that's wise?"

Emboldened by God's Spirit, Miah stood up to the hulking Gabriel, "It's not only wise, it's what I'm supposed to do."

Surprised by Miah's audacity, Gabe said nothing.

Juan, being the most accustomed to Miah's special gifts, repeated, "What do you want us to do, Jeremiah?"

Miah looked at Juan, "Juan, I want you to come with me." Turning his head to the others, "Gabe and Caleb, take Nora to Jim's lodge. Juan has the compass readings. Break camp as soon as you can, and put everything on Mary's back. She's strong enough to carry the load. We'll catch up with you later."

Miah turned back to Juan, "We'll travel light: weapons, ammo, food, and water. That's it."

Juan started gathering everything without question. Gabe and Caleb remained motionless; perhaps it was the suddenness of Miah's authority or Juan's willingness to blindly follow Miah, but the two men showed no compulsion to move. They stood next to the fire, rigid as marble statues.

As Miah and Juan left camp, Miah said to the intel guys, "If you want to remain here, that's your prerogative, but I can't take Nora with me. No matter what you think of me, I'm counting on you to protect my sister tonight." Without wasting another minute, Miah and Juan disappeared into the woods in search of Bill's hunting party.

൞ඬ൞

It didn't take too long to find Bill's group. Maybe the young troops felt no urgency to hide their presence (or maybe they doubted Bill's assertions) but whatever their reasoning, Juan found the PeaceKeepers in less than an hour—tracking them in the dark no less. As the pair drew near the solders' camp, Juan placed a finger to his lips, signaling absolute silence. Miah nodded once.

Miah stepped ahead of Juan to study the camp. Kneeling behind some bushes, both men watched the PeaceKeepers. Five young troops and Bill, all asleep and snoring. Incredible.

Miah closed his eyes to pray. When Miah reopened his eyes, Juan handed the young man his knife. Juan pointed to Bill and pantomimed a slashing movement across his neck, indicating the quickest way to end this battle, but Miah shook his head. He didn't want to kill his father.

Miah motioned for Juan to stay in position behind the bushes be-cause the Lord gave Miah a different plan of attack. Miah walked calmly over to the men's horses, releasing their hobbles and untying their leads. After he patted them on the rumps, they walked toward the road, in single file, as if they were still attached to each other.

Then Miah saw something that made him smile, encouraged him. For just a few seconds, he saw a figure in fine white linen leading the horses away from the camp, out of danger. Stepping quietly around the fire, Miah bent down and picked up his father's rifle.

He looked at the troops. He noticed almost everyone placed their weapons beside their bedrolls, only one soldier, a corporal, slept with the strap of his weapon wrapped around his arm. *Smart guy*, thought Miah. He cautiously picked up the PeaceKeepers' four loose M4s and Bill's shot-gun, taking them to Juan, until Juan had all the weapons except the M4 fastened to the corporal's arm.

Encouraged by the troop's deep sleep, Miah proceeded to look through backpacks. He removed cell phones and Glocks from several packs and discovered a drone and its controller. Once he placed these items in his own pack, Miah backed up slowly, never taking his eyes off the sleeping PeaceKeepers. Silently, Miah slipped back into the forest.

Without speaking, Miah carefully picked up three M4s from the pile, leaving the other M4 and Bill's shotgun for Juan to carry. The pair moved swiftly through the woods until they reached a hilltop, fifty yards from the slumbering troops, still hidden in the dense forest. When Miah signaled to stop, Juan stopped. The Latino watched his friend, trying to anticipate Miah's next move, but Juan didn't expect what Miah did next.

Miah raised his voice, calling his father, "Dad, wake up!"

Bill roused, confused. He looked around to get his bearings then asked, "Miah?"

"Why are you pursuing me?" asked Miah. By this time, the young PeaceKeepers were falling over themselves trying to find their weapons; yet only the corporal held his weapon firmly. One private rolled over to his backpack, looking for his pistol. He pushed items around in his pack, but couldn't locate the weapon. It wasn't until he dumped everything out of his pack on the ground that he realized his cell phone was missing too.

Miah called, "What have I done that you need to hunt for me with government troops?"

Bill looked for his weapon. *Where's my shotgun?* He patted the ground by his sleeping bag. Nothing. He looked up the mountain, toward Miah's voice. *Where's Miah?*

While he frantically searched for his rifle, Bill responded, "Is that you, my son?" trying to sound kindly, fatherly.

"You see that the Lord delivered you into my hands. I was urged to kill you while you slept but I only took your weapon. I haven't done anything to you, yet you're hunting me down to arrest me. May the Lord judge between us; and may the Lord avenge the wrongs you've done to me, but I won't touch you."[1]

Again Bill asked, "Is that you, Miah?" Bill began to weep. "You're more righteous than me. You treated me well but I treated you badly. The Lord brought me into your hands but you didn't kill me. When a man finds his enemy, does he leave him unharmed? May your God reward you for the way you treated me tonight."[2]

Miah stood erect, watching his father intently. He didn't trust his dad, but he didn't want to kill him either. "Go back to your post. You don't have horses but you have enough food and water to survive the trip. Don't pursue me anymore and you'll live."

1. 1 Sam 24:12.
2. 1 Sam 24:16–19.

Bill raised his right hand in the air, "I'll do what you ask, only spare my life."

"What about our lives?" a private hissed angrily to Bill. "Don't we matter?"

Disgusted with the outcome of this evening, Bill automatically snapped, "No, as a matter of fact. You don't matter at all!"

Juan and Miah cast one more glance at the pathetic squad surrounding the campfire. They knew no one in this PeaceKeepers unit would be greeted warmly when they returned to post. Finished with their business, Juan and Miah turned, quickly disappearing into the dark forest.

☙◦ⱺ◦❧

In the early morning, Marcus woke up from their eagle's perch on a cliff edge and surveyed the panorama. "Beautiful," he sighed. From this vantage point, he could clearly see three states: Tennessee, North Carolina, and Virginia.

And what a sight to behold. The Smoky Mountains truly look smoky in the morning; clouds filled hollowed valleys, giving the entire mountain range a ghostly, almost surreal appearance. Birds fluttered about in trees and twigs snapped as deer moved through the brush. As Marcus inhaled deeply, he smelled the fresh, earthy scent of decomposing leaves mixed delicately with the fragrances of wildflowers. He closed his eyes, smiling.

"Mornings smell good, don't they?" remarked Ryan.

"They do. If we didn't have so many people countin' on us, I'd like to stay in these woods a few more days, just enjoyin' God's creation."

Ryan laughed, "I hear ya, brother!"

Brant and Toynell started to rustle when they heard the men talking. Toynell snuggled deeper into their blanket. She wanted to sleep a little longer. Their bed was warm and cozy; she saw no reason to get up early when a fire wasn't even started yet. Despite his wife's reluctance, Brant rose, slipped on his boots and joined the other men.

"How long before we get home?" Brant asked.

"Two days at a nice, rolling walk," answered Marcus, "we're not in a big hurry."

"Good," the young man said. "I kinda like spending time with you old guys."

Ryan scoffed. Chuckling, Marcus put Brant in a headlock, "Why? So you can learn how to take care of yourself?"

"No," Brant said joking, "so I'll know how to take care of you." Marcus shoved Brant aside, smiling.

The three men began preparing for the day. As Brant gathered firewood, Ryan unpacked dried meat and fruit for breakfast. Marcus filled his teakettle with water and picked out an herbal tea Talia packaged for him. He preferred a steaming cup of coffee in the morning but in these days of scarcity, he was just glad to drink something hot.

As the men sat by the fire talking, Toynell listened drowsily, too comfortable to move. Sometimes it's just nice to hear relaxed banter without planning any daily projects. Eventually, she too slipped out of bed, patted her hair slightly, and pulled her boots on.

When she joined the men, she smiled shyly. Marcus offered her a hot mug of tea which she gladly accepted. Traveling with these three hardy men filled her with joy.

She loved Brant without question, but this trip really helped her to appreciate Ryan and Marcus. Both men treated her with courtesy but they never excluded her from decisions. Just one day after Nellie's death, they included her in all their discussions, even the unpleasant ones. Toynell treasured that respect.

Although barely five feet tall and not quite a hundred pounds, she liked that the men viewed her fairly. She carried her share and helped with all the work. One time when she tried to reach a tall branch to hang a clothesline, Marcus picked her up saying, "Let me help ya, little mite."

After she tied the final knot, he set her down again and returned to his business without a second thought. She valued Marcus's kindness—she finished her job but he didn't do her work for her. She was part of the team, not some tagalong slowing their progress.

They sat by the fire, sipping hot tea and nibbling on dried food. During this reflective moment, Ryan started talking. "You know I've heard about an interesting, old guy that lives somewhere in these mountains."

"An old man that's some kinda priest?" added Marcus.

"Yeah."

"I've heard the same stories."

"Maybe we'll see him since we're goin' cross country instead of keeping on the roads," said Ryan.

"Maybe we will." Marcus placed another log on the fire, "We'll keep our eyes peeled."

As Marcus's group drank their tea, the PeaceKeepers began packing their supplies for the walk back to post. The five men without weapons felt vulnerable but no one admitted his shame; they just squabbled with each other over minor offenses. Bill and the lieutenant snapped at the privates, ordering them about while the corporal kept to himself. As the only man left with a weapon and ammo, the corporal watched their surroundings, listening for intruders but he usually ignored Bill and Lt. Anderson's needless commands.

Noticing the lieutenant's hesitant decisions, the corporal finally stepped up to the officer, "When we head back, why don't you let me take the lead? If there's danger in front of us, I'll take care of it."

Lt. Anderson nodded his head, "Ahem. That was what I was going to suggest, corporal. Carry on."

The corporal took point and started walking back to the main road. The path was narrow through the forest so the company hiked single file: Lt. Anderson followed the corporal, then Bill, then the private with the flask, his hamburger buddy, and at the very end, walked the skinny private.

Uncomfortable with the lineup, the private in front of Skinny offered to take up the rear, but Skinny replied affably, "No, that's okay, I kinda like watching all you guys in front of me."

The guy in front of him mumbled, "Why because we're dinner?"

The private with the flask laughed to himself, thinking, *Man, it's so much fun screwing with people.* He whistled a tune, disregarding his buddy's hot breath on his neck. *Imagine, a grown man afraid of some harmless, scrawny kid.*

♠

Jim and Mattie moved with more caution than the PeaceKeepers. They stayed in the woods, following a deer trail over the mountains. Jim referred to his map and compass throughout the day, making good time toward the Tennessee River, ever mindful of human and animal predators prowling the forest. Jim suspected that they'd find Juan and Miah in a few days, but he never let his guard down.

Jim's serious attitude only heightened Mattie's instinctive reflexes. She listened intently to every sound, responding quickly to anything that might cause them trouble. Despite her sore nose and chest, she darted back and forth, investigating her surroundings, checking on Jim then running ahead to blaze a trail. They made an excellent team, a warrior and a scout, a man and his dog.

Sensing Mattie's presence, Sydney sniffed the air suspiciously. Somewhere within a five-mile radius was another dog. Both Shadow and Sydney understood the implications of an intruder. Although pups, the collies already assumed their roles as shepherds and they intended to keep their flock of people and livestock in a tight circle for protection. It was their duty. Their calling.

The dogs' vigilance was not lost on Juan. He noticed Sydney's nervous behavior when he and Miah returned from their foray with the PeaceKeepers. At first he thought Sydney would calm down once the men resumed their normal routine, but she didn't. She kept stopping to listen, keeping the smaller animals in a tight group, accounting for every creature. Agitated, she paced stiff legged with the hair on her back raised, looking around quickly at every sudden noise she heard.

Juan mentioned to Gabe, "Have you noticed how weird Syd and Shadow are acting?"

"Yep. There's something in the forest that worries them."

Juan tightened his hold on an M4, "I think I'll get up on the ridge to take a look."

Gabe agreed. "Take Shad with you; I think he wants to have a look-see too."

Juan gathered extra ammo and whistled for Shadow. Shadow ran over to him, anxious to explore the mountains. As Juan and Shadow left the others, they mirrored Jim and Mattie's behavior, a warrior and a scout, a man and his dog.

24

As Jim and Mattie crested a mountain, Jim saw a beautiful sight. Below him—in a grassy meadow with a small creek—grazed six, sleek horses. Jim began walking carefully into the ravine, talking with a gentle tone to reassure the horses.

Surprised, the horses looked up at the man approaching them but they didn't run away; they were tame horses used to people. A buckskin gelding nickered a greeting. When Jim drew closer to the herd, the buckskin walked over to him, expecting a treat—maybe oats or alfalfa.

Jim stroked the gelding's neck. "You are a friendly fella. Handsome too." As he ran his hands over the horse's legs and body, Jim quickly noted the care someone gave this horse. "You're a fine-looking animal. Strong, healthy. Somebody gave you a lot of attention."

The other horses began pressing closer to Jim. The tall man continued to talk with the horses, admiring their fitness, petting their noses, running his hands down their backs. Unsure about what to do, Mattie stood near Jim, whining, fidgeting, worrying about these new acquaintances.

She also smelled something else, *"A wolf? A coyote? Another dog?"*

"It's alright, Mattie. We just found six of the nicest horses I've seen in years." He picked up their hooves, examining their new shoes. "A farrier? You guys actually saw a farrier? Where did you come from?" Just then he heard a noise in the bushes.

"Don't shoot," rang a voice.

Jim turned swiftly. Reflexively, he placed his right hand on his sidearm. He didn't pull the pistol from its holster because out of the dense growth stepped another surprise.

"I'll tell you where they've been, Mr. Special Ops Guy," Juan answered amiably, "in PeaceKeeper stables." Juan stepped out of the brush, followed by Shadow.

Jim ran to his buddy and the men hugged each other, smiling broadly. "Juan, as I live and breathe." Jim stopped a moment trying to find the right words to say without appearing too sentimental, "You're a sight for sore eyes."

"I'm some kinda sight," agreed Juan. Realizing that Jim shouldn't be wandering around in the mountains, he asked worriedly, "Is Rosa okay?"

"Rosa and Sara are both fine. Actually since you left, some people showed up at our doorstep looking for a place to stay. Lucky for us that lodge is so roomy, we had enough beds for everybody."

Juan grinned, wondering what Jim would think of his next bombshell. "More people, huh? Any new animals?"

"Just this fine team of horses," beamed Jim, petting one of the horses nuzzling his arm.

"Well, let me tell ya what's happened with Miah and me since we saw ya last—"

⌁⌀⌁

After only one day of walking back to the PeaceKeepers post, Bill wanted to change strategies. He knew the unit would face retribution for losing a team of horses and supplies, or worse: accusations of conspiring with the enemy. He'd lose all the purchase he gained with the commander, and might even be thrown in jail for past crimes. Upon reflection, he decided that returning to post without prisoners eliminated his chances of promotion.

As Bill mulled over his options, Lt. Anderson considered his career—his short-lived, and sadly, unfulfilling career. *I can't return empty-handed, the commander will have my head. Literally.* The thought of standing before that brazen, unrelenting blade of steel made the lieutenant's knees knock together involuntarily. He had to sit down.

"Let's take a five-minute break," the lieutenant announced loudly. After sitting briefly, the lieutenant stood up feebly—still trying to present a commanding presence. When the officer stepped into the trees alone, Bill and the enlisted men removed their backpacks, and sat down on rocks or logs. The privates razzed each other, shuffling through their packs to look for smokes or snacks.

Although he sat down near the group, the corporal kept nervously scanning the landscape. Throughout the morning, he imagined he heard somebody following them, a twig snapping or a crunch of leaves. He couldn't shake the feeling that someone, or something, was watching them, tracking them. Hunting them. He studied the forest suspiciously. *This place is too wild for me to feel comfortable. I can't wait to reach civilization again.*

The three privates had no such worries consuming their minds, they just followed orders. They teased each other about weekend activities or their exaggerated experiences with women. When they returned to post, they'd assume their regular duties. For all intents and purposes, they were on bivouac with three stuffed shirts. The corporal was edgy and the lieutenant untested, but the privates unanimously agreed that Bill won the "biggest pain in the neck" award, hands down.

Speaking quietly to his buddies, one of the privates said, "Forget about Bill, he's nobody. I overheard a captain say that if Bill comes back empty-handed, he'll be standing in front of a firing squad anyway."

"No kidding?" asked the skinny kid. After Bill swatted him on the head three times for petty insults this morning, he thought maliciously, *That would be one job I'd love to volunteer for.* "Well, if you hear anything more about punishment for Bill, let me know."

As the skinny kid walked into the woods, whistling softly, the other privates studied him apprehensively. "Man, that guy gives me the creeps," said one of the soldiers.

His friend retrieved the flask of alcohol pressed against his chest. He passed the flask to his friend, "I wouldn't worry too much about him. He's just stupid."

Still gazing after the whistling man, the doubtful private responded, "A stupid person that knows how to kill with his bare hands? That scares the beans outta me."

◌◌◌

As dusk fell over the Smokies, blanketing everything with somber shades of gray, Gabe, Caleb, Miah, and Nora prepared their evening campsite. Although a little girl, Nora learned the men's routines quickly and imitated their behavior. She helped gather sticks for the fire, talked endlessly to the animals, and laid a blanket on the ground for sitting.

Now trekking through a state park, the group no longer found abandoned houses so the men stopped playing their "finders' keepers" game, but this didn't stop Nora. She continued sighting oddities on the trail: paper-thin rocks, fallen leaves as big as her head, or sun-bleached animal bones. When she uncovered treasures (usually when Gabe lifted her off Mary during a break) she stuffed items into her jacket, giggling secretly, her eyes sparkling.

Once she spread out the blanket, the toddler arranged her strange discoveries in a line, babbling to the curious dogs and geese that looked at her goodies. Sometimes she lost an interesting bone when she turned away from her task but this was a game that Shadow and Sydney played together.

Unfortunately, Shadow was with Juan tonight. When Nora set a small skull on the blanket, Sydney just looked at the bone, growled at the curious geese pecking at the skull, but the pup didn't bother stealing it. How could she enjoy this game without Shadow to chase her while she flaunted the stolen bone? Sydney exhaled and stretched out on the blanket. The puppy watched Nora's chubby fingers fidget with her playthings and she listened to the men talking with each other.

After being in Nora's jacket, most of her treasures were broken or tattered but the men never tired of her show-and-tell before dinner. Despite her rudimentary vocabulary, they understood her simple words now. In just a few short weeks, the hardened soldiers developed that uncanny, parental skill of understanding a toddler's language.

One day Nora garbled something unintelligible and Caleb just looked at her, confused. Gabe said casually, "She wants to show you a flower." Nora grabbed Caleb's hand, leading him to a lovely purple flower still in bloom, sheltered from harsh weather within a protected alcove.

Miah laughed as he watched. "Hey, Gabe, you've got the gift of interpretation."

"Huh?" the big man glanced at Miah, uncomprehending.

"You translated an unknown tongue," Miah joked.

"She made perfect sense to me."

"Yeah," smiled Miah, "that's what interpreters say. They hear an unknown language and know exactly what's said."[1] Although the Bible describes interpreting tongues as the translation of an inspired word of God, Miah couldn't resist teasing Gabe.

Gabe looked at Miah, shaking his head. "I don't understand half the things you say."

"That's okay. Juan tells me the same thing every day, but we're still best friends."

---

1. 1 Cor 12:8–10.

Gabe smiled at the young man. "Well, I'll keep trying. I understand your sister's baby talk; maybe someday I'll understand your Bible talk."

⋘⋙

Pastor Greg sat by the fireplace in Ryan and Jason's house, frustrated and tired. Without Ryan or Marcus to talk to, the normally vigorous pastor felt overwhelmed with his current problem. Ever since the compound residents began trading their valuable food for the settlers' new age paraphernalia, he battled with demons.

No one was more susceptible than anyone else. As a reprieve from their daily grind, women were enticed by Eastern philosophies and fortune-telling, men found smoking hallucinogenic herbs and drinking white lightning a pleasant pastime, and teens devoured books extolling witchcraft and self-empowerment.

Within days after their first meeting with the settlers, the community's tightly woven fabric began to fray. Neighbors argued over insignificant matters. Children talked disrespectfully to mothers. Fathers ignored families. Yet, not everyone adopted this new lifestyle, just those who were weary, afraid, or undiscerning.

"What's the use of living anymore?" a young mother asked herself. She held a crying baby in one arm and looked achingly out the kitchen window for her long-overdue husband. She sighed heavily, dirty clothes soaking in a washtub, cows bawling to be milked and not enough food for dinner tonight. Disappointed with her life, she watched the sunset drearily; *I really need to ask Monica how I can control my life better. To create my own private peace.*

Monica and Alisha quickly became a new support system for many women in the compound. Already respected as soldiers, they established routines of developing their own inner goddesses and instructed other women in the growth process. Monica and Alisha chanted the mantras they learned from Gaya and Kali; they danced and sang. They evolved. They no longer volunteered to post sentry at the gate because they were balanced, in total control.

"We no longer need weapons to kill others. We're too busy becoming one with our world and our environment to destroy life," purred Monica, a soft glow radiating from her face. A small clutch of women sipping tea shook their heads in accord; they admired this kind, mysterious woman and wanted to be just like her.

At the same time, in a grove of hardwood trees within the compound's perimeter, two men sat together watching the sunset. "This is such a good life," murmured a farmer as he shared a rolled cigarette with his neighbor. He shut his eyes contentedly.

"Yeah," responded his buddy, relaxed, unhurried. "Hey, do ya think our cows need to be milked about now?"

Both men cackled.

His friend answered, "Maybe if we don't go to the barn tonight, somebody else will milk our cows."

"Didn't we do that last night?" Both men laughed even louder, but neither one bothered to get up. They were having too much fun to bother with cows.

ↄ෨෨ᕬↄ

After he finished his chores, Jason noticed the same nine milk cows standing outside his barn door, lowing mournfully, shifting uncomfortably. He didn't want to continue milking the cows of lazy owners but he couldn't let the poor animals suffer either. Relenting, he unfastened the doors and called the engorged cows to enter. As the cattle hurried into the barn, bumping each other impatiently, he caught a glimpse of Talia walking back to her house.

"Hey, Tal, would you mind helping me milk a few extra cows tonight?"

Talia smiled. She walked over to her friend, "Naw, I don't mind. If you didn't share your milk with all my baby animals, they'd starve."

Jason remembered her small herd, and its one special member—her young stag. "How's Amos?"

"Great! He's growin' like crazy."

When she entered the barn, she set her bottles and buckets down, picked up a pitchfork and helped Jason toss alfalfa into feeding troughs. Once the cows settled into their stalls, they swished their tails back and forth to chase away flies and chewed their fodder steadily. Speaking kindly to the cattle, both teens sat on stools and began milking by hand.

Without electricity, milking was a labor-intensive job done twice a day but milk was absolutely essential to their diet. The entire community needed milk for drinking, cooking, and processing. They made various cheeses, churned butter, and cultured yogurt from milk. Sometimes cheese and yogurt provided their only daily nourishment; consequently, delivering milk to the community was a vital job.

Lacking modern refrigeration, every family also knew how to make kefir but Jason still preferred to drink raw milk. Every day he poured milk into a glass jar, sealed it tightly, and placed the jar in a frigid creek. Before he unscrewed the lid, he shook the jar briskly to mix the cream and milk together. When he tasted the creamy, savory milk on his tongue, he closed his eyes and thanked God softly. He never tired of this daily practice; it was Jason's simple act of worship, his honest appreciation of God's provision.

While they milked, the teens talked. They compared notes on changes happening to their friends and neighbors, not really understanding the implications, just tossing around ideas—trying to make sense of their world. Long after sunset, they finished milking.

Both tired and stiff from another busy day, the pair secured the barn and walked toward their respective houses. Talia stopped to look at Jason, "Ya know, it's weird, Jay. Both you and I work overtime to cover for our dads while they're away. But some of my other friends won't lift a finger to help their parents."

Jason stared at the ground, ashamed of this reality, "I know."

Talia bent her head sideways, studying her reserved friend. Then out of the blue, she asked, "What books are you reading now?"

Jason met her gaze, "I'm just readin' my Bible. I don't have time for much else."

"Yeah, me too." She paused, "I read a romance book about vampires. It was kinda disturbing."

Jason looked at Talia, shrugged his shoulders, "That's because Satan's disturbing."

Talia arched her eyebrows, surprised by his response, "Yeah . . . I guess so."

ᗑᗙᗙᗷ

That evening, Bill voiced his concerns to the PeaceKeepers in his unit. "I don't wanna return to post without the rebels."

Lt. Anderson sat down on a rock, ready to address this setback with his squad. He looked at his men, "If we go back now, empty handed, we'll probably face severe penalties."

The three privates thought with one accord, *You'll face penalties; we won't*, but they remained silent.

The corporal interjected, "LT, how do you expect us to do *anything* with only one weapon?"

Good, Bill thought selfishly, *no one knows about my pistol or knife*.

Unused to leading, the lieutenant argued, "We have no choice, corporal! Our careers depend upon our success in this campaign."

"Campaign?" the corporal countered, "this is no campaign! This is a Boy Scout Jamboree, a field trip!"

Busted! thought the privates, suppressing their grins.

"What do you propose we do?" whined the lieutenant resignedly.

"I *propose* we return to post with a story to cover the loss of our weapons and supplies, but say nothing about rebels. If we try to attack an armed group of experienced insurgents without weapons, we'll all die." The corporal stood up, towering over the lieutenant, challenging the young officer to defy his logic.

The lieutenant stood up, looked the corporal in the eyes, but said nothing. He seethed with anger yet he agreed with the corporal. Trying to regain credibility, Lt. Anderson said, "Let me think about it. I'll give you my final decision tomorrow morning." With that declaration, he stomped off into the woods, acting forceful yet hiding his trembling hands from his men.

Once the lieutenant left, the remaining PeaceKeepers just looked at each other, grumbling to themselves. Bill relaxed a bit, thinking that he may live to see another day. And three pairs of eyes, glinting in the shadows, watched this discussion a safe distance away: scrutinizing the situation, strategizing a scheme. Planning dinner.

25

Fᴀᴛɪɢᴜᴇᴅ ꜰʀᴏᴍ ᴛʜᴇ ᴅᴀʏ, Marcus's group looked for a place to sleep. After leaving Marshall City's outer suburbs, they saw very few people. They traveled through the forest but continued to walk near the road so they wouldn't get lost. They settled for the evening in a wooded clearing—grasses and flowers surrounded by a copse of trees. Not the finest location for security but certainly one of the most tranquil.

"When do you think we'll be home again?" asked Brant.

Marcus stirred a wispy fire, adding another twig, "Oh, another day or so."

After he sat on a rock, Ryan leaned back against a tree. "I don't know if I'm just tired, but I have a bad feeling about somethin'."

"Yeah?" Marcus said, acutely aware of Ryan's intuition. Marcus looked at Toynell, "Whatta you think, Toy?"

She answered flatly, "Nothing's felt right since I visited the settlers' farm. But the closer we get to home, the more oppressed I feel."

"Oppressed? That's a strange word," Brant wondered aloud.

She touched her husband's arm, reassured by his strength, "Something just feels dark. Heavy." Brant studied her with concern.

Ryan glanced up at the sky. "It looks like a storm's coming. Maybe we're just a little jumpy because of the weather. You know . . . the effects from barometric pressure?"

Marcus watched Ryan and Toynell, unconvinced, "Yeah, maybe . . ." He turned his face upward, and that's when a drop of blood splattered on his face.

⤷◎◑⤶

Although this storm already wreaked havoc in other continents, tonight marked its first appearance in North America. The storm behaved like a spoiled brat throwing a temper tantrum; but instead of hurling toys and stomping feet, the storm threw bolts of lightning followed by ground-shaking thunder. Moving south from Virginia, it rolled over the valley, advancing toward Marshall City and the Smoky Mountains with fury. Not an ordinary weather system; this was a storm of biblical portent, a storm of epic proportions. A vast, unearthly occurrence: a storm of hail and fire mixed with blood.[1]

Juan and Jim responded to the storm instantly. When they saw flames of fire falling from the sky, both men crouched down, their hands over their heads, and ran for cover under a rock ledge. It looked like a firefight. Beneath their rocky shelter, they gasped at the sight before them: baseball-sized hailstones slamming into trees, missiles of fire igniting vegetation, and dark, sticky rain saturating every surface.

Thinking quickly, Jim screamed over the pounding hail, "Juan, the horses!"

Juan nodded his head once; he knew what they needed to do. Jim immediately pulled a small canvas tarp from his backpack. They threw the tarp over their heads and dashed into the storm to rescue the horses tied to nearby trees.

The horses screamed, rolling their eyes back in terror. Several horses already had severe gashes and bruises but none of them sustained broken bones yet. Working together, Juan held the tarp over both Jim and himself as Jim cut the first horse's rope. Jim held the rope in his hands while Juan tried to protect their heads under the flapping tarp.

"Jim, this isn't working! The tarp's rippin' apart!" Both men ran back under the ledge with one rescued horse. They needed to devise a better plan.

As Juan tied the horse to a log under the ledge, Jim ran out to save the other horses. Running beneath a thick growth of trees, Jim covered his head with his arms as the icy clumps of hail pelted him mercilessly. Although Jim tried to release several horses at the same time, the horses refused to stand still for him. Eventually, Jim cut one horse free. While Jim ran back under the ledge with the second horse, Juan rushed back to the remaining horses. The nervous animals ran into each other, neighing frantically, jerking fiercely on their tethers. Juan finally grabbed another horse's lead and severed its rope with his knife.

---

1. Rev 8:7.

By this time, hail blanketed the ground. Round chunks of slippery, red ice created an impossible obstacle course for running. As Juan returned under the ledge with the third horse, Jim slipped and fell attempting to reach the other defenseless horses.

Regardless of his efforts, Jim couldn't get up. Each time he started to stand, the hail thrashed him to the ground, beating him relentlessly. Slumped on the icy surface, Jim could no longer move toward the horses or fall back under the rock overhang. Suddenly unconcerned about saving horses, Juan crawled over to his friend, put his hands under Jim's arms, and dragged him back under the ledge.

After reaching safety, the men gasped for air, panting from exertion. Juan touched Jim's arms and legs, "Anything broken?" he yelled.

Jim shook his head, "Don't think so." Jim looked at his shredded clothes and the welts starting to rise beneath his bruised, discolored skin. "But it feels like I was beaten with a club."

"Yeah. But we're alive." They both looked at the trees where the horses were tied. They saw a pile of spotted hail and sticky rain covering the horse's bodies.

The merciless storm knocked down trees, battered rock walls, and killed anything in its path. The exhausted men sat back against a rock wall beneath the ledge, bloody and beaten. The three rescued horses, glistening with sweat and rain, stamped their feet fretfully, huffing anxiously.

Juan looked over at Jim. Jim's face was streaked with blood, his eyes flashed with horror, his teeth clenched with rage. Jim wasn't a man to be trifled with anytime, but especially not now. He was furious.

"If you're not hurt . . . why are you covered with blood?" asked Juan.

Over Juan's shoulders, Jim could see the forest burning. Amazed at the sights, Jim noted, "There's blood everywhere. It's like the clouds are bleeding."

Juan furrowed his brow then looked at his own hands, his pants, his boots. He touched his hair, *Gooey.* He brought his sticky hand to his nose and sniffed. "Blood? Who ever heard of blood falling from the sky?" Juan asked incredulously.

Jim stared straight ahead, watching a mound of hail stack upon the dead horses. "Who ever heard of fire falling from the sky?"

⁌ↀⓒↀↄ

The PeaceKeepers faced even greater odds against surviving the storm. Sitting on a clear-cut mountaintop, they saw lightening striking inside tumultuous thunderheads but they didn't have rock outcroppings or trees to protect them. Watching the hailstorm rage through the lowlands and feeling tumultuous winds pelt their faces with debris, two privates ran down the mountain and into the woods hoping to escape the cataclysm. They left the skinny private, the corporal, Bill, and Lt. Anderson behind. The lieutenant screamed for his troops to halt but with the approach of this hellacious thunderstorm, the privates chose to desert their posts rather than follow orders.

As they ran downhill, one private told his buddy, "I'd rather face wild animals than this tornado!"

"I'm with ya!" hollered his friend, tripping over rocks, stumbling through razor-sharp brambles as fast as his legs could carry him.

Although technically not a tornado, this storm trumped any storm they ever experienced. The remaining troops took drastic measures to find safety. Arms flailing and legs tripping over stones, the skinny private ran halfway down the mountain into the woods. He sat on the ground, tied himself to a tree with cord he kept in his back fatigue pocket and pulled his BDU jacket over his head. The corporal copied the private's strategy but crossed his legs around a stout tree for stability; and the lieutenant frantically started digging a hole under a fallen tree root with a flat rock, tearing flesh from his hands, crying mournfully while he dug.

Bill ran downhill to a cave he sighted earlier. Although he saw the others desperately seeking shelter, he never mentioned the cave to anyone. Before leaving camp, Bill slipped behind the preoccupied corporal and stole his neglected M4. Now Bill had a knife, a pistol, and a rifle, protection in a dry cave, and no one to order him around. Once he hid his weapons in the cave, he sat down, and watched the cave entrance. Riveted by the storm's power, Bill secretly gloated over his victory.

If those guys gave me the respect I deserved, I woulda invited 'em here. Now they're outside in this storm and I'm in a dry cave.

"Fools!" Pride hissed in Bill's inner ear.

"Fools!" Bill yelled into the lashing winds.

As soon as Marcus and his group identified blood falling from the sky, they ran deeper into the forest. Unfortunately, they found neither fallen trees nor rock formations for protection. Scrambling up a gravelly slope, the four terrified people used their hands, knees, and feet to claw into dense vegetation.

Fighting gale-force winds, the foursome pushed into tangled brambles and tightly webbed kudzu vines. Shouting to each other and struggling to move through the vines, their advance was slow, grueling. The men's arms and legs became so entwined in the twisted, strong vines that they felt tied in a knot of steel cables. Unable to yank the plants up by the roots or cut the thick vines with knives, the men roared like lions caught in a hunter's snare. As they bellowed and struggled, their bindings pulled even tighter into their flesh.

Toynell, on the other hand, moved nimbly through this narrow, intricate environment. Petite and agile, she crawled on her hands and knees beneath the thickets. She negotiated through the inhibiting growth without kudzu barbs raking her skin or getting her ankles trapped in the vicious, knotted vines.

When Toynell escaped the undergrowth, she looked down the mountain at the trapped men then looked up at an ominous sound above her head. *What's that?!* The whizzing sound grew louder: wailing in pitch and thundering with intensity. She watched a fireball streak down from the sky, hitting the earth. KABOOM!

The ground shook from the impact of the collision. Dust, rocks, and sparks spewed into the air. Toynell fell to the ground, protecting her head from the rubble pummeling her arms and her shoulders. After the dust settled, she stood up unsteadily to see the men pleading for help, struggling to free themselves, becoming more helpless by the second.

Balls of fire streaked across the horizon. One after another. Lightning bolts of fire. It looked like a war zone—video footage of missile attacks on a TV news program.

Adding to the confusion, it started to hail. Fist-sized hunks of ice—sharp and jagged, wet and cold—fell to earth. Toynell dashed down the mountain, trying to avoid the hail, slipping on viscous, blood-coated rocks.

She scrambled under kudzu vines again—this time holding her knife—and she sawed the woody vines. Once she started to cut through the thick stems, the men finished freeing their own hands, arms, and shoulders with brute strength. They pulled the plants up from the ground, broke apart the webbing, and viciously cast off their constraints. When freed, they all crawled on hands and knees up a path she found leading them out of the brambles.

Still unable to find sanctuary, the weary travelers limped toward a dense thicket of trees. Huddling close to a massive oak, the group found protection from the wind under the tree's sprawling branches. Creaking under the strain of the storm, the oak lost thinner, younger branches; but the thick, lower branches—branches that children use for swings or tree houses—held firm, resistant to this pounding tempest, stalwart to the end. The tree didn't break. It weaved and groaned under the strain, but it didn't break.

Neither did the group of people clinging together under its branches. They didn't break their hold on each other. They grappled under the strain, but they didn't break.

⋘⊙⊙⋙

And a miracle did happen. But not under a ledge, or on a mountaintop, or beneath an unshakable oak, the miracle happened in an open, grassy field—the most vulnerable position in this wrathful squall. The miracle happened to a large herd of animals and small group of people.

Sensing danger, the animals amassed tightly together in the center of a grassy meadow. Rather than running frantically, madly, in multiple directions, the animals pressed close to Gabe's campfire, so close, in fact, that the goats stepped on Caleb's feet and a goose jumped into Nora's lap. Despite Nora's delight, Miah stood up, signaling for the others to not move. He listened, remaining silent.

Miah sniffed the air, "Do you smell blood?"

"Yeah," answered Gabe cautiously. Both intel guys grabbed their M4s and slung ammo belts over their shoulders but this was bizarre behavior. Before they created plans based on military training, the soldiers stopped to consider Miah's reactions first. *This kid knows something we don't.*

Although inexperienced in battle, Miah announced with certainty, "Don't be afraid because God is with us."[2]

Still standing, Miah closed his eyes and prayed. The young man lifted his arms to heaven and began praying in the Spirit. As he prayed, the soldiers watched him with confusion and curiosity. That's when everything became surreal.

From the corner of his peripheral vision, Caleb noticed—not one or two wild animals—but dozens of feral creatures sprinting, flying, or scrambling into their campsite to join the herd already nestled by the fire.

2. Isa 41:10.

Wolves, mountain lions, black bears, groundhogs, squirrels, birds . . . the convergence of incompatible animals defied reason! Predator and prey. Literally, a lion and a lamb huddled side by side quivering with fear; the lamb didn't fear the lion but they both feared the storm. Incompatible animals sat near the fire, touching noses with each other, even touching Nora's finger tips.

"What is *happening*?" whispered Gabe, unable to grasp what he was seeing.

As Miah continued to pray with his eyes closed and arms uplifted, the circle of animals grew larger in size and wilder in composition. Then a storm erupted in the meadow with such intensity that everyone froze, paralyzed with fear. Bolts of lightning knocked down trees on the mountainsides, hail beat the ground fiercely and pockmarked the soil, a shower of blood fell in torrential sheets. A series of fireballs struck the forest, starting major blazes throughout the area.

Yet, in the grassy field—within the circle of animals—not a drop of blood, not a wisp of flame, not even a fragment of hail touched anything, or anybody. It looked as if a gigantic, invisible umbrella opened over the meadow, protecting the people and animals under its cover. Staring wild-eyed at the storm beyond the circle, lions growled and wolves whimpered, but no creature, neither man nor beast, moved a muscle.

At the onset, Miah screamed into the gales, trying to overcome the unyielding winds with his voice. Thirty minutes later, Miah prayed in hushed tones because his throat was hoarse and scratchy. Eventually, Miah simply stood in the center of the "miracle bubble," not saying a word, but not lowering his arms either.

After what seemed an eternity to Miah, a hailstone struck a coyote standing in the far reaches of the circle. When the coyote yipped, Miah glimpsed at the injured animal. As he struggled to keep his hands up-lifted, his shoulders trembled with fatigue, and strained muscles burned up and down his arms. No longer able to maintain this strenuous position, Miah dropped his arms to his sides, and the miracle bubble popped. The savage storm lashed inhabitants within the circle mercilessly, animals cried out in fear, running into each other, terror filling their eyes.

Immediately, Gabe ran over to Miah and lifted Miah's arms high into the air again. Caleb brought a stone for Miah to sit on then each man held one of Miah's arms. As long as Miah kept his arms lifted toward heaven, the storm remained outside their defensive barrier. In time Caleb found two Y-shaped branches on the ground to brace Miah's arms. So there they stood, for hours, two men holding branch supports on either side of a young man. And a young man—filled with boundless faith—who prayed to God in heaven to protect them against this brutal, inexplicable, unrelenting storm.[3]

꙰

By morning, the storm abated. Bleary eyed but alive, the three men collapsed on the ground, completely drained. Although the branches helped prop Miah's arms, the demand of maintaining the same position for hours with limited movement, strained everyone's muscles beyond comprehension. Every part of their bodies screamed with pain.

For fifteen minutes none of the men moved. They just lay in a crumpled heap, three thirsty, hungry warriors, too tired to even think. They mumbled a few words to each other, but only to confirm that everyone was alive.

Nora toddled over. She squatted beside Miah, patting his face gently. "Mee-ah sleep." She lay next to her brother, sucking her thumb, "Me sleep."

Gabe rolled over to face the child, "We're all tired, baby girl." He draped a jacket over Nora; he had no energy to scrounge around in his pack for a blanket. "Can you sleep a while?"

"Hmm-huh." Nora smiled drowsily, waving her hand at the assorted animals in their camp, "Fends?"

Gabe observed some of the wilder animals walk hesitantly out of the lush, green grass within their perimeter. The creatures stepped lightly onto smoldering, blackened soil flickering with red-hot ashes, deciding whether to stay in the grassy area or leave. *Most of the animals are staying in the circle*, he noticed as he watched smoke rise from burned vegetation, *the ground must be too hot to walk on.*

Gabe answered Nora, "Not friends. Visitors. Just leave the new guys alone."

"Kay." Nora snuggled next to her brother, still sucking her thumb. Gabe grinned, *Whatta great, little kid.* He sat up, shifted his shoulders and sighed deeply. He would guard the camp until Miah or Caleb woke up then he'd sleep.

In the quiet, morning stillness, Gabe felt totally at peace. He smiled as he watched Griz wrestle with a slightly older cub; two clumsy, awkward bears playing together. Griz slapped the other cub playfully on the face;

3. Exod 17:10–12.

the older cub knocked Griz sideways with its shoulder. *Stupid bear.* Mary and Joe stood near the extinguished campfire; they looked like bronze statues in the morning light: ears erect, grazing calmly, and swishing their tails. The goats chewed on grass near Miah, preferring to stay in the close knit group, keeping a steady gaze on their primary caretaker.

Gabe laced his fingers behind his head; he felt the bright, welcoming sun warm his face. Taking a deep breath, he closed his eyes momentarily. He listened to the animals: lambs bawling, birds singing, pigs oinking.

"Wha . . . ?" Becoming more accustomed to weird things happening, he opened one eye warily, "We have pigs now?" he remarked resignedly. "Oi vey!"

26

AFTER THE STORM SUBSIDED, the Lord sat upon his throne. When angels came to present themselves to the Lord, Satan accompanied them. The Lord asked Satan, "Where have you come from?"[1]

Satan answered, "From roaming throughout the earth, going back and forth on it."

The Lord said to Satan, "Have you considered my servant Jeremiah? There is no one on earth like him; he is blameless and upright, a man who fears God and shuns evil."

"Does Jeremiah fear God for nothing?" replied Satan. "Have you not protected him? You bless the work of his hands, but if you stretch out your hand and strike his flesh and bones, he will surely curse you to your face!"[2]

The Lord responded, "Very well, he is in your hands, but you must not kill him." Satan left the Lord's presence, eager to inflict pain upon the young man.

❧

While Miah slept, pustules began to develop all over his body, throbbing with each beat of his heart. Miah woke up abruptly. He yelled as lesions sent searing volts of agony throughout his body, from the top of his head to the soles of his feet.[3] Trying to internalize his suffering, tears ran down his cheeks. He looked at the oozing sores on his arms, his legs, everywhere!

"What's happening to me?" he wailed helplessly, studying both sides of his hands.

1. Job 1:6.
2. Job 1:7–11.
3. Job 2:7–8.

Gabe gawked at Miah; the young man was almost unrecognizable. His once handsome face looked swollen, puffy—covered with fiery, red splotches. Ulcerated wounds coated his legs. His strong, powerful arms resembled weathered fence posts: ashen, peeling, and deteriorated.

Gabe stared, grasping for something to say. *Prince Charming fell asleep and turned into Frankenstein!* The big man stammered, but words failed him.

Nora woke up, looked at the abomination next to her, and ran into Gabe's arms, shrieking. She hid her face in the folds of Gabe's shirt, unwilling to look at the terrifying creature in their midst. Between sobs, she blubbered repeatedly into Gabe's chest, "No fend, no fend, no fend."

Gabe turned his back to Miah to comfort the small child. He pulled her away from his chest to look at her face, but he used his body to block her from seeing Miah. Although Gabe's heart pounded fiercely, he tried to talk steadily with her, "Nora, don't be afraid. It's Miah, not some new animal from the forest. It's Miah."

"Nooo . . ." she responded, "no fend. No Mee-ah." She pulled Gabe's shirt to her face, unwilling to look at the atrocity in their camp.

While Gabe soothed Nora, Caleb—wide awake from Miah's unnerving scream—started to help Miah. Caleb removed some of Miah's clothing to examine the extent of his problem. As he studied Miah's skin, Caleb shook his head, confused, "Miah, I don't know what could've caused this rash."

Gritting his teeth, Miah asked hopefully, "So you think this might be a rash? Maybe somethin' I ate . . . a weed that brushed my skin?"

"It's possible," Caleb said, doubtfully. "To be honest, I don't know what happened."

Miah's shoulders slumped with despair. Every square inch of his body itched or throbbed with pain. Miah nodded his head; he didn't understand but he tried to endure his misery quietly.

Caleb remembered, "Listen, I have a handbook and lots of herbs in my backpack. Maybe I can make a poultice that'll help you."

Pursing his lips to keep from crying out, Miah nodded his assent. Then through clenched teeth, he whispered, "Do it quickly! Please."

Caleb left hastily thinking, *There must be something I can do, something to ease his pain.*

Miah watched Gabe carry his sister to the far boundaries of their campsite. Nora kept her face buried in the big man's chest while Gabe bounced from one foot to the other, humming to her. Miah closed his eyes, still bone tired from the catastrophic storm, but now he imagined the storm's fireballs actually imbedded themselves under his skin.

Taking a deep breath to stabilize his voice, Miah prayed, "Lord, thank you for delivering us from last night's storm. You are so great, so awesome." He shifted his weight to find a more comfortable position, "Lord, please have mercy on me. I'm really hurtin'." He inhaled slightly because even breathing caused pain, "In Jesus' name, I pray. Amen." With his head bent down and his hands covering his face, Miah cried before the Lord.

Standing nearby to hear Miah's prayer, Satan roared with anger. He clenched his gnarled fist, extending his right arm upward, vowing to the heavens, "I will not relent until this miserable worm curses God!" He furiously left the grassy cove, uttering profanities, determined to make Miah's life a living hell.

❦

When the storm ended, Marcus and his three friends finally released their grip on the oak tree. Stiff and dirty, the bedraggled group began to assess damages. Their supplies vanished—swept away in the rainstorm—and their torn and bleeding flesh bore testimony of the sharp barbs on kudzu vines; but ultimately, no one died.

Wiping rain off his forehead, Ryan said, "We look like four wet mice saved from a rain barrel."

Marcus stood up, rocked his head left and right to loosen his neck. "At least we're all alive. I never saw anything like that storm." Everyone murmured in agreement.

Brant touched Toynell's face. He talked soothingly with her as he verified that neither he nor his wife had broken bones or life-threatening lacerations. After Brant helped her stand, Toynell brushed dirt off her dress and untangled twigs from her hair.

"Let's find somethin' to eat. I'm starvin'!" said Ryan.

The four automatically began searching the forest floor for edible greens: tender plantain or lamb's quarters. Of the vegetation remaining, they judiciously plucked leaves from nonpoisonous plants, popped the food into their mouths, and chewed listlessly, hoping to find something more appetizing. Fortunately, they also found black walnuts—still within hard shells, unbroken by the hail—so they stuffed walnuts into their pockets for cracking later.

Without grocery stores, finding edible food every day required effort, especially when roaming. Consequently, each person squirreled food
inside their clothing when they found it: dried fruits or nuts so when
they got hungry, they searched their pockets for snacks. This was less of a
problem for Toynell than for the men. It takes fewer calories to sustain a
hundred-pound woman than a two-hundred-pound man, so when starvation became a worldwide problem, men suffered more than women.

Marcus epitomized this reality. His clothes hung loosely on his thinning body. Once a hearty, stout man, Marcus now cast a much smaller
shadow. If they lost their farms, Marcus, Ryan, and Brant might become
like the thousands, maybe millions of men, starving to death because of
the lack of food to maintain their body size.

Fortunately, Jesus always provided for their basic needs. Today was
no exception. As Marcus's company scoured the forest for nourishment,
three people watched from a safe distance. Deciding that the food gather-
ers wouldn't harm them, one of the watchers stepped out of his hiding
place to introduce himself.

"The Lord be with you," a male watcher said boldly.

Startled, the group chewing on leaves looked up at the voice. Ryan
responded cheerfully with a wave, "The Lord bless you."

With Ryan's reply, two other watchers tottered over to the first man,
smiling their greetings. Three ancient people stood in front of Toynell.
Although she never saw such weathered folks before, Toynell was captivated by their energetic eyes shining from such ruddy, withered faces.

Toynell beamed brightly, "How do you do?"

A woman, even smaller than Toy, smiled sweetly, grasped Toynell's
hand with her knobby, arthritic fingers, and said, "I do fine, sugar. God
love ya', you ain't no bigger than a minute." The old woman looked at their
spokesman, "I think these young'uns need some food."

"Yep, that's what I be thinkin' too," replied the grizzled, old man.
Without any words of explanation, the three watchers turned back into
the forest, leaving Toynell and the others staring blankly at their departure. As he walked up the mountain, the old man called over his shoulder,
"You young'un's best get a leg up if ya wanna git some breakfast."

Never ones to refuse food, the valley group promptly followed the
ancient watchers. Despite their age, the old people moved swiftly up a
steep, rocky incline. Amazed, Marcus smiled as he watched three, white
heads bobbing ahead of them through the thicket. *It's like we're following*

mountain goats, not people. In his distraction, Marcus tripped on a rock and stumbled to his knees.

Ryan grasped Marcus's elbow and lifted him up. "Let's keep movin', buddy. I don't think our hosts are used to waitin' on stragglers."

⁙

The morning after the storm, Bill ventured out of his cave, leery. He sniffed the air, grimacing at the foul smell. Normally he enjoyed inhaling the fresh scent of rain, but not today. Today the air smelled like a war zone: dried blood and scorched earth.

From his mountain vista, he could only see a few yards in front of him. Everything was shrouded in thick clouds of smoke; the only things he identified clearly were embers glowing on the ground or forest fires still raging miles away. Bill gathered his weapons and left the cave. Watching his path, he stepped carefully around flaming logs, charred animals, and jagged rocks.

Bill decided to return to the mountaintop to check on the Peace-Keepers. Maybe some of them lived. He could invent a plausible story to explain his absence; *I'll just tell them I found a rock to hide under. It's not really a lie, a cave is a rock.*

"It's just a very big rock that you could've told them about," taunted Guilt.

Bill stuffed his hands into his pockets, pouting, mentally trying to justify his behavior. He stomped up the mountain, thinking of rational explanations for his decisions. As he walked, Bill's stomach grumbled and his swollen, dry tongue stuck to the roof of his mouth. *When I return to camp, one of the guys will probably have some food and water,* he reasoned.

"Yeah, if they'll share it with you," countered Guilt.

"If they won't share it with me, I'll steal it!" Bill shouted.

"What if they only have a few scraps of food or a single canteen of water that you can't steal?" asked another voice in Bill's head.

"Then I'll kill them!" thundered Bill, his words echoing into a holler.

"Hmm, that may be your only option," the voice murmured reassuringly. Guilt poked Murder in the ribs, both demons smiled.

The demons grew quiet when Pride interrupted them. Looming above the other demons, Pride lifted his chin, his lips moved silently as he counted the demons indwelling this worthless, sniveling human. Throwing a dark glance at Murder, Pride asked, "How many of you are living in this creature now?"

"We are legion," Murder responded.[4]

In the morning, Jim and Juan prepared to search for Miah's group. Before they left, Jim made two bridles from a roll of nylon rope he carried in his pack. Although primitive, the bridles would serve their purposes until they returned to the lodge. From a cowboy's perspective, it simply made no sense to walk when they had three, strong horses to ride; thus, the men each rode a horse and tied the riderless horse to Juan's mount.

The men rode side by side as they began their journey. Mattie continued to scout ahead of Jim but she didn't wander far away because she sensed danger everywhere. Shadow tagged behind Mattie, snuffling the ground she smelled, taking note of her reactions based on her nose.

She constantly sniffed the ground or scarred trees for Juan's scent. She pranced light footed—careful to avoid hot embers—on the path Juan had taken two days earlier. Although not a hound, she could still pick up slivers of his scent even in the carnage left by the storm. She perceived her task and preformed it admirably. Her dedication was not lost on either Jim or Juan.

"Mattie's a fantastic dog," admired Juan.

"She is. And look, she's teaching Shadow all her tricks. Before you know it, he'll be as sharp as she is."

"We can only hope," agreed Juan.

Jim knew Juan loved dogs. When Juan met Jim yesterday, Jim immediately noticed the absence of Happy, Juan's steadfast friend. Jim finally asked Juan, "Where's Happy?"

The suddenness of Jim's question caught Juan off guard. He sucked in his breath, swallowing with difficulty. Sometimes the mere mention of Happy's name gave Juan a jolt, his throat constricted and his eyes watered. After Juan cleared his throat; he related Happy's peaceful death and burial. When he finished, Juan detected Jim's reticence.

Jim didn't speak for a long time. They just rode behind the dogs, mired in their own grief. At last Jim said, "Beth died soon after you and Miah left."

Juan stopped his horse. Jim also stopped. Juan stared at Jim, incredulous. "How did it happen?"

"Snakebite. A rattlesnake."

4. Mark 5:9.

Juan sighed, staring up at the sky—blue as a robin's egg. Barely above a whisper, he wondered, "What's Miah gonna do when he finds out about Beth?"

"I don't know, but that's the main reason I wanna find Miah. I need to tell him." Jim licked his lips, his mouth felt so dry, "He's probably makin' big wedding plans in his head, dreaming of a family." Jim put his hand to his mouth, tears reluctantly filled his eyes. Whenever he remembered Elizabeth's sweet temperament or her lovely face, Jim grew misty.

Juan offered, "I'll go with you to tell Miah, if you want. You can do the talkin' but I'll stand by if you need anything."

Jim took another deep breath. "That might help."

As the pair started to move again, Juan added, "Miah once told me that he believed we'd see animals in heaven." Jim plodded along silently, staring at the ground. He didn't know what he believed about heaven, or Jesus, or God for that matter. "Well," suggested Juan, "maybe Happy found Beth in heaven and they're spending time together."

Jim smiled, uncommitted. He was hopeful that Beth was happy, wherever she was, but belief in a higher being required more faith than he could muster. He wasn't fooling Juan though, Juan identified Jim's reserve.

"Still haven't made that commitment to Jesus, have you?"

"No. I don't think I'm capable of believing in God."

Juan nodded his head, recalling all the miracles God performed on their trip to Tennessee. To pass the time, Juan told Jim about the deliverance of Miah's father in great detail. Jim listened intently. He asked questions, enthralled with Juan's testimony, but also highly skeptical; Juan had a terrible habit of exaggerating stories.

As the men headed toward Miah's camp, Jesus listened to their conversation. Jesus turned to Beth, "Child, Jim is still broken over your death."

Beth responded hopefully, "Will I see him in heaven, Lord?"

Jesus studied the earthly pair, deep in conversation. As Juan and Jim talked, their horses kicked up ash, covering the men's boots and pants with a thick layer of powder. "It is my heart's desire, daughter." He gazed at Jim, "I do not want anyone to perish, but everyone to come to repentance."[5] Upon hearing the Lord's words, Happy wagged her tail and lovingly licked Beth's soft hand.

5. 2 Pet 3:9.

27

BILL FOUND NOTHING AT the PeaceKeepers' former camp. The storm's impact—its powerful winds, battering hail, and raging fires—erased all semblance of life in the area. Dismayed, Bill scanned the panorama below him. He saw hundreds of miles of blackened woodlands, twisted, darkened trees; plumes of smoke rising from active fires, or remnants of dying embers; but oddly, he also saw green patches of meadows and forests completely untouched by flames.

These oases of vegetation, vibrant with life, caught Bill's attention. *How can this be?* he wondered. Acres of lush forests completely surrounded by charred soil; this made no sense at all! *Was there a sudden shift in the wind—in all four directions—to make a circle?*

Bill could not deduce a single explanation for these phenomena. The vista looked like a peculiar patchwork quilt between the sacred and the sacrilegious. Life and death. Contorted, charred trees standing beside healthy, stately conifers; nothing he saw made sense. There was no denying what he saw, yet he couldn't imagine how it happened.

Overwhelmed with curiosity, Bill sat down to stare at the forest, fascinated by the incongruence before him. *What happened here?* His mind flooded with questions, theories swarmed his thoughts, until ultimately in desperation, he whispered, "Is it true? Is there a God in heaven that can perform miracles?"

Without warning, his mind instantly switched his line of reasoning. He actually argued with himself, "Stop this nonsense! There must be a logical explanation for what I'm seeing." Scratching his head, "Maybe the fire jumped over the unburned land. Yeah, that's gotta be it! Some kinda weird, cluster of tornados that kept fire out of their vortex, or gaps in the clouds, or maybe . . . aliens put some kinda force field around certain areas of the forest to keep it intact."

Strangely, Bill felt comforted by these concepts swirling inside his head, "You are so creative, Bill," praised Pride. "It would take scientists years to hypothesize theories for this conundrum, but you just rattled them off in seconds. Amazing!"

Bill smiled smugly. *Well, there's always a sensible explanation for everything. It just takes a little intelligence, imagination, and flexibility to develop models for testing.*

Pride purred, "Only a little? Oh come on, Bill, don't be so modest. Your idea about aliens? Brilliant!"

Bill's smile grew larger. He leaned back on the ground with his eyes closed, enjoying the stillness of the barren landscape, pleased with his clever mind. Then something else caught his attention. *What's that I smell? Barbecue?*

The smell of food resurrected the gnawing ache in his stomach. With hunger overriding his distrust of strangers, Bill decided to investigate. He stood up and walked purposely toward the wonderful fragrances: roasting meat and tangy spices. Even smoke emanating from this fire smelled different from the burned forest; it had that pleasant scent of charcoal mixed with hickory that old timers used when barbecuing meat. Bill's mouth began to water.

He walked carefully through the scarred landscape. Although Bill seemed alone in this vast, dead world, something nagged his senses—a tingling threat that made the hair on the back of his neck stand on end. He stopped to study the curl of smoke a couple mountains away, rising lazily from an unseen valley, floating its tempting smells in his direction. He reconsidered his options, wavering a bit, but when another breeze passed over his head, surrounding him with the smell of hickory-roasted meat, Bill discarded his trepidation.

Since I'm downwind, they won't notice me coming, he speculated, *but I've got to eat whatever they're cookin' over there.* With renewed determination, Bill set off in the direction of the campfire. *At least I know I'm not the last, living soul in this forgotten wilderness.*

Although anxious to finish the final leg of their journey, Caleb and Gabe decided to wait a day before resuming their trek. Miah was in too much pain to travel. They justified their postponement by saying the animals needed to eat more grass before they left, but Miah understood their intent and he appreciated their concern.

Miah also knew that he'd ride Mary when they traveled, but every touch against his skin sent fiery bolts up his spine. Mounting the big mare would be excruciating, but that would only begin his trials. Even when he sat still, the feel of his clothes scratching his skin was agonizing. How would he endure the relentless sensation of his pants rubbing against Mary's back as she walked?

Rather than dwell on his misfortune, Miah desperately tried to distract his thoughts. He watched Nora play with different animals or gazed at the clear, blue sky; he even tried to sleep yet all these distractions led him back to Jesus. As he listened to the blowing wind or admired clouds in the sky, Miah couldn't help but revere the Lord's artistry.

In spite of his discomfort, he saw the Lord everywhere in his life; and Miah loved Jesus. Would he accept only the good in life and not the bad? He couldn't blame God for the troubles in life propagated by man's sin. His life was only a brief moment in history, but God was eternal.

He would never break faith with God; he needed to become more steadfast, more dedicated. He whispered, "Jesus, forgive me for my selfishness. Make me a man after your own heart, a man who seeks you first." After reasserting his faith, Miah closed his eyes and tried to rest.

❧☙

Although tired from the night's vicious weather, Marcus enjoyed the company of their new acquaintances. His team followed the surprisingly agile trio into a bustling community of elderly recluses. Nestled in a series of connected caves camouflaged by the forest, the community thrived without much disturbance from the outside world.

Marcus viewed the main cave with awe. The old man that led them to this strange place noted the admiration on Marcus's face. As they stood outside the cave's entrance, the old timer commented about his home, "She's a vision, ain't she?"

Marcus nodded respectfully, "Yes."

Marcus observed that the cave dwellers left little evidence of their presence in the forest. They cooked near the cave entrance and allowed small animals to live with them. They even tried to prevent creating paths near the entrance by stepping on rocks rather than tramping down grasses.

"It's the trash," explained the old man.

"Huh?"

"It's the trash that gives away a home," explained the man. "You was wonderin' how we stayed invisible, weren't cha?"

Smiling, Marcus admitted, "Yeah, I was."

"Whenever we 'uns have trash we cain't burn in the cave, we burry it. We dig little holes sommers away from our cave to let the dirt eat ever-thang. It's a purty good rule."

"I'll say."

Ryan joined Marcus and the old man. Extending his right hand, Ryan said, "My name's Ryan."

"Oscar."

Ryan said, "Oscar, maybe you two already introduced yourselves, but this is Marcus." The men shook hands. "And sitting over there in your cave are Toynell and Brant." The young couple—still talking with women inside the cave—waved to the men when they heard their names mentioned then returned to their conversation.

"Well, they's eight of us livin' here. Ya may meet everone, or not. Some of us is a mite skittish 'round newcomers."

"That's okay," said Ryan.

"We just appreciate your hospitality, especially after that brutal storm," added Marcus.

"Yeah, that downpour was a humdinger, weren't she? Did'ja see the hail missed our trees?" Oscar asked.

"Yeah, I saw that," marveled Ryan, placing his fingers on his mouth, thinking. The storm completely bypassed several mountains and valleys. "It's weird."

"It's God," answered Oscar simply. "We pray for safety all 'round these here hills, for us and the wild critters, and God answers our prayers." Without another word, Oscar headed toward the cave. Marcus and Ryan stared at the man's back; a bit perplexed by Oscar's sudden retreat.

"I guess living in the wilderness kinda robs a person of social graces," hinted Ryan, trying to defend the old man's behavior.

Grinning, Marcus said unperturbed, "Maybe he never had social graces but these folks sure live under God's grace."

"I'll say," remarked Ryan.

❧❦❧

As their mountain friends recuperated from the storm, valley residents living in the compound faced grave circumstances. The storm left them devastated. Exposed to the elements, the combination of hail, rain, lightning, blood, and fire wrecked their secure enclave.

The hail destroyed almost everything within their cloistered world. All the structures—houses, barns, fences, silos—bore major damage. Houses left standing lacked roofs or interior walls, barns creaked as winds blew around dangling oak timbers, and the perimeter fence—once the pride of the community—lay flat on the ground pulverized by the hammering, relentless hailstones.

Most of the inhabitants, both human and animal, perished. Those that lived fled into the mountains or found shelter before the storm ravaged the valley. By chance, some small livestock crawled under fallen lumber that served as barricades; but unfortunately, most of the large livestock never found suitable cover. Pastor Greg, who stayed in Marcus's house with Jason and Talia, rushed the youths to a storm shelter just as the winds began to blow fiercely. On her way down the shelter steps, Talia grabbed a fat, orange cat she saw shivering outside in the rain, and lugged the heavy, yowling cat with her.

Those living elsewhere in the valley fared no better. Earlier in the day, Monica and Alicia went to the settler's cabin for a party. Kali and Gaya invited several women to their house; women seeking their divinity. As the two instructors guided their eager listeners into deeper insight, they offered everyone assorted teas for refreshment. Some of the teas contained herbs the valley women already knew: spearmint, peppermint, and chamomile; but for the more adventurous, other teas included exotic combinations of hallucinogenic plants.

Not ones to avoid challenges, or excitement, both Alicia and Monica opted to drink the more exotic teas. Maybe they would discover their inner goddesses, maybe they would find the meaning of life, maybe they would simply enjoy themselves, but it really didn't matter; because ultimately, they had the right to do whatever they wanted with their bodies. No one would tell them what to do! And thus began their descent into a journey that neither woman could fathom or overcome alone . . .

28

DURING A SEGMENT OF their training, Gaya and Kali asked students to lie on mats. Relaxing in a prone position, students' minds wandered: some tried to attain a heightened awareness, others drifted to sleep, but Monica and Alicia fell into a catatonic, drug-induced state.

Surprisingly, both Alicia and Monica could hear voices in the room, visualize activities through their unfocused eyes, and feel the surface of their yoga mats, but they were paralyzed. They couldn't speak or move a muscle. Initially, this realization alarmed them, but after a few minutes, they relaxed in a wonderful, dreamlike frame of mind. They were safe. Their instructors wouldn't hurt them. What harm could come from a little recreational diversion?

And then the storm hit. As clouds released their terrifying mix of hail, rain, and fire, Bert ran outside to shutter windows. She nailed heavy sheets of plywood over several windows but didn't finish the job. She never returned. A hailstone, the size of a softball, hit Bert directly on the head, ending her life.

By this time, Kali and Gaya frantically tried to wake dozing students; unfortunately, none of the sleepers awoke. Their students rested in a deep sleep, unaware of the commotion outside: chaos shaking the house to its very foundation. In their muddled thinking, Monica and Alicia knew they needed to rise and take control of the circumstances but they remained incapacitated on the floor, two useless bodies laid out like corpses.

The man with wild, straw-like hair rushed into the room and grabbed Kali and Gaya telling them to run to a root cellar. At first the instructors tried to drag students with them, but self-interest quickly changed their attitudes. The instructors concluded that if these women didn't have enough fortitude to save themselves, they could die in the storm! Seeking refuge in their underground cellar, the three remaining settlers ran out of the house, leaving their students at the mercy of an unforgiving tempest.

Horrified, Monica and Alicia remained helpless. By this time, they knew exactly what was happening around them yet neither woman could move. They remained frozen. With glazed eyes and rigid expressions, they looked like two dead fish displayed on newspapers in a fish monger's market.

As the storm raged, the cabin slowly splintered apart. Unprotected windows broke, allowing torrents of rain to saturate the dwelling's interior. Wave after wave of rain mixed with hail broke lamps, smashed tables, and battered walls but the room where Alicia and Monica lay remained intact.

Inside her mind, Monica screamed, *"We're going to drown!"* But of course, no one heard her. She tried to lift up her nose, raise a finger, anything, but her body remained as still as a stone. *What can I do?* her mind screamed madly.

The same notions passed through Alicia's mind, but with even greater intensity. She was a well-tuned athlete, a fierce warrior, her father's daughter. This was infuriating! This shouldn't be happening to her.

But it was happening, and Alicia couldn't do anything to stop it. As water gradually filled the room, her panic grew incrementally higher. Inch by painful inch, the water rose, until at last, her nose was submerged. Her mind fought a valiant battle, but when her lungs filled with water, she died. After her last breath, Alicia felt herself falling, plummeting downward.

Unable to control her descent, she saw others falling with her. The farther they fell, the faster they accelerated. It seemed as if wherever she was going, someone wanted her trip to pass quickly. Although unable to move her head, Alicia spotted Monica in her outlying vision. Her friend was below her but also dropping at tremendous speed.

Monica wanted to grab the walls of this dark pit, somehow hold onto oily rocks to prevent tumbling any farther, but she couldn't move, couldn't speak. Thus she kept falling into this deep, stinking trench, a trench that got hotter the deeper she fell. She heard all the people falling with her, screaming in anguish but just like Alicia, Monica had no voice.

Finally Monica reached the opening of a gigantic pit; the opening looking much like the rim of an underground crater. Perched on the crater's rim, stood the ghastliest creature Monica ever beheld. A drooling, green, lizard-like beast extended it long, knobby arms upward, pulling shrieking people into the hole. It stuffed people into the large opening, one terrified person after another. The lizard spoke a crude, vulgar language but, inexplicably, Monica understood the creature's hateful words.

I'm going to hell! she realized. *How can this be? I was always nice in life! I helped old people, gave to charities, volunteered for every community project. Wasn't I good?!* She cried out hysterically in her mind.

"Stupid human!" laughed the drooling beast. He grabbed a handful of her long, black hair, and held her inches from his repulsive face, "It's not about being good." Swinging her petite body above his monstrous head, he threw Monica into the blazing pit, laughing maniacally, counting every lost soul as another gift for his dreaded master.

Panic stricken, Alicia summoned all her strength to speak. Just before she reached the pit's opening, she said one word. The word passed her lips as a whisper, a barely audible utterance, a mouse's squeak.

"Jesus!"

She stopped in midair. Her body lay flat, as if stretched out on a bed, hovering over the pit's entrance. Her wide eyes stared upward and her back faced the wretched creature that, only moments earlier, hurled terrified people into the rotting, pestilent hole. The beast temporarily ignored the other falling souls, as it anxiously tried to yank Alicia into the trench. The claws on its fingertips raked Alicia's shoulders, making every nerve in her body quiver with revulsion, but she continued to float slightly above the beast's grasp.

With her pulse pounding in her ears, Alicia inhaled enough oxygen in that choking, sulfurous ether to say two more words. In a shaking breath, she pleaded, "Save me!"

That's all she needed to say. Immediately, Alicia's body began its rapid ascent out of the putrid pit. She felt someone's strong arm holding her waist as she shot upward, out of the hole. The presence beside her glowed like the sun and nothing—vile or slimy clinging to the walls of the pit—touched her or her radiant savior.

Although they flew with great speed, a minute passed before they reached the earth's surface. Alicia felt a cool breeze upon her face but her body continued to fail her. She tried to flutter her eyes in attempt to see where they were going, but her eyelids remained tightly sealed.

The kind presence laid her body down in a pasture of soft grass. She heard the sound of quiet waters, not torrential rains. The combination of residual drugs, complete exhaustion, and tranquil sounds lulled Alicia into the deepest sleep she ever experienced.

Opening her eyes the following morning, she yawned, thinking absentmindedly, *I slept like the dead.* Instantly the horrors of the preceding night invaded her thoughts and she screamed at the top of her lungs. She screamed in abject terror. She screamed for Monica; she screamed for those souls hurled into hell; and she screamed to hear her voice again. After the screams raked her throat raw, Alicia buried her head into the soil, clutched green grass between her fingers, and wept hysterically.

✺

The vehemence of Alicia's screams shocked Jim and Juan. Reacting at once, both men jabbed their heels into their mounts' flanks, leaning close to their horse's necks. The horses responded perfectly: they flew over a desolate field then plowed up a mountain with the strength and endurance of trained cavalry horses. Accustomed to riding bareback, Jim pressed his knees into his mount's withers, lifting himself off the animal's back which allowed the horse to run with less restriction. Juan, a novice rider, could only follow Jim's trail. Fortunately, Juan knew that Jim had his medical pack and a weapon with him so Juan pulled his horse back to a pace he could manage.

In the meantime, Jim pushed his horse to run as fast as possible toward the panicking person. After cresting a hill, he spied the wounded screamer. The wretch (curled up on the ground in a fetal position, trembling violently) could be either male or female, but from his standpoint, Jim couldn't distinguish the person's gender.

When he reached the victim, Jim noticed the person's head pressed against the ground, revealing horrific gashes on the shoulders. Jim pulled his horse to a sudden stop and slid off the horse's sweating back. He dropped to his knees, lightly touching the despondent person with one of his hands. The crying person slowly brought her head up, just as Juan and the two dogs joined the pair.

Looking into her eyes, Jim gasped. Never in all his years as a trauma medic had he seen such manifest horror exposed on a person's face. The stunned woman clutched his shirt in both her hands, screaming uncontrollably in a hoarse voice, "There is a hell! I've seen it! It's real! Hell is a real place!"

Jim pressed the woman close to his chest. As she bawled, Jim held her convulsing frame protectively next to his own sturdy body. Unwilling to release her, Jim continued to whisper kind words into her ears, rocking her in his arms, reassuring her that no one would hurt her. After some time, her muscles began to relax. Once her heart-wrenching wails became more subdued, he loosened his hold on her.

Pulling away from Jim's wrinkled, tear-soaked shirt, Alicia looked up at a man she didn't know. When she glanced over at Juan, her face brightened; she recognized Juan immediately. Sighing with relief, she reached out to hold Juan's hand, "Juan, I'm alive."

She looked down at her shredded clothes, her muddied hands. She stared into Jim and Juan's eyes with such intensity that both men automatically leaned away from her. She whispered, "Jesus saved me!"

Juan responded encouragingly, "Praise God!"

"No. No you don't understand . . . Jesus came down—into hell—and saved me!" Both men leaned back, incredulous.

Through tears of fright and joy, Alicia told them her story. She remembered every detail. While she related her testimony, she held their hands or touched their faces. Suddenly she craved the touch of living, breathing people. She admired the beauty of creation, even a forest badly burned by fires; in fact, she never felt more alive than she did that very hour. She was saved from an eternity of torment by a God that loved her. Loved *her*!

After she finished her account, Alicia closed her eyes, slowly adding, "I will never take life for granted again." Reopening her eyes, she stroked the two dogs standing timidly beside her, "I changed." She continued slowly, realizing the magnitude of her next words, "In one night, I became a different person."

Jim and Juan looked at the distressed woman sitting in front of them. His forehead creased with worry, Jim inquired patiently, "May I examine your shoulders?" Alicia smiled easily, nodding her consent.

For modesty's sake, Jim removed a clean shirt from his pack. Alicia turned away from the men, removed her ragged tank top, and wrapped Jim's shirt around her breasts and abdomen. When she was ready, Jim studied the inflamed, red claw marks on her shoulders and upper back. Assessing severe infections in the gashes, Jim knew that simply touching her skin would inflict pain.

"This is really gonna hurt, but I need to clean your wounds thoroughly before I close 'em up."

She nodded her head, understanding. "Do whatever you need to do. I'll try not to flinch."

Juan offered her some homemade whiskey to drink, but Alicia declined. As Jim methodically cleaned and sutured her lacerations, Alicia closed her eyes, never flinching, saying nothing. Juan and Jim noticed tears rolling down her cheeks, but she remained quiet, not uttering one word of protest.

At first, both men assumed she was weeping because of discomfort, but they were mistaken. As Jim ministered to her injuries, Alicia thought of her friend, Monica. *No matter how much this hurts me, I'm not suffering like Monica. She'll face unspeakable agony without relief. Every day. For eternity.*

This realization—this cruel acknowledgment of hell's existence—made Alicia burst into tears again, just at the moment Jim tied her last suture. Intuitive, Jim clearly recognized that her tears came from wounds much deeper than those on her shoulders. He retrieved a small vial of salve from his medical bag. As he rubbed lotion on Alicia's back, Jim hoped the treatment would hasten the healing of her sutured wounds and his touch would soothe the pain of her broken heart.

29

BILL CAREFULLY ADVANCED TOWARD the campfire billowing with the aroma of roasting meat. The smell was tantalizing, irresistible! Nowadays, people seldom smelled charbroiled food, but to sniff seasoned meat sizzling on a spit usually announced a rare occasion: a wedding or a child's birth. Bill inhaled the aroma again. With his eyes closed, he breathed deeply, savoring images of flavorful food invoked by the smoke. Lost in his fantasy, Bill didn't hear the footfalls behind him. When a man jabbed Bill in the back with a rifle barrel, Bill popped his eyes open and looked at the stranger fearfully.

"What brings ya into our neck o' the woods?" asked a grouchy man holding the rifle.

In one of the few times of his life, Bill answered honestly, "The fantastic smell of whatever you're cookin."

"Ya like barbecue?" the bearded man asked, easing his grip on the trigger.

Bill turned on his charm, "Doesn't everyone?"

The man lowered his weapon. He spit tobacco on the ground, "Reckon so. Do ya want somethin' to eat?"

Bill unconsciously licked his lips, "Yes, sir." Assuming a slight drawl, "That'd be mighty kind."

The bearded man cast Bill a disparaging look, shrugged his shoulders, and motioned for Bill to follow him. As they walked toward the fire, the man spoke, "Me and my two cousins is out huntin' rat now. Ever' day we find fresh meat; we roast it o'er the fire or dry it in the sun. Soon's we got us enough meat, we'll head back home."

Feigning interest, Bill asked, "Where's home?"

The man turned to study Bill carefully, narrowing his eyes suspiciously. He replied tersely, "Not here."

A few feet outside the camp's perimeter, the bearded man yelled, "It's just me and another feller, put yer guns down!"

Bill fell directly behind the bearded man, just in case someone decided to pepper the area with buckshot just for spite. As they ambled into the campsite, Bill noticed long strips of meat drying in the sun and a fine roast hissing over the fire. Bill took a deep breath, enjoying that rich, smoky fragrance.

"Ahhh, that smells good," Bill sighed.

The two men in the camp looked at their cousin questioningly. Although they didn't say anything, their nonverbal communication implied, "*Why'd you bring a stranger here?*"

Interpreting their expressions, the first man said, "This skinny feller looked like he needed a good meal, ya know, needed to be fattened up a bit." Accepting his explanation, the others tolerated Bill's company without further comment.

Bill looked at the three men, but he could barely tell them apart. They all wore black and red flannel shirts, muddy blue jeans, and scruffy boots. Each man had a tangled, curly beard covered with tobacco stains and all three wore baseball caps. *It's like they're wearing some kinda hillbilly uniform*, pondered Bill with an air of superiority.

None of the men seemed to care about Bill. They attended to their business of salting, curing, and wrapping meat. Off to one side, they even had a large cauldron of water to boil meat off the bones; apparently, they let nothing go to waste. When Bill glanced at their wagon, he noted that it was already half full of packaged meat.

"When are you fellas goin' home?"

"Soon."

While the men stayed busy preparing the meat, Bill decided to clean his pistol and rifle. He kept a small cleaning kit in his coat pocket, and since no one seemed interested in eating yet, he decided to stay busy too. Bill found a flat rock where he could disassemble, clean, oil, and reassemble his weapons. As Bill concentrated on his work, the three men occasionally looked in his direction, spoke quietly together, and continued working.

Finishing the assembly on his M4, Bill looked up when he heard the men laughing covertly. He almost stood up to join them when he saw them share a drink from a whiskey flask. Bill stiffened. *I know that flask.* His throat constricted, *It's the flask that private hid in his pocket.*

Bill started to look around for more evidence of the other soldiers. Bill stared longingly at the roasting meat one more time then scanned everything in the camp: a boiling kettle, sharp filleting knives, butchering saws, a freshly scrubbed table. Nothing out of the ordinary in a typical hunting camp, so why was the hair on Bill's neck standing up? Why was his spine tingling?

While the three cousins joked loudly, Bill announced that he needed some private time in the woods. The cousins chuckled and turned their backs to him. Before he stepped into the forest, Bill quietly slipped his pistol into its holster and slung the rifle over his shoulder. Not too far from the campfire, Bill spotted a pile of discarded bones, stripped clean from the boiling water. Stealing a glance over his shoulder, Bill checked to make sure no one followed him.

He squatted down to inspect the bones, careful not to make any sound. Although not a specialist in anatomy, Bill watched enough crime shows to recognize a human femur—and his blood froze. Swiftly looking over his shoulder again, Bill remained crouched on the ground, petrified. He crawled away from the bone pile, his breathing unsteady, his lips dry.

Just past the bone pile, Bill made another heinous discovery. A pile of discarded clothes. A pile of PeaceKeeper uniforms. Summoning all the courage within him, he reached into the stack of uniforms to retrieve a BDU jacket. Above the left pocket, he read the name tag, "Stevens," and on the arms were the chevrons of a corporal. Bill dropped the jacket as if plague-ridden.

By this time, Bill knew he had to get away before the three cousins noticed his prolonged absence. He stood up and sprinted down the ravine, trying to avoid stepping on brittle twigs or branches. Once he came to a river at the bottom of the hill, he stayed in the river. He ran on river rocks, slipping and falling on their mossy surfaces, but never slowing his pace. Initially, Bill didn't care which direction he ran, all he wanted was a lot of distance between him and the cousins. Preferably miles.

When he reached a rocky slope, Bill splashed out of the water. Scrambling uphill, he used his hands and feet to climb up boulders to the top of a mountain. Tearing his hands and face on thorny vines and prickly shrubs attached to rocks, Bill blindly pressed forward without slowing down.

All that mattered now to Bill was survival. He didn't care about food, or Miah, or Nora, or even his vanity. He just wanted to live. When he reached the top of another mountain, he lay down and looked back at the diminishing plume of smoke over a mile away. He didn't know if those three hillbillies would follow him—but he suspected they *could* find a needle in a haystack—so he kept moving. For the next five hours, Bill jogged or walked briskly without stopping, up and down mountains, through burned forests, over singed, blackened earth. All the while, he used the sun's position as a compass to move in a northeasterly direction. Bill assumed that someday he might run into Miah, but right now, he just hoped he'd never meet those three cousins a second time.

❧☙

On the first day after the storm, Marcus and his group ate dinner with the cave dwellers. Even though several residents told Marcus he probably wouldn't meet everyone, he did. The most withdrawn individual, a man that looked older than time, introduced himself to Marcus after the evening meal.

The man's appearance intrigued Marcus. Beneath fuzzy eyebrows (which looked like fat caterpillars), the elderly man's eyes sparked with good humor, and the long, kinky, white hair on his head and beard looked more like lamb's wool than human hair. His tanned arms and legs still retained lines of tendon definition, but the flesh covering those tendons had more wrinkles and brown spots than a dried, shriveled apple.

As the pair talked, they walked toward a smaller cave. Marcus reflected on the man's contrasting qualities: dark eyes that radiated light, ancient words that predicted events, and an aged body that typified vitality. *Is he ageless?*

The sage smiled at Marcus, "Not ageless, my son—but highly aged."

Marcus gasped; the old man read his mind. Widening his eyes, Marcus asked apprehensively, "Are you a prophet?"

"No, I'm a priest of God Most High."

When they reached the entrance of the smaller cave, the priest—bent with time—entered without effort, followed by Marcus, who crouched a bit to avoid bumping his head. Once inside, Marcus could stand upright but he noticed the round cave could only seat about ten people comfortably. Three rows of benches hewn from logs served as seats and a four foot high, chiseled, stone block sat in front of the seats. A wooden cross leaned against the curved wall behind the stone altar.

Marcus assessed the room. *Pews, an altar, the cross . . . this is a church.* Marcus looked at the priest, who now stood behind the altar, "You built a church!"

The old man laughed, "Christ built the church. We just found a perfect place to worship him."

Knowing he was in the presence of a true priest of God, Marcus boldly requested, "Before we leave, may I have your blessing?"

"You may have my blessing now," answered the priest.

Marcus knelt before the altar. The priest placed his right hand on Marcus's head and lifted his left hand toward heaven. The priest prayed, "Blessed be Marcus by God Most High, Creator of heaven and earth. And praise be to God Most High, who delivered you from your enemies."

After the blessing, Marcus stood up; he fished around in his pockets for something to give the priest. Although he possessed very little, Marcus set everything he had on the stone altar as an offering to the Lord. Embarrassed by his meager gift, Marcus said, "Let me go home and bring back a tenth of everything I own."[1]

The priest smiled, nodding his head. "It's good to bring your whole tithe into the storehouse; but first go home to measure your wealth before you return with your tithe."

Marcus thanked the priest. The godly man smiled and left the cave to visit with others. Marcus stayed behind in the church to consider their conversation. A man of his word, Marcus pledged to bring his full tithe to the Lord's house. He intended to fulfill his promise to the priest, and to God.

Humbled, Marcus prayed, "Lord, I never imagined your house as a cave, miles from anywhere, or your priest as an old man living in the mountains." He whispered reverently, "But your ways are much higher than my ways."

Falling to his knees again, Marcus thanked the Lord for his goodness and mercy. Leaning his head against the hard, granite altar, the big man closed his eyes to pray. Sometime during the night, Marcus woke up from a peaceful nap. Noticing that someone covered him with a woolen blanket, Marcus grinned, wrapped the blanket tightly around his body, and fell back to sleep.

---

1. Gen 14:18–20.

30

FEELING MORE ANXIOUS THAN ever to find Miah, Jim wanted to break camp early the following morning. Fortunately, Jim traveled with Juan and Alicia, two hardened veterans, who recognized the restlessness of a soldier on a mission. After drinking a hot cup of coffee, the three companions packed supplies into dual backpacks and prepared to leave.

Since Jim didn't have enough nylon rope to make another bridle for the third horse, Alicia rode on the horse fastened to Juan's gelding. Actually, no one minded this arrangement: both men wanted to keep a close watch on Alicia's fever and Alicia didn't want to concentrate on anything. She only wanted to hold the mare's mane, sit upright, and watch the scenery. She underwent enough excitement in the last twenty-four hours to last her a lifetime.

By noon, the trio spotted Miah's camp from their vantage point on top of a mountain ridge. The entire valley below them, an oasis of deep, plush vegetation, was surrounded by a grotesque landscape of misshaped trees and charred earth. Dozens of animals, wild and domesticated, stood within the perimeter of the grassy area, grazing, sleeping, or frolicking.

As Jim and Alicia gawked at the huge herd of animals, Juan smiled broadly, "That's why it's takin' us so long to get back home!"

Alicia exclaimed, "Do I see bears down there?"

"Yep."

Jim watched in disbelief, "You have a mountain lion and sheep living together?"

"Crazy, huh?"

As Jim leaned back on his mount, he pushed the brim of his cowboy hat up with one finger. "I've never seen anything like it. This is completely . . . unnatural."

"I agree," responded Juan, "but I told you all kinds of wild things happened to us on this trip."

"Yeah, you told me," Jim laughed apologetically, "but I didn't believe you." Juan grinned; he didn't mind a little ribbing.

Transfixed by the animals in the valley, Alicia started to name creatures she recognized, "Bears, goats, horses, wolves . . . you mean to tell me, Juan, that you don't have a giraffe in this menagerie?" She gave Juan a sideway glance, "Giraffes *are* my favorite animals."

Happy to see a playful glint in Alicia's eyes again, Juan responded offhandedly, "We're not home yet."

૮૭૦૭৯

Before Jim's group started their descent into the plush meadow, Sydney heard them. She yipped sharply and ran as fast as she could toward the ridge. Surprised by Sydney's actions, Miah, Gabe, and Caleb readied their weapons and tried to pinpoint what alarmed her.

The men were not alone in their concentration upon the ridgeline; all the animals in the grassy meadow clustered together to watch the puppy. But in another astounding move, the animals formed two circles, a protective barrier of adult beasts surrounding the smaller, more vulnerable animals. In the outer perimeter, Mary stood between an alpha wolf and a mountain lion. This perimeter also included: Mary's foal, Joe, several smaller wolves, a wild boar, a coyote, a ram, and three raucous ganders. Standing within the inner circle were chickens, ducks, geese, and a large assortment of babies—including Nora and a tiny skunk Nora held closely.

If the humans couldn't resist an enemy onslaught, the bigger animals would fight to the death. Although the humans didn't understand the animals' unusual behavior, the animals realized the task at hand. Yes, they communicated with each other, verbally and nonverbally, but this organization set precedence; they moved in the formation of a trained army. They followed orders.

They received a command from the same voice that told them to join this traveling zoo. Offering no resistance, each animal faced the present threat without considering their normal impulse to leave the area, eat the creature beside them, or kill the men guarding them. Every animal heard a small voice and obeyed that voice with absolute fidelity. It was their master's voice.[1]

Miah stopped running toward the ridge because he heard that voice too. He turned to look at the two circles of animals standing in the meadow, a ferocious wall of fangs and sinew protecting a tight cluster of babies and birds. Miah gasped at the wonder of it all. God was here. No harm would come to them.

Miah relaxed; he held his rifle in a low stance. As he turned his glance away from the animals, he looked at Gabe and Caleb running ahead of him to set up secure firing positions. Unlike Gabe and Caleb, Miah remained completely relaxed. He looked into the clear sky with awe, "My God, my God, how faithful you are!"

Miah walked back to the meadow, he knew the battle belonged to the Lord. First he approached Mary to stroke her broad neck; afterward, he smoothed the coats of her brave cohorts, the wolf and the lion. Before long, Miah talked with all the animals, petting each one gently, reassuring them of their safety. As he touched the animals, he sang a song thanking Jesus for his protection and giving praise to his Father in heaven.

⟡

Aghast, Satan stared at Miah with disbelief. Once a beautiful angel but now a contemptuous gargoyle, Satan stood in the Lord's presence without saying a word. The Lord's throne room vibrated with a tense silence until the Lord looked down upon mankind's nemesis. God didn't repeat Satan's earlier accusations; they both knew what Satan said.

The Lord spoke, "You no longer have authority to afflict pain upon my servant, Jeremiah."

Summarily dismissed, Satan left the presence of the Lord. He vowed to continue to roam the earth, seeking to destroy those miserable creatures God was so willing to die for. "There must be other ways to inflict pain on that worthless human, Jeremiah," he muttered to himself. "There must be someone . . ."

Unexpectedly, an idea hit him, of course there was someone, there were two "someones"! Incapable of joy, Satan's grin appeared as a snaggle-toothed grimace, a cruel sneer. He couldn't touch Miah but Satan knew two people that he would drag down with him to hell to wound that selfless, singing, animal-loving Jeremiah!

---

1. Joel 2:11.

CRGRD

When they saw Caleb and Gabe running toward them, their weapons drawn, Jim's team realized what would happen if anyone made a misstep. As a result, Jim did the most unaggressive thing he could think of: he started to whistle. Immediately, Juan and Alicia sang the same melody in boisterous, off-key voices—a no-talent trio that wouldn't hurt anyone.

Adding to the excitement, Shadow bounded toward his sister. When the puppies met, they tumbled to the ground: wrestling and growling playfully. Afterward, the pups jumped up and started to chase each other in circles: biting tails, nipping ears. They took turns tossing each other over and playing tag. Their joy was infectious!

And occasionally when chaos knows no bounds—Mattie added to the confusion. She saw a waddling creature some distance away that she wanted to chase. Mattie blasted downhill into the grassy area but when she approached the animal, she stopped so quickly, she did a summersault. After she recovered from her surprise, Mattie ran swiftly back to Jim, never looking back at the offensive creature.

Still watching the incoming men and singing loudly, Alicia glanced at Jim, puzzled by Mattie's outrageous stunt. Jim stopped whistling. He chuckled then turned to Alicia and said knowingly, "Porcupine."

By this time Juan jumped off his horse, spread his arms open wide, and yelled, "Hola, mi amigos!" While Juan announced his return, Jim and Alicia slid off their mounts. They stood quietly behind Juan as the old friends greeted each other.

Panting from their run up the mountain, Gabe and Caleb calmed down when they heard the ridiculous singing but relaxed completely when they recognized Juan. They laughed and jostled their brash friend.

"It's so good to see you, buddy," Caleb exclaimed, slapping Juan on the back.

"After that storm, we didn't know what happened to you," Gabe added, also relieved to see Juan. When Gabe lifted his eyes from Juan, he saw the most gorgeous woman in the world: a tall, lithe, blonde knockout with light grey eyes and the barest hint of a smile. Gabe stood in front of the woman, his arms hung limp at his sides. He stared at her—speechless, breathless.

Juan looked at the big, flummoxed man. Smiling, Juan said, "Alicia, I'd like you to meet my friends. This stupid lookin' guy is Gabriel and," motioning toward Caleb, "this is my other buddy, Caleb."

Alicia beamed the most stunning smile Gabe ever saw. Her eyes twinkled; her face glowed. When she shook his hand, Gabe admired her firm grip beneath the softest skin he ever felt. Gabe lost his heart forever.

Juan nudged Jim in the ribs, casting a sly look at the love-struck man. Both men recognized Gabe's fumbling motions from their own awkward displays in the presence of "that one special someone." Alicia appeared nonchalant as she talked easily with the men, laughing at their conversation, enjoying their company. Not once did she embarrass Gabe with an off-putting comment or dismiss his deer-in-the-headlights expression as foolishness.

Juan introduced Jim to his intel buddies. Recognizing his need to speak for the two of them, Caleb talked with Jim, letting his big friend stand aside to discretely admire Alicia. Jim appreciated Caleb's quick wit and before long the two men realized they had a lot in common—especially regarding medicine.

While they talked, the five strolled casually back to the meadow. Even though most of the landscape looked bleak and foreboding, the green oasis cheered them. They saw Miah's head bobbing amid a continually rolling sea of animals, holding his little sister, waving his hand high in the air.

Jim waved back to Miah, thankful for the young man's safety. His smile faded slightly when he got a closer look at Miah. Jim asked Caleb, "What happened to Miah's face?"

"Aw, man," sighed Caleb, "that's a long story."

⋘◉⋙

Tired and starving, Bill finally stopped to rest in a boulder field. He found a dark recess where he could slip into the shadows just in case the three cousins searched for him. Glad to be alive—but utterly disappointed in this whole reconnaissance—Bill fell back on his regular default behavior: pouting.

As he watched the sun set, he flipped pebbles down a hillside. With each toss, he enumerated his problems: "I'm hungry. I'm alone. I'm lost. I'm pathetic . . ." the list might've stretched on for minutes, but Pride got tired of listening to his petty grievances.

"Shut up!" growled the demon. Bill closed his mouth but he continued to sulk. He threw bigger rocks, making more noise as the rocks chipped boulders, bouncing and rolling downhill, eventually splashing into a creek.

Keenly aware of the danger presented by the three cannibals, Pride barked louder, "Shut! Up!" Bill tucked his hands into his lap, pressed his chin to his chest, and heaved a pitiful sigh. Changing tactics to get this idiot to move, Pride purred into Bill's brain, "Have you already forgotten why you're here?"

"I wanted to find Miah," Bill said in a petulant tone. Not the least bit bothered about speaking out loud to no one but himself.

"Yes. Where do you think Miah is right now?"

Bill thought a moment. The light switched on, "He's going back to his home. That lodge he told me about in the mountains."

"Did he tell you how to find it in case you got lost?"

Suddenly Bill remembered, "Yeah, I recall a few details."

"Could you find the place now?"

Bill brightened, "I'll bet I can!" Bill crawled out of the recess, unbuttoning his jacket, and pulling on his ball cap. "If I find Miah, I may even locate another rebel hideout. There's a big reward for that!"

"Atta boy!" congratulated Pride. "You're too smart to let a few obstacles stand in the way of your success."

As Bill scuttled over the boulder field with renewed vigor, Satan watched. The epitome of pride, Satan knew the strategies his general used on this insignificant, human pest. Satan licked drool from his lips; he could almost taste this pitiful bug. *One down*, counted the Prince of Darkness, *now for Miah's second someone.*

When Marcus woke up the following morning, he felt totally refreshed. As he regarded the primitive church in the morning light, he remembered his discussion with the priest. After he stood up, Marcus folded the woolen blanket neatly, placing it under one arm. Shutting his eyes, he said a simple prayer then exited the cave.

Outside, the fresh air braced him. Marcus heard birds singing and fluttering in this undamaged section of forest. Walking toward the large cave, he heard the murmur of Ryan, Brant, and Toynell's voices before he saw their faces. Sitting by a fire near the main cave, his friends cradled steaming mugs of hot drinks, talking quietly together.

Marcus waved silently to them as he walked to their campfire. His friends returned waves, motioning him to sit with them. Ryan reached into the coals to retrieve a fire-blackened kettle and poured dark tea into a tin cup for his friend. Ryan gave the tea to Marcus and Marcus sat down on a log bench to visit with his friends.

"Well, whatta ya say?" Ryan asked brightly. "Ready to go home?"

Marcus nodded his head, "I am. I wanna get back to see Talia and check on our animals."

"You and me both, brother," added Ryan, worried about his son after that tragic storm two nights ago.

Toynell gazed around the peaceful forest surrounding the cave, saying wistfully, "We've only been here a day but I'm going to miss these nice people."

"I plan to return," Marcus stated. "Once we get things in order at home, I'm gonna bring back some food and livestock for these folks."

Ryan raised his eyebrows. "Do you have enough supplies to share with them?"

"On paper, it probably doesn't sound like a very good idea, but it's my tithe. I'm bringing a full tenth of everything I have; I'm not gonna cheat the Lord."

Ryan studied Marcus carefully. "What about the tithe you give to our church in the valley?"

"That won't end either. Tal and I can get by on less this year; these poor people need more food and supplies. I understand that other people come here on Sunday to worship and share a meal together."

Ryan pursed his lips, *This is a new wrinkle.* He shook his head, "Jason or I will come back with you. We'll give them some dairy cows."

Brant smiled, thinking of his own herd, "A dairy cow is a great gift."

Toynell stood up, shaking pine needles off her long dress. Marcus smiled as he watched her. After Brant once bragged about her illustrious days as a fashion designer, Marcus still caught glimpses of her need to stay clean and presentable.

Admiring her smooth, dark skin and her tidy clothes, he said, "You're very pretty, Toynell."

She snickered, removed her floppy, disreputable hat and gave him a sweeping, formal bow. "Thank you, kind sir."

His smile broadened; he laughed heartily. Marcus looked at his three friends; people he trusted with his life. "Man, I love you guys! I'd be proud to go anywhere with you." Referring to Ryan's salvaged red and white polka-dot shirt and Brant's lime green, polyester slacks, he added, "Even these two fashion train wrecks."

31

ADVERSITY OFTEN PRODUCES DEEP, sustainable relationships among people. Jim discovered this fact many years ago when he served his country. Although no longer in the military, he still found this truism with civilians. Certainly not with all civilians, but with the select few he accepted into his life.

Miah was one of those special individuals Jim loved and respected. Very rarely did Jim freely give his love to others, but he openly admitted that he loved Miah as a son. If he and Sara ever had a son together, Jim hoped the child would become a man like Miah.

So when Jim approached the meadow, he ran to Miah and hugged the young man tightly. Although casual onlookers watching the two men laugh and slap each other's backs may not recognize the depth of feeling between the pair, Juan understood. Here stood a father welcoming his son after a long, grueling separation. Both men were euphoric.

After their initial greeting, Jim took a step back to look closely at Miah's face. Even though Jim scanned him with compassion, Miah cast his eyes to the ground, ashamed of his shocking appearance. Swollen and blotchy, his face felt better but it remained disfigured with scaly, scratchy lesions.

When Miah looked back into Jim's face, Jim asked sympathetically, "What happened, Miah?"

Miah shrugged, "Honestly? I don't know. One day I'm fine. The next day . . . I'm covered with these awful sores."

Even though Caleb gave Jim a sketchy background of Miah's illness, no one could identify Miah's affliction. Was Miah allergic to something he ate or touched in the forest? Did some airborne disease fall down from that dreadful storm? Was it a skin reaction to stress?

Nobody knew the answer, but oddly, the disease seemed to be disappearing almost as quickly as it arrived. Today's scabs covered yesterday's open wounds, his fever subsided, and the incessant itching lessened. The entire life cycle of this unidentified disease remained a mystery.

Jim scratched his head, "Caleb, did you treat Miah's blisters with natural remedies?"

Baffled by the abrupt change in Miah's appearance, Caleb said, "I gave Miah some herbal tea to relieve his discomfort, but I didn't have any salves to treat his blisters. None of this makes any sense."

"Huh." Jim pursed his lips. "Well, whatever you did, Caleb, it seems to be workin." He patted Miah on the shoulders, "Drink Caleb's tea, Miah, because it looks like he gave you the right prescription to fix your problem."

Miah nodded. He didn't know what happened but he trusted God. Sometimes God heals a body miraculously, and sometimes, God uses the miracle of medications to treat diseases. Miah didn't care about the process; he was just grateful that the pain ended so quickly; because in truth, he doubted if he could endure the agony much longer.

࿐

In the late afternoon, Miah loaded all their plastic water containers on Mary's back. Since the group planned to leave the following morning, he wanted to make sure they had enough water to reach the lodge. Days earlier, their caravan passed an artesian spring. Despite setting up their camp several miles from the spring, Miah remembered its location; consequently, he told Gabe where he would go to fill their water bags. Miah hoped the storm didn't destroy the spring's opening because he absolutely loved the taste of clean water.

Fortunately when he returned to the spring, Miah still found water flowing freely. He led Mary to the center of a clearing where he unloaded the water bladders. He threw the bladders over his shoulders and walked briskly to the spring.

He didn't bother to tie Mary to anything. With only burnt tree stumps in the area, Miah found no place to attach a rope, but he knew Mary would stand nearby to wait. And she did. Mary placidly swished her tail, listening for strange noises, idly watching Miah.

That's the scene Bill observed when he saw Miah from the shadows: a big horse standing and his son working. Concentrating on filling containers, Miah faced the artesian well with his back turned away from Bill. Miah whistled a tune, completely unaware of his father's presence. Each time he topped off a container, Miah screwed on its lid and laid it on the ground beside the spring, repeating the procedure with another empty container.

Suddenly, Mary jerked her head up, her ears erect, her attention riveted. Mary's nostrils flared as she sniffed the air, she whinnied cautiously, stomping her feet. Something was very wrong. Sensitive to Mary's irritation, Miah turned around and swiftly stood up; that's when Miah saw his father walking toward him. Bill pointed his Glock at Miah's stomach.

Miah caught his breath but said nothing.

Bill strolled into the clearing, his pistol still aimed at Miah's gut. He taunted Miah sarcastically, "What? No words of welcome for your old man?" He walked past Mary. "Did you enjoy leaving me at your grandpa's house? Oh by the way, I led a detachment of PeaceKeepers to your granddad's farm. He's in prison now."

Miah clenched his fists, controlling his fury.

Bill planted himself about twenty feet from Miah. With a steady hand, he ratcheted a bullet into the chamber. "I've been thinking about this moment for . . . oh, I don't know. Seventeen years?" Bill scoffed.

Miah stared at his father without flinching.

Like a cat toying with a mouse, Bill enjoyed tormenting his son. "You and your pretty mom were so much alike. Devout Jews! Freaks! Now look at you . . . a pimple-faced troll." His lips curled into a sneer, "I wish she were here to see this."

Miah considered Bill's rigid expression. At first, Miah was simply startled by his father; now he realized the seriousness of his dad's intentions. *He wants to kill me.* He remembered Jesus's warning that "brother will betray brother to death, and a father his child."[1]

Rather than shrink back, Miah straightened his shoulders, accentuating his full-grown height. Standing almost four inches taller than his father, Miah no longer feared Bill's threats or his fists. Now also a man, Miah returned his father's cold stare, standing firm.

Momentarily startled by his son's boldness, Bill instantly regained his composure. He laughed scornfully, "You're such a fool!" Tapping his chest, "I'm the one holding the gun!" He took a few steps closer to Miah, his anger building. "I'm the one in control . . . you're nothing!" Bill vented, "You're nothing more than a pitiful excuse for a son!"

1. Mark 13:12.

That's when Miah spotted Mary behind his father. Responding to Bill's tirade, Mary's nostrils flared with indignation. She sensed an evil presence within the loud, vicious man standing in front of Miah. Then somewhere in the back of her mind—from the recesses of her Percheron ancestry—Mary became a warhorse. She would fight and die for Miah on the battlefield. As long as she had breath in her lungs, no one would harm her companion!

As Mary reared up on her massive hind legs, screaming; she threw crashing blows to Bill's head, neck, and shoulders with her front hooves, lashing him mercilessly. After Mary's first blow to his shoulders, Bill re-flexively pulled the trigger, hitting Miah on the right side of his abdomen. Doubling over, Miah fell to the ground, clutching his stomach.

Bill also fell to the ground, but Mary wasn't finished with him yet. She kicked and stomped the lifeless man, pulverizing his body. Finally, when Mary felt satisfied that Bill no longer threatened her human, she stopped. Still highly agitated, Mary danced away from Bill, his ragged body pressed into the ash-covered soil; she grunted, tossing her head in disgust, shaking her withers to settle her nerves.

Taking one final look at Bill, Mary snorted angrily, "*Snake!*"

⋯⊙⊙⋯

Nothing draws attention faster than the scream of a horse or the crack of a pistol. But to hear both those sounds so close together, sent an electric tremor straight up Jim's spine. He dropped everything in his hands, picked up his medical bag, and ran toward the tethered horses. Slipping a bridle over his horse's head, Jim jumped on the steed's bare back, and headed in the direction of the noise.

It wasn't a difficult sound to follow. The bellows from Mary's lungs echoed throughout the valley. As he listened to Mary's outbursts, Jim felt the hair on his neck bristle. Leaning over the stallion's neck to increase their speed, Jim and his horse moved in unity; its hooves chewing through soft cinders on the ground, flinging ashes into the air.

Within minutes, Jim spied the clearing. He saw Mary prancing in the area, blowing dust from her nose, exhaling loudly. Jim drew his stallion to a stop near Mary and slipped off his mount's back to help Miah.

Jim rolled Miah onto his back to inspect his injuries. A gunshot wound. The wound was fairly clean (the bullet exited through Miah's right side and missed vital organs) but Miah was still bleeding. Jim stanched the blood flow with direct pressure, then applied dressing to the wound, but he needed to do more. Jim needed to find another place—anything better than the ashy ground where Miah lay—to give Miah proper medical treatment. While he checked Miah's airway and treated the young man for shock, Jim considered alternate locations but waited for the others before making any final decisions.

When Juan, Caleb, and Gabe bridled their mounts to join Jim, Alicia volunteered to stay behind to protect the camp and watch Nora. Although Alicia wasn't especially motherly, after experiencing hell, she quickly agreed to play with a toddler rather than face another life-and-death situation. *The kid's okay*, she told herself. *Besides, I'm not completely useless; I can still help my friends.*

Jim barely noticed when the men arrived on horseback. With only two bridles left in camp (Jim made another one the night before), Juan and Caleb rode together, allowing Gabe, the heaviest man in the group, to ride alone. When the three men dismounted, Caleb and Juan rushed over to help Jim while Gabe settled the snorting, stomping Percheron. Gabe grabbed Mary's lead rope, held her tightly, and talked to her. Once he calmed Mary, Gabe noticed Bill's lifeless body then stepped back slightly to watch Jim, Juan, and Caleb attend to Miah.

Gut shot, Gabe thought grimly. *That's not good.*

After firmly securing Miah's dressing, Jim told the others, "We need to find a better place to take care of Miah."

The three other men looked at each other, thinking. Suddenly Juan exclaimed, "Hey, Jim, I saw a scorched farmhouse not far from where we met these guys!"

Jim looked up at Juan, "I sorta remember seeing the place . . . a brick house. It wasn't completely destroyed, was it?"

"I don't think so."

"It's only a few miles from here," Jim said, his hope renewed. Jim got onto his horse, "Lift Miah up to me carefully and we'll ride over to that farmhouse."

The three men on the ground picked up their unconscious friend and slid him in front of Jim. Miah's body slumped against Jim but Jim held him securely in his arms. Juan gave Jim the stallion's reins. Jim held the reins in his right hand, supporting Miah with his left arm. Jim's heels gently tapped the horse in the ribs and the stallion started to walk out of the clearing, back toward camp.

Alicia, holding Nora on her hip, walked briskly toward the men as they rode back to camp. Noticing Miah's limp body in Jim's arms, Alicia quickly distracted Nora's attention with a shiny can opener. Immediately enthralled, Nora tried to grab the tool from Alicia's hand, ignoring everything else around her.

Jim said, "Caleb, let's go up the mountain to find better cover for Miah. I need to stretch Miah out—on a cleaner surface—to tend to his wound." Everyone agreed. "Allie, could you pack some food and water for us? Enough for a few days?"

She shrugged, "No problem." Still holding Nora in one arm, Alicia swiftly turned to scrounge up provisions and keep Nora distracted from discovering her brother's injury.

Jim looked at Caleb, "Get your medical supplies, Caleb. Miah needs all the help we can give him." Pointing his head toward the mountains, "I'm gonna head over to that house now. You won't have any trouble catchin' up to us. I'm gonna go slow so Miah won't start bleedin' again."

"I'll be right behind you, Jim," assured Caleb. He dismounted his horse and started to locate essential items: his med pack, dried herbs, and pharmaceutical prescriptions he found in deserted houses. As Caleb assembled his kit, Alicia gathered enough food and water to sustain the group for days.

When he finished packing, Caleb mounted his horse again. Jim and Mattie crossed the valley quickly, but Caleb could still see the tall man's outline in the dusky shadows. He rode swiftly toward the mountains. Caleb reached Jim and Miah before Jim's stallion began its assent up the mountain.

Worried, Alicia asked the others, "Will Miah be okay?"

"He lost a lotta blood," answered Juan, watching Jim and Caleb ride up the mountain together. "But we can pray," he said.

Gabe, Juan, and Alicia stared at the figures slowly fading into the distance. Alicia reached over to hold Juan's hand. Closing their eyes, the three remaining soldiers took turns speaking with God. Each person brought a different element to the prayer but God listened to them. The Bible promises that the prayers of the righteous are powerful and effective[2] and true to his word, God heard their righteous prayer.

---

2. James 5:16.

32

MARCUS AND HIS TEAM arrived back to their valley late in the afternoon. Standing on the road above their farms, they looked at the destruction of their once fair community. Battered beyond repair, the fortified fence no longer served as an obstacle; blackened remnants of houses and barns smoldered. No life stirred.

Shocked, Toynell said nothing. Brant wrapped his arms around his distressed wife to let her cry freely against his chest. He bent his head down to whisper encouraging words into her ears, looking at the devastation from the corner of his eyes, tears seeping beneath his eyelashes.

Marcus removed his hat, placing it over his heart, "Dear Lord, help us."

The only one who didn't stop to survey the damage was Ryan. He ran toward destroyed homes, yelling names loudly, hysterically. "Jason! Talia! Greg, Alicia, Monica!" He called everyone's name; not just once or twice, he recited names without stopping. He yelled until his throat burned with the same raw intensity he felt inside his heart.

As Ryan screamed, he searched for survivors, plowing through the wreckage. He overturned metal panels, kicked charred posts, flung canvas tarps aside, desperately hoping to find living souls. Despite his efforts, he found nothing. The landscape remained deathly still: no people, no animals, no nothing, not even the chirping of crickets.

The late afternoon shadows stretched across barren, burned fields obscuring visibility even further. Desperate to find his daughter, Marcus joined Ryan's pursuit. Every time he entered a burned house or barn, Marcus shouted names, beginning with Talia, but he too found no one. The area was deserted, lifeless.

After an hour of sifting through the rubble, the four travelers came together in the crumbled remnant of Ryan's dairy barn. Ryan sat on a cement block, his hands covered his face. He thought despondently, *My barn. I talked with my children . . . my wife, my friends . . . and my cattle in this barn. This was where I worked. This was my life.* With his eyes shut, tears ran down his cheeks. Everything was gone.

Marcus understood his friend's misery. His family, his home, his life was gone, swept away by the storm. Where would he go from here? Bone tired of the struggle, Marcus sat beside Ryan, but neither man spoke. What could they say? There were no words left to speak, no grand plans to tackle, no homeless wanderers to house, no dreams for the future. Nothing. Absolutely nothing.

Then from out of nowhere, without any prompting from the men— in fact, never entering the men's imaginations—Toynell began to sing. The tiny woman extended her arms, singing a song of praise to the Lord of heaven. She didn't stop with one song, she continued to sing, and after a few songs, she did something unimaginable: she started to dance!

She kicked off her clunky boots so she could slide across the barn's cement floor in her stocking feet; she pushed straw away with her toes and swayed with her melody. She stepped over to Brant, still singing, her eyes inviting him to join her. She faced him, putting her right hand in his left hand, and her left hand on his shoulder, and the couple began to waltz. One-two-three, one-two-three, their feet moved in choreographed rhythm, reminding them of their wedding.

As they twirled, Brant sang with his wife—a flowing, picturesque couple. They looked like miniature, glass dancers spinning on top of a music box. Beautiful. Extraordinary. Exquisite.

Astounded, Marcus and Ryan watched the profiles of the two young people, dancing and singing, in the fading light. Just like the older men, the young couple had nothing: no home, no livelihood; yet they chose to dance, rather than despair. They chose to sing, rather than cry. They chose to live, rather than die.

Ryan nudged Marcus. The brooding thoughts each man carried seemed to fade in the presence of joy. Reluctantly, heaviness began to lift from their shoulders. A slight smile trembled on Ryan's lips; before long, Marcus found himself humming Toynell's song. Their spirits slowly brightened.

Unable to resist the music, Marcus's hum grew louder. When he opened his mouth, the sweet lyrics glided over his tongue, filling his heart with gladness. All the garbage he kept inside, all the insecurities he masked, all doubts that clouded his thinking evaporated while he sang his praises to the Lord.

Ryan joined his friends. He stood, lifted his hands upward and sang with abandon. His hoarse, scratchy throat reminded him of his earlier screaming but it didn't matter. He didn't care. Tonight he would sing to the Lord and celebrate life because, despite everything, he was alive! He was alive in Christ Jesus!

Demons lingering in the demolished valley cringed at the enthusiastic singing emanating from Ryan's barn. Disgusted by what he heard, Depression wrapped a cloak around his withered carcass, covered his ears, and fled the barn to escape the loathsome music. No one from the unrighteous hordes, not even his master, can remain in the presence of godly praise.

Satan would accept Depression's need to leave the barn but he would continue to emphasize the importance of music. Because Satan—the epitome of manipulation—exploits the power of music to change hearts and divert thoughts. He commonly applies this knowledge to pervert human perceptions. In their vanity, many people think that they can listen to offensive music and remain untouched; they believe they have complete control of their thoughts and actions.

"It's a wonder humans don't make the connection between lewd lyrics and deviant beliefs," smirked Satan. "Stupid, stupid slugs!" He snarled, wiping drool from his lips, "Sometimes my job is just too easy."

In the glimmering, morning sunshine, Ryan, Marcus, Brant, and Toynell decided to search destroyed farms for any clues to the whereabouts of their friends and families. The group noticed a few strangers nearby, leering at them from the road, but the strangers never approached them. Very little was left in aboveground structures but Toynell discovered some food in collapsed storm shelters and root cellars: canned vegetables, fresh potatoes and carrots, kefir, cheese, an occasional loaf of bread or crackers. Nourishment. *Thank God!*

For her starving group, Toynell's discovery lifted everyone's spirits; but even more amazing: she found her own root cellar completely intact. Several large trees fell over the door of the underground hole so no one disturbed their foodstuff. After she and Brant removed the wooden planks and tree branches blocking their root cellar, she asked Brant to tell the others her good news. With the promise of food, the men rushed to Toynell's cellar, eager to eat again.

When the men arrived, panting from exertion but smiling expectantly, Toynell glowed. She brought out a basketful of fresh vegetables and canned fruits, plus a crock of sauerkraut. Her face shined: *Look what I did! I preserved food. Me, a woman with no domestic training whatsoever, preserved food for the winter!*

Sensitive to nonverbal clues, Marcus admired Toynell's accomplishment. He examined all the food she brought up from the cellar, exclaiming, "I don't know where to begin with this feast!" And he really didn't; Toynell had outdone herself.

Ryan smoothed out a rumpled, canvas tarp on the ground so they had a place to sit down. Once the men seated themselves, Toynell spread out different jars of fruit, giving everyone a chance to examine their choices. The jars kept tipping over because the tarp—so stiff and lumpy it looked like a mountain range—wasn't the best picnic blanket in the world, but Toynell tried to create a banquet.

She placed the heavy sauerkraut crock in the middle of the tarp. Except now all the jars fell over, rolling everywhere, helter-skelter. Fortunately, the glass jars didn't break or lose their lids; but everyone laughed at the absurdity of it all. While Toynell fussed with a decorative presentation, the men just wanted to eat.

Brant reached over to touch his wife's hand, "Toy, you don't have to do anything else. You laid out a beautiful breakfast for us." He put a jar of peaches into her hand, "Here, this one's yours." She smiled sheepishly at him, embarrassed by her fussiness.

After saying grace, Ryan fished a multi-tool from his pocket, unfolding it, "Lucky we have these gizzies to open lids." As he pried open a lid, he asked, "Does everyone have a fork or spoon?" In unison, Marcus, Brant, and Toynell pulled out their camping sporks just like a bunch of first time campers.

"Alright! Let's eat!"

⌘

A funny thing happens when people fast for long stretches of time: they can't eat much at one sitting. After eating one pint of apples, Marcus—once a big, hulking man—was completely full. He stared at all the jars laying on the tarp, "I wanted to eat fruit from a dozen jars this morning, but I can't. I'm stuffed."

"Me too," admitted Ryan.

Brant shrugged his shoulders in agreement. Toynell simply resealed her jar with half the fruit still uneaten.

Brant stood up, drank the thick syrup from his jar and licked his lips with satisfaction. "We'll eat more later. I'll tell you somethin' though . . . that sugar gives me enough energy to run a marathon!"

With his hands clasped on top of his head, Marcus teased Brant. "Whatta ya plan to do with all that energy?"

"I'm gonna look through our house now. See if there's anything valuable left inside."

Ryan stood up, grunting, his back stiff. "Yeah, I'm gonna do the same thing. Once I saw Jason wasn't around, I really didn't feel like pokin' around our house." He frowned, "Maybe I'll find something worth keeping today."

Somethin' worth keepin', Marcus pondered, dismally, *that's what I'm afraid of finding.* A shirt, a hairclip, a baseball glove: memories hidden within the most innocuous items that can bring a grown man to his knees. He sighed, "Yeah, I 'spect I should go through my house too."

Slipping a cap on his head, Marcus stood up. He twisted his waist left and right to stretch. Afterward, he rocked his head back and forth, making crunching sounds in his neck.

Ryan laughed, "Good grief, Marc, your crackin' bones sound like an army of marchin' skeletons!"

Looking at his baggy clothes, Marcus replied, "I don't think I'm too far away from becoming a skeleton."

"Not if I can help it," Toynell countered, her chin lifted defiantly.

"Don't worry, little lady," Marcus patted her arm, "I'm not goin' anywhere without you." The big man sauntered toward his house; he wasn't in a rush. Having another thought, he turned around adding, "If anyone finds anything special, ring yer dinner bell. We'll come see whatcha found."

Before Marcus reached his house, he heard Ryan frantically ringing the bell on his front porch. Ryan wasn't just ringing the bell, he shouted loudly for everyone to hurry. If ammunition wasn't so scarce, Ryan might've fired a shot into the air for extra emphasis.

Marcus turned swiftly, running as fast as his long legs could carry him. He couldn't run too fast in his tight, cracked boots but he didn't care about blisters or leg cramps, he just wanted to hear what all the excitement was about. When he reached Ryan's porch, Marcus saw his friends laughing, crying, hugging each other.

Panting, Marcus yelled, "What's goin' on?"

Ryan jumped off the porch, picked up Marcus in his arms, tears running down his cheeks, "Jason and Talia are alive! So is Pastor Greg!"

"Wha . . . ?"

Ryan set Marcus back down, "Jason left me a note in our house. He said that every day, he or Talia would come back here around noon to look for us."

Incredulous, Marcus murmured, "They're alive?"

"They're alive and so are a few of the animals!"

"Where are they?"

Ryan opened his hands, "I dunno. They're hiding somewhere; but everyday someone comes out of hiding to see if we've come home."

Now it was Marc's turn to pick someone up. He squeezed Ryan in a bear hug, lifting him off the ground. "My daughter's alive! Your son's alive! My God, you kept our children alive! Thank you . . . Thank you . . . Thank you!"

The fathers danced around the singed barnyard, swinging each other around, kicking up ash, laughing, screaming happily. Brant and Toynell watched their friends' amusing behavior from Ryan's front porch. Smiling, Brant wrapped his arm around Toynell's shoulders, "Ya see? That's what happens when smart people have children; they go nuts."

Toynell smiled, "They're not nuts; they're men in love with their children. Two different things."

33

LOVE HAS MANY WAYS of expressing itself; for Jim, it meant constant vigilance. Jim never left Miah's side. After he and Caleb located the partially-burned brick farmhouse, they set up temporary living quarters in its basement to care for Miah.

Although crude, the basement consisted of three rooms. The largest room contained a wood-burning stove, a clothesline—with faded clothes attached with clothespins—and walls lined with hundreds of jars filled with food. A medium-sized room housed the usual household appliances—a washer, dryer, and water heater—and, almost appearing as an afterthought, the smallest room held a bed, dresser, and vanity.

The most wonderful feature of this basement was its condition: it remained completely intact. The basement had a few window wells with windows, but other than the filmy light from the sun, the entire area was protected underground. Within this cellar, they found a thick, homemade quilt covering the bed and a hand pump in the laundry room washbasin to draw well water. They couldn't ask for better conditions, especially in the ravaged forest.

Despite the basement's uninviting cement floors and walls, someone threw rugs on the floor and hung pictures on walls to make the place more welcoming. But feeling welcome wasn't Jim's primary concern, he needed a surgery and a recovery room, and this basement filled his needs better than he ever dreamed.

After laying Miah on the bed under its thick comforter and starting a fire in the stove, Jim and Caleb organized the cellar. They found a wooden picnic table (probably used for folding clothes) next to the washing machine. They moved the table near the stove and spread a cotton sheet over the table. As the room warmed, Jim and Caleb carefully carried Miah to the table and began to seriously clean and suture his gunshot wound.

Fortunately by this time, Miah's bleeding stopped but the young man's pulse was weak, his body temperature low. The men added wood to the fire but Miah needed extra fluids to replenish his blood loss. Fluids they didn't have.

That first night, Caleb and Jim took turns attending to Miah; one man slept in a chair while the other watched the fire and monitored Miah's vital signs. Despite their watchfulness, Miah's conditioned worsened. He needed fluids. Miah needed the Ringer's lactate solution Jim kept in his surgery but didn't bring on this trip.

At 3:00 in the morning, Mattie started to growl under her breath. She listened for a while, sniffing the air, moving about fretfully. Suddenly she perked up her ears, stood in a crouching position and barked loudly at the basement door. That's when Jim and Caleb heard the horses snorting outside nervously, yanking violently on their tethers.

Instantly aroused from sleep, Jim grabbed his rifle, following Caleb outside to check on the horses. One of the horses already snapped its rope and ran away, chased by a small pack of wolves. The second horse—its eyes open so wide the whites showed—whipped its head around wildly trying to break its restraints. The horse flailed its legs at a group of circling wolves, who snarled menacingly at the pinned animal.

As Caleb untied the frightened horse, Jim shot a wolf, killing it; he aimed his rifle again and killed another. The remaining wolves fled the immediate area but Jim knew they would return; the pack was too hungry to ignore a large, meaty horse. Still terrified, the last horse pranced in place as Caleb held it firmly. Caleb watched as the wolves ran a safe distance away but then stopped to observe the vulnerable horse, guarded by dangerous men.

"Whatta you want to do, Jim?"

"The horse is gonna hate this but we'll bring him into the basement until the wolves leave."

The two men practically dragged the horse into the basement's largest room. Stamping and snorting the animal was afraid, mad, and confused; but Caleb held his reins tightly, trying to keep the horse from destroying the basement. Fortunately by this time, Miah slept in the back bedroom, away from the action, but the situation was clearly not sustainable and both men knew it.

Jim offered to hold the horse's lead rope and Caleb gladly handed it to him. As Jim talked with the frightened animal, stroking its nose, Caleb asked, "Do you want me to ride back to your lodge?"

Jim nodded, "You read my mind, Caleb. I'm hoping the other wolves will follow their pack right now. The wolves will work as a team to bring down the horse that ran away. While their bellies are full, you'll probably have time to escape before they return."

Caleb didn't bother to look out a window. All he'd see was a window well anyway; there was no view aboveground from the cellar. Caleb decided to wait until daybreak so he could see where he was going and keep a close watch on predators.

Jim spotted a jar of apples within his reach. He grasped the jar with his free hand and pried the lid off with his other hand, still holding the horse's lead rope between his thumb and palm. The horse started to sniff the contents of the jar, relaxing a bit. When Jim placed an apple slice in his palm, the horse swiftly ate it then looked expectantly at Jim for more.

Jim smiled, "It's pretty good, isn't it, big fella." As Jim continued to feed the horse, he said, "Caleb, try to get some sleep. I'll make a list of things you need to bring back here. I'll give you directions to our place, but you might run into Juan's group before you get back anyway."

Caleb nodded. "I'd like to leave early; especially if those wolves are sleeping somewhere else."

"I understand."

"You know, it's odd; but ever since that storm, I was getting used to seeing wolves in our company. I could even pet 'em. I'm from the city, so what do I know about wolves?"

Jim glanced over at Miah, his unusual, adopted son, "Nothin's normal anymore. I couldn't believe I saw a mountain lion sleeping next to a goat in your camp." Returning his gaze to Caleb, he warned, "But the wolves outside that door? Those wolves are actin' like regular wolves so don't trust 'em. They'll kill you as fast as they'll kill a horse; they have pups to feed."

"I know. I'll take care of myself."

"Get some shut-eye. If you're lucky, you'll be sleeping in a soft bed tomorrow night."

"I'll drink some coffee before I head back here, but you won't be alone for too long."

"You're a good man." Jim shook Caleb's hand, "Mattie and I have plenty of food and water; we could survive here for weeks. But I'm really worried about Miah. I want to get him into a clean bed, hooked to an IV, and let Sara and Rosa dote on him."

Caleb studied Miah's pallor; a worried look crossed his face. "We'll get it done, Jim." Caleb sat down in a rocking chair close to the fire.

Jim tied the horse standing in a corner of the room, near the doorway. He walked over to the wash basin to clean his hands. After he dried his hands, he added more wood to the stove, and sat in another rocking chair, next to Caleb.

Jim studied the basement. It contained all the necessities for survival: food, water, heat—even a bed. He remarked, "I wonder what happened to the people who lived here."

Caleb closed his eyes, "It's hard to say, but I hope they're okay."

"Yeah, me too."

∞

On the same morning Caleb set out to find Jim's lodge, Ryan found Jason's note. Now the foursome waited anxiously in the valley to see if someone they knew would return to the decimated compound by noon. Midday came and went, but no visitors arrived. The afternoon sunshine lingered for hours but the light eventually morphed into evening shadows, and the shadows melted into a pool of nothingness.

At dusk, Marcus and Ryan sat on the porch steps watching for signs of life, someone moving cautiously in the darkness, anything. Throughout the day, they talked, daydreamed, or slept, but they never left Ryan's house. They rooted around Ryan's old barns and house for anything of value, packing whatever they deemed worth saving.

Brant and Toynell gathered a smattering of food and supplies found in dark corners of abandoned root cellars around the destroyed community, but most of the provisions were already gone. Other people took the foodstuff, leaving only scraps. The couple judiciously stowed goods in their root cellar. Since they planned to take the remaining rations with them, they wanted to consolidate everything in one place.

As evening approached, the group gathered together to discuss their plans. Ryan built a small fire and they ate a scant meal in the dim light of flames. While they ate quietly, Brant stopped chewing for a moment, he sensed something. He stood up and looked down the road that led to Marshall City but didn't see anything.

"I thought I heard footsteps," he said warily.

Ryan and Marcus stood up, craning their necks, hoping to hear a familiar voice or voices. For a few moments, they heard nothing. And then they did. Finally!

"Hey there," whispered Pastor Greg walking out of the gloom. Before he said another word, the young man was surrounded by his four friends. Everyone touched the pastor, wishing him well, wanting to hear the latest news about other valley residents. "Whoa, whoa, guys, one question at a time." Putting a finger to his lips, "You need to quiet down."

Grabbing both of the pastor's arms and looking him straight in the eye, Marcus asked, "Is anyone else alive?"

Greg smiled, "Yep. Jason and Talia are still alive; they're with me. Those that didn't die in the storm left already. It's just too dangerous to live here now."

"Where are they?" implored Ryan.

"They're safe in a rugged, little niche we found in the mountains. I would've come here earlier, but a few of the cows wandered off this morning. It took us most of the day to locate them." He glanced at the fire, "Look, we have to find a better place to sleep tonight. Put out the fire. We don't need to advertise our presence."

Toynell stammered, "But we stored everything in our root cellar today, we can't just leave it!"

"Yes, we can, and we will. Hurry up and grab your things, we gotta get outta here."

Heeding Greg's advice, the four threw on hats and coats while they picked up small parcels of food lying carelessly on the ground. Ryan tossed a bucket of water on the fire, releasing a hiss of steam; afterward, Marcus pushed loose soil over dying embers. Pastor Greg stomped on the smoldering coals with his boots to further extinguish the campfire.

"Is this really necessary?" Ryan questioned softly.

"You can't believe the people roaming the valley now," warned the pastor. "Follow me but don't talk. We're already too exposed." Without saying another word, the young man stepped into the inky darkness. The others followed his lead, slipping away without pausing or making noise.

34

ALONE. AGAIN. JIM LIVED much of his adult life alone, but that didn't mean he preferred isolation. It just happened to him, again, and again, and again.

Trying to rally his spirit, he thought, *I'm not actually alone; I have Miah and Mattie with me.* Then reality slapped him. *Miah and Mattie: my dying son and my faithful dog.* No matter how many times Jim checked Miah's pulse, the young man's heartbeat consistently grew fainter and weaker; and despite Mattie's loyalty, she couldn't do anything to help.

The futility of his predicament felt like the weight of the world sat on his shoulders. He held Miah's cool, white hands. Overlooking callouses and scars, Miah's fingers were amazingly long and supple. *The hands of a pianist*, Jim thought absentmindedly, *not the hands of a laborer or a farmer.*

Unable to contain his emotions, Jim held Miah's hands tightly, weeping. "How can I let you go? You're my friend; the son I never had!"

Still holding Miah's hands, Jim fell to his knees, beside the bed, crying. There was nothing else he could do for Miah. Nothing. He did all he could but it wasn't enough. All he could do now was hold Miah's chilled hands.

As he cried, another thought flashed into Jim's head. "Look at Miah's hands again."

Through his tears, Jim looked at Miah's hands: studying his fingers, his nails. He rolled Miah's hands over in his own hands, tracing lines and blood vessels, trying to imagine what caused some of the scars on his palms.

"Now try to imagine the scars on my hands," a voice said gently in Jim's ear.

Jim gasped. He opened his eyes wide, astounded. *What did I just hear?*

"Try to imagine the scars on my hands," the voice repeated.

Unable to grasp the enormity of the words, Jim sat perfectly still, not breathing. *Am I going mad?*

"No, you are not mad. You are a father watching your only son die. But you are not alone. Your Father in heaven also watched his son die. He saw my hands and feet nailed to a cross, making the scars I shall always bear."

Recalling his Sunday school lessons, Jim trembled uncontrollably. His mouth parched, Jim could barely murmur the name, "Jesus?"

"I Am."

Still on his knees, Jim crumpled to the floor. Terrified by the presence of the Lord, Jim was paralyzed with fear, reduced to a shuddering hulk. Jesus placed his right hand on Jim and said, "Do not be afraid. I am the First and the Last, the Living One. I was dead, and now look; I am alive for ever and ever! And I hold the keys of death and Hades."[1]

Summoning his courage, Jim opened his eyes and whispered, "Forgive me, Jesus, I'm a man of unclean lips."[2] Accustomed to the dim basement light, Jim blinked repeatedly, his eyes watering from the brilliance of Jesus. Jim reached out to touch the scars on the Lord's feet, "I'm so sorry for all the terrible things I've done." Jim cried from the depth of his soul, "Please forgive me," he paused then whispered humbly, "if you're willing."

Jesus answered, "I am willing." He smiled kindly, "Your faith has saved you."

Jim looked into his savior's resplendent face. As he grasped the Lord's feet, holding the only sure foundation in his life, Jim pleaded, "Lord, please heal Miah. He's a good person. A man after God's own heart, a man I would like to be."

Jesus smiled, "Do not be afraid, just believe."

Jesus turned to face Miah. He held Miah's hands, "Young man, I say to you, get up!"

Miah opened his eyes; he yawned and stood up! Astonished, Jim sat back on his ankles, his mouth wide open. He watched Miah's every move with awe, speechless. Although seated on the floor, Jim turned his head to look back at Jesus, but the Lord vanished.

Only he and Miah remained in the bedroom, but Miah was alive! Jim grabbed the bed to pull himself up on his shaking legs. Standing in front of Miah—but still shivering violently—Jim fingered the bandages

1. Rev 1:18.
2. Isa 6:5.

covering Miah's wound. When Miah didn't flinch, Jim started to clumsily unwind the bandages; slowly at first, then faster, faster; until he finally ripped the bandages from Miah's abdomen. Standing on the discarded, bloodied bandages, Jim examined Miah's torso; but all that remained of the gunshot wound was a scar.

A scar, Jim gasped as he touched Miah's flesh, tears filling his eyes again. *A healed, white scar!*

Jim grabbed Miah and hugged him with all his strength. Laughing and crying, Jim screamed, "Thank you, Jesus! Thank you, Jesus! Thank you, Jesus!" Miah hugged Jim, grinning.

After hours of fading in and out of consciousness, Miah was bewildered. The last thing he remembered was Mary rushing toward his father. Unaware of Mary's charge, his father held a pistol on him and then fired his weapon. Miah recalled grasping his stomach and falling to the ground; now the realization struck him: *My dad pointed a gun at me.*

Miah took a step back to look at Jim. Although dark circles under Jim's lashes revealed a lack of sleep, the cowboy's tearful eyes showed unmasked joy. *Jim's joyful?* Miah thought vaguely, trying to grasp the state of affairs.

Miah looked at the side of his abdomen, the place he grabbed when he fell. Huh. *Some dry, crusty blood around a lumpy scar but I'm okay.* Then he looked at the floor. Miah saw shredded bandages strewn over his feet, covering Jim's boots—the bandages Jim yanked off his waist moments earlier.

Muddleheaded, Miah scratched his head, but flashed his effervescent smile. "Uh, Jim, you're going to have to fill me in on some details because I don't know what's happenin'."

"My pleasure, Miah," laughed Jim, "but I warn you, you'll hear this story a thousand times before I die." Jim hugged Miah again, "Miah, I know you have a Father in heaven and you had a dad here on earth; but if you ever need anything, call on me. I'll do whatever I can to help. I love you. You're like my son."

"I know. I love you too," Miah added thoughtfully, "Pa."

Satan's underling grimaced. Supremely disappointed, she turned and left the basement, afraid to report back to the master on her actions. Tasked to harm Miah through the two father figures in his life, the demon failed on both counts. A massive horse trampled the first father—who could see that coming?—and the second dad gets a visit from Jesus. *Really? The Son of God? What're the chances of that happening?*

No matter, the fallen angel gave up her happiness eons ago. As she slunk back to hell to report her dismal results, she tried to create plausible explanations for her failure but inwardly she knew: *Now it's my time to be tortured. Again.*

At the same time Jim held Miah's cold hands, a bullet whizzed past Toynell's head and shot straight through Brant's heart, killing him instantly. She stopped to stare at her husband's body, but before a scream escaped her lips, Marcus picked her up and started running back to their smoldering campfire. Ryan threw Brant's body over his shoulders, following Marcus closely. Pastor Greg ran behind them, keenly aware of the danger surrounding them.

Someone fired more shots but the bullets missed their marks. Marcus sprinted straight to Toynell's root cellar for safety. When they arrived in front of the cellar's oak doors, Marcus set Toynell down and shoved the heavy doors open. He pushed Toynell forward, helped take Brant off Ryan's shoulders, and ushered Greg into the small, snug enclosure. They shut the doors securely, bracing them with wooden planks used as shelves.

Dug ten feet underground and lined with cement blocks, the cellar provided storage for root crops during the winter and canned foods year round. Right now, Marcus only wanted the cellar's solid doors and underground position to serve as a barrier against flying bullets. The food provided sustenance, but honestly, with all the jars Toynell collected earlier in the day, the room was crowded.

"Who was that?" screamed Ryan.

Pastor Greg shook his head bleakly. "Renegades. People who came here after the storm."

He related what happened the day following the tempest. When he, Talia, and Jason came out of their shelter, they found a few community residents wandering around wreckage looking for family members. They guessed the majority of inhabitants either fled the area before or after the storm, but no one wanted to remain in the valley anymore—only Greg, Talia, and Jason stayed behind. Over the next few days, the trio buried a few unfortunate people they found dead under debris but the livestock deaths caused far greater problems.

With the valley littered with dead animals, predators fell upon the area with veracity—not just the wild variety of predators—human hunters too. Within a day, starving people fought over food: they skinned dead animals in the fields and raided root cellars and houses. Vultures, wolves, coyotes, crows—a wide assortment of carrion-eating animals—also filled their stomachs on the carcasses. Regrettably, those scavengers squatted in the vicinity to fight over food scraps.

"As it turns out, Jason found some living dairy cattle huddled in a ravine so he led them into the forest for safety. He's still keeping a close watch on those cattle." The pastor looked at Ryan, "He tried to save as many cows as he could for you."

Ryan's stern expression softened, "He's a good son."

"What about Talia?" Marcus asked nervously. "How's she doin'?"

"She's fine. A real trooper." Almost as an afterthought, "Oh yeah, Talia took a fat, orange cat with us. She saved him during the storm."

At that moment, Marcus remembered Toynell; he turned to gaze at her. She sat in the corner, holding Brant's head in her lap, stroking his hair distractedly. Her eyes held a vacant appearance, a hollow stare.

Marcus sat beside Toynell, "How are you?"

She looked at Marcus as if she didn't know him. "Hmm?"

"How are you?" he repeated, touching her hand softly.

She stopped stroking Brant's hair, "I need to pick peas before the next rain comes. If I don't, I won't have enough time to can them before they get old." She shook her head sadly.

Marcus put an arm around her shoulders, "Let's not worry about those peas tonight. It looks like we got us enough food to eat for a long time."

She glanced around the room, looking at everything, but seeing nothing. "Brant really likes peas; that's why I fuss so much with them."

Marcus gently pressed Toynell's head against his shoulder. "Why don't cha rest your head right here for a while and forget about those old veggies. There's nothin' a little sleep can't handle."

Toynell shut her eyes resignedly. She sucked in air deeply, saying nothing more.

Pastor Greg and Ryan watched Marcus and Toynell. They listened to the gunfire and fighting outside their underground bunker, thankful that no one tried to break into the cellar—yet. Without speaking to each other, Greg and Ryan automatically closed their eyes and started to pray quietly, each hoping for safety or deliverance from this dreadful place.

⟿⟆⟆⟿

Jim and Miah sat in rocking chairs by the wood burning stove. They left the stove's grate open so they could watch flames dance over dry logs, hypnotizing their minds, and trying to make sense of the last hour. Although exhausted, Jim told Miah what happened after the shooting. Once he related his story, Jim waited for Miah to say something.

Unfortunately, when Miah spoke, his first words sucked the breath out of Jim, "I've been dying to ask you: how's Beth?"

Stripped of all his defenses, Jim told Miah about Beth's accident as tactfully as possible. Miah stared blankly at the flickering fire, listening to Jim, twisting his hands together. As Miah watched the flames, tears rolled silently down his cheeks.

Neither man spoke for a long time. Jim's words punched Miah in the gut. As Miah fought to catch his breath, his body slumped in his chair, too weary to move. Miah's reaction pierced Jim's heart. Struggling to control his concern for Miah, Jim sat straight in his chair, too worried to move. The wounded and the recovered, the weak and the strong. The son and the father.

When Miah finally shifted in his seat, Jim paused a few moments then confessed his initial intention to commit suicide. That's when Miah stopped watching the fire to stare directly into Jim's eyes. Heartbroken and mournful over Beth's death, Miah still appreciated the larger implications of Jim's confession, "If you'd done that, I wouldn't be alive today."

"Yeah . . . ?"

Miah reflected, "And Sara wouldn't have anybody. Sara. You know that nice lady everybody loves? Who takes care of ragged children and wounded animals? She wouldn't have Beth, or you, or me. She'd be devastated. She would lose a second family and it would kill her."

Jim sucked in a deep breath. He never considered the impact of his death upon Sara, or upon Miah; but Miah was right. "I'm such an idiot," he admitted.

"We all are, Jim." Miah said, his voice shaking, "You can make it up to her when you see her again." Still thinking of Beth, he choked, "Hold her, kiss her, treat her like a queen—she deserves it."

"I will," promised Jim.

Both men gazed at the glowing logs, lost in their own thoughts. Jim dreamed of things he would do for Sara as soon as he returned home: build drying racks for her herb collection, till her garden, but most importantly, apologize for neglecting her feelings and ask for forgiveness. Miah thought of what he'd do for Beth when he saw her again in heaven:

he'd touch her soft hands, gaze into her blue eyes, and once again, profess his love for her.

Despite their pain, neither man accused the Lord of Beth's death. They blamed no one; life ends with death but death doesn't end with nothingness. Another life begins after death, it's a different life to be sure, but for believers, it's a better life. So instead of wallowing in their loss, they began to talk about Jesus and their conversation drifted to the bigger picture, the eternal battle for people's souls.

Miah said, "Most people don't realize the depth of this warfare." He smirked without humor, "People fight over territory, money . . . nationalities. Some believe if they throw stones at others, they'll be considered intellectuals, innovators, world changers." Miah shook his head, "But these reactions aren't the battle, they're only smoke and mirrors, covering a deeper division."

Thankful to hear Miah talking again, Jim prompted him, "Whatta you mean?"

"I mean there are hundreds, thousands, of governments in this world but there are only two kingdoms: the kingdom of this world, which is Satan's domain, and the kingdom of God."

Confused, Jim asked, "But what's the battle?"

Miah pursed his lips seriously, "It's a battle for souls. Satan wants nothing more than to bring as many people to hell with him as he can. He'll lie, cheat, and manipulate people into believing that they are gods in their own right."

"We don't control our own destiny?" Jim pondered.

"Naw, but Satan tells people that they command their own lives."

"But what about death?"

"Satan tells folks there's a floating, nonexistence into the great beyond." Miah sighed, "Kind of a oneness with the cosmos, I guess."

"Okay, I kinda remember my Sunday school lessons." Still terrified by the Lord's earlier appearance, "But I never heard of Jesus makin' personal visits to save sinners."

"Jesus made several appearances after his resurrection. But a lotta people don't like to talk about supernatural things."

"I do now," said Jim vigorously.

Miah leaned forward to rest his forearms on his thighs; he looked directly at Jim. "You probably heard all the right things in church about God. God is three beings with one mind: God the Father, God the Son, and God the Holy Spirit."

Jim glanced at the fire, "That always confused me."

"Yeah, I think it confuses everybody at first." Miah continued, "But after God created the heavens and the earth, he created people. He made people to look like him because he wanted to share eternity with a family."

As Miah talked, some puzzle pieces started to fall into place. Jim recalled his earlier lessons, "Okay. God loved Adam and Eve like his own children, but he gave them rules."

"That's right. When Adam and Eve decided not to follow those rules, they broke fellowship with God and sin entered the world."

"But a perfect God can't look at sin, right?"

"That's right. To mend the relationship with his sinful children, our perfect Father came up with only one plan of reconciliation. He sent his son, Jesus—a man without sin—to die on a cross to pay for everybody's sin once and for all. So as one man, Adam, brought sin into the world, one perfect man, Jesus, took that sin away."[3]

"The sacrificial Lamb of God," murmured Jim.

"Yeah."

Jim talked slowly, "So the battle isn't economic differences or gender equality."

"It's also not contagious diseases or climate control."

"What about political corruption? Business monopolies?"

"Nope. Those are only symptoms of the battle."

Jim ended, "It's good against evil. It's God against Satan. It's a war between the world's two opposing, *supernatural* kingdoms. That's the battle!"

"Yeah. And the battle belongs to the Lord."

Jim leaned back in his chair, absorbing these concepts. Finally he said, "Let's get some sleep. We'll head back home in a few hours. We'll probably run into Caleb and the others coming back to rescue us." Jim chuckled, "Won't they be surprised to see you riding down the road?"

"I was meaning to ask you about that. Why's there a horse in the laundry room?"

---

3. Rom 5:19.

35

Although Marcus, Ryan, and Greg endured an entire night of screeching and scratching at the cellar door, no intruders broke into their shelter. When morning arrived, their tormentors disappeared. Claw marks gouged into the hardwood door and fruitless holes dug into the soil displayed the only evidence of their oppressor's presence. But now the enemy left them alone, at least for a while.

Seizing the opportunity, the men promptly attended to last-minute business before leaving. While Toynell slept, the men buried Brant then assembled all the food they could carry. Packed and ready to move, Ryan and Greg waited outside the cellar for Marcus to retrieve Toynell.

After Marcus roused Toynell, he looped his arm around her waist, and escorted her out of her cozy corner. Still in shock from the tragic evening, the young woman plodded next to Marcus kicking up dust, staring straight ahead but disclosing very little. Attentive to Toynell's fragile state of mind, Marcus encouraged her to follow Ryan as he stationed himself at the end of the line.

Wary of adversaries, all three men continuously scanned their surroundings as they walked hurriedly toward the Western mountains. Sometimes, the men noticed a vagabond shuffling over the singed landscape or a pack of coyotes running together, but no one bothered them. They escaped the valley without further incident.

Once they entered the forest, they relaxed a bit. Navigating over streams and rocky terrain, the quartet pushed deeper into the hills. They hiked steadily, occasionally taking breaks, but never resting for long periods.

By early afternoon, Ryan spied a few dairy cows grazing in a small, grassy nook. Craning his neck to look around trees and foliage, Ryan spotted Talia sitting on a rock, idly daydreaming. Ryan nudged Marcus, pointing at the young woman lounging in the sunshine on a large, warm boulder.

Marcus ran out from his cover in the trees and called his daughter's name—startling her at first. Upon hearing Marcus's voice, Talia stood up on the boulder waving her arms wildly, smiling broadly. She jumped down from her perch, running to the safety of her father's strong arms.

At that moment, Jason came out of the trees, bearing his rifle. When he saw Marcus running out of the forest toward Talia, he looked around expectantly for his own father. Then he saw him. His dad. Ryan ran toward Jason: his arms outstretched, his face beaming with joy.

For the second time in less than a year, the father and son reunited after a challenging separation. Ryan and Jason hugged each other, laughing. Ryan stepped back to examine his son—*no injuries, his hair a little too long, has he grown an inch?*—and Ryan ruffled Jason's shaggy head.

"You look good, Jay," Ryan grinned.

"It's great to see you again, Dad!"

Pastor Greg and Toynell joined everyone in the little mountain clearing. The pastor kept a protective arm around Toynell's shoulders while she observed the others passively. When Toynell glanced at Talia, a wisp of recognition glimmered on Toy's face. The detached woman watched the reunion between fathers and children with curiosity. The pastor noted the slight change in Toynell's behavior and he patted her shoulder to encourage her.

Toynell stared into the pastor's face, trying to recall his significance in her life. Although she couldn't remember him, she wasn't afraid. She turned her head to watch the people in front of her again; people kissing each other, talking simultaneously, and laughing together. Her countenance brightened. Despite her confusion, Toynell smiled.

Marcus announced, "Let's take the cattle back to your campsite. After we finish milking, we'll have dinner and catch up on our news. Tomorrow, Ryan and I wanna take you to meet some really nice people who live in caves."

"Caves?" Talia asked excitedly.

"Yeah, caves," her dad said grinning.

Jesus strolled easily through the massive stone temple where he and his Father reigned. Beside him walked two lovely young women: Beth, a blonde teenager with sapphire eyes, and Beth's thirty-year-old friend. Beth wondered how her friend always looked so fresh and lively because she completely ignored her appearance! Even today—a very special day for both women—her friend entered the room with her hair blowing carelessly around her face and her eyes glittering with mischief.

Jesus, charming and intelligent, walked with the women, asking them questions, laughing at their responses. The pair talked about the wonders of heaven, the songs they heard in the wind, even the remarkable fruits they ate. They chattered endlessly about everything. Jesus basked in the warmth of their company, totally in love with both of them.

At the end of the corridor, they entered the Lord's throne room. Sitting upon the throne, God dwelt within an unapproachable light, brilliant as jasper and ruby, encircled by an emerald rainbow. Twenty-four elders, wearing white linens and golden crowns, sat on twenty-four thrones which surrounded God's throne. In front of God's throne blazed seven lamps and a sea of glass sparkling as clear as crystal.

The creatures inhabiting the throne room defied imagination! Four living creatures covered with eyes, one looked like a lion, the second like an ox, the third like a man, and the fourth like an eagle. Each creature had six wings and they never stopped saying, "Holy, holy, holy, is the Lord God Almighty, who was, and is, and is to come."[1]

Overcome by the majesty surrounding them, the women fell to the floor, quaking with fright. Jesus touched each woman, saying, "Do not be afraid." Clutching each other as they stood, the women gazed with wonder at the Throne of Heaven.

Jesus walked up the steps. He sat at the right hand of his Father, high and exalted, with the train of his robe filling the temple.[2] He smiled cheerfully at Beth's friend and held his hand out to her, "Daughter, come to me." Nellie released her hold on Beth and stepped forward, drawn by the Lord's irresistible love and compassion for her.

As she walked toward Jesus, Nellie's silky, white garment flowed gracefully around her body. "*She looks like a princess*," admired Beth. In fact, everyone in the throne room—the four creatures covered with eyes, the twenty-four elders, and the seraphim—thought Nellie looked like a princess. When she reached the top of the stairs, Nellie knelt on the floor and rested her forehead on its glorious gemstone surface.

1. Rev 4:1–8.
2. Isa 6:1.

"My lord," she whispered.

"Arise, daughter," Jesus said kindly, "and come to me." When Nellie raised her head, she noticed Jesus still reached for her, smiling warmly. As she walked closer to him, Jesus said, "Do you remember what you asked of me when your husband passed away?"

Nellie stopped, furrowing her brow as she reflected, "No, Lord, I don't."

"Right after you gave your life to me. Try to remember what you asked me."

She glanced upward, thinking. "Uh," a glint of remembrance flashed in her mind, "I think . . . I remember." Embarrassed, she smiled awkwardly, blushing, "I was in so much pain; I thought my heart would break."

"I remember your pain," he looked gently into her eyes, "and I remember your request. When you wept, you asked if you could sit on my lap. You wanted to feel my comforting arms around you. And you wanted to listen to my heart."

Tears welled in Nellie's eyes, "I remember."

"Come to me, sweet child. Listen to the heart of your Father who loves you so much."

Nellie reached up, taking the Lord's hand. He lifted her into his arms. At first she sat upright in his lap, studying his hands, turning them over, touching the holes in each palm. She kissed his hands. Nellie closed her eyes, whispering her thanks, acknowledging his suffering for her salvation.

As Nellie sank into the deep folds of his velvety, kingly garment, she felt his powerful embrace. She pressed her head next to Jesus's chest. As she listened to the rhythmic beating of his heart—his good, pure heart— Nellie wept tears of joy. She felt the same reassurance, the same peace, the same love she experienced the day she made this bold request. Now she rested in his embrace. A beloved child in the arms of her father.

From within the company of witnesses watching Jesus hold Nellie, a rather unimpressive man stepped forward. He spoke assuredly to everyone in the throne room, "I am convinced that neither death nor life, neither angels nor demons, neither present nor the future, nor any powers, neither height nor depth, nor anything else in all creation, will be able to separate us from the love of God that is in Christ Jesus our Lord."[3]

And the multitude bowed in reverent agreement, "Amen, Lord Jesus. Amen."

---

3. Rom 8:38.

www.ingramcontent.com/pod-product-compliance
Lightning Source LLC
Chambersburg PA
CBHW051145030726
47504CB00004B/1042